# NORTH OF DAWN

Also by Nuruddin Farah

# NORTH OF DAWN

Nuruddin Farah

RIVERHEAD BOOKS
*New York*
2018

RIVERHEAD BOOKS
An imprint of Penguin Random House LLC
375 Hudson Street
New York, New York 10014

Library of Congress Cataloging-in-Publication Data

Names: Farah, Nuruddin, 1945– author.
Title: North of dawn : a novel / Nuruddin Farah.
Description: New York : Riverhead Books, 2018.
Identifiers: LCCN 2018028026 (print) | LCCN 2018028946 (ebook) | ISBN
9780735214248 (ebook) | ISBN 9780735214231 (hardcover)
Classification: LCC PR9396.9.F3 (ebook) | LCC PR9396.9.F3 N6 2018 (print) |
DDC 823.914—dc23
LC record available at https://lccn.loc.gov/2018028026

Printed in the United States of America
1   3   5   7   9   10   8   6   4   2

Book design by Cassandra Garruzzo

*In Memory of Basra Farah*

-----

*My beloved younger sister, killed by
Taliban terrorists in Kabul in 2014*

Leaving the scene, Imru-ulqais says,
"In the beginning was the word.
In the beginning of the word was blood."

—*Concerto al-Quds*, Adonis

# PROLOGUE

-----------

IN SOMALIA, THE BOMBS HAVE BEEN GOING OFF FOR MONTHS, ROADSIDE devices killing and maiming anyone unlucky enough to be in the vicinity. The frequency of the detonations and the unpredictability of where or when the blasts may occur have left the residents of Mogadiscio, the capital, constantly on edge. No one knows how many people have been injured or how many have been killed. People no longer delve into the details unless they recognize the name of a victim or that of the perpetrator.

My wife, Gacalo, however, would spend hours poring over articles about the bombings, fixated on any that might name anyone known to be active in the terror group Ashabaab. She was searching for news of our son.

It had been five or six years since Dhaqaneh had fled to Somalia, though I had cut him off totally from the moment he made clear to me, during his final visit to Oslo, that he would kill anyone, including our friends Johan and Birgitta, in the name of Islam. I refused to take his phone calls or answer his emails, and told Gacalo that I had no interest in discussing him, though later I would run across his name when he published his diatribes on the various Somali websites that report Shabaab's doings with alarming frequency. But for Gacalo it was impossible to cut ties. She remained in touch with him, even occasionally wiring funds to an intermediary who delivered the moneys to him.

I would learn only recently from Timiro, our daughter, that in order to communicate with Dhaqaneh by phone, Gacalo would key in a set of numbers known only to her, to him, and to some other designated person, whose name Dhaqaneh would update almost on a monthly basis whenever she wanted to speak to him. If he was not there to take her call, she would use a set code and then leave a message. She hated it when she had to leave a voice message, unsure whose mailbox she was entrusting her secrets to, secrets that could eventually be traced back to her.

Gacalo was more relaxed after Dhaqaneh contracted a marriage to a woman named Waliya, who has two children, a girl and a boy. It was the humanness of the woman's voice when Gacalo spoke to her on the phone that made an impression on her, that gave her some comfort and the illusion that she could trust her, even though she had never met her and did not know her from any Somali-speaking Eve.

When Dhaqaneh's Norwegian passport expired, Gacalo suggested that he have it renewed at the Norwegian Embassy in Nairobi. Dhaqaneh, however, was keen to sever all ties with Norway. In a letter Gacalo has shown me, he writes that he cannot bring himself to carry a passport whose cover is adorned by a cross, such a flagrant Christian symbol. Gacalo saw his action as more than a rejection of Norway; she saw it as a rejection of her too. And when she pleaded with him to reconsider and he insisted he would not, she disengaged from him for a while.

The next time they spoke, Dhaqaneh was holidaying in Nairobi with his wife and stepchildren. He had recently purchased a Somali passport, resolute in his determination never again to set foot in Europe, believing that Somalia, as he put it to his mother, "was the closest we have to an Islamic state, after Iran." Then came another long break in communication, during which both Gacalo and I, unbeknownst to each other, monitored Somali websites for news of him. He had risen quickly in the ranks and was soon made deputy head of the entire Benaadir region, of which Mogadiscio is part. The explosions in the capital city became more frequent and deadly, with fingers of blame pointed at him. When he and his mother did finally speak, she hoped for her own sake that he would deny that his men were responsible for the carnage. But he did nothing of the sort. Instead, he made a request of her: that she promise to take care of his wife and stepchildren if he were to meet his death either at the hands of his foes or in an attack on his command post on the outskirts of the city.

A month after that conversation, several of his men were en route to firebomb a target close to the international airport when their vehicle ran over a roadside explosive device and they were all instantly killed. As word would have it and as the Somali news websites and the world press would relay it, Dhaqaneh blew himself up at the entrance to the airport "to avenge his men." He died on the spot.

The shock of this hit Gacalo so profoundly that for the first few days after Dhaqaneh's death, she ran high temperatures and was so unsteady she had to hold on to the back of chairs or walls to go from one point of the house to another. Her health declined so rapidly that her doctor had her admitted to hospital and, because of her weak heart, kept her under constant observation for nearly a fortnight. When she finally recovered and seemed able to navigate her way out of her grief, she reminded everyone of the promise she had made to Dhaqaneh before his death: that she would bring Waliya and her children to Oslo and look after them.

At present, Gacalo and I are at loggerheads over whether to allow his Waliya and her two children to join us here in Oslo on the basis of a family reunion ticket. I have no idea what position to take, fearing what may become of us if Waliya turns out to be a troubled person, or, even worse, a terrorist.

# OSLO

----------------

# CHAPTER ONE

----------

GACALO WAGES AN UNRELENTING CAMPAIGN FOR SEVERAL MONTHS, HOP-
ing that Mugdi will not stand in the way of Dhaqaneh's widow,
Waliya, and his two stepchildren joining them in Oslo. Knowing
Gacalo, she will not hesitate to recruit the support of their daughter
Timiro, visiting from her home in Geneva; Kaluun, Mugdi's younger
brother; their Norwegian friends Johan and Birgitta Nielsen; and
Himmo, a Somali woman residing in Oslo whom Gacalo and Mugdi
have grown close to and who is of the view that Gacalo should continue supporting the widow and her two children where they are, in
Kenya. But Gacalo is adamant that she will not give up until Mugdi
and everyone else accedes to her demand.

Inflexible, Mugdi repeatedly asks, "Why would I sponsor the
wife of a son whom I forsook first and then denounced as a terrorist?"

A former ambassador in Somalia's Ministry of Foreign Affairs
just before the collapse of the state structures, Mugdi is used to
having his own way. It is no secret that it irritates him to see people

opposing him when their rationale does not sit well with his reasoning.

The longer the standoff lasts and Gacalo makes it obvious that she won't settle for anything less than Mugdi's full public endorsement of her plan, the more everyone becomes concerned. Gacalo's inability to convince Mugdi to share her vision upsets her so much that she feels diminished, unloved, to the point that one afternoon, after yet another explosive argument, she storms out of the house, not knowing where she is going.

When she doesn't answer her mobile phone or return home for a long time, Timiro goes out in search of her mother in the two parks close by. Not finding her at either park, she telephones Birgitta, who confirms that Gacalo is with them.

On Timiro's way home from her search, she runs into Himmo, who has just alighted from the tram after a night shift at the hospital where she works as a nurse. Delighted by the chance encounter, the two women decide to find a café where they might chat for a bit. Timiro explains what has brought her to this area of the city, filling Himmo in on the tension at home with regard to Waliya. She says, "The atmosphere has lately turned so toxic, I can't stand it, and I've told them so. I don't recall my parents ever rowing as much as they've done of late, or of Mum ever raising her voice in anger, except perhaps once, when I was a child."

"Oh? Were you a difficult girl?"

"It was more that I was young and obstinate, and desperately wanted a cat for a pet. Mum put her foot down, as having a pet would interfere with our weekend travels. I went behind her back, pleading with Dad, and he agreed without consulting her and arranged for the pet shop to deliver one. I had never heard her so angry as when she arrived home and saw the cat. In the end, however, Dad won the day and I got to keep it."

"Maybe it is only fair that your mother has her way this time round."

"Perhaps, but you never know with Dad, a man given to changing his mind at the very time you least expect him to."

Himmo says, "I know what you mean. But at his heart, he is such a mild-mannered man, and I feel certain that rather than continuing to disappoint your mum, he will give in."

"I hope so for both their sakes," says Timiro. "Mum broods all the time, is constantly at the office, and when she does return home, lapses into self-isolating silences. She goes to bed soon after dinner, if, that is, she is around to eat with us. She wakes up early and then goes off again. Then Dad retreats into his study to devote more time to the translation he's working on of his favorite Norwegian novel, *Giants in the Earth*."

Himmo predicts, "Time will come when they will both want to be on each other's good side. Don't worry. They love each other so."

"I just wish they wouldn't spoil my visit."

"Give their anger time to find its own home," says Himmo. "Your dad is incensed she kept a secret line open to Dhaqaneh; she is furious that he disowned the boy. Still, I'm sure he won't stand in the way of the family reunion."

Timiro's mobile phone rings. Answering it, she says in an aside to Himmo, "It's Dad." Then she addresses her words to her father, telling him not to worry, that Mum is with Birgitta, and she is at a café with Himmo, whom she ran into by chance.

The waiter brings them their pot of tea at the very moment when Timiro feels nauseated. She holds her breath and places her hand before her mouth in the manner of someone preparing to vomit. Himmo takes notice of this but keeps her thoughts to herself. Instead, she pours the tea and watches as Timiro brings her cup to her lips then puts it down in silence.

Himmo says, "Enough about your parents' quarrels over Waliya. I want to hear your news. How are you, and how is Xirsi, and where is he?"

Timiro shifts in her seat, and then with a beam of happiness shining in her eyes says, "I'm pregnant."

Himmo stretches out her right hand toward Timiro until their fingers touch. Then she congratulates her, wishing her good health and an uncomplicated delivery, given her age—Timiro will be thirty-four by the time the baby is due. She adds, "Your parents must be happy."

Timiro says, "Not as happy as I hoped."

"No? Why is that?"

"Well, as I've said before, I've flown into a stressful situation, and they're much too preoccupied with their own set-to, to be fully engaged in my condition. I don't completely blame them. After all, Dhaqaneh's death, my mother's promise to him, and whether Waliya is or is not welcome to join the family precede my pregnancy. And besides all that, they're not overly fond of Xirsi."

"So what do you plan to do?" asks Himmo.

"I'll sit them down and tell them that I do not wish to give birth to my baby in a hostile environment."

Himmo says, "I'm sure they'll see sense when you talk to them, and I hope that Xirsi sees sense too, and is able to step up and keep his side of the contract, both as a father to the child and as a husband to you."

"Xirsi is a bad lot and I'm unsure he'll mend his ways and

act responsibly toward me or our child," says Timiro. "I know it'll be tough to be a single mother and a professional. But I take courage from women like you. You've done it and done it well."

"It was easier having children back home, with an extended family to assist. Here, in Europe, it has been hard for most of the Somali women, whether they are married or not. Many couples come to a head because the husbands don't put in their fair share in holding the family together; they seem unable or unwilling to play their role, many showing more interest in clan politics, not in raising their young families. This is why women with professional careers have found themselves in impossible situations, with many choosing to divorce. Personally, I salute the mothers that persevere and work tirelessly to put food on the table, look after children, make sure they attend school, stay out of trouble, with little or no help from male partners. I think of these women as the unsung heroines, every single one of them."

"I'm done with Xirsi. I'll divorce him."

In her empathic response to what Timiro has just told her, Himmo's outstretched hand comes into a gentle contact with Timiro's and the two women remain silent for quite a while.

Timiro needs no reminding that Himmo has been married and divorced three times, the men in her life having failed, time and again, to act responsibly toward their offspring, which Himmo is now looking after by herself. Now Himmo says, "Of the men I know, your father is exceptional in this regard."

Timiro is happy to hear Himmo say that, and after a few more minutes of small talk, the two women go their different ways. At home, Timiro finds her father in his study, working on a moving scene of *Giants* in which the first Norwegian migrants to settle in the Dakota territories meet Native Americans for the first time and are terrified, suspecting that the band of natives will scalp them.

Timiro makes dinner and when her mother has returned, albeit in low spirits, Timiro invites her parents to the table. As they eat in silence, she worries that she cannot sense her parents' togetherness the way she used to; she can only feel their doubts about the future, their fears. Why allow a third party to pull them asunder at the very time when, with their mourning over, they should be showing their connectedness?

So she ambushes them with unexpected news: that she is returning to Geneva as soon as she finds a flight. Gacalo is the first to find her tongue, stammering, "But you said you would be here for a while. You're in no state to be on your own, feeling sick, staying up late, and working."

"I know why she is leaving," says Mugdi.

Gacalo looks from Mugdi to Timiro and back at Mugdi. "Am I missing something? Have the two of you been conspiring?"

"Our daughter is leaving because she can't stand being around when the two of us are fighting to the bitter end, neither of us prepared to allow the other to have his or her way."

"If that's the case, what are *you* going to do about it?"

"What are *we* doing about it, Mum," says Timiro. "Remember, this concerns every member of the family, including my unborn baby."

Timiro will forever time the moment her father's resistance buckled to when she used the inclusive pronoun "we," in "What are *we* going to do about it?" It is true that she has run out of patience with her bickering parents. Still, she feels that her father has put on himself pressure unlike any other, understandably—he will do his best not to allow outsiders to intrude harmfully into their lives during the auspicious period when they are expecting a grand-child. Later, she will claim she knew he would concede to Gacalo when she saw the twinkle of his eyes. As it happens, he acquiesces to all of her mother's dictates: renting a vehicle to fetch them from the airport; taking Waliya and the children to their new home, a three-bedroom apartment Gacalo has obtained for them; and what's more, doing all of this alone, as when the day finally comes that Waliya and her children are to be picked up, Gacalo will an-nounce that she is chairing a meeting that she cannot afford to miss. And so there is nothing left for Mugdi to say but "It'll be a pleasure to welcome them, darling."

How sweet of him!

As Gacalo gathers her papers to leave for the office, she offers Mugdi a multipocketed leather purse heavy with coins.

"What is this? Gold?"

Gacalo replies, "Coins for your parking."

Mugdi has never known Gacalo to be fretful, yet now she is as antsy as a mother hen, clucking protectively at anyone approaching her chicks.

She says, "Will you promise not to ask them any embarrassing questions—not when you first meet them, nor later, when you are in the car on your way to the apartment, where I'll be waiting to welcome them?"

"I won't."

"How I wish *he* too was coming!"

He says nothing, knowing she is referring to Dhaqaneh. She turns away from him, the well of her eyes filling with tears. Before she departs, she says, her voice moist, "Be sure to call me anyhow."

On the drive to the airport, Mugdi brims over with sadness and not for the first time thinks of himself as a man born to grief, a

Somali concerned about the death of a son or the arrival of a widow and her children when he should be sorrowing over the terminal cancer that has infected his nation. He detests Somalia's dysfunction, unrelenting since 1991, the year the country collapsed after its clan politics had gone awry, and Mogadiscio became a killing field.

Mugdi arrived in Norway in 1988, before the start of the strife. Norway was a different country then. The majority of its Muslim population consisted of a homogenous community of Pakistanis, who had come as indentured laborers. Soon after Mugdi's arrival, he learned of a nineteen-year-old Norwegian member of the right-wing National Popular Party who had launched a bomb attack on Nor Mosque in 1985—a forewarning of the attacks that would increase in frequency.

Johan Nielsen, his friend, said at the time, "There's nothing new about this. Nowadays hate groups perceive Muslims as an existential threat to Norway in the same way similar hate groups of old perceived Jews, with contempt and fear."

"Still, it is worrying," said Mugdi.

His wife, Birgitta, went on, "The year before, a prominent Norwegian politician of extreme right-wing persuasion falsely claimed to have received a letter from a Muslim, in which the author forewarned that one day mosques will be as common in Norway as churches are today and that the heathen cross in the flag will be gone."

Mugdi felt so unwelcome and unsafe hearing of such incidents that he even considered returning to Somalia, and perhaps would have, if Gacalo hadn't pleaded with him not to for the sake of the children. Instead, he did what he could for his country from afar, writing articles and editorials in which he advocated for peace among the warring clan militias. Then he joined a group of former

Somali ambassadors, politicians, and intellectuals whose aim was to deal with the rupture in Somalia's body politic, to stop the hemorrhage, but to no avail. Still he did not give up, and was soon in New York to provide background documentation for the United Nations Security Council meetings on Somalia. He was traveling constantly and saw less and less of his family. It was during this time that Dhaqaneh began acting out, skipping class until his frequent truancy led the school to threaten his expulsion.

When Mugdi was home, the tension in the household made him edgy and irritable. His sense of failure took the shine off his work for the nation. Frustrated and depressed, he cut himself off from the Somali community, spending more of his time in his study, at the gym, walking in a nearby park, or ensuring that Dhaqaneh was back on the straight and narrow.

But despite his efforts, all was not well with the boy, whose offenses began to increase in severity until he was charged with a minor felony, accused of injuring an elderly lady when he and his two Pakistani friends were tussling for a ball. Mugdi promised to Gacalo he would have a word with Dhaqaneh, but did not, busying himself instead with a new Somali political collective engaged in yet another peace dialogue. But when the collective's efforts ended in disaster and the men and women who formed it blamed one another along clan family lines, Mugdi vowed yet again never to have anything more to do with Somali politics or self-serving politicians.

The next time Gacalo had reason to plead with Mugdi to be firm with their son, Dhaqaneh was in another pickle with the police, accused of being the leader of a group caught in an unpremeditated fistfight with swastika-bearing skinheads. It soon became obvious that nothing Mugdi or anyone else could do would reverse the path their son was on, as it was not beyond Dhaqaneh to act violently toward everyone, including his own father, whom he took to describing as "a dud politician, incapable of succeeding where his peers had excelled," and whom he could not hold in respect.

When Dhaqaneh was in his teens and Mugdi was serving as Somalia's ambassador to West Germany, based in Bonn, Dhaqaneh was often described as his mum's boy, the two becoming quite close. Then, when puberty took total command of his mind and body, he spent more and more time alone in his room, the curtains drawn, listening to loud music, surfing the Internet, and watching porn. One night, during a visit home, Mugdi entered the boy's room and found his son completely in the nude, with a blue film on. Gacalo thought that a sabbatical away from Timiro—the two had been fighting ceaselessly—would very likely bring the best out of the boy; maybe he was finding living in close proximity to her daunting. For she was dutiful and he was not; she was hardworking at school and he was not; she excelled in everything at which she tried her hand and he did not; she showed future promise, he did not. Dhaqaneh hated being compared to her and he hated her guts too. What if Gacalo and Dhaqaneh returned to Mogadiscio? Would he benefit from being in a different place, with fewer amenities? They could try it for a few months, staying in the studio apartment they still owned in the city, which Mugdi used whenever he had occasion to return to Somalia, usually for work.

Dhaqaneh raised no objections to this plan, reasoning that he would deepen his knowledge of Somali, and perhaps learn to play the guitar and write his own lyrics in the language. His parents knew of his growing interest in music, sharpened after meeting one of his favorite Somali singers, who had come to give a concert in Cologne. He was fascinated watching the singer playing the pear-shaped, many-stringed instrument known in Arabic as *oud*, but commonly called *kaman* in Somali. Now Dhaqaneh said that he wanted nothing more than to apprentice himself one day to someone who could help him realize his commitment to singing and writing lyrics in Somali.

Gacalo and Mugdi were delighted he was eager to go to Mogadiscio, though Mugdi was considerably less pleased with his son's singing aspirations.

Mugdi asked, "What about school?"

"No school. I want to become a singer."

"It's all settled then," Gacalo said, and she purchased a kaman from a Lebanese shop specializing in Arab musical instruments. A fortnight later, mother and son were off. But they were back in Bonn before three months elapsed, Dhaqaneh having lost all interest in guitar playing and lyric writing. Besides, Somalia was not to his liking. Dhaqaneh was born and brought up abroad, and Mogadiscio was so different from the European cities he was accustomed to from his father's postings—Moscow, London, Brussels, Rome. Neither Gacalo nor Mugdi was surprised when Dhaqaneh said that he couldn't think of Somalia as his country.

On reflection, Mugdi would hand it to Gacalo that she had succeeded in her interventions with the boy early in his youth, when he worked and she was a housewife. When the roles reversed, she the breadwinner and it falling to him to be patient, tactful, and loving to the boy, he had failed.

Just as Mugdi and Gacalo tried one more time to improve their relationship with their son, Dhaqaneh started to become a fervent frequenter of the mosque. He divided his time between the local university, where he was doing a degree in media communications and taking his studies seriously, and the house of worship, where he avidly prayed. Yet neither of his parents knew that an imam notorious for his radical views was influencing his behavior. Dhaqa-neh was in his penultimate year of his studies when he displayed the first signs of displeasure at his family's secular behavior. Over the coming weeks, he became increasingly outspoken in his criticism of them, until finally their irreconcilable differences came to the fore.

Dhaqaneh, who had always been a person of extremes, would say, "I love this and no other," or "I hate this like no other." As a child, he'd insist on eating nothing but spaghetti for weeks on end, only to announce that he wanted no more spaghetti, would not touch spaghetti for months, nor explain why. Eventually, there came a point when everyone asked fewer questions about his choices.

Nearly fourteen years later, in 2003, Mugdi summoned Dhaqa-neh, by then a bespectacled and gangling man, with a full beard that had not known a blade, home for a private talk. He was calmer than he'd been in his youth, more pensive, following four years' uninterrupted stay in Mogadiscio.

In those years, once the imam's influence had taken hold, Dhaqa-neh loved Somalia, returning to Oslo, to Gacalo's delight and relief, only when he needed to replenish his depleted income. And when he was home, he remained secretive about his doings and where-abouts in Somalia. It irritated Mugdi no end when his son pontifi-cated about his wish to "purify Islam from the Western influence that is ruining the religion's originality."

One evening at dinner, when conversation touched on Al Qae-da's bombing of the US embassies in Nairobi and Dar es Salaam and the 9/11 massacre, Dhaqaneh declared that Islam was the one faith that would save the world and everyone on it from perdition and, if need be, he was prepared to kill to achieve this.

A row ensued, tempers were lost, strong words were used, de-spite Gacalo's pleas to her son to stop provoking his father and to

Mugdi to see what was happening for what it was: a son separating himself from his father, making his way in the wider world. At the time, Dhaqaneh worked as a volunteer at a Saudi-funded Muslim charity in Oslo, living in a one-room studio near the mosque, where he gave free instruction to young Somali students in math and science and ran evening classes for adults, earning just enough to pay the bills. To supplement his income, he drove a taxi. Gacalo sensed that Mugdi was unhappy about their son's lack of ambition. But she was pleased that he was at least popular among the Somalis, who adored him.

A few months later, Mugdi sought Dhaqaneh's opinion when the boy's religious mentor was reported to be under investigation, turned back from the airport, suspected of links to one of the 9/11 bombers. Was his son aware that Imam Yasiin had been headed to Mogadiscio when he was turned back? Mugdi asked, "Were the two of you planning to meet up there?"

The silence that followed was as deafening as it was prominent, as father and son stared at each other, neither willing to be the first to blink.

Mugdi broke it first, reminding Dhaqaneh that the people and government of Norway, in bold defiance of right-wing politicians and xenophobes, continued to admit into the country thousands of migrants and refugees, many of whom were Muslims. "I hope you and many others like you appreciate the government's open-handed and left-leaning policies."

"I've no idea what you're on about."

"How do you think Muslims should respond to Norway's current climate of openness and welcome?"

Dhaqaneh said, "The point is moot, Dad."

"What do you mean?"

"I view all non-Muslims as creatures bereft of souls and, as such, they are in no position to decide what they do. Rather, it is Allah's will that makes them host Muslims, and feed the multitudes starving in the famines in Somalia. In short, they have no choice in the matter."

Stunned once more into silence, Mugdi reminded his son of the non-Muslim friends the family had, like Johan and Birgitta. "What do you think about them? Are they also creatures bereft of souls?"

"I don't think of them as full humans," said Dhaqaneh, "and yes, if it came to it, I wouldn't hesitate to exterminate them."

The option of throwing his son out of the house and asking him never to show his face again crossed Mugdi's mind, yet he knew that such an idea would never fly with Gacalo.

As he walks into the arrivals hall, Mugdi cannot recall what he did or said in the immediate aftermath of that conversation. He knows Gacalo knows that he and Dhaqaneh had a falling out, but she has no complete understanding of what happened between father and son, and his determination to never share it fully has remained unshakable.

Mugdi finds a café facing the flight information board, gets himself a cup of coffee and a croissant, and watches the hordes of men and women also waiting at the arrivals gate, some holding placards in the air with the names of the persons they have come to pick up.

He assumes Waliya and Saafi, her daughter, to be loyal to a religious disposition of the sort that discourages physical contact between men and women unless they are married. Recently he has had the displeasure of extending his hand to shake that of a woman whom he has known for years, only for her to say, "I'm sorry, no handshakes." Not that he sought an explanation, but she said, "We were bad Muslims before now, but now we know better." On the contrary, he felt Somalis were better Muslims before the 1991 civil war poisoned their minds and ruined their hearts.

As his eyes move from the face of a Caucasian woman to a man with Middle Eastern features, and from a woman in a sari to an African man in an agbada, Mugdi is sad that scenes such as this, where a variety of races congregate at a public arena, are unavailable in Mogadiscio. As he watches the expressions on the faces of some of the Norwegians, he can spot some whose gentle features stiffen, turning ugly when they come face-to-face with a Muslim woman in full Islamic gear. Maybe a woman with a Muslim headscarf is seen as a threat, whereas a sari-wearing woman is viewed as unusual and fascinating in this part of the world. Mugdi remembers reading about a judge in the state of Georgia in the US who barred a woman with a headscarf from entering his court. Would the same judge turn away a Jewish man with a yarmulke or a nun in her habit? Mugdi thinks of himself as a spiritual man, even though he lacks the discipline to turn his sense of spiritualism into a formulaic faith with defined rituals and places of worship, where like-minded throngs professing to believe in the same faith congregate and pray on specific hours and days of the week. Mugdi doesn't like any form of regimentation.

His phone vibrates and he answers it after checking the identity of the caller. "Yes, darling?"

"We're having a tea break and I've just entered the flight details into the internet and I understand that there is a delay in the ETA," Gacalo says.

"Yes, I can see that on the board."

An hour later, the public address system announces that the flight Waliya and her children are supposed to be on has landed. Mugdi sends Gacalo a text message saying, "They're here."

# CHAPTER TWO

----------

A MOMENT LATER MUGDI DEBATES THE CORRECTNESS OF HIS STATEMENT given that Gacalo never received confirmation that the three did in fact leave Nairobi, from where Waliya was expected to call once they had passed through Kenya's rigorous security checks—Somalis boarding aircraft to most destinations are made to go through a more strenuous interrogation. Moreover, Waliya or one of her charges was also to make contact soon *after* landing in Brussels and *before* connecting with their flight to Oslo.

Mugdi is prepared to wait for as long as it takes, maybe several hours, remembering that Waliya and her children have been traveling for almost a fortnight, their journey having begun in Nairobi and from there to Entebbe, Uganda, on three forged Tanzanian passports and air tickets that Gacalo had paid for. The tickets would take them to Damascus, where they were to spend a little over a week at a hotel frequented by traffickers who specialized in ferrying illegals to their European destinations. Gacalo rang them daily, and Waliya kept her abreast of what was happening, informing her of the identity of those whom she met and bargained with, and what they said and did, but also if there was an immediate need for funds to be wired.

From Damascus they flew on to Nicosia, Cyprus, with a minder representing the trafficker in tow. The family lay low for a couple of days, hardly leaving their hotel in the Turkish-run portion of the island. From there they flew to Rome, where they arrived late at night, because the minder escorting them knew that the Italian immigration officer manning one of the counters would facilitate their entry into the city. In Rome, they put up at a hotel in the suburbs of the city near Fiumicino. Not that any of them would be interested in sightseeing, with their bodies in a free fall and their minds exhausted, unsure that they would ever make it to Oslo. Waliya advised patience when her son Naciim raged and Saafi almost joined him in a riotous mutiny. "Allah is on our side," she said.

Two days later, a taxi driven by a Somali whom Waliya suspected of belonging to the smuggler's ring fetched them from their hotel and drove them to the Stazione Termini. The driver provided them with sleeping car tickets, and they traveled by train from Rome to Brussels, where they would finally board their flight to Oslo.

Waliya and her children had no idea about the cantankerous communications between Gacalo and her immediate family members or that Timiro spoke her mind about the extravagant expenses incurred. "Close to nine thousand dollars! Are they worth this costly excursion?"

There was no guarantee, of course, that the three would not end up shortchanged by a wily trafficker, or even in a detention cell. And even if they do arrive safely, Gacalo believes they will likely be detained, as most asylum seekers are. In that case, access to them may not be granted until after they have endured a harrowing interview with the Norwegian Police's Refugee Department, with a Somali-speaking translator in attendance.

Mugdi would not be the right person to answer the questions the Norwegian authorities would be interested in, should they decide to interview him, as he was not party to the minutiae of the travel arrangements. He is convinced he has done the right thing by refusing to know the details of their progress. Both by nature and because of his diplomatic training, Mugdi is loath to take shortcuts. It is against his principles to go against the laws of Norway, the country that kindly hosted him when he couldn't return home. It won't surprise him if the family's standing suffers yet more devastation if something goes terribly wrong and Waliya and her children are deported back to Nairobi or, in the worst case, sent back to Mogadiscio.

Mugdi thinks that the apartment Waliya and her children will move into is perhaps the largest they have ever occupied, and surely much nicer than any place they previously called home. There will be plenty of food for them too, prepared with Gacalo's generous hand. Mugdi will feel that he has done his part and will leave them as soon as they are safely ensconced.

He now sits on a bench facing the exit the passengers are due to come through. He takes out a printout of the scene he is currently translating from *Giants in the Earth,* in which the Norwegian Per Hansa encounters a group of Indians camping a mile away from the Norwegians' recently established homestead. The presence of the Indians stirs fear in his wife, Beret's, heart. As with many of the impoverished, hardworking Norwegian fisherfolk who ended up as migrants in the Dakota Territory, fleeing not only poverty but also the terror associated with the midnight sun in summer and the debilitating winters, there is much to admire about Per Hansa's steadfast spirit, the spirit of a man born to lead and to endure, and while enduring, make something of his life.

Mugdi rereads his translation out loud and decides that the opening sentences lack the natural rhythm of the original. Furthermore, they do not enjoy the pathos of the scene, in which there is mutual suspicion and fear—nearly all the Norwegian homesteaders ascribe terrible thoughts to the "band" of Indians, fearing that they will scalp them, rob them of their handful of cattle, and deprive them of the swaths of land for which they paid only half a dollar an acre. Per Hansa is a singularly sensitive man, yet at no point does he seem concerned that they, the Norwegian homesteaders, are the ones who have dispossessed the Indians and pushed them off their land.

Mugdi remembers telling Gacalo that he started with this scene because of his interest in the initial encounter between the Norwegians and the North American Indians. Per Hansa and his fellow Norwegians represent a mightier and stronger Western way of thinking. When he thinks of what passes for mutual exchange—Per Hansa provides a sick Indian with ointments and bandages, and receives tobacco for a pipe—Mugdi can't help questioning whether there is fairness to their trade.

Presently, Mugdi hears the scuffle of a number of persons with signs bearing the names of arriving passengers. And suddenly, for reasons he cannot explain, he feels his brain fogged up, his mind leaden, weighed down with more questions than answers. He asks himself what he will do if Waliya and her charges were not allowed to board their flight to Oslo. He knows that the woman at the desk won't know, and even if she does, she won't share with him the names on the flight manifesto.

Then a fresh uncertainty imposes itself on Mugdi's mind, and his eyes darken as he concentrates on it fretfully. He tells himself that there is no way of knowing if Waliya is or is not an imposter, a mole assigned to perform a job on behalf of the jihadi group to which Dhaqaneh belonged. There is the possibility too that things may not work out to Gacalo's satisfaction or that, even assuming she is not a "sleeper," the family members may not find her and her brood to their liking. It worries him that the woman, a sympathizer, clearly, of the radical movement of which Dhaqaneh was a loyal member, is coming into their lives without being vetted. Forever an optimist, Gacalo trusted that everything would work out in the end. And whenever she couldn't give adequate answers to his questions, she merely advised him not to worry. She said, "Waliya and her children won't lose sight of the fact that this is their once-in-a-lifetime opportunity to enjoy peace. We'll provide them with all the assistance they need to find their feet and place the children in school."

"What about the widow?"

"She'll learn the language and work."

Mugdi does not have as much faith in Waliya as Gacalo does. Even so, he promised Gacalo that he would keep his runaway hatred of the Somalis, who, in his experience, seldom work when they can receive handouts from the state, in check. But he couldn't help speaking his mind. "I bet she won't want to work."

"Not if she wants to be on my good side."

From the little Gacalo had told him about Saafi, the girl's situation was more complex: she had no basic education and little English. Her best option was to attend the compulsory language classes to improve her chances of getting a job.

And when Gacalo felt truly backed into a corner, she attacked, saying, "Do you think that this is the kind of conversation to have a mere fortnight before their arrival? You're all making it sound as if I am the only one who has to find solutions to the myriad problems their presence will impose on us."

Timiro, as if speaking for all the others, would say, "Because, Mum, you're facilitating their coming."

Mugdi feels Gacalo is wrong, but he will not challenge her, lest she accuse him of elitism, of lacking empathy or being a moaner. Birgitta even once labeled him as perhaps the closest she had known to a self-hating Somali.

Johan, witness to one of these frequent arguments, said in defense of Mugdi, "He wants the Somalis to do well and to grab every opportunity with both hands, and there is nothing wrong with that. While today it takes only several hours' flight from any corner of the earth to the farthest corner of the planet, true integration requires several years."

The vibrating phone in the pocket of his jacket pulls him out of his thoughts. He checks the time on the phone and is surprised at how late it is. But there is still no sign of the widow and her children.

"News about their whereabouts?" he asks.

"The Immigration Police at the airport have been in touch with me and they've detained all three of them," she responds.

"That can't be a good thing. But go on."

"The officer instructed me that we must present ourselves in two days at their office at the airport for an in-depth interview."

Mugdi senses that her voice is imbued with a sense of triumph, as if she has succeeded in getting them over the first and most difficult line.

"Does that mean they won't deport them?"

"Not right away."

"So can I head home now?"

"Of course, darling."

As Mugdi drives home in the stop-and-go rush-hour traffic, he switches the radio on. There are riots in the US, right-wing vigilantes in cahoots with the KKK on a rampage in Virginia, and three hundred Africans and Middle Easterners have drowned as they attempted to cross the Mediterranean. In Myanmar, Buddhist monks massacre Rohingya Muslims; a bus full of schoolchildren veers off a high mountain in Serbia; and a high-rise in Cairo has collapsed because of structural flaws. Mugdi turns off the radio, convinced that the world is headed the wrong way and that perhaps the best news of the day is that the widow and her children have at least been allowed to enter the country and await a decision on whether they qualify as refugees. He hopes that they will.

# CHAPTER THREE

----------

MUGDI IS IN HIS UPSTAIRS STUDY, INTENT ON RENDERING A HANDFUL OF select scenes from *Giants* into Somali. Gacalo had assured him before she left for work that she had not received any further news from the Federal Police Post inside the international airport, whose officers had promised to provide them with an interview date, on which they'd be required to speak about their relationship with the new arrivals, their own income, and their willingness to help. He has now been at his desk for at least three hours, the text of the Norwegian original open side by side with the English translation, now reading the Norwegian, now the English, and now the Somali.

Now he rereads a portion of the scene he has just translated into Somali. In it, a group of native "Injuns" arrive and camp nearby. But when they depart and the half dozen cows on which the Norwegian settlers rely for their milk mysteriously disappear, some of the Norwegians suspect the "Injuns" of cattle rustling. A deep despondency reigns in the settlement when the cows do not return, with Beret, Per Hansa's wife, beset with fear that the untamed land, the prairies that stretch endlessly in every direction, is not meant for human existence. No wonder she nearly goes mad. Mugdi scribbles a note in the margin that, like the Norwegians in the Dakotas, Somalis too felt sundered from their previous lives when they first arrived in Norway, with its snowy landscape, half a year of sunless darkness, and the old truism about Norwegians' openheartedness being difficult for foreigners to gauge, especially those who do not drink with them or know their tongue.

He decides that it is impossible to predict how Waliya and her children will fare, though surely Naciim will have it easier than his sister, Saafi. Gacalo has told him something of the gang rape the girl suffered at the refugee camp in Kenya and the subsequent trauma to her psyche. She will require tender, loving care of the specialized sort. As for Waliya, his sense, based on what he knows of other Somali women of Waliya's age and background, is that she will behave tortoise-like, withdrawing into an unreachable domain, seldom sharing her thoughts with him. He'll keep a respectable distance and leave all the important decisions to Gacalo, as Waliya and Saafi will surely be more comfortable in her company. From what Gacalo has told him, Naciim is intelligent, hardworking, outgoing, and ambitious. On top of this, his stepfather Dhaqaneh accorded him a greater preference, inducting him into the position of a Mahram, the male head of the household, from an early age.

Now restless, Mugdi goes down to make coffee, only to discover there is no milk. He decides to go out, but first he remembers that Timiro is still here after deciding to extend her stay in Oslo. He knocks on the door to her room. Her voice weak and barely audible, she asks, "Who is it?" He tells her that he is stepping out to get some milk and wonders if she would like to go with him and get a bit of fresh air.

"I don't feel like leaving this room, Dad."

"Anything I can get for you?"

"No. Thanks."

When Mugdi arrives at the shop, he finds it closed—the note pinned to the door says "a family wedding." He pauses, crosses the road and heads south to the nearest supermarket that he knows, often walking past it on his way to or from the tram stop.

As he walks, he thinks of the similarities between Beret's life in the Dakotas and that of Somali women in Norway. Beret, in her fear of the prairie, covers the windows of her sod house and bars the door at the slightest worry whenever her husband is away. And the Somalis conceal their bodies with all-enveloping tents when they are outside the house, afraid of whom they may run into.

At the supermarket, having gotten his milk, Mugdi stands in line to pay as the TV replays news of two terror attacks that appear to have just occurred in Britain—one in London, the other in Glasgow. According to the newscast, the attackers, "who may have been radical Muslims," reportedly tried to detonate bombs in London using cell phones, but did not succeed, whereas in Glasgow, an SUV carrying bombs burst into flames after slamming into one of the entrances to Glasgow Airport. British officials are of the view that the two attacks are connected.

When the newscast moves on to international sports, the stunned silence is at first quite deafening. Mugdi immediately thinks of his younger brother Kaluun, who, last he recalled, was traveling in Scotland. He can't remember if he was supposed to be in Edinburgh or Glasgow, training a group of young Africans on some British Council stipend in radio reporting. He thinks that he must telephone him, see if he and his partner Eugenia are safe, when a woman with a pierced tongue, who is at the head of the line, turns round and addresses the other shoppers, her voice filled with rage. She says, "Imagine what will become of our country if Muslims and blacks are the majority, which they will be in another two decades, unless we stop them from coming in. At the high rate they breed, they are already a threat."

A young tattooed man says, "You can't be serious."

"I am very serious," says Pierced-Tongue.

A debate erupts, with several people talking at the same time and taking sides. The majority of those who speak are opposed to the view held by Pierced-Tongue. A young woman says to her, "You take us for fools when you and your lot say stuff like that. There is no way Muslims and blacks will ever form the majority in Norway. Come on, talk sense."

Mugdi wonders what Pierced-Tongue might say or do if she knew that not only was his Norwegian-raised son a terrorist, but now his family has helped his widow and stepchildren to come to Oslo.

Pierced-Tongue looks from Mugdi to the Pakistani shop manager and says in a voice marked by pique, "We host *them*, clothe *them*, provide *them* with food and do you know what *they* do? Instead of showing *their* gratitude, they bomb our subways, attack our buses, and kill thousands when they destroy our buildings. A plague on their faith."

Then she stomps off, leaving her purchases behind on the counter, despite the manager's attempt to call her back.

Mugdi remembers the frightening effect 9/11 had on nearly every Norwegian he talked to, including Birgitta and Johan. Then just four years later there were the attacks on London's underground and the bombing of the double-decker bus, in which more than fifty people lost their lives. And even though there have been many more suicide bombings in Iraq, Somalia, Afghanistan, Yemen, and Pakistan, the Norwegians thought little of these. They may have empathized with the victims—just never as much as when the killings took place close to home, and the dead were Europeans.

When finally it is Mugdi's turn to pay, he feels a quiverful of hostile arrows directed at his back. He begins to relax only when he leaves the store.

Mugdi arrives home and finds Timiro making a bowl of miso soup. Her movements are a bit slow and uncoordinated and her complexion is pallid. She is in a bathrobe, her hair wet, straggly, and short at the back. As he moves with speed toward the phone to make the call to Kaluun, Timiro asks, "Why do you look gloomy? What's happened?" When he tells her about the attacks in Glasgow and London, she says, "Are they okay, Uncle Kaluun and Eugenia?"

"That's what I'm trying to find out."

As the landline in his brother's apartment rings and he waits for either his brother or Eugenia to answer, he asks Timiro how she is feeling. "I'm tired, no energy at all." About to head upstairs, she waits, eager to know that all is well with Kaluun and Eugenia, until she figures out from the conversation between her father and uncle, now that Kaluun has answered the phone, that everything is okay. She says to her father, "Give them both my love, Dad." Then, taking the bowl of soup with her, she trundles up the stairs to her bedroom without much ceremony.

Mugdi, pausing, picks up faint footsteps as his brother explains that he is going out on the balcony overlooking Abney Park cemetery, a woodland memory park in east London where the two brothers often took long enjoyable walks together.

"Everything is okay with me and Eugenia," Kaluun says.

"When did you get back from Scotland?"

"We took the night train and arrived this morning."

"I am glad you are safe and resting."

Kaluun says, "My head of division wants me to help out, relieve a colleague who was on the night shift."

"The bells of panic are sounding all over Europe. We've heard them loud and clear here in Norway," Mugdi says. "And even though the perpetrators haven't as yet been apprehended, my feeling is that it will be someone who looks like us, whom we wholeheartedly condemn. But of course all of us will be painted with the same brush. I hope that things settle down soon."

"I think it'll be a long while before it does. But tell me how Timiro is doing. Eugenia and I were glad when she telephoned and gave us the news that she is pregnant."

"She is out of sorts and fatigued," says Mugdi. "But apart from that she is all right. She sends her love."

"Last time we spoke, she confirmed to me and Eugenia that her marriage is a dud. Myself, I've inquired about Xirsi's whereabouts, but my search hasn't produced any good results. No one I know seems to know where he is."

"You introduced them, didn't you?"

Kaluun changes the subject with formidable speed. He says, "Tell me about the widow and her children."

"There is nothing much to tell."

"They are in Oslo, right?"

"They are indeed, but we haven't seen them yet. They are being held for interrogation. I don't know how long the whole process will take, but let me say that it will most definitely take longer now that this has happened in Glasgow and London. You can be sure the right-wing groups will bay for Muslim blood, for deportations and draconian laws of surveillance."

"You paint a dark picture, my brother."

A skirmish of sorts insinuates itself into Kaluun's voice. Something has happened to him, Mugdi thinks. Back when he first moved to England, he used to be as hardy as winter fodder. But lately he has softened.

"What are you thinking?" asks Mugdi.

"We are thinking of selling our house here in London and pur-chasing property on an island, somewhere in the Caribbean, for when we retire."

Mugdi knows that Kaluun seldom plans his trips well in advance and therefore he often pays over the odds for his airline tickets for his impromptu travels. When he does decide to travel, he can afford it. He has a good job with the BBC and no children to bring up. He has never married, but has shared his life with his partner, Eugenia, whose parents are from Montego Bay, though she was born and brought up in London, where she is a reputable barrister. From what they have told Mugdi, the two of them have no plan to wed. But they are happy together and that is what matters. Mugdi is very fond of Eugenia too.

"Why the Caribbean? Because of Eugenia?"

"Because it is also the one cosmopolitan place in the world where everyone is welcome, and where I would feel less tense, less fearful. People in the smaller islands have learned to live and let live. At least that is how I felt whenever I went there."

"It is one thing to visit for a week, and altogether something else if you move there in a permanent way."

Kaluun says, "I am aware of that." Then after a pause, he goes on, "Anyhow, it is time you came to visit us in London. You haven't been here for a long while."

"Not when everyone is nervy, thank you."

"It won't be like this for long."

Mugdi notes that Kaluun has contradicted what he said a couple of minutes ago, when he guessed that things would take a long time to settle.

"I'll believe it when I see it."

"Big cities have a way of adjusting to shocks far better than small towns or more homogenous communities. If this were to happen in Oslo, then that would almost be the end of Norway, as we know it. That is my feeling."

Again, the timbre of Kaluun's voice undergoes a noticeable change. It is as though someone has joined him on the balcony. As if to prove this, Kaluun says, "I must go. Please give my love to both Timiro and Gacalo."

And they both hang up.

Sixteen years separate the two brothers. Their father was a police officer from Galkacyo in the central region of Somalia, the first member of his family to abandon the pastoralist lifestyle and join the youths migrating to the cities, landing a lowly position in the police force. Much hard work and dedication, night school, and eventually his conscription into the first police academy in the country set him apart from the other new recruits receiving on-the-job training. Later, he would be selected as one of a handful of officers to go abroad for further training, returning home after five years, just as Somalia was put under United Nations trusteeship in 1950. Within a year of his return, he was being groomed as one of the first officers to gain a command and soon after was appointed as the officer in charge of an entire suburban district. And when Somalia was granted its political independence, their father was second in rank to the Commandante Della Polizia.

Kaluun was a problem to his parents and a pest to his sisters—the brothers had five sisters between them. As a child, Kaluun was involved in more fights than most of his peers. Not only did Mugdi try his hand at molding him, but eventually he succeeded in guiding him through the difficulties he faced in his teenage years. What is more, he protected him from their father, who had such a temper you would not want it turned on you lest it destroy you. When Kaluun skipped class, Mugdi would cover for his brother by forging their father's signature to excuse his absence. Then one day Kaluun got into a fistfight with a much older boy and broke his opponent's nose, which resulted in the headmaster inviting their father for a conversation, a situation Mugdi could do nothing to shield his brother from. Kaluun got no less a punishment than he deserved, receiving his father's wrath in the form of lashes on his back and the soles of his feet that were so severe he couldn't walk for a week or sleep without feeling pain. The fear of what his father might do if he misbehaved again kept him on the straight and narrow from then on.

It so happened that half a year after Mugdi landed his first posting as a junior diplomat in West Germany, Kaluun took his high school finals and his results were good enough to have him admitted into the National University's Faculty of Journalism.

Gacalo, a housewife at the time, was very unhappy and felt unfulfilled, in that she desperately wanted to become a mother and couldn't, despite their attempts. She consulted doctors several times and then convinced Mugdi that he too should take a test. But the results were inconclusive. For his part, Mugdi had no worries on this score. He was in his early thirties and Gacalo was six years younger. He was convinced there was plenty of time for them to sort out whatever problems there were in this area. But Gacalo's anxiety was starting to cause daily frictions. After an all-night, air-clearing conversation, Gacalo, who was now inclined to try alternative approaches, suggested that she return home to Somalia. Mugdi said he had no objections, suspecting that she would in all likelihood take counsel from an herbalist, since modern medicine had failed her.

When Gacalo met Kaluun and he told her that he and a girl, a classmate, were reckless and she was now past the possible date for safe abortion, Gacalo decided to step in and help. Luckily the girl was large, and so far it was not obvious she was that far along, especially to her elderly grandmother, who was half blind and almost deaf. Gacalo, following a brief meeting with the girl, agreed to wade into the mess with a solution that might benefit them all. She rang Mugdi to update him on how matters stood: that the school term had just ended and classes would not begin again for another three months. Perhaps she had a window in which she could do something, provided fortune was on her side.

"So what is the plan?" he asked.

Gacalo said, "Possibly I can arrange to whisk her away, take the girl away on some pretext—say, that the girl, being exceptional in her studies, has received a three-month scholarship to study in Mombasa, Kenya."

"Are there no other options?"

"For one thing, Kaluun doesn't wish to marry her, and for another, the girl is prepared to do anything to bring an end to the mess. My plan is safer than a backstreet abortion."

"Be careful. That's all I am saying."

She said she would be very careful.

Mugdi always admired his wife's pluckiness and promised he would support whatever decisions she took, but it would be wise if she didn't tell him everything, lest he worry.

The next time he heard from her, Gacalo and the girl were in Mombasa. Gacalo hoped no one would ask her or the girl too many questions.

In Mombasa, they put up in a hotel the first week and then found a friendly estate agent who helped them rent a ground-floor two-room apartment in the suburban village of Mwembe Tayari, where there were fewer residential homes, giving them more privacy. They met no difficulty registering the baby as Gacalo's at the municipality, thanks to a junior clerk's willingness to assist after payment of a palm-greasing fee.

Once the girl had healed, Gacalo sent her back to Mogadiscio on her own; she stayed behind for three more months, spending the last two of these in Nairobi to apply for the baby's visa to be put in her ordinary Somali passport. Again, she bribed Kenyan immigration officials, this time to leave the country, the baby wrapped in layers of clothing. In Mogadiscio, Gacalo arranged adoption papers. Mugdi was delighted to be the father of a baby girl, named for Gacalo's late mother, Timiro—the one who is as sweet as dates.

Gacalo bottle-fed the baby, who was easygoing and slept and fed well. In secret, however, she put the baby to her nipples and "suckled" her in the mythical belief based on well-worn Somali wisdom that she might bear a child. Gacalo still believes that it is thanks to "suckling" the baby that she became pregnant four years later and gave birth to Dhaqaneh.

Gacalo would eventually learn from Kaluun that Timiro's birth mother had met a sad end: she died in an car accident a year and a half after giving birth to Timiro. She had been on her way to the airport to travel to Bucharest, where she was to study at a medical college after finally graduating from high school.

It never occurred to either Mugdi or Gacalo to wonder if Kaluun would let it slip to Timiro that he was actually her biological parent. It was always explained that she was adopted as a baby. Why tell her more than she asked answers to? She is happy as their daughter and that is what matters to all concerned.

- - - - - -

When Gacalo returns home after a very long day at the office, her heart appears so heavy that she seems to be carrying an extra load.

Timiro times her entrance well by arriving just as Mugdi is making tea for himself and Mum. She says, "Make it three, Dad."

Mugdi gives them Kaluun's affectionate regards.

"Have you spoken to him and how are they?" asks Gacalo.

He says, "They're well and safely back in London from the West of Scotland, where they were holidaying."

"I'm hoping that the paranoia resulting from the bombings in Glasgow and London does not impact negatively on Waliya and her children's application to stay in Norway," says Gacalo.

"It worries me too that the specter of fear in the West will be raising its head again," says Mugdi. "We could do without these provocations, SUVs ramming into airports or devices exploding in underground stations, barbarous acts that complicate matters for the widow and her children and many like them. And us too—we are all vulnerable."

After a few minutes, Gacalo pleads exhaustion, bending double. She stoops her head, closes her eyes, tightens her jaws, and grinds her teeth as if in pain. Mugdi and Timiro know of her weak heart. Mugdi remembers a similar flaring up of the condition when they received news of Dhaqaneh's suicide. And as if confirming his conclusions her hand goes to the left side of her chest, squeezing it. Mugdi goes over to her and holds her hand in his, saying, "Not to worry, darling. Everything will work out."

Gacalo straightens, shifts in her chair, breathes in and then out, her eyes opening, as if amazed that she is still alive. "I hope so."

# CHAPTER FOUR

----------

THE FOLLOWING MORNING, GACALO, FEELING MUCH BETTER AFTER A REST-
ful night, is downstairs having a light breakfast with Timiro. The
young woman gets herself a glass of water and sits across from her
mother. She says, "I had a bizarre dream last night."

"Why bizarre?"

"I was at a party in Geneva and the heel of my right shoe came
off. When I took it to the shop to have it repaired, the woman
working there told me it was a knockoff."

The phone rings and Timiro falls silent as Gacalo answers. The
caller identifies himself as the deputy head of the Politiets utlend-
ingsenhet (PU)—the Police Foreign Unit responsible for registering
newly arrived asylum seekers.

He says, "I have a couple of preliminary questions for you
about Ms. Ahmed and her two underage children who've claimed
to be your relatives. She is your son's widow—he was a Norwegian national and so are the other members of your family. We're
going to need you to appear in person to answer some more
questions."

"I know of their presence in the country, because Waliya has been in touch with me by phone."

"The widow claims they are your guests."

"She and the children are our guests, yes."

"She says that you've found them a place to live and that you'll be responsible for their expenses until the Norwegian Directorate of Immigration determines their status. Is my understanding correct?"

"Yes, your understanding is correct."

"You realize that the widow and her children are not entitled to economic support from the state from the moment they come with you until their asylum papers are issued?" he asks.

"Yes, I am aware of that."

The officer says, "Please bring along all the necessary documents, including the rental contract for the house or apartment where your relatives will live. If and when you meet these conditions, then you can come and collect them from custody," and he gives her the address.

"Is it okay if my husband comes with the signed documents and fetches them from there?" she asks.

"Yes, of course," and he hangs up.

She has hardly put down the phone when Mugdi comes into the kitchen. He is in his pajamas and rubbing his eyes, awakening to the new reality about which he is sure Gacalo will tell him. He hugs her—there must be a special occasion, he thinks, because she is dressed the Somali way, in a frock with flower patterns—and then embraces Timiro before taking the seat facing them. Gacalo gives him a rundown of what the officer has said.

"Darling, will you be able to pick them up from the arrivals hall at the airport today?"

"Of course," he says.

As Mugdi stands once again within view of the arrivals hall exit, a mobile phone with the tone of a muezzin calling all Muslims to afternoon prayer starts chiming and he looks around the terminal, curious whom the phone belongs to and how non-Muslims in the vicinity will react to the summons for prayer. His eyes alight on a young man sporting a full beard and no mustache standing close to an elderly woman in the habit of a nun—her cowl sky blue, her scapular white with black fringes. Born a Muslim, albeit seldom practicing the faith, the ringing of the muezzin stirs memories within him.

Mugdi wants to know what the nun makes of all of this and as he watches her, her cheeks widen into a sweet grin and her eyes light up with genuine amity. He can't tell if she is from the South of India or from Sri Lanka, but given that there is a very old man in a wheelchair beside her, he decides she is his caregiver. On further scrutiny, he thinks the two of them look alike; maybe they are related.

Mugdi asks, "How old is he?"

"Just turned ninety," she replies.

"What of the family resemblance?"

"He is my older brother."

"Are you from South India or Sri Lanka?"

"We are from Sri Lanka."

"Have you been here a long time?" he asks.

"We've been here much too long."

"So have we," Mugdi says. "My wife and I."

"Lately, however," she continues, "my brother has been finding the weather too unwelcoming. And now that the civil war in our country has more or less ended and he has attained the ripe age of ninety, he wishes to spend his remaining days in Colombo, where he wants to be buried."

The old man drops the straw through which he has been drinking and his sister picks it up, cleans it with a paper napkin and gives it back to him. She asks, "What about you? Will you be going back to where you came from—to die and be buried there too?"

"I wish I knew I could go back."

"Your accent—it sounds Somali. The strife continues to rage in your country, I understand."

Mugdi hesitates. "Yes, I come from Somalia."

"Your Bokmål is excellent," she says.

"I've been here for twenty-odd years."

She says, "I am Tam, short for Tamannah."

"Everyone calls me Mugdi," he says.

Tam takes out a cloth and gently wipes the saliva of her brother's chin. He wakes in a startle, opens his eyes, and says, "What?" She says something to him in Tamil. In response, the old man nods, his jaws moving in the manner of a baby chewing something in its sleep.

"Is every second Somali named Mohamed?"

"Do you know many Somalis?" asks Mugdi.

"I have a few acquaintances in my neighborhood, in Groenland. It seems that out of every three Somalis, one is called Mohamed. Besides, many have nicknames. Do you have a Mohamed somewhere among the names you bear?" she asks him.

He says, "As it happens, my given name is Mohamed too, but I answer to Mugdi, a nickname, meaning 'midnight black.' I was named so by my mother, after she clapped eyes on me and said, 'My God, I gave birth to midnight.' Then she had a good laugh."

"Do you live in Groenland too?"

"We live in Bislett."

"Many of the Somalis in my block are too noisy and unruly," she says. "Some seem to court unnecessary trouble. As a result of this, half a dozen of them have recently fallen victim to the Child Welfare Services, their school-age children now placed in foster care."

Mugdi has heard of a number of Somali parents who have fallen afoul of the Barnevernet. He has also heard of Somalis who, fearing that the agency may place their offspring in state care, have sent their young ones either back to Somalia or to their kith and kin elsewhere in Europe.

Tam asks, "You're not traveling, are you?"

"I am meeting my son's widow and children."

"How old are the children?" she asks.

"The girl is fourteen, the boy twelve."

"Will they stay with you?" she asks.

"We've found them a flat in Groenland."

The airport public address system advises the passengers flying to Colombo via Dubai to go to the gate, with departure expected on time. The nun looks at her brother, who is enjoying his sleep. She prepares to wheel him away, but not before she places his carry-on bag at his feet, checks that she has the tickets and passports, and then wakes him up with a loving whisper. Then she bids Mugdi farewell, saying, "All the best to you and your son's widow and her children."

Shortly after the nun's departure, Mugdi observes a teenager who bears a likeness to the photo he has of Naciim, pushing a trolley loaded sky-high with unruly suitcases. A young girl and an older woman, both in body tents, walk behind him, keeping their distance, though it is clear they and the boy are together. Mugdi lets them walk past him, as he makes a quick phone call to Gacalo saying, "They are here," and hangs up just as fast. Then he calls out a greeting in Somali. "*Nabad*, Naciim!"

Naciim turns at hearing his name, sees and wraps himself around Mugdi in an emotional embrace. Waliya and Saafi, meanwhile, retrace their steps with deliberate slowness, pausing, then exchanging hesitant looks and words that Mugdi can't make out, their hands making sure that their face veils are in place.

Mugdi advances toward them slowly, his hands behind his back—he does not expect either woman to greet him physically, as Naciim has. He says now to Waliya, now to Saafi, "Welcome to Norway."

Naciim says, "Are we taking the train?"

"We have a rental car, waiting."

Mugdi leads the way, with the boy following and the women trailing behind. Mugdi and Naciim wait as two lifts come and depart.

Mugdi knows that for a boy who has spent much of his life in a refugee camp in a dusty border town, far from cities with great amenities, being driven in a car is a big deal. Growing up in Somalia, those of Mugdi's friends with cars were the ones who attracted all the girls.

"Where *are* they?" says the boy, miffed.

They watch the women walking slowly toward them.

Naciim says, "Look at them. Stepdad Dhaqaneh used to say that in Europe time is money. They must learn to move fast."

When Waliya and Saafi arrive, the four of them step into the lift. Mugdi observes fear in the women's eyes when three huge, loud Norwegian men step into the lift as well, one of them pushing his way farther in as he speaks to his companions, his gesticulating hands nearly coming into contact with Waliya. The widow with-draws in panic and says out loud in Somali, "Will someone talk to him please?"

Mugdi, behaving with paramount propriety, does not address his words to Waliya but says in a whisper to the boy to tell his mother that the men that have come into the elevator are just shar-ing a good-natured banter among themselves and that there is nothing to give them worry.

In the parking garage, Mugdi offers to help Naciim with the trolley. But the boy says that he can do it all on his own. When they reach the car, Waliya and Saafi get in the back and the boy takes his seat in the front.

Naciim says, "A beautiful car."

The boy passes his hand admiringly over the dashboard and touches the inside of the vehicle. He says, "When I am grown, I will buy a car just like this."

"You'll have to earn a lot to own a car."

"I have five dollars I've saved from my share of the travel allow-ance Grandma Gacalo has sent us and I'll buy a lottery coupon and will win the lottery jackpot."

Waliya speaks for the first time since the lift, saying, "Gaming is a crime in Islam and I won't allow it."

Naciim twists his mouth into a sneer. Mugdi is tempted not only to tell the boy off about his unacceptable behavior, but also that no one in Oslo will sell a lottery ticket to him until he attains the age of eighteen. He thinks better of it. and decides to wait for the right opportunity.

Then Mugdi's mobile phone rings and he converses briefly with Gacalo in Italian, a language Mugdi assumes Waliya and her children will not understand, letting her know that they are on their way.

He tells Naciim to put on the seat belt and asks that he tell his mother and sister to do the same. He finds it tedious that the new social convention prevailing among Islamists in Somalia nowadays discourages men from speaking directly to women except via a Mahram.

As Mugdi drives, he observes in the rearview mirror that the women's lips are astir, seemingly reciting verses from the Koran. He directs his eyes back to the road. He has scarcely gone half a kilometer when Naciim asks if he was talking in Italian before.

"Do you understand Italian?" he asks.

"Not yet. But I want to learn many languages," the boy says. "Norwegian, French, Italian, and I will improve my English."

Now Saafi pipes up for the first time, asking in a small voice, "What about Arabic?"

Naciim asks, "What about it?"

"It's the Prophet's tongue, may Allah's blessing be on him. And it's the language every Muslim must learn."

Naciim makes a face and his sister's expression darkens.

Mugdi, in the meantime, has observed that Saafi and Waliya do not have their seat belts on. He pulls over, but does not turn off the engine. He tells Naciim to tell his mother and sister to please put their safety belts on, as it is obligatory in Norway.

Waliya retorts, "We'll die on the day that Allah has ordained for us to die, whether we wear this thing or not."

"I'll be made to pay a heavy fine if you don't have it on," Mugdi shoots back. "Would you like me to pay a heavy fine?"

Grudgingly they comply, and the rest of the car ride is silent.

When they reach their apartment building, Mugdi rings Gacalo once more. She confirms that she is inside and ready to let them in.

When they enter, Gacalo, not veiled, but dressed in the Somali way, in a flower-patterned frock, a shawl, and her head covered welcomes Mugdi with a hug and she says, "Thanks, darling." Then Waliya and Saafi greet Gacalo cursorily and then take off at the first opportunity. Naciim, however, stands close to Mugdi, behaving as if he belongs to the old man's world rather than the one into which the women have taken refuge.

The boy moves about, peering out the windows, touching the walls, and admiring the airy cleanliness of the place. He paces back and forth, as if taking measure of how spacious the apartment is in comparison to the shacks in the refugee camp. Then he says to Mugdi, "Please come with me and let us go round and see the rooms, because I want to choose mine."

Naciim leads Mugdi by the hand and they go first into a room that is sparingly furnished, Naciim looking around and saying, "Maybe this will be Saafi's."

Leaving the room, he turns left, Mugdi following, and they come to a door that is locked from inside. Naciim gently taps on it and with no one answering walks on, saying, "Maybe that is the room where Mum and Saafi are now."

Eventually, they come to an en suite room overlooking a garden. Naciim sits down on the double bed in the farthest corner. Excited, he speaks with the brazen tone of someone determined to have his way. He says, "This will be my room."

"Why not consult your mum first?"

"But it is the room with the best view."

Mugdi understands the boy's meaning: that the best of everything goes to the man of the household and, since he is male, the largest room with the best view is his by right. Mugdi is upset, not so much with the boy as with the tradition that pampers the male species.

Mugdi says, "Where have you learned this machismo? You make me unhappy when you badmouth your mother and sister, who treat you as though you were their Mahram, their male guardian. In our family, we don't approve of this sort of behavior."

Naciim frowns in mock anger and says nothing.

"How would your stepdad have reacted if he were here and you talked this way? Would he call you out, or would it not bother him at all?"

"He would find nothing wrong with it. In fact, Stepdad Dhaqaneh would encourage me to think of myself as the man of the house, the boss of the womenfolk, the Mahram."

Mugdi has heard men described as the protectors of the womenfolk and that the man's first job is to preserve the honor of the family in every possible way. Mugdi can't help thinking that he and Gacalo have their work cut out for them.

Naciim continues, "Stepdad Dhaqaneh would want me to be his stand-in."

"What does that entail?"

"It means that my mother and sister can't do anything without my express permission and I can punish them if they are out of line," says Naciim.

"Do you think that's the right way to behave for a boy your age?"

"Once in his absence," says Naciim, "my mother and Saafi attended a wedding without letting me know beforehand, and when he returned and I reported what they did, he told them off. He said that in his absence they should take orders from me."

"Did he ever hit or maltreat your mother?"

"He disciplined her often," says Naciim.

"Did the disciplining include smacking?"

"Yes, but not as often as he smacked me."

"Why was that?"

"Because he saw me as his 'selectman.'"

"What did he mean by that?"

"That I was worth more than the women."

From the hallway, they hear Gacalo wondering, "Where are the men?"

Mugdi calls, "We are here, darling."

She asks, "What are you up to?"

"The young man and I are getting to know each other. I can't help thinking that this fellow has a lot to unlearn."

After a few minutes of small talk, Gacalo walks off in the direction of the kitchen and Mugdi and Naciim follow her. In the kitchen, Gacalo turns her gentle gaze on Mugdi and she says to him in Italian that he may go home now, thanks.

Naciim works out that Mugdi is preparing to depart and asks if he can go with him today. Mugdi says, "Not today."

"Do you have TV at your home?"

"We do," replies Mugdi.

"Can I come and watch it sometime?"

"You'll watch it when you visit us."

"I hear you own lots of books."

Gacalo says, "We have plenty of books."

"What kind of books?"

"Books of all sizes in every genre, in Italian, English, Russian, Somali, Arabic, and Norwegian."

"Stepdad Dhaqaneh had more books than anyone else I knew,"

Naciim says, "and he read a lot. He taught me to read and write. But I had difficulties reading and was never good at it until he started to help me. Reading used to bore me, but not anymore."

"What do you like doing, when not reading?"

"I love watching soccer on TV."

"Do you play soccer?"

"I love playing it too."

Mugdi says to Gacalo, "See you at home."

"Thanks for picking them up and bringing them home," she says.

And he is out of the door before Naciim has a chance to ask him when he will see Mugdi again.

# CHAPTER FIVE

----------

FOR THE THIRD EVENING IN A ROW, GACALO ARRIVES HOME LATER THAN usual, pleading exhaustion and explaining that after work she has gone to visit the widow and her charges in her effort to help them find their feet. It is unlike her to be away from her home and husband this often, but she feels she is justified in devoting time to the three new arrivals, each with a different set of demands and interests. Nor, as Mugdi might have expected, has she been sharing the details of her exchanges with them, only that there have been problems.

Mugdi is in the upstairs bathroom, the door open and the lights off. He cleans his teeth, using the over-spilling brightness from the bedroom. He likes to walk about in scarcely lit spaces. When the lights are on downstairs, he may not turn the upstairs ones on. He argues that he feels rested that way and that he sees better. Timiro teases him by comparing him to a cat moving with stealth: for he is on top on you, she says, before you know it.

Of late, Gacalo and Mugdi have met in near silence, their heads crowded with thoughts that neither wishes to put into words. Last night, Gacalo accused Mugdi of envying Waliya and her children the care she has given them; of being so bitter that he couldn't even refer to the widow by name. Gacalo wished there was a way for him to allow his good-natured side to come out on top, as it used to.

They meet on the landing, just as Gacalo gains the topmost stair and Mugdi is about to enter the bedroom. Gacalo steps out of his way and then follows him into the room.

He gives her enough time to put her handbag on the windowsill and to change out of her outdoor clothes and into pajamas. He stays silent until she has cleaned her teeth, washed her face, and taken her place under the covers on the left side of the bed.

"How have things been?"

"Timiro is going through a bad patch."

Gacalo furrows her brows in the dim light and gathers the top sheet around her. Married for five years, Timiro remained loyal despite Xirsi's constant lies and straying from the conjugal bed for months at a time. Mugdi and Gacalo never could abide the fellow, and even Kaluun, who introduced the two and appreciates Xirsi's charm, acknowledges that he has credibility issues. Kaluun insists that Timiro knew what the man was like before getting involved with him, but that she saw no reason not to forge ahead. "There is no womanizer who can't be cured of his profligacy," she'd say.

Gacalo thinks that Dhaqaneh's dying before giving them a grand-child has been an irksome thing. Now she says to Mugdi, "And what a grand delight it will be for us to welcome Timiro's baby into our lives, a grandchild to love and pamper in our old age. I can't wait."

Mugdi, suppressing a yawn, says, "Like you, I look very much forward to the baby, which will be both a blessing and a joy in our hearts."

Then she turns her back on him and fluffs the pillows, and placing some distance between them, she says, "Night, honey." But she is unsure if he heard her.

When Mugdi finally falls asleep, he dreams of visiting Kaluun and Eugenia, and walking through Abney Park Cemetery. He calls at several graves of abolitionist men and women buried there. At some point, a sudden downpour erupts and he seeks shelter in a cave as large and dark as a basement apartment.

Soon he is joined by a group of men, women, and children dressed in white, the men heavily bearded and with skullcaps, the women veiled and barefoot, and the children carrying books with the titles of sacred texts on their spines. Mugdi leaves the cave only after it has stopped raining and returns to Kaluun and Eugenia's home.

The following morning, Mugdi and Gacalo are up early. Timiro joins them and asks, "When can I visit Waliya and her children? What is she like? Do you reckon she'll do well here and integrate?"

"I think it'll take her a long time to adjust," says Gacalo. "Not many unlettered women of her age do well, if they put into their heads that they won't do well. And Waliya strikes me as someone who has already decided that."

"How old is she?"

"She is twenty-nine, thirty."

"For all she's gone through, I assumed she was older. And where was she raised?"

"According to her personal details in the forged Tanzanian passport, she was born in Mogadiscio," replies Gacalo. "But then can you trust the biodata in a false passport?"

"And what of the children, Saafi and Naciim? What are they like?"

Mugdi says, "He is something, the boy."

"I think the boy has as much to learn as he has to unlearn," says Gacalo, "if he is to navigate his way around this new environment."

"Saafi is a peaceable sort, mild-mannered, too easily intimidated, but petite and pretty."

"Do they fight, Saafi and Naciim, the way Dhaqaneh and I used to fight, like rats in a sack, no holds barred?" Timiro asks.

Gacalo says, "You fought with the ferocity of a cat marking its territory, if Dhaqaneh preyed on your insecurities, like when you got your first period."

Timiro says, "Dad always protected me—even when I was at fault. All I had to say was, 'Dad, Dhaqaneh is mean to me,' safe in the knowledge that Dad would punish him."

Mugdi says to Timiro, "You knew no better."

Gacalo says, "But you were a soft touch."

Mugdi trains his full stare on Gacalo and then goes up to his study without another word.

He and Gacalo often disagreed about how best to solve the mystery that was Dhaqaneh, and now that their son is dead, each assigns a portion of the blame to the other. Neither wants their closeness to suffer irreparably. Yet Gacalo hectors him about how he favored and cherished Timiro more. In a particularly heated moment, he once said in defense, "Because she was a pleasanter person, let us face it."

"How could you say that?" she demanded.

Before he could stop himself, he fired back with "Where is he now and where is Timiro, as we speak? One of them is here and alive, the other is dead after causing so much death to other communities."

Even though Mugdi's forthrightness unnerves Gacalo, she failed to come up with an immediate riposte to his remarks. As a result, she averted her eyes, and avoiding meeting his gaze, she stared into space, her senses benumbed by what Mugdi had said.

# CHAPTER SIX

----------

TWO DAYS LATER, THE MOOD IS GOOD AND LIGHT. GACALO IS PLEASED THAT Timiro is well enough to make a courtesy call on the widow and her children. Timiro says, "It's high time I met her. And it'll be a welcome distraction." Timiro has just gotten off the phone with Eugenia, who is setting up an appointment with a lawyer so Timiro might start filing for divorce from Xirsi.

Mugdi waylays the two women with a question. "Did you not say to me that Saafi is suffering from terrible nightmares?"

"Yes, I did," replies Gacalo.

"What shape do they take—the girl's nightmares?"

"In the dream," says Gacalo, "it is all pitch dark and she is chased by a bearded man carrying a torch and he lusts after her."

"What do you plan to do to help the girl?"

Timiro interjects, "I've been in touch with a psychologist friend of mine, Qumman, who's agreed to see her. You remember Qumman, Dad, don't you?"

"I thought Qumman was based in Stockholm," says Mugdi.

"Has she moved base, come to live in Oslo, where she now consults?"

"She consults in both cities, given the frequent need of Somali-speaking therapists in Scandinavia," says Timiro.

"Have you thought of how Waliya might react to her daughter consulting a psychologist?"

"That's Mum's concern, not mine."

Mugdi says, "It seems to me that the only acceptable cure to Waliya would be the one Saafi might receive from a reading of the Koran. Which brings me to the question as to how you will go about arranging consultations, if Qumman wants to see her regularly, once every month say or something?"

"I'll find a way," says Gacalo confidently.

Just before Timiro and Gacalo leave to walk to the tram, Mugdi comes down to the kitchen to top up his coffee. Before he heads back upstairs, he says to Gacalo, "I would be curious to know what the widow and Timiro make of each other."

He remembers Timiro describing Waliya as "a victim of circumstances." He wonders if their encounter will change Timiro's perception of the woman. He hopes that their conversation will be civil, and that there are no fireworks that Gacalo cannot cope with.

Timiro and Gacalo derive great pleasure from sauntering toward the tram, their arms locked, the daughter happy in the company of her mother. After they reach Central Station, they decide to walk the rest of the way, rather than take another tram. There is no need for them to rush. Their outing gives more joy to Gacalo than she assumed possible. After all, she has fulfilled her promise to her son in enabling Waliya's safe arrival in Oslo. And it delights her that Timiro, who is pregnant with her grandchild, is with her, visiting a woman who mothered Dhaqaneh's stepchildren—the closest her son came to siring his own offspring.

When Timiro suggests that it might be a good thing to call the widow ahead of their arrival at her door, Gacalo gives the impression that there is no need. She says, "They'll be there, for they have nowhere to go and are even unlikely to take a walk in the neighborhood."

Timiro whips out her mobile phone and says, "No harm in alerting them to our coming, Mum. Just in case." But no one answers the phone.

Finally, they are at their block. Gacalo presses the four-digit code on the apartment complex entrance pad from memory. In the lift, they meet an elderly woman who does not return Gacalo's warm greetings. Timiro, notorious for her quick uptakes, says to her mother in Somali, "What an unfriendly lot, the residents of the block, if this woman is a representative of them." Gacalo pleads with her daughter to be amicable toward the widow and not to say anything that might be construed as provocative. "No showdown, please, as is your wont." Gacalo recalls Mugdi's warning that Timiro will pick a fight with Dhaqaneh's widow, as though guaranteeing that there is still life in their sibling rivalry.

The lift stops on the third floor and the old woman gets out. Gacalo and Timiro stay on until they hear the *whumph* noise the lift makes when it arrives at Waliya's fourth-floor apartment.

Gacalo knocks on Waliya's door, first gently and then harder, as Timiro stands uncertainly behind her. When a few minutes pass and there is still no answer, Timiro says, "Enough waiting, Mum. Let's go. Very wise of Dad not to come." Eager to depart, she calls the lift.

Unprompted, Gacalo says, "Lately, many Muslims are practicing a different Islam from the one you and I have been raised on.

Whereas in former times, Somalis were relaxed about the genders mingling and spaces were not necessarily allotted to specific genders, our people have recently adopted the more conservative, stricter Wahhabi tradition, which stipulates that different entrances are assigned to the two genders."

"And so what happens in a situation in which there is only one door? How are the comings and goings managed?"

"Well, when there is only one entrance, as is the case here, only a male may let an outsider in."

"I don't like it," says Timiro.

Gacalo says, "Just keep in mind this is the first time that groups of Muslims numbering in the millions have come into contact with other faiths. It's become fashionable to talk of preserving Islamic culture in its purest form. This is why more and more Muslims have opted for the Wahhabi strain of conservative Islam, in which the sexes aren't allowed to mingle, and women require male guardians."

"Is this why Naciim thinks he is a prize asset, because Islam says so, according to some of the sheikhs?"

"Yes. And according to conservative Islam, neither Waliya nor Saafi will be able to open the door to let us in, in the absence of Naciim, the stand-in guardian."

Timiro says, "The mind boggles."

The lift takes ages coming and Timiro presses the button persistently and continues cursing. Gacalo's eyes are trained on Waliya's apartment door, hoping it will open.

Gacalo says, "I can understand Waliya's sense of caution, a mother whose daughter has suffered rape. Besides, in much of Somalia, old men your father's age have lately been marrying girls even younger than Saafi."

Timiro, tired of waiting for the lift, kicks at its door and then at

Waliya's apartment door. The sudden, aggressive movement brings Naciim, who opens the door and apologizes. "I was showering and had no idea you were outside."

The sense of occasion clearly overwhelms the boy. Visibly happy to meet Timiro and welcome Gacalo, he is of two minds as to whether to shake hands or wait until they decide whether he is worth a hug. Then Gacalo discerns a slight frown on his face: can it be that he is trying to work out how his mother will react to Timiro, who is dressed more like a Norwegian than a Somali?

After a moment, a broad smile settles on Naciim's face once more and he says how pleased he is to make Auntie Timiro's acquaintance. But to Gacalo's displeasure, Timiro's rage flies at the boy. "Why did you make us wait at the door, when we knocked and knocked and waited and waited?"

Timiro adds extra insult by passing up the chance to shake Naciim's outstretched hand. She walks past him into the living room, her forehead creased with anger. She takes the couch closest to her and makes herself comfortable. Looking about her, she spots bare walls everywhere, two threadbare rugs, cheap furniture on display, an empty potato chips packet, and naked light bulbs dangling from the ceiling, one of them directly above her head.

Gacalo tells Naciim, "Go call your mum and tell her she has visitors."

Naciim is back before long and sits in a chair not very far away. He says, "I've told them you are here."

Still angry, Timiro says, "Something doesn't make sense to me."

"Let the boy be, darling."

Timiro asks him, "At least, could you tell me who designated you as the one and only person to answer and open the door?"

He says, "It falls to me, as the only male in the household, to protect the womenfolk against anything that might bring dishonor to the family name. This is the correct way, the Islamic way."

"How do you guard them?"

"I decide who comes in and who doesn't."

Naciim remembers the maxim his stepdad often repeated: that, in his absence, he, Naciim, is the Mahram to his mother and sister, and therefore their boss.

Eventually, there is the shadow of a movement and Saafi reveals herself: a sweet thing delicately put together, doll-like. Prim and proper and discreetly veiled only with a headscarf, she touches Gacalo's and Timiro's hands to her lips in turn and then sits down on the chair farthest away from the women, her legs pressed, feet facing forward, and hands resting in her lap. The girl is blessed with breathtaking beauty and alluring eyes. A pity she has to hide all her beauty from the world's view, Timiro thinks to herself.

Waliya, meanwhile, times her entrance, conscious of how important it is to make a good impression on one's sister-in-law on first meeting. Though thick around the waist, her gait is dainty, and her veil is made out of gauzy dark-colored material, with her eyes peeping through, prompting, or rather subtly insisting, that you give her a second look. She is barefoot. As she moves farther into the room, wrapped in the hush surrounding her, she addresses her words to Gacalo, purposely intending to charm her. She stands a good distance from Timiro, nods her head and then mumbles a few words of welcome.

Waliya and Timiro size each other up, neither saying anything for a long while. Waliya sits on the edge of the chair farthest from Timiro.

Waliya asks, "What will you have? Tea?"

"I can also make coffee," offers Saafi.

Gacalo says, "We've just come to find out how you're doing. We should be having you over for a meal at our place."

Waliya says, "We are doing very well."

"The stove is working, you can make food?"

"Naciim has figured out how to make it work. He doesn't tire until he gets the hang of how devices like a stove or a fridge or a mobile phone work. Dhaqaneh has taught him well."

As she speaks, Waliya keeps Naciim under her observation. Finally, she decides she has had enough of his gawking at Timiro, and she says to him, "What are you doing sitting among the women? Please go to your room and make sure you commit to memory the verses of the Koran your instructor has suggested you learn by heart."

"Yes, Mother," he says begrudgingly, and leaves.

Gacalo is impressed that Waliya has found the boy a teacher who can help with his Koranic education, and she says so.

Timiro surveys the scene, looking from Saafi to Waliya before saying, "Now that we're on the subject, perhaps you can speak a little more about Saafi and Naciim's education."

"Saafi has had homeschooling," Waliya says. "We withdrew her from the certificate-based school system in Kenya."

Timiro can't help having a go at Waliya. She says, "What you're telling us, plainly speaking, is that you've kept your daughter at home and chose not to send her to school, like the other girls at the refugee camp?"

"I am not saying that," says Waliya.

Timiro says, "So what're you saying?"

Because Waliya does not answer immediately, Gacalo steps in and countermands her daughter's insistence that Waliya elaborate her statement. Gacalo advises, "Let us move on, darling," and then turns to Waliya, whom she asks, "What about Naciim?"

Waliya changes tack by pleadingly looking at Saafi and suggesting, since Timiro's way of questioning is making her hot under the collar, that she answers the question about the boy. Saafi, obliging, says, "He is twelve years of age and is in grade seven."

"Let me rephrase my question. What kind of education do you want for both your children now that they are here in Norway?"

Waliya motions for Saafi to leave the room.

"I want a good education for both of my children and we would appreciate any help," says Waliya. "My priority is to make it possible for them to master the blessed, sacred language of the Prophet and the Koran and then take courses in Islamic theology."

Timiro says, "I am afraid you are in the wrong country for the type of 'good education' you have in mind for your children."

Gacalo is in some distress, and wishes that she and Timiro had spoken about the topic before it came up here.

Waliya asks, "Why do you say that Norway is the wrong country? Aren't there in this land Muslims who teach the Koran and the Prophet's traditions to their children?"

Her voice almost failing her, Gacalo explains to Waliya, "You see, the state schools here do not provide the kind of 'good education' you have in mind for Saafi and Naciim."

"How do other Muslims do it?" says Waliya.

"Mosques and Islamic centers offer such courses, but only as part of their extracurricular after-school activities, not as main subjects of study," says Gacalo.

"Are there no other options?"

Timiro says, "Their best option would be to wait until their first degree at university and then to take a degree in theology at master's level."

From the expression on her face, Timiro suspects that Waliya has no idea what first degrees or master's are or where you acquire them.

Changing the subject altogether, Timiro asks, "Why did you expose yourself and your children to so much danger to come to Oslo in the first place?"

"What's this, darling?" Gacalo cuts in, as Waliya repeats that she wants the best for her children.

"The education you have in mind, if it were available, would qualify them only to belong to a large underclass in Norway," says Timiro.

Gacalo and Waliya are silent, as Timiro charges on. "Why did you not go to a Muslim country, like Saudi Arabia, where your children would receive the benefit of the 'good education' you desire?"

Finally, Gacalo interjects more forcefully. She says to Timiro, "You sound to me as if you are reading from some right-wing manifesto intended for the undecided voters in a marginal constituency."

"You stay out of it, Mum."

Waliya, appearing visibly uncomfortable, but still defiant, says, "We came here at your mother's invitation."

Timiro, fired up, begins to interrogate Waliya. "How old were you when you fled Somalia and sought refuge in Kenya?"

"I was fifteen, sixteen."

"Did you ever work outside the house?"

"Why do you ask?"

"Aside from being a call girl?"

"Who said I was a call girl?"

"My brother, in one of his rare phone calls, told me what you were like, both when your kids were younger and you were a party girl at the camp, keeping the top brass entertained, and later when they were a bit older, and you came to many a lavish shindig with the expats who party every weekend in Nairobi. My brother assured me that it was he who made a good woman of you. So don't come here acting hurt and veiled and pretending you are a saint, because you are not. My brother was no fool and didn't share these details with my parents, but he and I were closer than we let on."

Gacalo tells Timiro, "I think we should go."

"We'll go when I am done, Mum."

Gacalo falls quiet, as Timiro says, "You never held a job as such until you met and married my brother?"

"That is right."

"Then you lived for two years and a bit in Nairobi in relative comfort, thanks to the remittances my mother sent to my brother."

"That's right."

"You are now my brother's widow, in a country that has offered you and your children sanctuary. But because of the illicit manner in which you arrived, you do not qualify for the state welfare benefits that refugees are entitled to. Not immediately. So tell me. What is your plan? Are you going to register for one of the adult courses that Oslo offers?"

"I am too old to study."

"Will you look for a job, then?"

"Depending on the jobs that are available."

"My mother, who is much older than you, is still working, and I too put in many hours of work every day. Let me ask you again. Will you look for work?"

"I am not qualified to do any work."

"You can work as a saleswoman at a supermarket or as a carer at a home for the elderly."

"I can't do that."

"Why not?

"I am not good at that sort of work."

"What do you mean, that sort of work?"

"I can't work where they sell liquor, nor where I have to deal with the needs of elderly men in their natural state," says Waliya.

"Would you work as a dishwasher?"

"I've always been a stay-at-home mother."

Timiro says, "You know that we know this not to be the case. My brother told me there were times when you went out to work after dark and returned home in the small hours, your pockets bulging with cash. We are not asking you to do anything as degrading. But what is wrong with earning half of what you will cost my mother to keep you and your children in this apartment until your refugee papers come through? Then we know that your children will qualify for state welfare benefits."

Gacalo chimes in. "Not to worry, darling. I've set aside sufficient funds for them to live on for a year."

"Still, it's our family's money, not hers."

Waliya is unmoved and stays silent.

Timiro says, "When I was in New York and taking my second degree, I worked as a dishwasher and cleaned other people's toilets and dealt with men in their natural state when I bathed them and changed their soiled bed sheets, all to support myself. If I, the daughter of an ambassador and a senior administrative official of the Norwegian government, was humble enough to work in such menial positions, why not you too?"

Waliya stays silent.

"As I see that you're unprepared to speak of this any further, would you be willing to tell me something about Dhaqaneh's death?" asks Timiro.

"We agreed not to go there," says Gacalo, alarmed.

"Mum, he is dead. She's alive and I want to know. I have the right to ask her questions, the right to demand that she answers them."

"What is your question?" asks Waliya.

"How much did you know of, and how much hand did you have in, the suicide that ended my brother's life? I've heard it said that you were the one assigned to perform the job and you refused, because you didn't want to leave your children motherless, and so he agreed to do it. Is there an element of truth in this?"

"No truth in that," says Waliya.

"Did you keep his suicide belt hidden for days and, because he had misplaced the instructions, showed him how to detonate it?"

"I had nothing to do with suicide vests."

"One final question."

"Go ahead."

"Are you a member of a jihadi cell operating in Europe?" says Timiro.

"I am a widow with two children."

There is a very long silence.

Waliya breaks it when she says, "No wonder Dhaqaneh never had a good word to say about you all his life." Then she excuses herself, saying, "Give me a minute, please," and walks out of the room. She does not reappear. Eventually, Gacalo and Timiro leave in silence.

A sense of agitation dominates Gacalo and Timiro's travel home, with the younger woman muttering all sorts of maledictions until Gacalo says, "Why didn't you speak of any of this before?"

"What was the point?" says Timiro. "You were determined to bring her here whatever the cost and whatever the inconvenience, because you made a promise to your son that you would care for his widow and her children."

When they reach the house, Timiro heads upstairs, tired and looking sick, and Gacalo walks into the kitchen, her head hanging as if in shame. Mugdi hugs her with warmth and then makes her tea the way Somalis like it, with at least two spoons of sugar. He serves it to her along with digestive biscuits without speaking a word.

# CHAPTER SEVEN

----------

GACALO DECIDES THAT SHE IS WELL POSITIONED TO INVITE SAAFI AND NA-
ciim out on the pretext of buying them clothes. She has wanted to
purchase several dresses, undergarments, shoes, and other items for
Saafi; also Naciim's first brand-new pair of jeans, shoes of his
choice, a couple of shirts, socks, underpants, and tops, and then
bring them to her home, where she and Mugdi will have a chance
to talk to the children away from Waliya. She is determined to help
them settle in. And with the apartment rent paid for a year, new
clothes and shoes, a weekly allowance for the mother, and a little
pocket money for the boy and the girl, surely Waliya's worries will
be lessened.

To this end, she phones Waliya's apartment. The phone rings for
quite a while until Naciim finally answers. Gacalo identifies herself
and chats with him for a bit, then asks how everyone is at home.
When he hesitates, she requests that he put his mother on the line.
Then, because she is rather keen on being on the right side of Waliya
following yesterday's set-to, she rehearses the words she will use to
calm the widow's nerves.

"Mum can't come to the phone," says Naciim.

She pauses, suspecting either the phone is on speaker or the boy is holding the receiver away from himself. She searches for the right question to ask that will prompt the boy or his sister, who is surely listening in on the conversation, to open up.

Gacalo says, "We talked, your mother and I, the other day, about my taking you and your sister shopping for clothes, seeing that you both very badly need new things to wear. I am thinking of coming around in a short while and taking you out shopping, then perhaps going to McDonald's. Then I will bring you here to see where we live."

In the background Gacalo can hear Saafi's words, but she can't make out what she is saying. "My sister says, and I agree with her, that it will be okay with Mum if we go out with you today to buy clothes. So please come. We will talk to her, in the meantime, to let her know our plans."

Naciim is waiting for her in the parking lot when she arrives. As he leads her by the hand into the lift, he says, his voice bouncing with eagerness, "I can't wait to go shopping, but Grandma, we must go up to the apartment first, in order for you to say hello to my mum and also because Saafi will be comfortable only if we are with her when we come back down. This is the first time she is setting foot outside the apartment since our arrival."

"How is your mum?"

"She is unwell. She says she has a most terrible headache, like hammers on a metal drum."

They enter the apartment. Saafi knocks on the door to her mother's room, announcing that Grandma Gacalo is here. Through the door, they can hear Waliya's muffled voice saying, "I have a headache and am not properly dressed and so I can't come to greet anyone."

Naciim barges in on the conversation between his mother and sister. He says, "Can we go with Grandma, Mum? I need jeans, Saafi needs dresses, underthings."

"Of course," she says. "Please go."

A determined young fellow for one so young, Gacalo thinks. She permits him to run ahead with the car keys and open the car by pressing the button before they reach it.

This being their first drive in the city, Saafi and Naciim listen as Gacalo serves as their guide, naming the streets they are on, pointing distantly in the direction of the tram or Metro or bus, and explaining how they will need to learn to move around in this place which is now their home.

As they approach the main entrance to the department store, Gacalo senses a hint of fear in Saafi and Naciim. Saafi tightens her facial veils and recoils from any physical contact with the hordes of eager shoppers, while Gacalo observes how the boy's fingers rest assuredly on his sister's spine, speaking to her in a low voice. Saafi nods her head and walks forward, Naciim's hand still on her back, guiding her. Then Naciim points out to Saafi the presence of a young Somali-looking woman with a niqaab working the cashier's till, ringing up purchases and exchanging a few words with the Norwegian customers in their native tongue. Gacalo feels their closeness as they communicate with each other in a secret code whose meaning evades her. But when they spot a man in uniform moving in their direction, they freeze, fear again crossing their faces, and appear helpless as he speaks to them first in Norwegian and then in English. "Can I help you?"

Gacalo rescues them, saying to the children in Somali, "He works in the department store as security," and then saying to the man in Norwegian, "They are with me. Thank you."

Then Gacalo leads them farther into the department store, repeating to Saafi, "No reason to panic, I am with you." She advises Naciim not to move ahead too fast; she is worried they might lose each other.

Gacalo, with Saafi willingly following and Naciim tagging along despite his wish to slip away and do his own thing, follows the signs to the junior women's section. She wants to get Saafi several sets of underwear, half a dozen pairs of socks, a skirt or two, but is determined not to force her. She would like to show Saafi the items, let her feel their softness, and then leave it to the young woman to choose.

Saafi appears delighted with almost every undergarment shown to her. But when it comes to going into the fitting room alone, fresh panic sets in. To allay her worry, Gacalo goes in with her. Still, Saafi finds it embarrassing to disrobe and waits until Gacalo turns her face away.

"Do you like shopping?" Gacalo asks.

"I haven't done much shopping in my life."

"Grandma, can I go and get my own things?" Naciim calls from outside.

"Patience. I'll come with you in a minute."

Naciim makes a long face but waits. As Saafi tries on the various items, Gacalo entertains her with amusing tales, telling her about Mugdi's attitude toward clothes shopping—or any shopping for that matter. He will walk into a store, hands empty, grab the first items he sees, and within a few minutes head straight for the till, without ever stepping inside a fitting room.

When they are done, Gacalo and Saafi go with Naciim—she makes a point of extolling the virtue of patience—so he can make his choices: two pairs of jeans, a Levi's jacket, and a pair of canvas shoes that light up in the dark.

He says, "See, I am done in two seconds."

Saafi and Gacalo laugh and give each other a high five. Naciim is annoyed that he does not know why they are slapping their palms against each other.

He says, "I've always meant to ask someone. Why do women take ages to make up their minds?"

"Do you play chess, Naciim?" Gacalo asks.

He says, "I do and I'm good at it."

"Did you bring along your set?"

"I never go anywhere without a travel set."

"Can you name the most important chess piece?"

"The queen, of course," he replies.

She lets this sink in for a moment.

"And what's the least important piece?"

He answers, "The pawn or the foot soldier."

Again, she allows silence to do its work.

"When you pack the chess pieces, don't the most important and the least important pieces go into the same box, with the king, the queen, the knight, and the castle all fitting together?"

He takes his time before answering. "Yes. I am sorry. I won't speak like that ever again, I promise. Please forgive me."

She pats him on the shoulder. She asks, "By the way, where did you learn to play chess? Or rather, who taught you to play it?"

"Stepdad Dhaqaneh," says Naciim.

"Naciim was good at it. At his school in the refugee camp, he was the junior chess champion," says Saafi, with pride.

After driving for a hundred meters, with Naciim in the front, Saafi in the back, Gacalo takes a furtive look in the rearview mirror and decides that there is a newfound degree of self-awareness in the way Saafi carries herself. The girl leans backward, her eyes closed, as though she has already taken a good measure of who she wants to be. Then she adjusts the positioning of her facial veil, pushing it ever so slightly aside so she has more of a peripheral view. Gacalo turns her head away just before the girl's eyes can meet hers. She does not want to be accused of planting the idea of dispensing with the veil into the girl's head.

Naciim, the first to break the silence, asks with the bravura of someone who knows what he wants, "Where are we going?"

"We're going home," says Gacalo.

"Whose home, yours or ours?"

"Where would you like me to take you?"

Naciim says, "Yours, please."

"Can we find out what Mum thinks?" asks Saafi.

"What objections can Mother raise?" he says.

Gacalo says, "Would you like us to call the apartment to find out what she thinks?" When Saafi nods her head, Gacalo brakes and parks by the side of the road. Turning to Naciim, she says, "Please allow Saafi to have her opinions and please no bullying." Then she gives the girl her mobile phone to make the call to her mother.

As Saafi dials the apartment number and it rings on and on, Naciim says, "I look forward to putting my new clothes on."

Gacalo knows from her conversations with Dhaqaneh that her son often took special care of the boy, pampering him with visits to restaurants where he could order a hamburger and chips, two of his favorite foods, of which Waliya did not approve, and buying him everything he needed. Waliya would tell Dhaqaneh, "You are spoiling the boy," and Dhaqaneh would retort that he was delighted he had a boy to spoil.

Gacalo is sure that Dhaqaneh would approve of the way she is looking after his family.

Saafi finally says, "There is no answer."

"I know Mum won't object."

Gacalo says to Saafi, "What would you like us to do?"

Saafi replies, "I don't mind if you take us to your home first," even though she does not sound at all enthusiastic at the prospect.

Gacalo starts the car and drives. Then after a while, she asks Naciim, "Have you and your sister explored your neighborhood yet?"

"Mum advises us against going out in the area."

"Why?"

"You'll have to ask her."

"Mum is worried for us," says Saafi.

"Worried? About what?"

"She thinks we will be beaten up by the white gangs who rape black girls and do not like blacks or Muslims. Though I think she worries more for Naciim than for me. She says that Muslim boys are always suspected of being up to no good, when all they do is roam about."

Gacalo thinks that Waliya's fear is not unlike that of parents living in areas notorious for drug turf wars. There, the parents advise their children to take all precautionary measures to stay safe. It is understandable that Waliya would assume such a stance, given what the children went through in the refugee camps.

Gacalo parks the car close to the gate.

Mugdi warmly greets Saafi and Naciim, bowing his head, his hands behind him. Timiro stands at the lowest step of the stairs and says, "Welcome," in their general direction. After which she zeroes in on Saafi, smiling and asking, "What have you bought?"

Mugdi engages Naciim in similar talk, saying, "Now let's see what you've got." The boy leads the old man into the living room and shows off his purchases.

Gacalo is happy that Saafi and Timiro are engaged in a tête-à-tête in a corner on their own, separate from the men, and that the girl is finding it easier to open up. In the right mood, Timiro exudes an air of authority, balanced by empathy, and Saafi seems to benefit greatly from this healthy mix.

Gacalo offers the children a choice of food, including fish, salad, and a variety of cheeses. Neither shows interest in the items offered. Then Gacalo asks, "What about T-bone steaks?"

Saafi asks what that is and Gacalo brings a steak to show to her, still wrapped in its foil. The girl asks if it is halal. An amused look passes between Gacalo, Mugdi, and Timiro, since they had not given that aspect much thought. Naciim says he has no problem eating the T-bone and Saafi stares at him with disapproval.

The thought of describing Saafi as "a religious bore" to her mother in Norwegian crosses Timiro's mind. But on second thought, she says aloud, "Mum, didn't you get that from the Pakistani butcher?"

"Yes, I did, because halal meat is healthier."

Saafi doesn't seem convinced and doesn't want it.

As an alternative, Gacalo takes half a dozen frozen chicken drumsticks out of the freezer and puts them in the microwave to thaw.

Soon after eating, Naciim goes to the TV room to change into his new clothes and he is back in a flash, eager to display them in sequence, as if he were on a catwalk. Mugdi is having fun applauding and Gacalo comes out of the kitchen and joins in. Naciim then makes as if to dump his old clothes and his worn sneakers in the garbage. Mugdi is about to put them instead into the recycling bin when he asks, "Have you checked if you may have forgotten something in your trouser pockets?"

Quick on the uptake, Naciim retrieves the trousers and out comes a five-dollar bill he has saved from his share of the travel money Gacalo sent them before they left Africa, which he wants changed into Norwegian kroner.

"What will you buy with that kroner?"

"A lottery ticket."

Saafi says, "He is very tiresome, my brother."

Timiro says, "Lottery tickets, eh? But you must be eighteen to buy a ticket."

"I'll work on the means to make a fortune legally."

"I want to win a fortune."

Saafi speaks a warning firmly. "In Islam, games of chance are on par with wine drinking and pork eating and both are forbidden."

Naciim says, "If I win, you'll get your share too."

There is a term the residents of the refugee camp use to describe young boys like Naciim: *buufis*, thinks Mugdi—a perilous type of protracted daydreaming, in which the dreamer confuses the real with the imagined. It's clear the boy has much promise—his charm and ambition attest to that. But he must be guided with caution.

"Do you own a chess set, Grandpa?"

"Why? Are you good at it?" asks Mugdi.

"I've won games against many adults."

"Bet I'll make your five-dollar bill ten?"

"Too early to bet with you, Grandpa."

Mugdi brings out the chess set and Gacalo and Timiro watch them play with interest. Soon enough, Mugdi is in trouble, but he is lucky not to lose his queen in just seven moves, as Naciim lacks the attentiveness the game requires. Shortly, Mugdi checkmates him. In spite of this, the old man believes that with more training, Naciim can do very well.

As Mugdi and Naciim begin a new match and Gacalo washes the dishes, Timiro turns her full attention to Saafi. She asks the girl, "How do you feel here?"

"I'm not sure about Oslo yet, but I am comfortable in this house. More comfortable than I believed I would ever be in your parents' home."

With the knot in her niqaab undone, Saafi seems to relax, her new purchases spread out on the floor in front of her as if to be admired, not worn.

Timiro asks, "Would you like to go to the bathroom and model them for me?"

"Can we close the door please?"

"Of course we can."

"Can we lock it with a key? Please."

Timiro grunts in frustration. She says, "We're not used to locking doors in this house and I don't know if anyone even knows where the keys are."

Timiro has known people who have keys in every door, who lock themselves in when they are in the shower, the toilet, or the bedroom at night, not because they are worried about an intruder, but because they do not trust those who share the house with them. In their own home, they have never locked doors. Does that define who they are? But Timiro wants to gain the girl's confidence. So she asks her mother to locate the key to the bathroom, and to bring it along. When Gacalo hands her a bunch of keys, Timiro, choosing to speak Norwegian, tells her mother that she wants the men out of the house for at least an hour.

"Why do you want the men out of the house?"

"Please trust me and send them out," says Timiro.

A look at Saafi, who is curled in the bathtub, tells Gacalo all she needs to know. She says, "I'll tell them to go to the park."

Her mother gone, it takes Timiro twenty minutes to find the right key for the door, aware, as she feels the girl's eyes on her, that much is riding on how Saafi reacts from this moment on. The door finally locked, Saafi moves with the gliding unease of an inexpert skater as she peels off her old clothes one item at a time until she stands in her underpants.

Timiro says, "I am going to run a hot bath for you to soak in. You will love it, because of the scents and oils and the soap suds."

"Auntie, please stay when I sit in the bath."

"I won't leave you for a single moment, dear."

"Thanks, Auntie."

Timiro notices a gradual reddening in the water, enough to worry her. However, she can't determine the cause of it: is the girl having her period? Is it because she didn't wash properly after her most recent menstruation and the unwashed-off encrusted blood is now coming out in the bath? Or is there a more innocent explanation: the girl has a cut somewhere on her body?

Timiro asks, "Do you have your period?"

Saafi is positively abashed, when, in a flash, Timiro has a tampon between her fingers. "Familiar with this?"

Saafi nods. "I know what they are."

"Have you been washing yourself?"

Saafi shakes her head no, her cheeks aflame.

"Why ever not?"

"There were strange men everywhere, in the plane, on the trains, and in the hotels we stayed in on our way to Oslo," says Saafi. "I couldn't bring myself to bathe, afraid some man would intrude on me."

"And since you got to Oslo?"

The girl then haltingly explains that she had her period on the day they arrived at the airport detention center. There was one bathroom for twenty or so women, the queue was always long, and by the time you got your turn, the water was tepid or cold.

"And since moving into the apartment in Oslo?"

"Mum and I don't know how the shower works."

"But doesn't Naciim know how it works? He had just taken a shower on the day Mum and I went to see you."

"He does. But he has a mean streak and when Mum and I have asked him to show to us how it works, he calls us 'bush women' and refuses to help."

Timiro fights hard not to roll her eyes in frustration. But at least she understands why the girl's body is emitting a fetid smell.

Timiro then demonstrates how to run the shower, repeating the process more than once until Saafi has mastered it.

Once she is washed, Timiro lends the girl a dressing gown in which Saafi wraps herself, her hair jet-black and shiny from the shampoo.

"Try one dress. Then we'll try a second one. Take your time; there is no need to hurry. The men are out of the house on a long walk to the park, only you and me. And Mum is downstairs, guarding the entrance."

Saafi takes her time putting on the dress.

Timiro changes the subject. "Know how to swim?"

"No. I don't."

"Dad says he wants to teach Naciim. Maybe you should go with my mum to learn."

"My mother would never allow it. She never permitted me to do any kind of physical activity that meant I had to bare my face or my arms."

As Timiro struggles with the zipper on Saafi's dress, their bodies touch. Saafi gives a startle and shuns any physical contact for a second or so. Then she stands stiffly, uncertain of her next move, as Timiro continues to tug on the zipper. She holds the girl's waist with her open palms, and suggests that the dress needs a little adjusting. Timiro then tells her to try yet another dress, her third. A moment later, Timiro asks, "What do the devout Muslims, like you and your Mum, give much priority to?"

"Being a good Muslim. And if you are a woman, you want to be a good wife."

"And how does one evaluate that?"

"Well, a very good wife, as we understand it, is a wife who is caring of her husband; forever and unfailingly obedient."

"Would you say your mother was a good wife to my brother?"

"I'm in no place to answer that," says Saafi.

"But you would like to be a good wife?"

"If God ordains that I find a good man."

"In your view, who is a good man?"

"A devout Muslim."

Timiro asks, "Does the niqaab decide whether you are a good Muslim and therefore potentially a good wife, or does your behavior in all things Muslim determine that?"

"There is a lot of peer pressure," says Saafi. "And if you don't dress in the Muslim way, you can be subjected to verbal and physical abuse."

Timiro knows of a Somali woman living in a suburb of Oslo

who was beaten up by four men at a petrol station because the men believed she was not dressed in the proper Muslim way.

"I can't take any more verbal or physical abuse after what I have been subjected to in the refugee camp," Saafi continues. "According to some people, I was being taught a lesson, because of some of the terrible things my mother had done before marrying Adeer Dhaqaneh."

Timiro does not wish to embarrass the girl by making her repeat things she knows only too well: that every woman associated with a radical husband—whether a foot soldier of no high standing or one at higher ranks—is kept unsure of her status as a wife. This is to force the women to work harder to please their men, knowing if they don't, they could be demoted to a lower station in the kitchen or as a house cleaner, or simply divorced. Wives serving radical religionists know that they must not allow themselves an instant of security.

Saafi changes out of the new dress and into her old clothes. As soon as she does that, she loses her open personality and begins to look like a shabbier shadow of herself. Timiro remains silent, watching as Saafi takes her time to debate whether to wear the niqaab and on top of it the facial veil. In the end, she decides against the facial veil, but puts on the niqaab and replaces the safety pin to make sure that everything is in place.

Then they hear the downstairs door slamming. Mugdi and Naciim are back and Gacalo shouts to alert Saafi to the fact that she will be taking them home shortly.

Saafi says, "I am ready when you are, Grandma." Then she gives Timiro a warm hug. Timiro imagines that the girl won't tell her mother how much she has enjoyed being in this house. Saafi goes down to join her brother and Gacalo in the car.

When Saafi and Naciim are back in their apartment and their mother asks them if they enjoyed the outing, both agree that they did. They show their mother the clothes they bought. Waliya keeps her thoughts to herself about Saafi's choices, assuming that Gacalo is to blame for putting pressure on the girl.

Naciim speaks at length of how big and beautiful Mugdi and Gacalo's house is. "There is a TV with as big a screen as the sky, there is everything. I liked the house a lot."

"I agree, it is beautiful and big," Saafi says. "But I saw no prayer rugs anywhere and no articles honoring the Muslim faith."

Later, when Naciim and his sister are alone in the kitchen, he calls her a killjoy and says, "Why mention to Mum that there is no prayer rug in that house and no one prays in it? I bet Mum will never want to go there, if invited. Good going."

# CHAPTER EIGHT

----------

A FEW DAYS LATER, VERY EARLY IN THE MORNING, MUGDI SLIPS OUT OF bed, puts on a robe, and tiptoes softly down to the kitchen. An incident with Waliya weighs heavily on his mind.

The first Mugdi learned of it was when he answered the phone and a man describing himself as a policeman asked to speak to Gacalo or Mugdi. Mugdi identified himself to the officer and asked what the problem was.

The officer said, "Some of the neighbors in the apartment complex where I understand your daughter-in-law and her children reside have filed a complaint against her for unruly behavior."

Mugdi asked the cause, who filed the complaint, and whether his daughter-in-law and her children were currently in police custody.

"No one is in custody at present," the officer replied. "Apparently your daughter-in-law was disturbing the entire neighborhood through a recitation of the Koran via a loud sound system. We brought her and the complainant in for questioning and decided that your daughter-in-law deserved to be given a warning in writing and allowed her to go home."

Mugdi was relieved that he did not have to go to the police station in Groenland to bail the widow out.

The police officer went on, "We're calling to warn you that, in future, if your daughter-in-law disrupts the peace, we'll hold you, as the apartment tenants, responsible for her actions."

Mugdi thanked the officer and hung up.

Now he makes a cup of tea and sits at the kitchen table to reread some of his translation extracts from the day before. Scarcely has he reread the first three paragraphs, made slight modifications, and taken a sip of tea, when he hears soft footsteps coming down the stairs. Gacalo is still in her pajamas, rubbing the sleep out of her eyes.

"What are you doing here?" he asks.

She retorts, "What are *you* doing here?"

"I can't sleep, just can't."

Gacalo asks him to make her a cup of tea too.

"What are we to do about Waliya?" he asks, as he offers her the tea.

"We tend to think only of what Waliya says or does, not how the two children behave," says Gacalo. "What are your thoughts on them?"

"They are of a different generation and of a different mindset, especially Naciim."

They sip their tea in silence.

Mugdi thinks of the night the news about Dhaqaneh's death reached them. It was dinnertime. Gacalo rose from the table to answer the phone, let out a heart-rending cry, and collapsed. That night neither went to bed, each playing host to recriminations, each blaming the other, Gacalo hysterical and weepy, and Mugdi defiant and stone silent. The next day, Kaluun and Eugenia, Timiro and Xirsi flew in from London and Geneva. Friends and relatives came in droves to show their support. Himmo, whose eldest brother had been Mugdi's best childhood friend, arrived soon after first light and Gacalo let her in. Johan and Birgitta flew back from Paris, where they were holidaying, there to remind everyone how much they adored the deceased as a young thing full of life. Dhaqaneh was their son Frederik's playmate and fellow mischief maker. Many others whom Mugdi and Gacalo had not visited with or spoken to for years showed up at their door.

Contrary to Gacalo, Mugdi refused to mourn, despite the outpouring of support from friends and family. And when one day Johan asked him why he wouldn't show sorrow for his son's death, replied, "How I can mourn a son who caused the death of so many innocent people? It makes no sense to grieve his death. I explode into rage every time I remember what he did."

A man he didn't know very well said, "Your son is your son forever and you are his father forever, no matter how much you try to deny this or keep your distance from him."

Mugdi snapped back, "I couldn't mourn a son who has caused the deaths of so many people. If anything, I am grieving for those who died at my son's hands."

Gacalo's grief, in contrast, was so intense as to be indescribable. She barely slept for days and suffered so many chest pains that it became necessary to have her consult her doctor.

Now, as they consider what to do about Dhaqaneh's widow's mishap, Mugdi observes a sadness of the sort he hasn't seen her express for a long time, taking semipermanent residence in her eyes.

He will admit that what is happening now is not on par with

what occurred when the family lost Dhaqaneh. However, there is no denying that Waliya and her children's arrival is a product of their son's passing. Earlier in bed, pretending to be asleep so as not to disturb Gacalo, he kept turning angry thoughts over and over in his head, hoping to wish away the nightmares that continued to call on him, and from which he couldn't awaken.

Now Timiro enters the kitchen and wishes her parents "Good morning," and then says, "What a night!," rubbing her eyes with vigor and yawning. "A very strong cup of coffee brewed with love by your good hands, Dad, would do me wonders."

Mugdi suspects that even though he didn't hear Timiro's mobile ringing, the bad night has something to do with Xirsi, the perennial culprit. Neither he nor Gacalo ask Timiro to elaborate. The last time Mugdi advised his daughter to lock Xirsi out of her life, Timiro threw the book at him and charged him with indifference to her happiness.

They eat in silence for a while. Then Timiro says, "I dreamed I was burning Xirsi's shoes last night, several pairs of them. You see, he lives for his shoes and loves them and I can't stand the sight of them still sitting in our wardrobe. And guess what, Mum?"

"What, my sweet?"

"In the dream, you were so unhappy with what I had done, you wept and wept."

Then Timiro looks in her father's direction, expecting him to make a comment, but he has nothing to say. A moment later, the phone rings in the living room and Timiro starts, as if she imagines it is Xirsi. She dreads the thought of having to speak to the man whose shoes she set on fire. Gacalo says, "Leave it to me. I will deal with Xirsi, if he is the one calling."

Gacalo answers it and then says "My God" a couple of times, and that she will share the news with Mugdi and Timiro. When she rejoins them, Gacalo says, "It was Himmo. A pig's head and a Nazi flag have been left inside the big mosque in Groenland that she worships at."

"Do they know who the perpetrators are?"

"Himmo has no idea," answers Gacalo.

This is not the first time that groups allied to right-wing skinheads in Norway have dropped off a dead pig's body at a mosque. Such actions seem to be escalating—in the past few years there have been multiple cases of a right-wing assailant knifing Pakistanis or Arabs in different areas of Oslo.

Silent, all three are aware of the battle lines that have been drawn between two minority groups: on one side, the neo-Nazis, with their anti-Islamic, anti-immigrant smear campaigns, and on the other, the jihadis, small in number when you think of the world's Muslim population of a billion plus. These two are at war and the rest are victims.

Then Gacalo tells Timiro not to forget that they have an appointment with Qumman, the Somali psychologist with whom the family has been speaking, with the aim of assisting Saafi to overcome her personal difficulties. Qumman specializes in dealing with victims of rape among the Somali diaspora; she has published a booklet that has become a go-to in the field.

Gacalo and Timiro take a taxi to fetch Saafi to the psychologist's office. Gacalo, to diminish Waliya's worries about her daughter going out, tells the widow, "We'll do a bit more shopping and Saafi will be back within two hours, if not before that."

When they are in the taxi, Gacalo says to Saafi, "I hope you don't mind, but I've talked to Timiro about your recurrent nightmares."

"I don't mind you sharing it, Grandma."

After she and her mother exchange a free-from-anxiety glance, Timiro asks, "Have you told your mother about them?"

"No, I haven't dared to."

"Why?"

It seems the question makes Saafi uncomfortable or embarrassed and she covers her mouth with her hand, as if to hide her thoughts this way. Finally, she says, "I thought she might accuse me of inventing the story."

"Are you given to inventing stories about men, Saafi?" asks Timiro.

"Of course not."

Gacalo says, "Now this is what we're going to do: we're taking you to meet a friend of Timiro's, who we think will help you get better. She is a psychologist."

Timiro says, "Do you know what a psychologist is, Saafi?"

Saafi's eyes increase in size and she asks, "Am I sick, Grandma? Is this what you are telling me?" And she looks from Gacalo to Timiro and back.

"No, my sweet. You're not sick. But you need a form of help only a psychologist like Qumman can deal with."

"I am willing to see anyone who can help me."

"All you have to do is to talk to her, answer her questions," says Timiro.

"We went to university together, Qumman and I and I'm sure you'll like her."

"Is this to remain a secret between us three and just to be sure, you don't want me to share it with anyone else, especially my mother?"

"That's right," says Gacalo.

Saafi wears a bring-it-on look, but says nothing.

When they arrive at Qumman's office, Gacalo, as previously agreed, wishes to know more about what the psychologist has in mind for the girl. She also wants to make Qumman's acquaintance, since she will be the one bringing her after Timiro has gone back to Geneva.

Qumman says to Gacalo, "It's my job to know how to make a subject relax and talk. I am trained to do that. It may take a couple of sessions, but in the end I succeed. But I don't want either you or Timiro to be in the room with us."

Timiro asks, "Any idea how many sessions you'll require before we decide whether she is making progress or not?"

"Leave it to me to decide," says Qumman.

Gacalo wishes Saafi "Good luck," and takes a taxi to work. Timiro stays behind and, when the psychologist invites Saafi in, she waits in Qumman's anteroom with a book to read, lest the girl take fright if she came out and didn't find her there.

When Saafi reemerges after what seems to Timiro longer than eternity, the girl's sweet smile makes every second she has waited worthwhile. Saafi looks relaxed as Qumman escorts her out of the office. Timiro says nothing to Qumman, happy that the first session has worked to Saafi's and everyone's benefit.

Saafi takes Timiro's hand in hers and they walk side by side and ride the lift down to the ground floor. Timiro, thinking that she needs to talk a bit with the girl, finds a bench in a small park and they sit. As soon as Timiro feels that Saafi is visibly relaxed, she asks, "What do you think about Qumman?"

"I like her. I felt I could trust her."

"What do you like about her?"

At first Saafi's smile hardens into a frown and then she gives herself a moment's pause to think. Then she says, "She is the kind of woman to whom I can talk about the terrible night in as much detail as I can bring back."

"I'm glad to hear that."

"She has tried to make those memories scare me less than before," says Saafi.

Timiro watches the girl to see if there is fear in her eyes or in the rest of her body, but there is nothing of the kind.

Timiro drops her off at her apartment and makes sure that she is home safe.

As they part, Saafi shares a confidence. She says, "I'll show Mum the scarf and the perfume and won't talk about meeting 'Auntie' Qumman."

# CHAPTER NINE

----------

THE HOUSE IS QUIETER THAN IT HAS BEEN IN DAYS, NOW THAT TIMIRO HAS returned to Geneva and Gacalo is back at work. Mugdi spends more time in his study, making up for the hours he lost in helping Gacalo with all matters Waliya and attending to his visiting daughter.

It is just as well. Alone in his study, he doesn't need to pretend that all is right with him, or share the devastating dream of the night before. In the dream, Mugdi is hiding in a chest as waves of locusts descend on a farm he owns in the Lower Juba region of Somalia. When the assault is over and he reemerges to assess the damage, a Waliya look-alike appears out of nowhere and says not to worry, even though life as the family lived it will never be the same. Mugdi hasn't been able to put the dream from his mind all morning, worrying if the prophecy might come to pass.

Then he observes Gacalo standing in the doorway of his study. Perhaps she has come to remind him that she is on her way out to meet up with Himmo. Gacalo has lately decided she needs someone to cultivate the widow's trust and act as a mediator, someone who, as Somali idiom has it, might be in a position to "carry fire" between the widow and the rest of the family. Can Himmo play the part? For one thing, Saafi's father is her blood relative, who, like Waliya, has been unlucky with her marriages. For another, he and Gacalo are close to her and they have faith in her. But will Waliya be willing to listen to Himmo? And will Himmo be prepared to carry the fire between the two parties?

In their telephone conversation, Gacalo told Himmo that the director of the language school Saafi is supposed to attend has written to say that the girl has not shown up or even registered. It is after hearing this that Himmo offered to intercede, since it became obvious that while all three are meant to attend the language classes for newly arrived asylum seekers, only Naciim has done so every day without fail. Saafi has been irregular in her attendance, now pleading sickness, now finding another excuse not to leave the apartment. Waliya has never even registered.

Mugdi asks, "You off to meet Himmo then?"

"Yes. I'll take the tram to Central Station, where I will meet Himmo at a café there before going together to the widow's place."

"Good to have friends like Himmo."

"We don't have many friends, do we?"

"Perhaps not, but there are no friends better than the ones we have—Himmo, who is there for us, and Johan and Birgitta, on whom you can depend. You don't want your life to be full of unnecessary clutter, with friends who are really no more than acquaintances. One stands to gain from deep friendships and the takings are greater that way."

Gacalo consults her watch, turns on her heels and says, "I don't want to be late."

"Give my warmest to Himmo," says Mugdi.

With Himmo standing alongside her, Gacalo rings the doorbell to the widow's apartment. If her heartbeat quickens, it is because she has no idea if, in the likely absence of Naciim, who is supposed to be at school, Waliya will open the door to them. She stands back and listens for footsteps approaching, waiting for what feels like ten minutes, when in real time it is even less than three. She presses the bell again, waits another moment, then taps hard on the door thrice, and finally in exasperation takes hold of the handle, turning it. When none of these have produced results, she decides to knock on the door at the same time as she calls out to Waliya by name, evidence of her impatience. "It is I, Gacalo. Open the door. Now please."

At last, the door opens—Saafi, in the absence of Naciim, has taken the initiative after peering through the peephole to let them in. It appears the girl has not forgotten Timiro's tirade when they were not allowed in the last time.

When Gacalo and Himmo step inside, Saafi, smiling regretfully, explains, "Naciim is not home." She looks uncomfortable and is aware, no doubt, that she should have opened the door to them sooner. Then she says, "I'll tell Mum you are here."

No hug, no shaking of hands.

And no sooner has she run off than Waliya, her fingers busy tucking a cowl into place with the help of safety pins, comes into view, appearing a little perturbed.

Never the one to blink first, Gacalo braces for an unpleasant welcome, remembering the last visit. She recalls Himmo's advice at the café that perhaps the best way to deal with Waliya was to grow a thick skin and to ignore her behavior, however gruff. After all, as Himmo said, "You and Waliya have a long-term relationship, she is your daughter-in-law, you her mother-in-law, and, what is more, you are bound to each other in this country's bureaucracy, because you share files."

Waliya says, "We did not expect you."

"This is Himmo," says Gacalo. "From what Himmo tells me you are distant cousins several times removed. In addition, Himmo is an aunt to Saafi on her father's side."

Himmo steps into the conversation and mentions the relevant consanguinity, naming the ancestors.

"Himmo has lived in Oslo for a number of years and she is a registered nurse, much loved at the hospital where she works," says Gacalo.

Waliya says, "I had no idea you lived here. I know your name from my former husband, Saafi's father, and I am delighted to meet you in person." Then she says after a brief pause, "Where are my manners?" Then she points the two women to their seats. "Please!"

As the women sit down, Saafi, her smile broad and her features cast in a pleasanter mode, shyly offers them tea.

Gacalo says, "Thanks. Tea black, no sugar."

"Somali tea, one sugar," says Himmo.

Waliya says, "Same as Himmo, three sugars."

The widow's fingers are frantically counting her rosary, her lips moving rapidly, maybe praying or perhaps rehearsing her replies before speaking them, Gacalo can't decide.

Gacalo says, "Where is the young man?"

"He is hardworking and at school," answers Waliya. "He seems to be enjoying it and tells me about the Syrian, Iraqi, and Palestinian refugee families who attend the language course with him."

"I am happy to hear that," says Gacalo. "How many hours does he attend daily?"

"Four to five hours daily."

"When does he leave home?" asks Himmo.

"He leaves home earlier in the day, became he likes to play soccer with the other boys in the class, many of them Arab," says
Waliya.

There is joy in her voice—a proud mother. It is clear that she is
delighted with the progress Naciim has made.

She adds, after a pause, "He is a very adventurous boy. However, he is much too forward and that upsets me."

"Too forward—how?" asks Himmo.

Waliya says, "There are these Palestinian twins whom he has
befriended and to whose home in the vicinity of the school he
has been. Only yesterday did he tell me that the twins are Christian
and he has been eating their haram food. And they have an older
sister. It angers me to hear this."

Saafi arrives with the tea and hangs around for a couple of minutes, until a subtle shake of her mother's head lets the girl know
that she is not welcome to listen to the conversation of adults, and
so she leaves.

Gacalo redirects the conversation. "I understand that although
the stove in the apartment is working, there is a problem about the
water heating system."

"Everything is fine with the water heater. We are happy."

"I am happy that you are happy," says Himmo.

Waliya turns to Himmo. "This is the first time that each of us
has a proper bedroom, with beds much larger than any we've ever
slept in. This is also the first time when we've lived without frequent power outages and when we could pray without fear. We're
very grateful to my in-laws, especially Gacalo, for providing us
with so many of these comforts."

"Have you been out and about?" asks Himmo.

"Naciim has."

"You haven't been tempted to go out yet, not even for a walk? Surely, it gets lonely in the apartment."

"Saafi and I have been to the mosque on the odd Friday to pray," says Waliya, "and Imams Fanax and Zubair have come together to visit us at the apartment: the first time to pay a courtesy call and to know of our needs and the second time to bless the house with a reading of the Koran. But Saafi and I are not like Naciim. The boy has no worries and knows no fear."

Himmo says, "You'd want that in a boy."

Waliya asks Himmo, "Do you have children?"

"Two girls and a boy."

"How old are they?"

"One of my two daughters is older than Saafi, and the boy, who is in the middle, is close to your daughter's age. My youngest, the second girl, is younger than Naciim," says Himmo.

"We should bring them together some time."

"Yes. We should and we will."

"Where were they born and raised?"

"All three of them in Europe."

"Then they won't have anything in common."

Gacalo thinks that Waliya is hostage to the traumas a longtime resident of a refugee camp in Kenya suffers. Unaddressed, the damage haunts the memory forever.

Himmo, changing the subject, asks, "How is Saafi doing?"

"She is at a difficult age, in an awkward space, and she happens to have come to an alien land," says Waliya.

Himmo says, "We've talked about Naciim's schooling and how much he enjoys it. Why is Saafi not in school like her brother?"

"Saafi feels trapped and panics easily."

Himmo, as agreed between her and Gacalo, alludes to the benefits Saafi might receive from talking to a psychologist. She says, "Would you approve if we consulted psychologists to help Saafi? A lot of research has been done in Norway on Somali refugee girls who feel trapped in their own bodies, following the horrid experiences they have had back home in war-torn Somalia or in the refugee camps."

Waliya cuts her off and says, "Only the Koran can help, no one else can. It is to this end that Imam Fanax of the mosque and I are working on a plan."

Gacalo is ill at ease, knowing that she and Timiro have already taken the girl to Qumman. But then she is relieved that Saafi did promise Timiro that she wouldn't speak of the visit to her mother. When next Gacalo looks at Waliya, she sees that the woman has resumed counting her rosary with more fury than before. When they hear the muezzin announcing the call to afternoon prayer, the sound is so loud Gacalo figures that it has emanated from within the apartment. Saafi remerges, as if in a choreographed move, seemingly eager to say her prayers, her mother leading.

While Waliya doesn't bother to ask Gacalo if she will join them, she asks Himmo, "If you are joining us and you need to perform your ablutions, then we will wait for you?"

Himmo says, "I would very much love to join you, with you leading."

With the start of the praying postponed until Himmo has performed her ablutions, Waliya trains a disapproving look in Gacalo's direction before bringing out a bigger prayer rug now there are three of them. When Himmo returns, she and Saafi stand behind Waliya, who speaks the iqaamah ritual, reciting the phrase, "Prayers are now ready." Saafi is more intense and very attentive, whereas Waliya seems more relaxed, almost casual.

When they have concluded their prayer, there is a standoffish, albeit silent, moment between Waliya and Gacalo. To Waliya, it is as though she shares nothing with the woman she is supposed to think of as her mother-in-law.

To break the tension, Himmo asks Saafi, "How do you fill your day, if you don't attend school?"

All eyes trained on her, Saafi becomes self-conscious and stammers slightly when she starts to speak. "I am keen on improving my reading of the Koran."

"And your ambition in life?" asks Himmo.

"It is to become an Islamic scholar one day and to teach the Word of God to other women."

Waliya adds, "Saafi is always awake in the early hours, reading and praying, devoting a lot of time and thought to understanding the complexities of the faith and how to interpret it in the proper way."

Himmo says, "Such dedication is admirable. I wish my children developed similar dedication to anything. I suppose it shows a certain amount of maturity."

Waliya indicates to Saafi that it is time she returned to her room, because she doesn't want her to be present in the event their talk becomes adult talk. With Saafi gone, Waliya asks Himmo, "What school do your children attend?"

"They attend state schools near our home."

"Do you teach them Arabic and the Koran?"

"In the early part of the day, they attend the school proper and three times a week in the afternoon they study Arabic and Tajweed at an Islamic center close by."

"You describe state schools as 'proper schools,' not where they learn the Koran and Arabic Tajweed. Why?"

Himmo says, "I wish we had such a school, where they could learn to write and read Somali, but there is no educational facility of that kind here in Norway, only in America."

"What do they study the rest of the week?"

"The older girl takes piano lessons."

"And the other one?"

"She plays soccer in the afternoon."

"A girl playing soccer with boys?"

"She is on an all-girl team."

"She wears the niqaab, playing soccer?"

"To be honest, she doesn't."

Nervous about the turn the conversation has taken, Gacalo thinks that the time to leave has come. However, she wishes to put an important question to Waliya, one that she wants answered in Himmo's presence. Gacalo says, "We've talked about the children. We've heard you describe Saafi's panic attacks and the difficulties she has with attending language school regularly. And we know too that you are not interested in seeking a job or even working. Did it ever occur to you that attending the language school is compulsory and that anyone who does not attend it may not be issued with asylum papers?"

"I am almost thirty and feel too old to learn a new language that shares no roots with Somali or Arabic," says Waliya. "I find it difficult to contemplate sitting in a classroom at my age and learning a new alphabet."

Himmo seems shocked. She says, "I was much older than you are now when I first arrived, with no Norwegian and no profession to speak of. I was a single mum, with two children to raise. Not only did I learn Norwegian, at which I am highly proficient now, but also I trained as a nurse and work at a hospital and earn enough to raise my children, pay for my mortgage, and send money home once every two months to my elderly aunt, who is bedridden."

Waliya says nothing. Himmo and Gacalo wait.

Then Himmo goes on, "You know of course that neither you nor your children will receive state support until after your asylum papers are processed and approved. You don't need me telling you that until that time, which may take at least a year, Mugdi and Gacalo are obliged by law to pay for all your bills, including the monthly rent of the apartment, and all your other needs. And let me say this, while I can. It was one thing living in a refugee camp in Kenya and receiving remittances amounting to a couple of hundred dollars monthly from Gacalo. But it is altogether a different thing to sit around now doing nothing—not attending school, not working, and just making the occasional visit to the mosque. You were brought here at great risk and expense. You could've been stopped from boarding your flight, arrested for carrying forged passports, deported, and all would have been for naught."

Himmo, in the pause she takes here, reminds herself that the tickets alone cost nine thousand dollars and counting; and the apartment run will run into thousands of kroners in the first year.

"You need to put in your share," she continues. "You don't want to be a burden on anyone, least of all Gacalo and Mugdi, who have already given so much. I suggest, for starters, that you go to the language school and then find a menial job of whatever nature so you share the financial burden with them."

Waliya wears a fresh new seriousness for the first time since Himmo and Gacalo have arrived. She says, "I've been talking with Imam Fanax. We're close to reaching an understanding."

"Is he offering you a job?" asks Himmo.

Waliya says, "I am thinking of starting a nursery for Somali children whose mothers work outside the home. But we are considering making provisional use of this apartment, having the children brought here in the morning and picked up when the mothers are back from work. The parents will be made to pay something close to babysitting expenses, the mosque will make a financial commitment to the project, it being Muslim-inspired, and perhaps the district will give us a grant."

Himmo says, "That is a brilliant, workable idea."

"Wait a minute," Gacalo interjects. "We must consider the legal ramifications of such a decision and inquire if it is even feasible to turn the apartment into a baby nursery."

Waliya looks frustrated. She says, "Why is everything in this country difficult? I keep hearing this is not allowed; this is not legal. Why?"

Gacalo is surprisingly impressed with Waliya's quick-fire questioning. "I'll consult a lawyer I know, see what she says, and come back to you with an answer."

Everyone relaxed, Gacalo and Himmo prepare to leave, their hearts less heavy than when they arrived.

As they wait for the train, Gacalo says, "There are moments in one's life when everything one considers to be a win is for all practical purposes a loss."

"In that case, we must make sure that the win you felt when Waliya and the children were not deported doesn't turn into a loss," says Himmo. "This is why it is incumbent on us to be patient when dealing with Waliya, so we stay the course and ultimately succeed."

Gacalo says, "How wise of you, dear Himmo."

# CHAPTER TEN

----------

A WEEK LATER, HIMMO MAKES A CALL AT MUGDI AND GACALO'S HOME. WITH her is her oldest daughter, Maimouna—Mouna, among her friends.

Himmo has news. But before she tells it, she wants her daughter out of the way, and suggests that Mouna and Naciim, who has just arrived, go play a game of chess. Mugdi finds the chessboard, leads the teenagers to the living room, plies them with their favorite soft drinks, and then rejoins Himmo and Gacalo in the kitchen.

Himmo says, "Waliya has confirmed to me that she has mustered the support of Imam Fanax of the mosque in Groenland; he is raising funds to hire her as a nursery teacher."

Mugdi asks Himmo, "Do you know Fanax and Zubair, his deputy?"

"I know Zubair, the deputy, fairly well. He went to the same school as Mouna, though he was a lot older than her and they were in different grades—he was four, five years above her. He arrived back in 1998, with a married Somali-Norwegian couple he claimed to be his parents. At first, he was a model student. His teachers spoke well of him and he had many friends. But when he reached fifteen or sixteen, his character suddenly changed. He was no longer the good boy everyone knew him to be. He became disruptive in class, started to fight with his teachers, and grew notorious for his tantrums. He was even sent to a psychologist for anger issues, but there was nothing they could do. Until one day, after quarreling with his parents, he held a knife to the throat of the man he addressed as 'Father,' threatening to kill him. The police were called and he was dispatched to a center for violent juvenile delinquents. Then to everyone's surprise, the couple insisted he was not their child—that they were not even related by blood. A DNA test proved this to be the case. Child Welfare Services removed him from the couple's home and put him into foster care. When the foster family couldn't cope with him, he was dispatched back to the center, where he stayed until his eighteenth birthday. After his release, Zubair sought out his adopted parents once more, but the father refused to accept him back as their son. Rumor had it that after the neighborhood got word of this, a kindly neighbor to whom the couple was indebted called round one evening during the holiest month of Islam and pleaded with them to take the boy back in. After much discussion, they finally acquiesced. In celebration, the neighbor held a prayer meeting at his home to which he invited the couple, the boy, and a few members of the community. Everyone present at the event described it as a moving ceremony well worth attending. From then on, Zubair's law-abiding behavior became exemplary."

"How do you know all this about Zubair?" says Mugdi, who feels overwhelmed with much of what he is learning.

"I met his elderly foster mother when she was admitted for a hernia surgery at the hospital where I work," says Himmo. "Her husband visited often and when we got to know each other a little better, they opened up to me and told me a lot."

Gacalo says, "You meet all sorts, don't you, at the hospital where you work?"

"I do. Sooner or later almost everyone comes, whether as a patient or as a visitor."

"Please go on," says Mugdi.

"After that latest incident, Zubair was much less boisterous. He became a Norwegian citizen, led a relatively quiet existence, and his grades improved. But he was no longer popular among his peers and cut a lonely figure in the halls, hardly speaking with anyone, much less girls. A year before he finished high school, he showed so much enthusiasm for religion that he dropped out of school and apprenticed himself to Imam Yasiin, who took him under his wing, taught him Arabic, and trained him to sharpen his mind so he could interpret the Koran. I have no evidence to support this, but I suspect it was during his first year as a budding Islamic scholar working with Imam Yasiin that the imam referred to Dhaqaneh as one of his brightest followers. Zubair would become acquainted with Dhaqaneh during one of his brief visits to Oslo. Six years after Zubair dropped out of school, he spent nearly nine months in the south of Somalia, before returning to Imam Yasiin's mosque. At this point, according to the kindly neighbor who had facilitated the easing of tensions between Zubair and his parents, the Norwegian antiterrorist unit took a great deal of interest in Zubair, especially his internet activities. The unit summoned him for an extended interview and held him for a couple of days before releasing him without charge. Less than a year later, the unit arrested him on suspicion of remitting funds to Shabaab. There wasn't sufficient proof to indict him. According to his mother, before dismissing the case, the judge warned him that he would be sent to jail for a long time if he was ever brought to court again on similar grounds and found guilty."

Himmo pauses to have a sip of water.

She continues, "A former follower of Imam Yasiin's, who prays at our mosque, has also confirmed to me that Zubair knew Dhaqaneh and may have worked with him in Shabaab. And when I saw Waliya not long ago at the funeral service of a man I was friendly with who was also her distant clansman, and I asked her if she had ever met Zubair before, she affirmed that she had, but only in passing, when she was residing with Dhaqaneh in a housing complex attached to the mosque in Eastleigh, Nairobi."

Gacalo says, "Perhaps there is more to Waliya than I imagined."

Despite the alarm that Himmo's information has raised in him, Mugdi remains silent, biding his time.

"There is another worrying factor," Himmo adds. "A photograph taken in front of the Finchley mosque, showing Imam Yasiin, who was Dhaqaneh's mentor, and Zubair with an extremist, charismatic cleric named Anjem Choudary, has appeared in a London newspaper. When questioned by Norwegian security about his relationship, Imam Fanax—the imam employing Waliya as a nursery teacher—claimed he had no idea that the cleric was praying in the same mosque as him on the day the picture was taken."

Gacalo says, "It makes no sense to me how these men and women can justify plotting against and murdering those who have shown them such kindness, providing them with the comfort of home and job security."

"They have no conscience," Mugdi says.

Himmo shifts in her seat. She says, "I don't know if Imam Fanax has yet done anything to warrant his comparison with Anjem Choudary. At least the Norwegian antiterrorist unit, according to one of the Somali websites, namely Goobjoog, has not so far come up with sufficient evidence even to question him, save the one time when he was pulled in and interrogated, following the appearance of the photograph in the newspaper."

"We're getting ahead of ourselves," says Gacalo. "We don't know the relationship between Waliya, Zubair, and the imam. So far, we are speculating without evidence. Would an imam even have the ability to pay a salary to an appointee as a teacher or community activist?"

"In Norway, all houses of worship, including mosques, are required by law to register their number of congregants, and are then allocated grants accordingly. So in a way, yes. Imams have some funds at their disposal, enough to pay for any community-related activity."

Himmo continues, "On top of this, extra funds often trickle into these mosques from places like Saudi Arabia, Qatar, and Kuwait. The Gulf countries have built the largest mosques in Africa, Asia, and Europe, and there are rumors linking some of their mosques to nefarious activities undertaken in the name of Islam."

Mugdi says, "I think I read somewhere that the government is averse to allowing a country such as Saudi Arabia to make large charitable donations toward the mosques in this country, since Saudi Arabia does not permit reciprocity. You see, Saudi Arabia, despite the presence of a million Christians and so many Hindus and people of other faiths, will not allow a single house of worship for any religion other than Islam."

Gacalo then makes reference to a recent incident that has provoked her ire and Mugdi's. She says to Himmo, "Have you heard about a Canadian woman who has decided to build a chapel for the Christians living in the Somali-speaking peninsula to worship in?"

Himmo says, "No, I am not familiar with the incident."

"The woman's well-meaning action has caused such uproar that every Somali has threatened her with immediate expulsion, detention, or death."

"We thought that was uncalled-for and unreasonable too," says Mugdi.

Himmo asks, "Why unreasonable?"

"It's silly and impracticable," says Gacalo.

Mugdi says, "Myself, I find it shortsighted, in that there are millions of us Muslims living in Europe and elsewhere and despite the existence of a few problems here and there, Muslims in the main are allowed to worship Allah as they please. Which is why it seems unreasonable to me for Somalis to prohibit the construction of a chapel or a church. Before the civil war, Mogadiscio had a splendid cathedral. It's a great disservice to our shared humanity to destroy a house of worship because it belongs to another faith."

The key phrase, "the unreasonableness of Somalis," leads them to speak about a number of things that have little or nothing to do with the topic under discussion. Eventually, Mugdi, observing that Himmo has heard enough and is perhaps eager to leave, falls silent.

Himmo pleads a work commitment and calls out to Mouna, saying, "Come and say goodbye to Uncle Mugdi and Auntie Gacalo."

Mouna and Naciim join them.

Mugdi asks Naciim, "So who won the games?"

"I did. I won four times, Mouna once."

"He didn't win. He cheated," says Mouna.

"I didn't," he insists.

"Boys are cheats," says Mouna, teasing him. "Cheating is what they are good at."

Gacalo says that she has some shopping to do and must also leave. She goes to the bedroom upstairs to fetch her handbag and wallet.

Himmo, as she, Gacalo, and Mouna depart, says to Naciim, "You must come and visit us. Bring Saafi along. She'll enjoy meeting the girls."

"Thanks. It'll be a pleasure," he says.

When the women leave, Naciim asks Mugdi to play a round of chess with him. The old man agrees, deciding it's a perfect opportunity to question the boy about his mother's plans to set up a nursery in the apartment, and her association with Imam Fanax.

On hearing the imam's name, Naciim says, "I don't like him at all. I find his behavior disturbing."

"Why does his behavior disturb you?"

"He seems to have eyes only for Saafi."

On hearing this, Mugdi grows disturbed. "What does your mother say about that?"

"Mum doesn't appear to notice it, even though I've pointed it out to her more than once," says Naciim.

Troubled, Mugdi messes up his next move, an error that the boy is quick to point out. "Now your queen is under threat. Just like Mai, who couldn't concentrate on her game, and when I took a piece the way I can take yours now, she says I am a cheat."

Mugdi asks, "Why do you prefer Zubair to the imam?"

"Zubair told me he was a friend of my stepdad's. And he doesn't act in a suspicious manner the way the imam does. Whenever Imam Fanax visits now, Mum sends me out of the house on some pretext or other, such as getting them soft drinks or a takeaway from the halal shop. She is worried I might put up a fight, in my capacity as a Mahram, and disallow him from visiting the apartment, especially after I warned her about his behavior toward Saafi."

"Do you eavesdrop on their conversations?"

"Sometimes I hear things not meant for me to hear."

"How's that?"

"And see things not meant for me to see," he says.

Mugdi, in his memory, revisits a conversation in which Gacalo and Timiro talked about how Saafi—out of worry that Waliya might accuse her of inventing stories—wouldn't speak to her about her nightmare. Naciim, on the other hand, hears things not meant for him to hear and sees stuff not meant for him to see. Mugdi wonders if he can infer from these two facts that Waliya unwittingly alienated their affections, and Naciim has resorted to eavesdropping on her, while Saafi does not trust her mother enough to talk to her about her nightmares.

# CHAPTER ELEVEN

----------

IT IS FREEZING COLD IN OSLO AND SNOW HAS BEEN FALLING HEAVILY FOR hours, clogging the roads and closing schools for the day. Naciim is delighted by the snowfall, his first, and is thrilled that he'll finally have use for his winter jacket, boots, and scarf, which he has looked forward to wearing from the day Gacalo took him to purchase them. He is as happy with winter's arrival as his mother and sister are desolate, neither willing to step out of the house.

Now six months to the week since his arrival in Norway, Naciim has lately experienced a kaleidoscope of mixed fortunes, mostly of the positive variety. His greatest achievement is that two of his teachers at the language school have recommended that he is now proficient enough in Norwegian to attend regular school and so he has been accepted into Vahl Skole, one of the best multicultural schools in Oslo. His teachers told him that it is rare for a beginner to do so well. Everyone is thrilled for Naciim, especially Mugdi, who asks what kind of school satchel Naciim would like as a gift.

"I don't need a new one," says Naciim.

"Are you sure?" Mugdi asks. "In one of the shops we frequent, there's a vintage school satchel on display. It's made of leather, with plenty of space for books and a laptop. We can get you one, as a gift."

"I'll never say no to a gift from you."

"Would your mother join the rest of the family here for a meal to celebrate your rare achievement?" asks Mugdi.

"I've no idea, but I can ask."

Waliya has always found one excuse or another to avoid setting foot in Gacalo and Mugdi's house. Naciim has previously hinted that his mother and sister are averse to "eating foods cooked in non-halal kitchens."

Mugdi is curious whether the widow included their kitchen among these. Naciim confirms that is the case.

"Would she come if we offered to take everyone to a restaurant that is decidedly Muslim?" asks Gacalo.

"I'll find out," says Naciim.

"What do you think will make her happiest?"

"She would be happiest if you invite Imam Fanax and Zubair to join us, whether we eat at a restaurant or have a catered meal here at your home. I don't like Fanax. He knows it, and Mum knows it too. But I'll be grown up about it, if you invite him and he comes, as this will probably make Mum happy."

Gacalo pauses, considering the options. Mugdi, however, has nothing good to say about the imam or Zubair after the information Himmo has given them. Now he speaks with a voice so firm it is obvious the decision is final. "No way will I allow the imam or Zubair to darken our door. And if you go to a restaurant, I will not join you. I refuse to liaise with terror suspects, especially ones so closely aligned with our terrorist son."

After a moment, Gacalo says to Naciim, "Here is what I'll do. I'll order a lavish meal from the most prominent Somali restaurant in the city and have it delivered to your apartment. Run along home and tell your mother to invite a few guests of her choice, people she is fond of or with whom she wants to curry favor. I'll have the food delivered after the evening prayer."

A few hours later, Gacalo receives a brief text message from Naciim. The message simply reads, "Mum has hurt herself." But the boy does not explain how, or how badly. When she shares the message with Mugdi, he looks confused and a little aggrieved, as if he has no idea what Gacalo expects him to do about it.

To his surprise, Gacalo remains silent, just when he assumes she's about to remind him that as Waliya is their son's widow, they are forever linked. The answer Mugdi has always given to such statements is this: that he did not mourn his son's death when he chose to blow himself up and that he cannot think of Waliya as his son's widow. Gacalo, for her part, views Dhaqaneh only from the perspective of a mother. She cannot and will never forget Mugdi's strident condemnation of the boy, a memory that shocks her to the core even now. Sometimes Mugdi thinks that the distance between them on this matter is irrecoverable.

When Gacalo arrives at the widow's apartment, alone, a sign on the door reads, in Somali, "It is open and so please come in."

She bets that Naciim has not told his mother or sister what he promised he would when Gacalo phoned him on her way here. He said he would leave a note on the door so she should just walk in. Still, she knocks out of politeness and waits for a moment before entering.

Naciim is on his way to his room when he and Gacalo meet. He says, "Welcome," and instantly apologizes for being in his bathrobe, his hair wet and dripping, as if he has just come out of the shower. As he retreats in embarrassment, Waliya, having heard a woman's voice, appears, looking the worse for wear. Gacalo observes black-and-blue discolorations on the widow's face, prominent contusions and ruptured skin. Her lower lip is swollen, as though repeatedly stung by a bee and then scratched. Now her tongue, red and sore-looking, emerges from her mouth to wet her lips, maybe to comfort them.

"How did you hurt yourself?" Gacalo asks.

When Waliya speaks, Gacalo has difficulty comprehending her and the widow has to repeat herself two, three times.

"I tripped."

Saliva runs down over her swollen lip and she sucks it back in, enunciating carefully, like a novice practicing a foreign tongue. It takes what seems like three minutes for her to say, "I slipped on a wet cake of soap and hit my head against the shower door."

"And then?"

Naciim, dressed, rejoins them and listens to the conversation in silence.

"As I tried to gain my footing," says Waliya, "I slipped again, hit my head against the shower wall, then felt woozy."

"It was my fault," Naciim says.

"How is this your fault?" Gacalo asks.

"I left the soap on the shower floor, intending to pick it up, but forgot to do so. She wouldn't have fallen if it weren't for my carelessness."

"Those bruises are bad," says Gacalo, not quite believing Waliya's story. She thinks that perhaps the widow hasn't shared what truly happened with Naciim. "Would you like me to take you to hospital?"

"I'll be all right," Waliya insists.

Saafi appears in the doorway, kitted out in the clothes Gacalo bought for her on their shopping excursion a few months ago. The young girl offers a smile to her guest and seems about to pirouette in the way models do, but stops just short of doing so. Naciim, forever incorrigible, says, "You look as if you're going out somewhere. Maybe next time you should come out with me in this beautiful dress and everybody will go, wow!"

Waliya says, "I won't allow it."

Ignoring his mother, Naciim says to Gacalo, "Saafi alternately puts on one of the four dresses you bought for her and spends several hours each day in front of the standing mirror in Mum's room, admiring herself. Can you imagine?"

Then they hear a knock on the door and within seconds, both Waliya and Saafi, nervous about who it might be, prepare to flee, in the way of criminals escaping a crime scene. Naciim turns to Gacalo and says, "Please give me a minute and I will find out who is at the door. It is either the man from the restaurant delivering our meal or Zubair, whom my mother invited to join us." The boy moves toward the door as though the entire world is at his command and asks in Norwegian, "Who is it?"

"I have a delivery to make," a man says.

Naciim gives his mother and sister enough time to go to their rooms before opening the door to the man, who advances into the room with nonchalance until his eyes clap on Gacalo. Then he stops short, shocked at coming face-to-face with a woman not dressed in the "Saudi" way that has lately become fashionable among Somalis. Naciim relieves the man of the food he is carrying, signs the receipt, and gives him a tip. The man takes one more look in Gacalo's direction to make sure that he is seeing a "naked" woman, not a ghost. Then he departs.

Just as Naciim lets the man out, Zubair arrives at the door. Naciim then leads the way back into the living room and presents Gacalo to a man in his early thirties, with a beard that has known no razor, a white conical hat, a baggy shalwar, and a long seamless khameez. He boasts a massive prayer mark on his forehead, evidence that he prays more frequently than most. Gacalo remembers Himmo talking about him at length, that this young man knew Dhaqaneh first in Norway and then in the battlefields of Mogadiscio—obviously a fellow jihadi. But she has no interest in speaking about her son this evening. She is here to celebrate Naciim's achievement: that he can now start regular school, having done exceptionally well at the language school in the shortest time possible.

Gacalo rises to greet Zubair. He keeps a respectable distance, nodding his head in acknowledgment. In the absence of the women of the household—she assumes that Waliya and Saafi are putting on the hijab before rejoining them—Gacalo takes the food to the kitchen and empties it into serving bowls, leaving Naciim to play host to Zubair.

Finally Waliya and Saafi rejoin them, clad in rather fashionable chadors. By then, the food is on the table, alongside colorful orange drinks and other varieties of soda. When Zubair and Waliya lock eyes, Gacalo wonders if there's more to the relationship than anyone has said. She also gathers from the way Saafi looks upon the scene that the young woman is more familiar with the man than she lets on.

Gacalo says, "*Bismillah*," to encourage everyone to serve themselves. Zubair rubs his palms together, his face showing his eagerness to eat. Then he says, "Just a moment," and off he goes to wash his hands. Because he does not ask where the washroom is, Gacalo notes that he clearly knows his way about the apartment. It crosses her mind that the truth is that the bruises are the consequence of a beating Waliya has received from Zubair, because it is a well-known fact that jihadis are often violent toward their women for the slightest religious infraction.

On his return, he and Naciim pile their plates high with food while Waliya and Saafi take tiny portions. Gacalo takes a single drumstick and a bit of salad. Zubair says *"Bismillah,"* and everybody else's lips, except Gacalo's, are astir with devotions, after which they start eating.

Gacalo is happy to be here for the boy's sake, but relieved Mugdi is not around to be discomfited by Zubair's presence.

Naciim is the first to speak. He says, "Sheikh Zubair has been involved in helping Mum start a nursery. And did you know," he says to Gacalo, "he and my mother knew each other back home."

Gacalo suddenly feels an intense sickness at the troubling thought that this fellow jihadi is alive while her son is not. She cannot bear the thought of engaging him in small talk, let alone asking him what Dhaqaneh was like just before his self-murder in the service of his faith. Her expression queasy, she fights back a wave of nausea. In an attempt to distract herself, she raises her glass in which there is water and makes a toast. She says to Naciim, "We are here to celebrate your admission into regular school in a much shorter time than expected and we pray that you'll do well."

Zubair trains his shifty eyes on Gacalo in a manner that makes her uneasy. As he watches her intensely, she thinks that perhaps she is misreading things and that he is anxious in the way of someone wanting to get something off his chest. When he speaks, his non sequitur doesn't surprise her, because he says, "I know Waliya from way back, when she and Dhaqaneh first met. And I was there when they married. So it is a great thing that she and her two children are here, thanks to Allah, the Merciful and the Beneficent. She is now among her people. Imam Fanax and I have always supported her refusal to accept social welfare benefits from a non-Muslim entity such as the Norwegian state. So we have decided to give her a hand in setting up her nursery for Somali and Muslim children, to teach them reading and writing in Arabic."

Zubair goes on, "So far a dozen children, some as young as two and others as old as five, have registered with us at the mosque. The children have working mothers and they need help." Then he turns to Saafi and adds, "Saafi will be hired as her mother's assistant."

"I love looking after babies," says Saafi.

"As far as Saafi and Naciim are concerned, the state will support them from the moment their asylum papers are issued. Saafi, like her mother, does not wish to receive a cent from the state. Needless to say, we're content with Naciim's progress, even if we are disappointed that he is not receiving the education a Muslim boy of his age requires."

Waliya agrees with Zubair and, speaking with difficulty, she says, "You know I said so when we first arrived. Nothing would give me more pleasure than giving my children a good Islamic education."

Then Gacalo's mobile phone rings. From the phone ID, she can tell it is Mugdi. Grateful for an interruption, she listens to him for a couple of minutes and then says, "I'll come home as soon as I can."

The plates have barely been cleared when she hastens to depart.

# CHAPTER TWELVE

----------

GACALO ARRIVES HOME IN A TAXI HALF AN HOUR LATER AND SHAKILY alights and wobbles past Mugdi through the gate. Seeing how unsteady his wife is, Mugdi offers Gacalo a hand, but she waves him away, asking him to please pay for the taxi. As she teeters forward, he hears her voice a lament that he fears will ring in his ears for a long time to come: "Everything is in ruins." As he waits for a receipt from the taxi driver, he recalls his own sense of doom upon first setting eyes on Waliya.

After collecting the receipt, he gathers Gacalo's hand in his and asks, "What's ailing you, darling?"

"I've no idea," she responds, her voice deep and pained.

Then Mugdi notices an overpoweringly musty odor whose source he cannot determine though it seems to be emanating from close to his wife. It is not the sort of smell he associates with Gacalo, who is always unfailingly clean. The pervasive odor that is interfering with his thoughts is worryingly suggestive of rottenness; there are intimations of death about it.

Gacalo mutters maledictions as he supports her—Zubair's name occurs several times in her curses. He assists her entering the house ahead of him and then together the two of them totter up the stairs, one unsteady step at as a time, until they gain the bedroom. Gacalo lies down on her back and he pulls the sheet over her, tucking her in as if she were a baby. When her breathing is no longer as erratic as before, he sits on the edge of the bed and asks, "Can I get you anything?"

Gacalo does not respond.

He waits for a minute or so, gets to his feet, dims the bedroom lights, and walks softly out of the room, leaving the door slightly ajar to admit a fraction of light from the hallway so that Gacalo will know where she is should she wake up alone.

Once downstairs in the kitchen, Mugdi is so perturbed he cannot remember what has led him there in the first place. Does he want to eat something? He wonders if someone at Waliya's has said something to fog her mind, darken her mood, and make her sick. Distractedly, Mugdi reaches for a large lemon and a chopping board. He cuts the lemon in half and squeezes the juice into a large mug, into which he pours some water. He takes the mug up to the bedroom, thinking Gacalo will be thirsty when she wakes. He'll leave the water on the nightstand next to her.

As he enters the bedroom, Gacalo says, "You're back?"

"With a glass of lemony water," he says. "I hoped you'd still be asleep."

It hurts him to watch her struggle to do something as simple as turn to face him. He holds her head with his firm hands and helps her shift and sit up so she can have a sip of the water. It is impossible for him to ignore how much she is trembling.

Her voice low, she says, "Enough. Thanks," and pushes the water away.

He helps ease Gacalo into a comfortable position. Then, as he's about to head downstairs, he hears her say, "Please."

He turns and watches as her arms flail like someone desperately trying to dispel cobwebs in front of her face.

"What is it, darling?"

"Help me to the bathroom, please."

"Are you sure I don't need to take you to hospital?"

"No need. I'll be absolutely fine."

He does as she asks. Even so, doubts enter his mind as he escorts her to the toilet and, having helped her sit, pulls the door shut and waits outside. He wonders if he is doing the right thing in agreeing with a sick woman's insistence that she has no need of an ambulance or a doctor.

She calls to him again. Mugdi supplies Gacalo with toilet paper and again steps out to give her privacy, then shepherds her back to the bedroom. Her voice is so weak he can barely catch her words without moving closer. She says, "I want to drink more water, lots of it."

He stays up for much of the night, sitting by the bed and ministering to her. She falls asleep, finally, at three in the morning. But Mugdi cannot bring himself to sleep and so he engages in what he does best when he is unhappy: revise translation texts or write something new. Eventually, he too falls asleep in a chair at her bedside.

In the morning, Gacalo wakes before Mugdi does. Her memory of the night before is fractured, and she has trouble distinguishing what happened at Waliya's and then later at home from the nightmares in her head. For the first time in a long while, she calls in sick to work.

When Mugdi comes downstairs to the kitchen and finds Gacalo

sitting at the table drinking tea, he hugs her tightly, as if, in his mind, he is welcoming her back from a trip to the uncharted territory to which she traveled alone. Gacalo tugs at his sleeves, happy to be back with him.

Several hours later, there is a knock on the door. Answering it, Mugdi is pleasantly surprised to find Naciim standing on their doorstep with a carrier bag containing what looks like a football and a large envelope. The boy is grinning in a way that suggests he has a secret he wishes to share with him. As Mugdi lets the boy in, he asks, "Is everything okay?"

Gacalo and Mugdi were delighted the first time Naciim turned up unannounced, praising him for identifying the right tram and underground line to take, then negotiating the labyrinthine streets near Vigeland Park, where their house is. Completely unaided, he avoided the cul-de-sac and followed the alleys leading to their home. At the time they asked how the boy, who had been in Oslo for less than two months, had accomplished such a task. His reply was as indicative of their expectations of him as it was of his ability to surprise everyone in a positive way. He said that the few times he visited them in the rental car, he had focused on the features of the area he needed to remember and that memorizing these had helped him map the way in his head. He admitted he had been unsure of the street to take once he left the train but asked a friendly-looking woman for help, who pointed him in the right direction.

"Excellent," says Mugdi.

Gacalo is equally impressed and compliments Naciim on his self-reliant approach to life in the new land. "What news brings you here?" she asks.

"You left so suddenly last night, I was worried. I've come to see how you are doing," he says.

"How sweet of you to visit."

Emboldened, Naciim says, "I was unhappy with the indifference Zubair and my mother showed to you. It was obvious you were unwell. And then after you left, Zubair made unkind remarks that I won't repeat here."

Gacalo asks Naciim, "Have you eaten?"

Mugdi is amused, knowing that his wife tends to think of feeding the young before engaging with their concerns. Timiro used to be irritated by her mother's questions about food whenever confronted with a serious topic, whereas Dhaqaneh always seemed hungry and had no trouble devouring a large meal regardless of the situation, earning him the family nickname "Hoover."

Before Naciim can answer, Gacalo takes off toward the kitchen to warm up the boy's favorite: chicken and rice.

Gacalo puts the food before Naciim, then asks if Mugdi would like a cup of coffee. He replies that he would love one.

Naciim, meanwhile, chews a bite of chicken with slow consideration and then says, "I would like to open a bank account in my name. I need your help."

Mugdi asks, "Have you come into money we don't know about?"

"I've saved some from the monthly allowance you give me and would use every bit of it toward my education or to buy an iPhone, a new computer, or books."

"That sounds like a good plan," says Mugdi.

"Where is it, the money?" asks Gacalo.

Naciim rummages in the carrier bag and brings out wads of cash held together by a rubber band. "Here," he says, and he offers it to whichever of them will accept it.

Gacalo receives it. She says, "A bank, eh?"

Mugdi informs the boy that he will not be able to open a bank account in his name until he has been assigned a national security number, which takes a long time to get, and requires more papers than Naciim yet has.

"No problem," the boy says. "Keep it for me and I'll ask you for the amounts I need. You see, if the money is with me, I may be tempted to spend it. I also do not want to keep it at home where anyone might find it."

"Fair enough," says Gacalo.

The boy's request makes Mugdi recall similar experiences with Dhaqaneh, who as a child would ask one of them to keep his pocket money for him, to reclaim it as his needs arose. But because he would ask for bits of cash so often, now from his mother and now from his father, it was difficult to know how much of it remained. Gacalo came up with the solution of writing down every sum he withdrew. So now Mugdi decides to give Naciim a notebook in which to jot down his withdrawals and remaining balance. Naciim says, "A good idea," and they all agree that there'll be no withdrawal without Mugdi, Gacalo, and Naciim all signing the slip.

Naciim suppresses a yawn. Then he says, "In our apartment, I wake up soon after four in the morning whether I like it or not, because the wall clock, as well as my mother and Saafi's phones, relay the message of the muezzin, urging us to rise and say our prayers. And then Mum puts on the Koran tape, recited by her favorite Sheikh Sufi."

Gacalo says, "I hope you say your prayers without fuss or fail when your Mum asks you to."

"Mum and I have rows," says Naciim, "especially when she insists that, for a Muslim, saying the five daily prayers must take priority over every other activity. I try hard to please her, knowing she is easily upset when we are discussing religion, and I talk back.

I tell her that if I am up until later, reading and rereading my Norwegian textbooks, and revising my math, physics, and chemistry, on top of working on the daily homework my special tutor assigns, then perhaps I can say my prayers later in the day when I have the time. Islam allows that, but my mother doesn't. I remind her that everyone would sympathize with me. I am only thirteen and I have four more years before I reach the age of majority. Then I will make sure that I pursue my religious responsibilities with more vigor."

He pauses to take a sip of water, then asks, "Was Dhaqaneh like me at my age?"

"At your age he never said his prayers," says Gacalo. "He wasn't in the least religious and I doubt he opened the Koran or read it with great enthusiasm until much later, as a grown man, just before he joined Shabaab. That is the truth of it."

Naciim says, "Likewise my mother."

"How do you mean?" says Gacalo.

"Mum was always more into nightclubbing than praying and she seldom set foot in a mosque until she met Dhaqaneh. These are two facts she cannot deny."

Gacalo remembers Dhaqaneh telling her about Waliya's nightclubbing and how he worked hard to make a good woman of her; she recalls Timiro confirming that Waliya was once a call girl on the day the two of them visited the widow together in her then new home. Now she says, "But your stepdad said you often prayed with him, and you made no fuss about going to the mosque before you got here."

"We were all under Stepdad Dhaqaneh's influence, when my mother was married to him and we lived together, as a family. I thought he was a good man, very kind to me, and I loved him."

"And now that he is dead?" Mugdi asks.

"Mum is under the influence of Imam Fanax and Zubair. These two men are charlatans and I don't trust either of them. I valued Stepdad Dhaqaneh's advice. He was a caring man, very kind and protective of me, something these men are not. Sadly, though, the point that needs stressing is that nothing you or I or anyone else does or says will make her change her mind about these con artists."

# CHAPTER THIRTEEN

----------

TIMIRO RETURNS TO OSLO UNEXPECTEDLY, CANCELING ALL THE PREVIOUS arrangements she and her mother had made during her last visit. Her mother was to move to Geneva in time for the delivery and to assist until her presence was no longer needed. That she is now back, eight weeks short of her possible delivery time, much too heavy for her own comfort, often fatigued, and on edge a lot—she has given an earful of grievances to her father since the taxi has dropped her off—means that he and Gacalo have their work cut out for them.

Gacalo comes home the moment Mugdi telephones her at work. He says, "Timiro has just come home, she is lying on her back on the bed in her room, looking like a beached whale."

Gacalo is treated with the spectacle of an oddly shaped stomach boasting of a protruding belly button. What's more, Timiro takes an eternity to change the position of her body in order to face her mother. "In Geneva, I felt alone with this body mass and I couldn't bear carrying this weight all by my lonely self."

The two women content themselves with an awkward handshake.

"Don't give it a moment's worry, darling. We're pleased you are here. But how are you feeling?"

"My doctor in Geneva says all is well."

Gacalo thinks to herself that the journey to a full term pregnancy, followed by delivery is long and tedious and maybe that has made Timiro impatient, especially since work colleagues, the nurses, and the lab technicians have kept repeating to her that she is nearly there, as if she was on a bus about to reach its destination.

In silence, Timiro strokes her stomach, and then with her eyes closed, her hand in her mother's, she says, "It's the not knowing how and when the baby will arrive and if everything will be fine that has gotten to me."

"You'll see everything will be fine."

Last time they talked on the phone, Timiro had complained bitterly about frequent heartburns, shortness of breath after doing sit-ups. Then, in anticipation of the day when she wouldn't be able to work, she told her mother than she had been working non-stop for the past two months without a break. This in part must have exacerbated the situation.

"Worry not, honey," says Gacalo.

------

Later that day, Timiro, feeling more rested, joins her father in the living room, watching the afternoon news. She says, "Good to be home."

When her father lowers the volume, Timiro, unprompted, explains that she has also come to Oslo with the aim of doing further tests, following her latest consultations with her obstetrician in

Geneva. He suggested that she get a second opinion on a couple of her complaints.

He turns the TV off. "You're okay though?"

"My doctor in Geneva has forwarded last week's tests to the doctor at the Rikshospitalet, whom I see whenever I am here. I've already set an appointment and expect to see in a day or so."

He keeps his thoughts about changing doctors at this late stage of pregnancy to himself. Still, he says, "I'm sure all will be well, darling."

"By the way, how are Naciim and Saafi?"

"They are at Himmo's," Mugdi says. "Saafi is now attending Norwegian language school and Mouna and the other children help her with her assignments. These young people's companion-ability has brought back the missing smile to our faces and has introduced a fresh light to our eyes, especially Mum's."

"Who's the center of attention, the one who entertains the other children? Naciim?"

"Everything actually centers around Mouna," Mugdi says. "And Naciim is infatuated with her. He follows her everywhere in the way egrets follow water buffaloes whenever he can. She is fond of him too."

"And how is Saafi faring?"

"The girl has found her way to a comfort zone all her own and her voice is stronger and surer than ever."

"They haven't made peace, she and her mum?"

"Since the situation with the imam, Saafi doesn't trust her mum anymore."

"And Naciim?"

"He is protective of his sister, giving her all the support she needs in hopes that she will continue being strong and defiant," says Mugdi.

"How have Mouna and the other children responded to the girl?"

Mugdi replies, "Never having known what it is to be a refugee, and born and raised by a caring mother, Mouna has been the most empathic toward Saafi. Because Saafi never misses a prayer, Mouna has taken upon herself to make sure that Saafi's choices and prayer times are taken into account and accommodated. Nor does Mouna allow Naciim or anyone else to tease Saafi cruelly. And when Saafi absents herself from the group, something she does every now and then, either praying or because she is uninterested in the rough and tumble games the others are fond of taking part in, Mouna never fails to forbid the others from pestering her. When any of the others describe Saafi as someone in the slow lane and Saafi is too timid to defend herself, Mouna steps in and retorts that Saafi will catch up and surpass them, no doubt about it."

Timiro says, "Does the fact that Saafi and Naciim have lately been spending more and more time in a home such as yours, where liquor is consumed, or at Himmo's, where there are free-spirited children, give Waliya worries?"

"There is nothing she can do about this and from what little Naciim has told me, Zubair and Fanax are biding their time and waiting for the day when they can punish Naciim, whom they label as the 'problem boy' without bringing the wrath of the Barnevernet down on themselves," says Mugdi. "After all, the two men are aware of the consequences if they harm a hair on the boy's head."

"But Waliya must be relieved to know that Naciim keeps a close eye on his sister," says Timiro.

"No doubt this gives her some comfort."

"So she isn't as heartless as I initially thought?"

Mugdi says, "Any way you cut it, life has been tough on her."

Just as Mugdi prepares to leave the room, thinking their conversation has come to an end, Timiro not only changes the subject, but she has something she wants to get off her chest. She says, "Dad, is it true that Xirsi was in Oslo, and that he rang, and you spoke to him and you scolded him?"

"I didn't scold him," says Mugdi.

"That's what Uncle Kaluun has told me."

"I told him you weren't around."

"Did he say why he telephoned?"

"I assumed he wished to talk to you."

"Now why did neither you nor Mum tell me about his call?" she asks.

"What would you have done if you were here? Would you have spoken to him and if he had suggested you got back together, would you have said yes to his request?"

"Of course not."

"Why the fuss then?"

She is short with him then, saying, "You won't understand where I'm coming from anyhow. So let's leave it at that."

That he did not understand where she was coming from was one of her favorite lines in arguments whenever anyone responded unfavorably to one of her demands. Mugdi, however, suspects that Timiro will not admit openly that she is finding it hard, to wean herself off Xirsi, to whom, maybe, she is still addicted.

------

The following day, a woman at Rikshospitalet tasked with the management of expectant mothers' health and safety calls Timiro and tells her that stress is the cause of her worries and she refers her to a team of in-house specialists who deal with these kinds of problems.

When Gacalo returns from work and learns of this, she asks Timoro how she feels. Timoro says, "The recurrent pain started at an exercise session with other expectant mothers, many of whom were younger than I. And the woman overseeing the workout suggested I immediately seek my doctor's advice."

"What did the doctor think was the matter?"

"He was initially worried about possible future complications," says Timiro. "And he ordered a series of lab tests capable of detecting a wide range of disorders to determine the cause of my discomfort."

"And the lab results have come back?"

"Yes."

"Well, what were they? And what is the likelihood of complications that may lead to premature delivery, given that you are already thirty-two weeks pregnant?"

There is a long silence.

Her voice shaking, sounding as feeble as a frightened baby's, Timiro says, "Mum, I want to have the baby here. I don't just want to get a second opinion here, I want to come home."

Gacalo feels a sudden wrench inside her, as though an invisible hand is tugging at the roots of her heart. She says, "Of course, darling. We are here for you and will do whatever is necessary to make sure you have a healthy delivery."

The truth is Gacalo had looked forward to relocating to Geneva before the birth of the baby and had bought an air ticket in advance. But instead of raising objections or even inquiring as to how Timiro's doctor will react to her request to have the baby in Oslo under the supervision of another doctor, Gacalo revises her plans, tries to have the ticket refunded, and failing, accepts in the end that her daughter's desires are paramount.

In the meantime Birgitta and Gacalo arrange for Timiro to meet with one of Oslo's best obstetricians. The obstetrician puts her on a waitlist, vowing she will see her if there is a cancellation. A day later, the obstetrician's secretary telephones to inform her that Dr. Anna Petersen will see her in three days' time, at nine in the morning.

On the day Timiro is to meet the obstetrician, Gacalo accompanies her, sitting in the anteroom and waiting. Nearly half an hour later, Timiro walks out, beaming with relief. That night, Timiro, Mugdi, Gacalo, Johan, and Birgitta all meet for dinner, Himmo joining them late on account of having a day shift at the hospital. They share the good news that all is well with the expectant mother and baby. Johan and Birgitta leave early, saying, "Timiro has an exhausted look, and we're exhausted as well, having just flown in from Portugal. We'll leave you to get some rest." Himmo departs shortly after.

Timiro does tire easily now, her breathing labored, and wakes often in the night, the baby's strong kick reminding her of the delivery waiting to ambush her at any moment. She's most relaxed in the company of the young people, who entertain her with their stories and antics as she puts her feet up and rests. As a first-time mother, Timiro takes childbirth classes, and she speaks with great intensity to her mother, to Birgitta and Himmo, and to her new obstetrician, whom she loved from the instant she met her, believing her very knowledgeable, with a voice that she has found comforting and a smile that has calmed her nerves. Adding to her comfort, Himmo has agreed to play the role of a doula, her nursing background proving indispensable in such matters. The two meet daily, Timiro subjecting herself to the rigor required to have a less than unpleasant labor, knowing that all labors are hard. Luckily she is blessed with a high pain threshold, though she refuses to confirm if she will get the epidural or not.

"I'll decide on the day, maybe on the spur of the moment," Timiro insists.

"Is that a good idea?" asks Gacalo, holding her daughter's hand.

"It is very unwise to make any decision about it until I assess the situation, because in any case, according to Himmo and all the reading I've done, epidurals only lessen the pain, they do not remove it." Changing the subject, she asks, "What were you like as a first-time mother, when you gave birth to me?"

Tense, Gacalo reclaims her hand from Timiro's tight grip, averting her whole body before saying, "No two births are alike, and yours was unique in its own way, my love."

"If I insist on knowing, would you tell me what was unique about mine?"

"For now, I want us to concentrate on the job at hand."

During the pause that follows this, Timiro looks at her mother with loving eyes. She says, "I agree with you absolutely. Nothing is as important as the current job I am doing and I must concentrate on it to the exclusion of everything else."

The day of the delivery finally arrives and Timiro is not at all anxious. With her are two people in whom she has total faith, Himmo on one side and her mother on the other. "I am ready for whatever may come," Timiro says. "Though not yet for the hospital. I don't want to show up too soon like most mothers do and spend an eternity waiting, when I can be comfortable at home." Then her contractions begin in earnest, one following the next in quick succession, and despite her earlier words, the pain numbs her senses in ways Timiro has never known. Her right hand keeps clutching her chest and she appears to swoon, wondering if this is what death feels like. "Would you like us to go to the hospital now?" Gacalo asks.

She mouths the words, "I am okay. Thank you."

Himmo does not speak at all.

"We won't rush you," Gacalo says. "You decide. We'll do what you tell us to do."

After another series of contractions wracks her body, her face ghostly pale, Timiro says, "Now, please. I think it's time."

The three rush to the hospital, where Timiro's labor lasts another seven hours, and she declines an epidural. Finally, she delivers a beautiful baby girl with a sweet cry, whom she calls Riyo.

Timiro returns home after three days and the house and everyone in it is happy to welcome a healthy mother and a cheerful baby. Streams of visitors come from near and far, the telephone keeps ringing with congratulatory messages, and gift parcels arrive too. But the debate starts as to whether Xirsi should have a place of pride among the girl's names. Mugdi and Gacalo make hardly any contribution when it comes to choosing the baby's name, both arguing that it is Timiro's prerogative to do so. Nor does either of them give an opinion—for reasons known to Kaluun, Timiro, and themselves—as to whether Riyo's surname is hyphenated so as to add Mugdi's and Gacalo's to Xirsi's.

# CHAPTER FOURTEEN

-----------

IT HAS BEEN A LONG, EXHAUSTING DAY FOR NACIIM, WALIYA, AND SAAFI. It is nearly three in the afternoon and Naciim, who is eager to join his Norwegian friends for a soccer kickabout in a neighboring sports complex, is at home against his will. Sulking, he watches his mother and Saafi chase after small children, some on all fours crawling away from the wet spot where a boy, not yet toilet trained, has just marked a corner with his urine. Their nursery is in full swing.

In the corner of the living room diagonal to where the boy has had his accident, there is a different sort of mayhem: two boys are throwing rubber balls at one another, and one strikes a girl in the face, who begins shrieking with wild abandon. Waliya picks her up and tries to comfort her without success. Meanwhile, the boys have now started upending the plastic tables and spilling juice boxes and milk bottles. Naciim, standoffish and bad-tempered, retreats to his bedroom where he finds his bed newly unmade, the covers torn off and a different group of boys jumping up and down on the mattress. A soft giggle alerts him to a little girl hiding in the cupboard, the floor brindled with some unidentifiable brown substance.

As he prepares to leave the boys to their own devices, keenly aware that there is no place he can retreat, another little girl, veiled from head to toe despite being a mere two years old, with a soiled diaper and dirty hands, takes hold of his trousers and refuses to let go. Her viselike grip is so strong that he fights off the urge to kick her so she will release him. He keeps himself in check and curses under his breath.

To his relief, his sister comes into view, with two other girls in tow, and he pleads with her to help.

Saafi looks cursorily at the toddler with the soiled bottom and asks, "Why don't you change her?"

"Why don't you?"

He turns his gaze away, annoyed not just by the chaos of so many children in such a small space, but by what the veiling of the toddler represents—he reminds himself of how lately Somalis have developed the bizarre habit of making little tykes don veils. It can only mean that baby girls are no longer looked upon as genderless munchkins but as young women. Otherwise, why make them cover up?

When it comes to sex, Naciim has been a sharp-eyed witness from an early age, when, while living in the refugee camp, his mother would go nightclubbing and return home late, smelling of cigarette smoke and beer. The body tent she wore over her party clothes served the purpose of concealing the truth from those who might encounter her on her way to meet up with various men in cars, who always parked a distance away from their shack. If he or Saafi fussed and his mother tried to comfort them, delaying her, the man would often tap on the window impatiently, return to his car and wait until she joined him. On occasion, she would wait to leave until Naciim and Saafi had fallen asleep. He remembers many fretful nights wondering when she would return.

The way Naciim now understands it, in order to survive and bring up her two children as a single mother, she has always held back the truth of who she is from everyone, save a few of her closest female friends, particularly Arla, who now lives in Copenhagen and with whom he's overheard his mother speaking on the phone quite often since their arrival. Compared to other Somali women at the refugee camp, Arla was fun and wild. He will forever remember the stories she told him, which unfailingly fired his imagination as a boy.

At least some of his mother's caution is justified, Naciim thinks. After all, Saafi probably never would have been attacked if it weren't for his mother having taken a white man as one of her lovers, which so enraged a group of vigilante youths that they determined to teach her a lesson. Half a dozen waylaid Saafi one night on her way home and raped her. This horror has provided him with a deep insight into the workings of men's minds, just as it has turned Saafi into an anxious girl, wary of all men.

"Fine." Saafi sighs. "I'll change her. But you take these girls back to the living room." Glad to be spared the unpleasant task, he leads the two girls at her side away. But before he can deposit them with his mother, he hears a knock on the front door. "Who is it?" he calls. A young male voice he is familiar with replies, "It is me, Edvart."

Naciim can't help remembering that he has let Edvart and his other playmates down by not turning up this afternoon as agreed. Disappointed that he couldn't join his friends to play soccer, because his mother wouldn't allow it, his heart is now heavy and his hesitation obvious. Still, he opens the door and then comes face to face with Edvart, who is clutching a ball and wearing his soccer boots. The sight of his friend kitted out for the game lifts his spirits. He and his friend quickly fall into rapt conversation, unmindful of what is happening around them, including that two little girls have squeezed out the half-open door, one crawling all the way to the lift.

Waliya, suddenly aware of the missing girls, moves fast, nearly colliding with the boys on her way out the door, and snatches the girl sitting by the lift and brings her in, gesturing for the other child to follow her. She prepares to close the door, but catches a glimpse of the two boys still engaged in their talk. Her stomach turns, and then, sick with rage, she shouts at Naciim in Somali. Before he's fully aware of it, she shoos Edvart away, rudely pushing him in the chest and closing the door in his face. Then she grabs Naciim by the wrist, forcibly pulling him until they are in her bedroom. She turns to face him in an apparent fury and makes as if to strike him, before taking a deep breath, actively trying to calm herself. Her voice hard and severe, angry that he wasn't watching the kids as they wriggled out, she says, "What am I to do with you, punish you?"

"Mum, please let me explain."

"I've told you many times. I don't want your non-Muslim friends in my house. Everything an infidel touches is haram." She goes on, "And I've told you not to go to their homes or eat their foods. I know you've disobeyed and done that. Saafi has said so. Why do you continue going against my instructions?"

"Mum, you do not understand."

"You are saying I am stupid?"

"I am doing no such thing, Mum," he says.

"You will cause us nothing but ruin."

"Why won't you let me explain?"

"How many times have you been to your Norwegian friends' homes and eaten their haram food? Just tell me."

"I've been to Edvart's only the one time."

"And you've eaten there?"

"Eaten out of politeness, Mum."

"What did you eat?"

"Chicken, not pork."

"I don't want you to do that ever again."

"His mother was nice and she welcomed me."

"What's that supposed to mean?"

"She treated me well, as a human being."

"Get out of my sight, before I change my mind and give you the smack you deserve."

Naciim, in a rage now, says, "Why do you have to be so rude to my friend? Why chase him as if he were a stray dog with rabies? Why can't you welcome him nicely, the way his mother welcomes me?"

"Because he is unwelcome in my home."

"Remember, Mum, this is his country."

"What are you saying to me?"

He turns on his heels and is about to walk away, when, more agitated than he can remember seeing her in a long while, Waliya grabs his wrist. For a moment he worries that she really will give him a beating. But she struggles for self-control, and eventually regains composure, releasing him. "Why did you open the door?" she asks, her voice more measured.

"I had no idea it would be him."

"What if one of the babies got hurt?"

"I said I'm sorry." After a long pause, he says, "Can I go?"

------

Naciim takes refuge in the toilet, where he hopes to have a quiet moment of reflection. No sooner has he bolted the door from the inside and readied to pull down his trousers than there is a quick, insistent rapping on the door—his mother, demanding that he come out because a child needs to use the bathroom. Annoyed, but determined not to enter into a new argument, he pulls up his trousers, exits the bathroom, and scoots past his mother without speaking a word.

Before she can stop him, he leaves the apartment and takes the lift down to the ground floor, not knowing where he is headed. He walks to the park in the neighborhood, sits down on a bench and, his head between his hands, revisits the afternoon's events. When he recalls how rude his mother was to Edvart, chasing him out of the apartment as if he were a tramp, merely because his friend is not a Muslim, he decides that her attitude is no different from that of the neo-Nazis, those nativist skinheads so violently opposed to foreigners in their midst.

When he thinks of Edvart hastily retreating, the image comes to him of a dog departing with its tail between its legs, and he regrets that he did nothing in defense of his friend. What does this say about him? Did he act this way because he lacks self-confidence? When he considers his mother's inexcusable behavior alongside the fact that he is a Mahram, the man among the women, then surely he can come to no other conclusion but that he has failed.

His sense of annoyance palpable, he whips out his mobile phone, a gift from Mugdi, and dials Edvart's number. When Edvart answers,

Naciim's right hand, which is holding the phone, shakes and his voice is rich with unvented anger.

"Where are you?" Edvart asks.

"I am in the park, sitting on a bench."

"Alone?"

"Yes. On a bench facing the fountain."

"Stay where you are and I'll come to you."

"I am sorry about what happened."

"There's nothing to be sorry about," says Edvart.

Naciim looks up from his phone and catches a glimpse of a ball rolling toward him, kicked by a small boy, and nearby a grown man who must be the boy's father. He kicks the ball back to the boy, who, in turn, kicks it to his father, and his father passes it to Naciim. As the kickabout develops, Naciim volunteers to chase the ball every time the little boy kicks it astray. Soon the boy's breathing becomes heavy and he breaks out in a sweat, before tiring completely, prompting the father to suggest they sit and rest a bit. Turning to Naciim, he asks, "Do you live around here?"

Naciim points in the general direction of his apartment building and says, "I live with my mother and sister, and we are new to Norway."

The little boy tugs at his father's trousers and fusses until his father lifts him up and seats him on his lap.

"You speak well, no accent at all."

"We've been here for a little more than six months now."

The little boy starts to fidget and whine once more, already restless. The man says something to his son, who makes a grumbling sound.

"Maybe he is hungry," Naciim says.

"Hungry and tired," agrees the man. He fumbles in his shoulder bag and brings out a bottle that the boy devours as soon as it is put in his mouth. Soon enough, the child closes his eyes and falls asleep.

Normally not given to begrudging people anything, Naciim finds himself overwhelmed with envy and bitterness at the tender scene. Envy, because he did not have as kind and caring a father as this when he was the boy's age. Bitterness, because while his mother was out partying, it was often left to the neighbors in the refugee camp to care for him and his sister. And while she no longer leaves them for such unsavory nighttime activity nowadays, he is more and more convinced that his mother is somehow colluding with Zubair and the imam, whom he suspects of unsavory radical religious politics, trading one questionable activity for another.

Yet as he sits listening to the boy's gentle snore, he reminds himself not to let anger overtake him. He knows he has already endured much more than most of his Norwegian friends, who have lived in comfort all their lives, never suffering the kind of displacement to which he has become accustomed, born in one country, brought up in another as a refugee, and now thrust into a third, a newcomer once more. As shameful as it is to admit, there is a part of him that would prefer it if his mother quit Norway, since she is clearly so uncomfortable here, and only alienates herself more from others. Perhaps he could move in with Mugdi and Gacalo—he is certain they would welcome him.

Edvart's voice calling hello shakes Naciim out of his thoughts, while also awakening the sleeping boy. The boy, thrilled at the new arrival—and the second ball Edvart has brought with him—wiggles off the bench, grabs the ball at his father's feet, kicks Edvart's ball hard ahead of himself, and runs after it. Edvart chases the ball and the boy, who is elated for a few moments, but soon comes to a stop, searching for his father in the far distance before bursting into tears. His father rushes to comfort him, reclaims the ball, picks up his son, and departs.

Naciim and Edvart kick their ball around and eventually transition into a competitive dribbling routine. When they have played to exhaustion, they sit on the bench to catch their breath. Naciim leans forward, fingers in the shape of a steeple, pauses for a moment, then speaks, his voice deep. "I know I said this over the phone, but I can't seem to stop thinking about it. I am very sorry about what my mother did."

"Please, don't give it another moment's worry."

"She was rude," says Naciim.

"We are never responsible for what our parents say or do," Edvart says, patting his friend on the shoulder. "Mine embarrass me, too, and you know it. My father can be snotty, and often says terrible things about blacks, and makes even worse comments about Muslims."

"Your mum was nice, though," says Naciim.

"She's certainly easier to be around than my father," Edvart agrees. "And she likes you. Do you want to come home with me tonight? My father is away so it will just be us."

"No, but thank you for the invitation. I will go to my grandparents'."

# CHAPTER FIFTEEN

----------

TOMORROW MORNING, THE SEVENTEENTH OF MAY, NORWAY WILL BE AFLUT-
ter with flags bearing blue crosses outlined in white on a red background, the colors borrowed from the French tricolor, seen as a
symbol of liberty. Throngs will be out in the streets to watch the
children's parades celebrating the 1814 signing of the constitution.
Naciim can hardly contain his excitement. His friend Edvart has
earned the honor of carrying his school's official banner in the parade, and he will be followed by half a dozen older students carrying flags, with a marching band hard on their heels. Then hundreds
of younger children will follow behind, waving miniature flags to
the older students' full-size ones. The bystanders, mainly adults
dressed in *bunad,* or traditional costumes, will line the streets,
watching the marchers pass and taking delight in listening to the
celebratory songs and to the whistling, drumming, and shaking of
rattles.

But Naciim's eagerness for tomorrow's festivities is tempered by
the fury he feels at his mother and the way she mocked him for
preparing to join the Constitution Day celebrations. She practically

forced him out of the house with taunts meant not only to wound his pride but also to question his very identity—for how could he now consider himself a Somali, or even a Muslim, his mother demanded. It has taken him more than ten minutes' ride on the Metro from Groenland to Vigeland Park, plus a five-minute walk to reach this bench where he decides to sit until he has calmed his nerves. He does not wish anyone, least of all Mugdi and Gacalo, whom he will join later, to see him in such bad spirits on a day that he wishes to mark with respect.

When he feels more relaxed, he unknots the carrier bag containing three Norwegian flags he bought the day before from the money Mugdi gave him and which he hid from his mother under the mattress. He brings them out now and unfurls them, proud of his forethought. However he will admit to having made a mistake in allowing his mother to see even one of them—and more specifically, the flag's emblem which she views as a Christian cross—to shred in the first place. After all, he knew she would utter anathemas before throwing a fit and tearing it to pieces—and accuse him once again of "un-Islamic" leanings. He would then refuse to admit he had done anything wrong, and after barely a few minutes, they would be locked once more in battle, dredging up quarrelsome scenes from the recent past, and on it would go, until he left the apartment. Even as he tries to calm himself, he can't help replaying this latest fight in his mind.

"No cross in my house," she said. Then Naciim argued that he did not see it as a cross, but as the symbol of Norway, the country that has hosted them in their hour of need. "Besides, we must give every country's flag respect, whether the country is small or large, whether the flag depicts a cross, a crescent and a sword, or Arabic script."

"It is a cross and no matter what you say, you won't convince me to respect this symbol of Christianity," she insisted, adding, "Give it here."

He refused.

"Give me this Christian thing."

"I won't."

"Give it now, before Allah curses us."

"Why do you people forbid every kind of fun?" It took all his self-control not to speak the blasphemous thoughts invading his mind.

Saafi, who seldom entered the fray, came out of her room at this point. His sister's silent presence distracted him for an instant and before he knew it, his mother had snatched the flags out of his grasp. "There," she said in a triumphant tone. Deflated, he watched her cut up the flags until they were no more than fragments of red, white, and indigo blue. But he was not completely dispirited because he knew he had three more flags concealed under the mattress. To save these from potential destruction, he snuck away when his mother was absorbed in her prayers, grabbed the flags, hastily packed a bag with his favorite clothes, and fled the apartment. He'll stash the flags and his clothes at Mugdi and Gacalo's house and pick them up early the following morning, so he may take his place in the line of his flag-waving classmates.

Significantly more relaxed, Naciim rises to his feet. There is a natural spring to his gait and he is convinced he will regain his happiness the instant he claps eyes on Mugdi and Gacalo. He is uncertain, though, if he will share with them the details of what his mother has done.

He knocks softly on Mugdi and Gacalo's door, which prompts Mugdi to shout, in muffled Norwegian, "Who is there?"

Naciim mumbles an answer, his voice betraying anxiety. Mugdi opens the door and instantly knows that the boy is in a world of trouble the moment his eyes meet Naciim's.

He lets him in without a word.

After a few moments' silence, Naciim staring at the floor, his head hanging, Mugdi says, "Out with it. Is there something you want to tell me?"

"There is," says Naciim.

"Go on, then."

He listens as the boy relays the afternoon's events, pausing every so often as if to weigh his words, proof that he has given much thought to what he is retelling. He shows Mugdi the spare flags and explains his plan to arrive at the school early and stand as close as he can to his friend Edvart.

"Where will your starting point be tomorrow? If you leave from home, there is no guarantee that your mother will allow you to join in the celebrations."

"There must be a way," says Naciim. "What if I leave the flags and my clothes here, and fetch them tomorrow morning before the parade starts?"

"That would be one way," says Mugdi, "although there is an easier solution."

The boy looks embarrassed and says, "I'd hate to inconvenience you."

"How are you going to inconvenience us?"

"I want you to remain blameless."

It amuses the old man that Naciim wants to keep Mugdi and Gacalo out of Waliya's bad books, when Mugdi does not doubt that they are already inscribed there, for such indefensible acts as allowing her son to question the principles of the faith, and exposing him to Norwegian culture.

"My mother tends to blame the world, never herself," says Naciim. "And I am tired of that. When will she take responsibility for her actions, admit that she is wrong?"

Mugdi, as much as he might share the boy's feelings, is loath to tread further down this avenue of finger pointing, and decides a change of subject is the wisest course of action.

"Tell you what, Naciim," Mugdi says. "Go and watch a bit of TV—and be sure to help yourself to a soft drink, you know where the fridge is—and I will return to my study upstairs and do some more work. We'll talk about this later. For now, just relax."

"Yes, Grandpa," Naciim says, noticeably lighter in temperament.

Three hours later, during a pause in the soccer program he is watching, Naciim hears a key turning in the lock and the voices of two women entering the house. He is able to identify Gacalo as one of the speakers, but can't quite place the other woman, though she sounds vaguely familiar. As the women move into the living room, Naciim now recognizing the other voice as Himmo's, he feels the urge to announce his presence, as he doesn't want Gacalo to think of him as an intruder. So he clears his throat loudly enough for the women to hear him without being startled.

"Hey, look who is here," Himmo says, shaking the hand Naciim has extended in her direction, then hugging and kissing him on the forehead.

Gacalo smiles at Himmo's warm greeting before giving Naciim a tight hug and several kisses of her own. The boy seems grateful for the embrace, gripping her so fiercely that after a moment

Gacalo steps back and appraises him, intuiting that something is amiss. She curses under her breath and asks, "Is it your mother?"

Naciim's eyes downcast, he nods.

"What was it this time?"

He is preparing to answer when Himmo takes him by the elbow, gently shakes him, and says, "A big quarrel or a small one?"

Seeing the boy hesitate, Mugdi, who has come down from his study after hearing the women's arrival, kisses his wife hello, hugs Himmo, saying, "It's been a long time, my dear," and then answers her question on Naciim's behalf. "I would say it was a very big quarrel, over whether his mother will allow him to join his classmates in the flag-waving celebrations tomorrow. From what he told me, he bought a couple of flags and she tore them to shreds and inveighed against crosses and alien gods."

Gacalo, filled with indignation, says, "The boy wants to have a bit of fun, that's all. He means no harm to anyone, nor to his faith, nor to the reputation of his community. What's wrong with his dressing up in his best clothes, joining his classmates, and having a good time?"

"Nothing wrong with that," Himmo agrees.

"The woman is mad," says Gacalo.

"Exactly. And let's leave it at that," says Mugdi, turning toward Himmo and asking, "Tea?"

As Gacalo excuses herself to go upstairs and change out of her work clothes, Himmo takes the tall chair, waiting for her tea, and Mugdi asks Naciim if he would like tea of his own or another soft drink.

"Another soft drink, please."

Mugdi hands the boy a Coke from the fridge, then sensing his eagerness to leave, says, "You may return to watching your soccer match if you'd like."

Putting on the water to boil, Mugdi brings out the teapot, tea cozy, cups and saucers, sugar for Himmo and milk for himself and Gacalo, who has returned in time to hear him say, "For a boy of Naciim's age, moments of small turmoil such as this feel like a day of reckoning."

"And the best comfort he can expect is empathy," Himmo says, "courtesy of a couple like you and Gacalo, a man and a woman with giant hearts."

Gacalo, still visibly annoyed with Waliya, says, "The irony is that Naciim perhaps still harbors the illusion of being the Mahram and therefore the most important member of the household. But he is what he is, a mere child, and his mother is the householder. It is time he acknowledges that this whole Mahram business is just religious fantasy."

Something like liquid rage now rises in Mugdi's entrails, as he relives the terrible memories associated with Waliya's coming to Oslo—the family members divided, forms filled out, funds wasted, relationships strained, tempers lost, promises made, favors called in. He thinks of Gacalo taking to her bed not so long ago, and the boy turning up, unannounced, seeking a place of refuge. Is it any wonder that they are all beginning to feel burned out?

Soft footsteps signal Naciim's return to the kitchen. "I have a few questions about tomorrow," he says hesitantly. "How and when did all this flag-waving start? Why is it the school-going children who lead the celebrations? How come the adults take a less active role?"

"The day has several monikers," Mugdi says. "National Day,

Constitution Day, and Liberation Day. It is tradition for each school to celebrate with a children's parade that passes by the Royal Palace, where the Royal Family greets the celebrants from the balcony. And while children march through the streets in colorful clothes, waving flags, adults don the Norwegian national costume."

"When did this holiday start and who started it?"

Gacalo says, "Was it not 1825?"

"You can't think of this day without also thinking of Henrik Wergeland, one of Norway's greatest poets, who is credited with the idea of a celebratory day primarily for children. To mark his importance, the Russ, the high-school graduating class of the year, call at his statue and place an enormous hat on his head," Mugdi says. "And he has earned legendary status among Norway's Jewish community, for his commitment to inclusiveness and the efforts he undertook to accommodate their presence."

"But he wasn't Jewish, was he?" Himmo asks.

"Nor was he Muslim, even though some of his fellow Norwegians believed he had converted to Islam, because in a letter to his father, Wergeland referred to God as Allah. He was just a man ahead of his time, a champion of multicultural Norway, who is seen today as the father of the Norwegian left."

Himmo says, "But there have always been dissenters, groups who oppose celebrating the constitution in the spirit with which Wergeland interpreted it."

Gacalo cuts in, saying, "I remember in 1983, Norwegian extremists incited their fellow citizens to rise up in arms against allowing immigrant children to be part of the celebrations. These groups made bomb threats in neo-Nazi propaganda pamphlets sent to the principal of one of the schools. The teachers of the school pleaded with the police to provide protection. But when the police declined to do so, the school authorities demanded that the celebrations continue as planned, without making the racist threats known to the public. The teachers, brave souls, would not back down, despite the threats from the racists. Luckily, everything went ahead without incident, though there were repeated bomb threats the following year too."

"What is wrong with these people?" Naciim says. "Why all this hate toward Muslims?"

Mugdi looks down at his hands, staring at his nails which are in need of trimming, while considering how best to answer the boy's question. After a few moments, he meets Naciim's eyes and says, "The right-wing ethnic Norwegians aren't the only ones who oppose Wergeland's inclusive, peace-abiding interpretation of the principles of the Norwegian Constitution. You have the mullahs on the Muslim side, whose challenge to the ideals upon which the pillars of freedom stand is just as dangerous as that of the right-wing extremists. A Salafist group that exists on the fringes, like Islam Net—a Sunni Muslim organization whose founder expressed support, in 2013, for the execution of homosexuals and adulterers—is no promoter of peace either, despite their claim. In short, you have native-born right-wing extremists and a handful of radical Islamists who are daggers drawn over 'ideology' and therefore make everyone else's life difficult. And you know what happens when two elephants confront each other and fight?"

"No. Please tell me," says Naciim.

"When elephants get into a wrestling match, it is the grass that suffers," says Himmo.

"I don't follow you," says Naciim.

"In other words, when the native-born extremists get into a no-holds-barred fight with the radical Muslims, the victims will be the innocent folks, who belong to neither group," says Gacalo. "We must all beware of provocateurs, no matter their allegiances, who are enemies to the nation at large and of peace everywhere."

Naciim, thinking over what he has just heard, says, "Wergeland and every peace-loving person here and elsewhere would oppose both groups. Am I right?"

All three adults answer in unison, "Yes."

An hour and a half after dinner, Naciim is given the choice of either returning home with Himmo, who is willing to offer him a bed for the night, and then joining her three children tomorrow at the celebrations, or spending the night at Mugdi and Gacalo's. The boy chooses to sleep at his grandparents', provided that they let his mother know where he is.

Mugdi makes the call to Waliya. When Saafi answers the phone, he asks her to tell her mother that "Naciim is well and is staying with us for the night."

Then he hangs up.

# CHAPTER SIXTEEN

-----------

THE FOLLOWING MORNING MUGDI AND NACIIM ARE IN THE KITCHEN AND the old man asks, "What would you like for breakfast?"

Gacalo has already left for work. Despite its being a national holiday, she has to file an urgent budget proposal. She and Mugdi woke early and ate together. Mugdi made her an omelet, and for himself, his favorite morning meal, porridge.

He is now on his third cup of strong coffee and has just greeted Naciim with a welcoming smile. The boy looks exhausted, having slept little the previous night. When Mugdi awoke around two a.m. and came downstairs to get a glass of a water, he witnessed Naciim tossing and turning and talking to himself in his sleep, shouting someone's name incoherently. To Mugdi, it sounded as if he were cursing Zubair.

"What's there to eat?" Naciim asks.

Despite his lack of sleep, Naciim is looking forward to the day's festivities, and to the fact that his best friend Edvart will be at the head of the line, carrying the flag. Mugdi replies, "I can make you porridge."

"What did Grandma have?"

"I made her an omelet."

"Can I have an omelet too, please?"

"Of course," says the old man.

Mugdi brings out a skillet and some butter, cracks two eggs, which he beats together in a bowl, adds a drop of water, and then seasons the mix with black pepper and salt. When the butter has melted, he pours the mix into the frying pan and waits until it is fully cooked on all sides and ready to serve. Naciim watches everything with rapt attention, perhaps keen to make his own omelet next time. Mugdi places the omelet before Naciim and asks, "Would you like toasted bread or a slice of untoasted baguette?"

"A slice of baguette, please."

The boy fidgets in his chair, looking slightly ill at ease. Though Mugdi does not inquire as to what is causing him discomfort, he assumes that Naciim is embarrassed to be sitting there doing nothing while an old man cooks his breakfast and serves it to him. In the culture in which the boy was raised, not only is the kitchen considered a woman's place, but it would be seen as the height of rudeness for a young person to sit idly while a man of Mugdi's age prepared and served them a meal. Mugdi derives solace from knowing that this type of confusion will soon come to an end for the boy and everything will be fine. Or so he hopes.

"Is everything OK?" asks Mugdi.

As suddenly as it appeared, the anxiety leaves Naciim's face, and he replies with joy, "I can make an omelet from today on, having watched you. But tell me, Grandpa, why do you put two or three drops of water in the beaten egg?"

"Because that will make it less runny."

"My stepdad used to put milk in it instead," says Naciim. "And I agree, it was a lot runnier than the one you just made."

When they have eaten and dressed, Mugdi consults his watch and decides that it is time to leave if they are to join Naciim's fellow students before the parade starts. "Are you coming too?" asks Naciim.

"I remember escorting Dhaqaneh from the first years of his schooling until his final years at high school. And it was always fun," says Mugdi.

"I had no idea you used to accompany my stepdad in the flag-waving festivities. Had I known of this, I might have told my mother about it."

"Do you want to call your mum now?"

"No. She'll just quote some religious thing at me, and find some new way to worry. She goes to bed worrying and wakes up worrying."

"All the more reason to call her now," says Mugdi, "to tell her that all is well with you and that so far nothing terrible has happened."

"Let me have fun first and then I will call her after the festivities are over," says Naciim.

Naciim offers to wash the dishes before they depart but Mugdi will not hear of it. He suggests the boy collect his flags and get ready so they can walk to the train station.

The first time Naciim took the underground, not long after his arrival in Oslo, he was full of fear and excitement, overawed to imagine that he was, as he put it, "in the belly of the earth, alive right inside its mysterious abyss." Since then, he has taken it more times than he can remember, though he still gets a thrill each time he descends below ground.

As he follows Mugdi, now walking on the old man's right and now on his left, he is determined to keep pace, lest he be left behind. Mugdi is fond of walking fast, and Naciim's steps are short compared to the old man's long strides. If it were up to him, Naciim would study his surroundings in detail. He'd happily sit on a bench by the side of the road and watch with care the men, women, and children going this way and that, carrying flags of varying sizes, crowding the streets with delight. His gaze falls on two girls his age, one wearing a short skirt and eating an ice lollipop, the other, a bit older, skimpily clad in a see-through dress and smoking a cigarette. Shocked to see such a young girl puffing away—and even more by the sight of her budding breast, which can be glimpsed through the side of her dress—Naciim decelerates to the point of stopping altogether, his eyes opening wide with awe. He is so focused on the girl that he forgets where he is headed and with whom, until he hears his name and sees Mugdi towering over him, asking, "Are you coming?" Naciim hopes Mugdi cannot tell what has held him captive. Even so, he apologizes and scurries after Mugdi, as the old man resumes his fast walk.

Soon the sidewalks grow busier, filled with crowds on their way to the nearby schools or to the T-Bane Metro. Mugdi eases his pace so the two of them can walk side by side.

At the ticket kiosk, Mugdi purchases a ticket for Naciim.

"What about you? Don't you need a ticket?"

"I have a pensioner's pass."

Assuming that Naciim may not know its intricacies, Mugdi begins explaining the history of Oslo's T-Bane to the boy. "It extends over more than eighty kilometers and the first line started operating in 1898," he tells the boy, "though the basis for today's network was constructed in 1928 and then added to, as the city grew and its population increased tenfold." He brings out a subway map and shows Naciim their present route, pointing out how the different lines are color coded. Then he falls into silence, because it is too noisy for them to hear each other, and looks around at the crowd. Everyone seems friendlier today; even the masses of people pushing into the train are politer than during usual rush hours, standing aside to make room for the younger ones waving flags. Maybe the extremists on either side of the Norwegian divide have chosen to stay away. The passengers remind him of soccer fans making their way toward a stadium where they are confident their team will win. Maybe Team Wergeland is the winning side today.

As agreed the previous night, they meet up with Himmo and her children in Groenland, close to where Naciim is linking up with his friend Edvart, and where Himmo's children will join their school parade. After seeing the children off, Mugdi and Himmo walk alongside the parade for a good quarter hour, liberally commenting on the sights and their fellow attendees.

At one point, they spot three generations of an African family. Himmo observes their harmonious appearance, the grandparents holding the hands of the youngest, the sisters walking arm in arm, and the husband and wife in loving communion, practically kissing. Then Mugdi overhears a Somali couple by the side of the road making racist remarks about the family. Incensed, Mugdi can't control himself. Storming over to the couple, he inveighs against their behavior, which white Europeans might use to justify their own discriminatory observations about black people. He adds, "Why don't you desist from this fascist behavior today of all days?"

"What business is it of yours to speak to us that way?" the man challenges him. "We can say what we want and you can't stop us."

An argument ensues and Himmo joins in. Mugdi and the man

are close to exchanging blows when other Somalis standing nearby intervene, pulling the two apart. As they walk away from the scene, Mugdi says, "We Somalis are xenophobic and chauvinistic. Often I wonder if we have the right to complain when or if others behave unkindly toward us."

Himmo agrees and says, "Our self-regard, as a people, makes me sick too. We look down on everybody—white, black, African, Arab, American—and do not defer to anyone's authority. To use the Somali word for slave, *adoon*, to describe a fellow African here in Norway, as that couple just did, is to denigrate ourselves as humans."

"An ill-educated, cynical lot," Mugdi says, "these Somalis have nothing to recommend them, whether here in Norway or anywhere else. They have no idea that the age-old certainties which they held at home are no longer valid here."

"What does one do with them?"

"What can one do about the byzantine contortions of their clan-based politics, when even they know the institution does more harm than good?"

Looking around, Mugdi awakens to the fact that, so absorbed in his anger, and in the conversation, he no longer recognizes where they have walked. "Do we know where we are going?" he asks.

"My place is three minutes away," Himmo says.

Himmo's three-bedroom apartment is located on the third floor of a small building. When Mugdi walks in, he is struck by how pleasant and airy it is, with large windows, high ceilings, and walls painted a light shade of beige. When Mugdi asks for the toilet, Himmo shows him to the bathroom and he remembers her saying a couple years ago, not long after she first moved in, that the apartment's one drawback was that it had only one bathroom—a massive headache when you have three children who need to get to school on time.

The bathroom is a bit of a mess, with wet towels piled on the floor, and on the sink a comb bearing traces of long curly hair. He hangs up the towels but leaves the comb for someone else to deal with. He tells himself that this is a lived-in place, with lovely young people who will grow to be responsible one day, maybe after they are married.

When Mugdi reemerges, he finds Himmo clearing up the young folks' breakfast mess and he offers to make her tea. Himmo works night shifts a few times a week. On those evenings she's at the hospital, her oldest daughter, Maimouna, looks ably after her younger siblings.

It is a shame that Himmo has been so unlucky in her marriages, Mugdi thinks. One of her three husbands had more blind spots than a vehicle with no side mirrors. He had a hand in the death of a Somali man, a fellow qaat chewer, and was later accused of raping a Somali woman and ended up in prison. Himmo sought a divorce, and with the help of a lawyer hired by Mugdi and Gacalo, received full custody of her children and a small settlement. Mugdi is very fond of Himmo and considers her family, the one person in Norway whom he has known for a great many years. She is the younger sister of his best childhood friend, and he treats her much as he treats his daughter Timiro.

Mugdi fills the kettle through its spout, as the lid will not give even though he pulls it hard. The gas turns on after two attempts and, with the water boiling, he searches for cups. "Tea's ready, dear," says Mugdi.

"Thanks," Himmo says, approaching Mugdi with her hands

held away from her. Mugdi steps out of her way so she can reach the washbasin.

"Here." Mugdi passes her a cup after she dries her hands. "Sugar?"

"Yes, please."

He stirs in a spoonful of sugar and waits for her approval. Himmo takes the cup, sips, and says, "Perfect." She pauses for a moment and then says, "How come you play host to me in my own home, serving me tea, when no other man I've ever known has done that for me?"

Mugdi says, "You deserve far better than the misfortunes you've met in the men that you've married. But you have three lovely children and that is worth all the gold in the world."

After a companionable silence, Himmo says, "From the window, you can see the apartment of that Iraqi-born Kurd who is often in the news for his controversial radical politics."

"Is he the one the CIA tried to kidnap so as to take him to Guantánamo for interrogation?"

"The same. I've never understood why the authorities can't deport him to Iraq, since his Norwegian citizenship has been revoked."

"Remember, Norway is a country of laws."

"Yes, and he exploits the legal system."

Mugdi says, "Remember also that his wife and children are Norwegian citizens and that judges in the courts do not look favorably upon separating a man from his family."

Hearing the voices of young girls and boys at the door, one of them turning a key in the lock, they bring their conversation to a halt. Here are Himmo's three children and Naciim, all politely saying hello and casting their flags aside, eager to tuck into the Big Macs each is unwrapping.

"Where did you get the money to buy these?" Himmo asks. Her children surely have not forgotten that their mother disapproves of what she calls "terrible, fattening food." She is a nurse, after all, and knows what she is talking about.

Maimouna says, "We couldn't say no when Naciim offered to pay for ours, and for his friend Edvart's. He described it as a gift on the happiest day of his life since coming here."

Turning to Naciim, Himmo asks, "And where did you get the money to buy all these?"

Naciim says, "I've saved some money from what Grandpa Mugdi and Grandma Gacalo gave me."

Half an hour later, Mugdi is ready to return home and he suggests that Himmo ring the widow to inform her that her son will be home before nightfall.

# CHAPTER SEVENTEEN

----------

IT'S BEEN TWO YEARS SINCE NACIIM'S ARRIVAL IN OSLO AND HE IS GOING to Johan and Birgitta's dinner party to welcome home their son, Fredrik, visiting from the US, where he teaches. Fredrik, as it happens, was his stepdad's playmate when they were both young. Lately, he has been spending more time at his grandparents' than at his mother's, following his set-to with his mother about the flag-waving festivities he took part in. And what a joy it has been to enjoy sleepovers at Auntie Himmo's, in the company of Mouna, with whom he is infatuated.

Mugdi and Gacalo haven't seen Frederik in years, though they were quite fond of him as a young friend of their son.

Over lunch, Mugdi and Gacalo's conversation inevitably leads them back to Naciim, their only topic of discussion as of late, and whether to take him along to visit their friends or send him home to his mother. Mugdi puckers his forehead in concentration and says, "What about school tomorrow? You realize his satchel and books are at his apartment."

"That is no longer a problem," says Gacalo. "I took him shopping earlier, when you were working in your study, and bought him a new satchel to replace his secondhand one. I also got him everything he needs for school, plus toothpaste, a toothbrush, and a pair of pajamas."

Mugdi lifts his arms from his sides in the way of a bird readying for flight, as his eyes focus on a distant patch of the heavens visible from where he is sitting in the kitchen. He extrapolates from her words that a room in their home will soon be designated as Naciim's and that the boy will occupy it whenever he visits. He allows himself time for this new reality to sink in and says, "So we're taking him along to dinner?"

"I want Naciim to get to know our friends."

"Then we must let them know."

"I've already taken care of it."

"Anything else you haven't told me?"

"I've booked a cab to take us there. It'll be good for Naciim to meet Fredrik, who knew his stepfather in his preteen years. And they are both so bright."

"He's done well, Fredrik," says Mugdi.

Gacalo interprets Mugdi's assertion as an implicit condemnation of Dhaqaneh. There is nothing new in this; Mugdi has always believed that their late son squandered his potential, whereas Fredrik stayed on the right path. Still, Gacalo finds this sentiment enraging. Unable to come up with a defense of her beloved son, she leaves the kitchen, no doubt to have a good cry alone in the upstairs bathroom.

It is not lost on Mugdi that Fredrik earned a PhD at the University of Chicago at the very same time that Dhaqaneh was becoming embroiled in radical extremism. The two boys were both keen on sports, Dhaqaneh on soccer and Fredrik on swimming, and they remained close during their formative years, when their parents were diplomats representing their respective countries in Bonn and Moscow. Mugdi and Gacalo were as fond of Johan and Birgitta's son as the two Norwegians were fond of Timiro and Dhaqaneh. At dinner, Gacalo will be at pains to show that she is happy for Fredrik, whose partner, a journalist, only recently discovered she was pregnant while traveling between Aleppo and Mosul on assignment. As fond as she is of Naciim and Saafi, how Gacalo wishes Dhaqaneh had been survived by his own biological child, "not," as she put it to Himmo, when Waliya first arrived, "two stepchildren that are part of a package."

As it happens, Mugdi and Fredrik have overlapping interests, and have been in close correspondence with each other. Fredrik, an associate professor at St. Olaf College in Minnesota, has been of great assistance with Mugdi's Somali translation of *Giants in the Earth*. Its author, Ole Edvart Rølvaag, taught for many years at St. Olaf, and the novel was even written at the college. Fredrik has been helping Mugdi to unlock the work's mysteries. And as Mugdi's interest in the history of Norwegian migration to North America has sharpened, Fredrik's concomitant interest in Somalis in Minnesota has taken shape. The two speak and write often to each other, each relying on the other's expertise.

As Mugdi waits for Gacalo to regain her composure, he joins Naciim in the TV room, where they watch Serena Williams in the finals of a tennis match, until Gacalo, calm once more, comes downstairs and suggests they turn off the TV. "Surely you can find a more useful way to spend the hours until dinner," she tells Naciim.

Later, in the taxi on the way to Birgitta and Johan's, with the boy sitting in the front and the elderly couple in the back, Gacalo asks Naciim, "So what did you do after I requested that you turn off the TV?"

He replies, "I've been busy writing."

"Writing? Writing what?" says Mugdi.

"A book."

"What's the book about?"

"It's about my life, from the moment I became aware of what was happening around me, and all the people who were there, the men and women, our neighbors," says Naciim.

"How did you come up with the idea of writing a book when you haven't yet read a great deal yourself?" asks Gacalo.

"I watched a program on TV earlier about several teen writers who have published books in the past," he replies. "The presenter gave summaries of their stories, which I did not find uplifting. By the end, I was sure I could write better. And so I decided then and there to start writing a book about the experiences I've had growing up in the refugee camp."

Mugdi exchanges a look with Gacalo and then asks Naciim, "In what language have you chosen to write the story of your life?"

"My plan is to write it in Somali now and, later, when I have mastered Norwegian, translate it," answers Naciim. He pauses and then adds after reflection, "I'll do the translation in reverse order to what you are doing, in translating from Norwegian into Somali, though I do not think that my book will be anywhere near as good as the classics you are working on."

Impressed, Mugdi imagines helping this ambitious boy any way he can, reading as many drafts as necessary until the book is licked into publishable shape.

Gacalo asks, "Do you remember the names of any of those young authors mentioned in the TV program?"

"A young Dutch author, something Frank?"

Mugdi says, "Anne Frank?"

Naciim says, "She died before the book about her experiences, which took her years to write, was published, didn't she?"

Mugdi says, "That's right. She died early."

"I want to finish writing before I die."

Mugdi hopes that the boy's frenetic intelligence does not dissipate in the way of his own son's squandered abilities. He says to Naciim, "We are here to help you in any way we can."

Naciim appears to be about say something when the taxi slows down and he falls silent. Having arrived at their destination, Gacalo, whose idea it was to take the taxi in the first place, tells Mugdi and Naciim to wait for her on the sidewalk. She settles the fare, giving a generous tip to the Ethiopian-looking driver, and collects a receipt. Then she joins them and they walk together, Naciim between them.

It has always disturbed Mugdi that Somalis in Norway tend to attract bad press, and seem relegated to the lowest rung on the economic ladder, unable to see beyond their ideological and religious constraints, and so unable to ever really advance. As Mugdi steps aside for Gacalo to enter the Nielsens' home, he feels certain that Naciim and his generation of fresh-faced ambitious young Somalis will change all that.

The Nielsens greet them exuberantly, welcoming them with hugs and solicitous pleasantries. Mugdi is attentive to the sounds and scents of the house, wondering if their friends have put their German shepherd in the back garden, suspecting that the animal might frighten Naciim, who is not used to dogs. As diplomats serving abroad, their hosts have always been considerate of their guests, hospitably accommodating their cultural and religious demands.

There are few people Mugdi has known who are as inclusionary as the Nielsens.

Fredrik is a giant of a young man, standing over six feet seven inches, close in height and bulk to his father. He has the bearing of an athlete, even if his movements are as elegant as a dancer's. He takes Gacalo's hand, as if they are about to perform a foxtrot, and follows Birgitta into the kitchen. Johan, meanwhile, is chatting to Mugdi and Naciim as he pours them drinks, an orange soda for the boy, red wine for his friend, and white wine for Birgitta and Gacalo. Naciim's anxiety level ratchets up as Mugdi takes quick mouthfuls of wine as though it were water, and Gacalo returns to the living room and does the same. Unfamiliar with wine drinking, Naciim assumes that anyone who has a sip of it will straightaway be drunk, and he asks himself what will become of him if Mugdi and Gacalo are unable to take him home.

Johan asks Naciim, "Do you like Norway?"

"I love it so far," answers Naciim, glad to have the conversation as a distraction.

"What do you love about it?"

Fredrik and Birgitta have also returned to the living room, and there is eagerness in their eyes as they wait for the boy's answer. Naciim plays his part, pleased with having such an attentive audience.

He speaks with the slowness of someone searching for the right words in Norwegian, and when he feels the language failing him, he lapses into Somali, occasionally requesting that Mugdi or Gacalo act as interpreter. He says that he loves the diversity and beauty of Norway's nature: the fjords, green valleys, mountains, and sea. Then he elaborates that he spent much of his previous life in a refugee camp, where one seldom saw a tree, as they were all cut down and used as firewood.

"Have you been out of Oslo yet?" asks Fredrik.

"On school trips, twice."

"Where did you go?"

Again he combines languages, now stopping as if in search of a word, now stammering and looking in Mugdi's direction for help. Eventually, with encouragement from the old man, he spells out that the school trip took him to the Borre National Park, where he saw Viking burial mounds, which he found fascinating. He loved the carefree nature of the place, the fjord, and the mature forest in the hills. He concludes that he has never seen anything quite like it.

"I'm curious, what did you find so fascinating about the Viking burial mounds?" Fredrik asks.

Naciim, feeling shy about addressing the young man directly, gives his explanation to Mugdi, who then translates his words into Norwegian. "Naciim says he remembers his stepfather Dhaqaneh stripping the hide of two Shabaab members accused of digging up the corpses of a number of Italians buried in a Mogadiscio cemetery and scattering their remains elsewhere."

When Mugdi pauses, Gacalo, who knows that her husband has no time for Dhaqaneh, thinks that he may be playing the role of a *tradutore traditore*—quite literally, a translator traitor. So she assumes that task of translating, saying, "Naciim says that when people discovered street children kicking these human bones around as though they were footballs, Dhaqaneh described the desecration as 'the work of a despicable lot.'"

As Johan tops up Mugdi's glass, Birgitta jumps in with a question about Shabaab, asking, "What's wrong with them, these barbarians?"

"I would say that the violent culture of right-wing groups here in Europe is very like Shabaab's," says Mugdi. "I am of the view that the two radical groups feed off each other."

"And we are their victims," says Johan.

"Both here and there," agrees Birgitta, heading into the kitchen to give the last touches to the dinner, before announcing "*à la table*." Just as everybody rises to obey, Fredrik, walking alongside Gacalo, says, "I was shocked to learn about Dhaqaneh's involvement in radicalism." Then he adds before taking his seat, "Who would have thought that would be his fate?"

Gacalo says, "None of us did."

Fredrik remembers Dhaqaneh as someone who thought of himself as a bridge builder, a bringer-together of peoples from different beginnings, a Somali proud of his place in Europe. There was the time when the two of them saw a film adaptation of Albert Camus's *The Stranger*. Dhaqaneh was very upset, not because Meursault couldn't care less about his mother's death, but that he was so uncaring and emotionless that he could bring himself to kill an Arab.

Fredrik now turns to Mugdi, who sits across from him to his left. The old man says, "The major regret in my life is not only that this did not cross my mind when something might still have been done for him, but also that I blamed Gacalo, among others, for failing to do their part in saving Dhaqaneh from ruin."

Dinner served, Gacalo and Johan attempt to shift the tone of the conversation, revisiting old memories that their two families have shared, until Naciim, who does not figure into the reunion stories being told, suddenly recalls the type of food Dhaqaneh cooked on special occasions, to celebrate a birthday or New Year's. A sense of unease spreads around the table and no one can think of anything to say.

Eventually, Fredrik finds his tongue and says, "Well, as you may know, I have some happy news—I'm about to become a father."

Tears spring to Gacalo's eyes, but no one is certain if she is sad, remembering her late son, or happy, because she is thinking of Timiro, who has given her a grandchild. She smiles at the Nielsens, sure they are looking forward to becoming grandparents when Fredrik and his partner have their child, then lets her gaze fall fondly on Naciim, before drifting to Fredrik.

She remembers the wonderful times they had when he was young and a constant companion to her son. She had always thought him a handsome youth, with his Cupid's bow lips, blond hair, athletic build, and charming personality, and she recalls many a girl wanting to kiss him. In her freer moments, she will not deny she had a crush on him as well, though this was no more than an occasional feeling and never lasted long. In life, there is always a lucky girl.

Of Fredrik's partner, Johan says, looking in his son's direction, "It is commendable that Fredrik seldom complained when she traveled on assignments to dangerous cities like Aleppo or Mosul, and spent such long periods away, the two often barely seeing each other." Then he rises, saying he needs a refill on his drink, and walks to the liquor cabinet. "Anyone else? What will you have?"

Mugdi would very much like a stiff drink, but is unsure if his mind approves of it, or if his heart can take it. In the end, he says, "A tall glass of mineral water, with a slice of lemon, please."

"Are you sure?" asks Johan.

"Give the man what he wants and don't needle him with your questions," Birgitta reprimands her husband. "He wants a tall glass of mineral water."

Gacalo wonders from this exchange if perhaps Johan has been

guzzling large quantities of alcohol and Birgitta suspects he wants Mugdi to partake as well. Drinking the hard stuff has never troubled Johan, who can manage any amount from morning until bedtime. It is amazing how little he would be affected by it. Not so Mugdi.

"What about you, Gacalo?"

"I would love some water for now," she says. She is pleased this meets everyone's approval, especially Birgitta's.

Johan doesn't bother to ask what Naciim wants. He gets water for Gacalo in a tall glass, like Mugdi's. They all sit in silence, until Fredrik says to Naciim, "Did your stepfather prepare you for life without him before he committed suicide, knowing that he wouldn't live long?"

Taken aback, Naciim stares at Fredrik, as Birgitta jumps in and says, "No doubt he prepared his family for the troubles they might have once they arrived, aware he would no longer be around," before falling silent once more, head down to avoid catching anyone's eyes.

Gacalo then steps into the breach and addresses her words to Fredrik, as though seeking his endorsement. "Dhaqaneh readied this bright-eyed boy for what was to come."

Mugdi is eager to change the thrust of the conversation. He wants Fredrik to talk about his interest in the stories of the Norwegian migrants to North America, a subject that served as the kernel of Fredrik's PhD thesis, whose publication will be in a few months' time. "Tell us also what you are currently working on, in terms of research."

Naciim sits back and listens, glad the focus is no longer on him.

Fredrik replies, "I am at work on a comparative analysis of the first Norwegians to settle in Minnesota and the Somalis—the most recent arrivals. And I'm coming around to the idea that you can't do well in a new country if you don't have a good measure of the one you left behind."

"Please explain," says Gacalo.

"The Norwegians who migrated to North America were poor farmers in need of land to farm. Their arrival in the US in the early 1860s coincided with the mass hanging of Native Americans at Mankato during Lincoln's presidency. That mass execution provided the Norwegians with land on the cheap, at times for less than a dollar an acre. Later, farmland in Minnesota was cheaper still when even more Native Americans were driven off the land and Europeans were arriving by the shipload. With land—that really belonged to others—given to them for next to nothing, and the easy availability of credit, it is no surprise that they were successful. And of course in terms of weather, winter in Minnesota is no worse than what the Norwegians had known back home."

"What about the Somalis then?" Johan asks.

Fredrik answers, "Both in Minnesota and Norway, the Somalis have come en masse as refugees, many with little or no education. They found the climate in both Norway and Minnesota disagreeably cold, very different from back home; nor was it easy to adjust to their new circumstances—the Somalis arrived damaged from the scars of war in both Norway and the US, while the Norwegians landed in the Dakotas full of hope and helped by the situation they found: plenty of land and support from the state. The Norwegians were welcomed with open arms, as a desired race that was good for the new country, whereas here in Norway, the Somalis are very much unwelcome, being black Muslim refugees at a time when migration is now viewed both as a political problem and as a threat to the Norwegians' continued existence as a 'pure race.'

Right-wing groups see the Somalis as real pests, worse than bubonic plagues."

Birgitta affirms what her son has said, adding, "Moreover, the Somalis are seen as a burden on the social welfare system, a lazy lot unwilling to adapt to their new country or integrate."

"In the Dakotas, the Norwegian migrants were told that they held their fate in their own hands and would either sink or swim. Here in Norway, because the state offers the Somalis enough to get by, they are not required to earn their upkeep by the sweat of their brow. There's no dignity in relying on handouts, that's for sure," Fredrik says.

"But there are no employment possibilities here," Johan objects, "unlike Canada and the US. Besides, Norway is too small to create jobs as an export-based market economy."

Now Mugdi jumps in, saying to Gacalo's mild annoyance, "And we Somalis refuse to do certain jobs on account of being Muslim."

Mugdi's words introduce a new elephant into the room, one occupying far more space than anyone is willing to allow it. Naciim, who has finished eating, fidgets restlessly. He wants to take his plate to the kitchen sink but waits for his hosts' permission.

Gacalo is the first adult to indicate that she too is done. They soon break into smaller groups as Naciim helps collect the plates and follows Birgitta into the kitchen.

Mugdi finally brings the evening to an end an hour before midnight, and they leave for home, tired and, despite the dinner's occasional awkwardness, mostly happy. Mugdi ascribes this happiness to the fact that, for the first time in a long while, no one has mentioned Waliya's name.

# CHAPTER EIGHTEEN

---------

GACALO TOOK ILL THE FOLLOWING DAY.

Timiro telephones her dad to ask after his and her mum's health, and to let them know that she is in London. He asks, "What urgent business takes you there?"

She says, "I'm just here for twenty-four hours to finalize the divorce."

"And how is that coming along?"

"Thanks to Eugenia," Timiro replies, "I've got an appointment with an attorney first thing tomorrow, and plan to fly back to Geneva late in the afternoon after the consultation."

"And how are Kaluun and Eugenia?"

"They send their love."

"And how is Mum doing?"

"Back to her usual self, full of gumption."

"Can I talk to her please?"

"She's gone to see her doctor for tests and such. But I'll let her know that you called and asked after her."

"And how is that woman faring?"

He knows who "that woman" is and he tells her that lately there have been new and positive developments that involve Saafi.

"New developments? Let me hear them."

He explains all the brouhaha involving Naciim, the flag-waving, and his mother and how Saafi entered the fray. He goes on, "Mum and I didn't think that Saafi had it in her to stand up to Waliya. But when Waliya threatened that she would give Naciim the beating of his life if he defied her instructions one more time, Saafi not only defended Naciim with vigor, but also reminded them that it was not their place to speak of matters that are not of their concern. She added that Naciim had the right to have a bit of fun so long as his actions are inoffensive to the community and our faith."

Timiro asks, "Your source for this?"

"Naciim is my primary source and when I met Saafi, she confirmed it."

"Where are they, as we speak?"

"He's at school," replies Mugdi, "but she is home with me and has just given me verse and chapter of what happened. My feeling is she is here to stay."

"She'll no longer help at the nursery?"

"I doubt she will."

"How is Waliya reacting to this?"

Mugdi says, "It's is fair to assume that she's understandably steamed up over what has occurred. And even though she views our stance as one of betrayal, she knows that we are much easier to deal with than the Child Welfare Services that would take them away and punish her. From what Naciim has told us, she is angry that we are allowing them to stay here, but she can't or won't say anything."

"Please help me get this right. Are you saying that Saafi has braved her mother's meanness and fought off the imam and his deputy all on her own, despite the obvious pressures?"

"She did," replies Mugdi.

"I wish I were there to witness it."

"We're happy to have her here."

"So you have both with you as you speak?"

"He is at school, she is home with me."

"If she's willing to be alone with you, can it mean that she is no longer afflicted with androphobia?"

"We're in no position to draw this conclusion. We can only say that Mum has the situation well in hand, and she's continued to take Saafi to Qumman, the therapist."

"Well, I'd like to help anyway I can," Timiro says.

"Perhaps Saafi can eventually join you in Geneva?"

"I'd love that," says Timiro. "It would be wonderful to have her around. She could go to a language school and help with Riyo. But tell me. How is Naciim doing?"

"He too is in a defiant mood and wishes to prove he is no pushover. According to the boy, the set-to between him and his mother started well before the flag brouhaha, when it became obvious that Fanax is sweet on Saafi, has made his advances to the girl known, and his mother didn't take the appropriate stand to discourage his moves."

"My God, how preposterous!"

Mugdi then says, "Wait, please wait," as Timiro hears him exchange a few words with a young female voice. Then he says, "That was Saafi on her way down to the kitchen. She sends you her best."

Timiro says, "Give her mine too."

Then before either of them hangs up, she adds, "And my love to Mum."

"Give ours to Kaluun and Eugenia."

------

In London that evening, Timiro, Kaluun, and Eugenia gather at the couple's favorite local restaurant, where Kaluun has booked a table. He orders sautéed scaloppini, Timiro arrabbiata, and Eugenia sole in white wine. As their drinks arrive, Timiro brings them up to speed on the latest goings-on in Oslo. Eugenia, for her part, updates Timiro on the arrangements she has made for tomorrow's appointment with the attorney.

Once the waiter sets down their plates, Timiro revisits her telephone conversation with her father and rehashes Saafi's difficulties. "Does either of you remember the riddle in which there is a man in a boat who has to ferry to the other side of the river a goat, a lion, and a tuft of grass, conscious of the intractability of each?"

"I've heard this riddle, yes, but told with a tiger instead," says Eugenia.

"In other words, how does one manage the continued safety of a girl as beautiful and as delicately put together as Saafi, who 'attracts' the violence that is of a piece with maleness?"

Kaluun cannot figure out the relevance of the riddle to Saafi's story and makes as if to interrupt, before Eugenia shushes him.

They listen to Timiro as she says, "The first day I set eyes on the girl, she didn't want to be anywhere near my dad. And when I pointed this out, Mum said that it is understandable Saafi would feel unsafe wherever men are. Keep in mind that she has already had to endure being ferried across an ocean, following a brutal gang rape at the refugee camp in Kenya. How can you guarantee that no further harm will come her way when her mother is determined to practically hand the girl over to Imam Fanax, who is lusting after her?"

Kaluun helps unpack the question in a bid to make Eugenia and Timiro understand. He says, "It is precisely because Waliya is determined to protect her daughter, knowing what she has been through, that she arranges for the imam to marry her."

"But that is absurd," says Eugenia.

"It probably is absurd and brutal, from where you stand. However, according to the Somali or Islamist tradition to which Waliya is loyal, a married woman is a 'protected' woman. Marrying Saafi off guarantees the girl's protection."

Eugenia comments on the shocking number of rapes that have recently come to light and says, "Girls whatever their age, women whatever their position in society, have never been completely safe, whether at home or in the streets or on public transport or in their workplaces. That we now can speak openly about these attacks and condemn them is something to commend."

A long, brooding silence follows, in which Timiro thinks of all the rapes that are the consequences of powerful men claiming their so-called rights to the bodies of women; rapes that are the result of civil wars; rapes that come about because young girls are married off to men in their sixties, seventies, or even eighties.

Then Timiro's eyes falls on a man with the physical features commonly associated with the peoples of the Horn of Africa. The man has in front of him a large meal and he samples now the meat, now the brussels sprouts, now the pasta, now the fish, now the rice, and now the T-bone steak. Timiro cannot make sense of what the man is doing, whereas Eugenia thinks the man is most likely a food critic writing for a journal, though perhaps he is consuming large quantities of food all on his own, attempting some feat like a Guinness world record.

Kaluun calls a waiter over, as he too is curious about what the man is doing. The waiter gives what Kaluun thinks of as a tongue-in-cheek explanation, saying, "The man says that he hails from a famine country to which he is returning, and having found himself in the land of plenty, wants to eat enough to keep him going for a week or so, like a ruminant, blessed with a stomach that has several compartments."

After the waiter is gone, Timiro says, "He is pulling our leg."

Eugenia says, "It reminds me that when I was young and I didn't eat the food my mother placed before me, she scolded me to think of all the hungry Ethiopian children who had nothing to eat. That used to frighten me out of my wits and I would eat my food."

------

The phone is ringing as they return to Eugenia and Kaluun's apartment. When Eugenia grabs it, it is Gacalo, saying she wishes to speak to all three of them separately.

Gacalo talks first with Eugenia, asking a number of questions about the business that brought Timiro to London: how the process of filing for divorce is going, and whether, in Eugenia's opinion, her daughter will stay the course or quit before the final resolution of the case. Their conversation lasts no longer than five minutes, then Gacalo asks her to put Kaluun on the line.

Gacalo shares with Kaluun the shocking revelation that Xirsi, Timiro's soon-to-be ex-husband, is in Oslo. "The scoundrel called our home on the off-chance that I would answer it, but he got

Mugdi instead, who rudely wanted to know why he was phoning. Xirsi said that it was his understanding that Timiro was in Oslo and could he put her on please? And because it took long for Mugdi to confirm that he would put her on or even to say anything, Xirsi volunteered that he was now in Lillehammer attending a conference and that before coming to Norway, he had called the flat in Geneva and there was no answer, rang her number at work and a woman informed him she had no idea where Timiro was. Mugdi said, "Timiro is not here," and left it at that. But when Xirsi continued to insist that he knew otherwise, and that, in fact, a mutual friend of his and hers assured him that he had seen her in town a day or two ago, Mugdi told him to sod off and hung up on him."

"Where are you going with this?" asks Kaluun.

Gacalo says, "I just want you to beware and to remember that Xirsi is a schemer, and you should do all you can to strengthen Timiro's resolve to file the papers if you sense that she is starting to waver in her determination to divorce him."

The phrase "O ye of little faith" enters his mind as his conversation with Gacalo comes to an end, and he tells Timiro that her mother wishes to speak to her.

Timiro, when she comes to the phone, senses that her mother is cross. Timiro is cross as well, though her anger is directed at Imam Fanax and Zubair, two men taking advantage of a confused woman.

"Dad told me earlier that Saafi is staying with you," says Timiro. "He seemed optimistic about her current state. Tell me, how do *you* think she's doing?"

"I think given the circumstances, she's doing quite well. Qumman has succeeded in helping Saafi regain her sense of self and encouraged her to stand up to the combined bullying of Fanax and her mother. And so she did, by saying she has had enough of it, and leaving to come here. She's no longer prepared to be submissive."

"And what have you been up to?

Gacalo says she has been teaching Saafi a few basic things, including encouraging her to grow in self-confidence in her decision making, something that Qumman has been trying to instill in the girl. She has been helping her with her Norwegian too, assisting her in accepting her new way of carrying herself, of dressing, and making sure that she is comfortable "in her new self, her new skin." She has taken her once to the gym to practice her swimming. There is some evidence that she has benefited from seeing Qumman and spending more quality with Grandma.

Timiro agrees with her mother's approach and says, "She'll do even better if you spend long, uninterrupted hours with her, if only to make sure she knows she is on the right path to wellness, mentally and physically."

"I will. Of course I will. I can't praise Saafi highly enough for what she did," says Gacalo. "Now it falls to us to support her."

# CHAPTER NINETEEN

----------

MUGDI HAS REASON TO REMIND HIMSELF OF THE SAYING THAT WHATEVER doesn't kill you makes you stronger. The cliché has never made sense to him before, but he appreciates it now more than he ever thought he would, when Gacalo walks in and drops a bombshell, telling him about the phone call she received at work.

"What are you saying? What's happened?"

"You won't believe it. You can't."

Then he listens to her ranting against Waliya's recent roster of gaffes, including her set-tos with her children and her lack of concern for their well-being. He is all the while on tenterhooks, wanting to know what the accursed woman has done.

"She's now committed her gravest blunder."

"Well, don't keep me in suspense! Tell me, what has she done?"

"She hosted Zubair, a wanted man! The officer who called told me that the Norwegian antiterrorist unit apprehended him when they raided Waliya's apartment earlier today."

He becomes quiet and then asks, "Where is she now?"

"The widow is not directly accused of engaging in any criminal activity," says Gacalo. "Still, the fact that she was taken in by the antiterrorist unit, fingerprinted, interviewed, and then released can only be an unwanted stain on her character—and by extension, on ours."

Saafi, who has just spent her first night in their home, seems relaxed in their presence, though her sense of relaxation slowly gives way to agitation as she realizes that something has happened. Though she can barely understand a word of Norwegian, she hears her mother's name mentioned repeatedly. Has her mother done something terrible, she wonders. Has she killed someone or been killed or taken into detention? She wishes her brother, who has been spending more time with Mouna at Himmo's home, playing chess and enjoying the company of the others, were here to tell her what's happened. Or that one of her grandparents will.

Finally Saafi cannot help herself and asks, "What's happened, Grandpa?"

"We'll explain things later," says Mugdi, "when we know more."

Then he finishes making Saafi's omelet and serves it to her. He thanks the heavens that Saafi has been spared the sight of bulky men breaking down her apartment door and storming in, barking out orders in Norwegian. He can imagine the fright this would cause the girl.

"Are we to blame?" asks Gacalo.

"We've harmed no one, hurt no one, and misled no one. How can anyone blame us?"

Saafi can barely eat the omelet before her as she struggles to understand their conversation.

"The guilt of one Muslim will be laid at the door of every Muslim," says Gacalo. "Who's to say we won't be viewed with suspicion by the authorities and seen as associates of terrorists? The agents who linked her to Zubair will surely link her to us, as we share a file."

Mugdi thinks of Beret, one of the two main characters in *Giants of the Earth*. A disrupter, she is in direct conflict with everything the landscape of Spring Creek represents. Just like Beret, Waliya is forever creating havoc, unable to come to terms with her new country's climate, culture, or faith, nor able to tear herself loose from all that defined her back in the land where she was raised. Mugdi retreats into silence and reflects on how Beret, in distress at being pregnant and away from her parents, seeks solace first in Per Hansa, the man who impregnated her, and then in religion. And Waliya, in her search for peace and shelter, came to a country she did not love, to the house of her husband's father, on whom she could not rely for support.

Saafi is now nibbling at her omelet.

Gacalo says, "I know that earlier today Naciim went to the apartment to pick up something he forgot, his notebook. Do you think the antiterrorist unit might question him?"

"Not without the presence of an attorney."

"Our turn to be questioned isn't far off."

"There's no way of knowing what the antiterror unit will do or if they will want to talk to us."

"Perhaps not, but challenging times are ahead." Her nerves frayed, Gacalo falls into a protracted silence of her own, before saying, "The media will cover the story from every possible angle now that one of the most respected Somalis, a former ambassador, no less, is a proven associate of a terrorist."

"I don't believe that the media in general is necessarily more hostile toward Somalis, only that a number of them tend to give the Somalis bad press. I wouldn't worry about any of this yet if I were you."

A brooding look on her face, Gacalo says, "Would you be willing to take the children in and look after them if I weren't around? Or if their mother is found guilty and sent to a Norwegian jail?"

"What do you mean if you weren't around?"

"No one is here forever, darling."

"Where would you be, if not here?"

"I could be dead."

Mugdi casts an irascible glance at her and his Adam's apple cranks up and down, as if it has suddenly become a bad-tempered mechanism. He says, "I won't respond to such speculations."

Shortly after, Naciim turns up and straightaway Mugdi can see his pained expression, which covers him like a shroud.

"Where's Saafi? Is she okay?" asks Naciim.

"She is easily broken, but she is okay on the whole. Grandma put on a film for her to watch and I've checked on her a few times. How about you?"

"Mum wouldn't tell me anything. She says I am too young to understand." Naciim looks at the door of the TV room, which is pushed shut. "Have you told Saafi what's going on?"

"We've spared her the trouble of knowing."

"You've done the right thing," says Naciim.

Mugdi stretches out his hand and pulls Naciim toward him for a hug. He says, "Just remember we're here, Grandma and I. Everything will be okay."

"I hope so. I'll go and see my sister now."

The TV is off and Saafi is curled on the couch, crying. Naciim steps into the room as Mugdi hovers just outside, uncertain as to how best to be of use to the boy, who has ably taken charge of the situation. The agitation he feels comes to an abrupt end when Naciim, leading his sister by the hand, comes out and says to Mugdi, "I've told her everything."

Wiping away tears and nodding her head, Saafi says, "Thank you." Then, to Mugdi's great surprise, her sweet smile turns on, bright as a midnight sun, and she says, "I've told Naciim of a decision I've made."

Naciim urges her on. "Tell Grandpa. Speak."

"I'll attend school and learn Norwegian."

"That's excellent," says Mugdi.

"I feel left out when I can't follow what the radio is saying, for instance, or today, when you and Grandma spoke about what happened to Mum and again I couldn't understand. I don't want to feel like that anymore."

"That's positive thinking," says Mugdi.

Later that morning, when it is time for Mugdi to leave for the gym and Naciim shows his keenness to go with him, the old man asks Gacalo if she has a reason to go out for a walk or to go shopping.

Gacalo turns to Saafi and asks, "Would you like to stay with me or go with Grandpa and Naciim?"

The girl says, "I am no longer the girl I was a couple of months ago and I don't want anyone to see me as a problem to solve. What if I came with you to the gym?"

"Wonderful. Come," says Mugdi.

"You'll enjoy watching the women swim or do their workouts on this first visit. Later, you can decide on the exercises that'll interest you," Naciim says.

"As if I need your advice," says Saafi.

"No offense. I meant well."

As they head out the door, Naciim and Mugdi each carry a bag with a towel and a pair of flip-flops, while Saafi goes as she is, albeit with a pair of Mugdi's headphones through which she is listening to a reading of the Koran. Naciim begins griping about his mother. "Every day, before I came here, Mum would spend hours on the phone with her friend Arla. I liked the colorful stories she told us. But there was something she often did that troubled me: she brought bad, white men, who would take the two of them away, maybe to bars and naughty places. This irked me no end."

"How inventive you are," Saafi says.

"I have it on authority from Stepdad Dhaqaneh, before he made a good woman of Mum," Naciim says. "Are you saying he was lying when he told me this?"

"Where is Arla now?" Mugdi cut in.

"Copenhagen, where she lives."

"I think it's good Mum has a friend to talk to," says Saafi.

Naciim says, "Arla, in light of what Stepdad Dhaqaneh said, feels the impulse to cause havoc wherever she goes."

"But Arla's your mum's close friend."

Saafi says, "Mum adores Arla."

"But the woman is wild. How can Mum?"

"Maybe she is no longer as wild as before," says Saafi.

Naciim shakes his head and says, "I doubt very much that she has changed her essential nature."

"If she's been in Europe for a long time, then it is possible. Europe changes people after a while," says Mugdi. "What don't you like about her, Naciim?"

"My mum is under her thumb," says Naciim.

"That's not true," says Saafi.

"Mum will obey Arla's commands. Stepdad Dhaqaneh never

liked her either. He would complain about how she chain-smokes, is always showily dressed, and does all sorts of forbidden stuff."

"What forbidden stuff?"

"Like wearing gold earrings and nose rings and rings on every finger and thumb. She even has a tattoo."

"That's rich," says Mugdi.

"I tell you she is wild."

"How on earth do you know she has a tattoo?" Saafi asks.

"A Somali woman tattooing her body? Isn't that rather unusual?" says Mugdi.

"Arla's tattoo is just above the parting of her bum," says Naciim.

"How do you know?"

"I was there when she showed it to Mum."

At this Mugdi stops in mid-stride. "You've learned quite a lot about this woman, haven't you?"

"He's always been obsessed with Arla," says Saafi. "Ever since we were young and she babysat us, when Mum would go out by herself," says Saafi. "Obsessed and infatuated."

"I know a lot more than I let on," Naciim says.

No one talks until they reach the gym.

At the gym, Mugdi fills in a lengthy form for Naciim and Saafi to be registered as his guests; he also pays a small fee. Then he leads the children through the turnstile, where he introduces Saafi to a female instructor, who says, "Leave her with me and I'll show her what she needs to see."

Then he and Naciim go to the men's section of the gym, where the old man points out the showers, weights, and swimming pool. He's about to step out of the changing room to give the boy privacy, sensing that he will not undress in Mugdi's presence, when a naked Norwegian man walks in. Naciim is visibly shocked. Then he sees more nude men entering or coming out of the showers. The boy has no idea whether to look, avoid looking, or act as if he is indifferent to all this. At school, nudity in the public areas of the gym is discouraged. He wonders if adult Norwegians are more relaxed about their bodies.

"If the women in their section are as naked as the men here, then Saafi is in for a shock," Naciim says.

"Never been to the women's section," says Mugdi. He has been to Turkish and Moroccan single-sex *hamam*s, but in Somalia there are no such bathhouses, and Somalis on the whole frown on male or female nudity, even if it is not beyond a Somali woman to display her assets by wearing a *guntiino* robe or transparent *dirac* dress, traditional clothes the religionists have lately described as un-Islamic and therefore forbidden.

The two men go their different ways: Naciim to swim and Mugdi to the treadmill. Later, Mugdi searches the boy out in the pool, where Naciim's technique strikes him as unrefined. He thinks that the boy would benefit from taking more swimming lessons.

On the way out, Mugdi inquires at reception about a swimming instructor, and the receptionist introduces him to a young man in his early twenties who agrees to give swimming lessons by appointment to Naciim, on times and days to be arranged in advance. As they walk toward the tram, Saafi is silent. Naciim, on the other hand, can barely control his excitement. "I think Mum will be shocked to her very core if we tell her where we've gone today, what we've done or seen. But there is no point telling her about any of this, is there, unless we intend to shock her?"

Naciim's rhetorical question reminds Mugdi of a Somali of his acquaintance, who had quite the shock of his when he came upon a nudist colony—and he tells the story to the boy.

"What is a nudist colony, Grandpa?" Naciim asks.

Mugdi explains, to the boy's considerable awe.

"Would men and women walk about naked in mixed company? And don't some men pester the women they see in the colony?"

"In nudist or naturist resorts, men and women who are comfortable with such things go there," says Mugdi.

"Have you ever been to a nudist site?"

Mugdi shakes his head. "No."

"I'd like to go to one," Naciim says. "It would be fun to take a burka-wearing woman along, wouldn't it?" he continues.

"How I wish you'd desist from being so crude in your comments about women," says Mugdi.

When they arrive back at the house, Saafi waits until Naciim is having a shower and then says, "All my life, I've been used to one way of looking at the world. Now the visit to the gym has shown me that there is an entirely different way of seeing."

"What makes you say that?"

"At the gym, the women struck me to be without fear and behaved, from the little I saw, as though they were equal to men."

Mugdi nods his head and says, "Interesting, very interesting."

Saafi, needing no encouragement, goes on, "Maybe they were raised, from a very young age, to do whatever men could do. All the time I watched the women, I kept thinking that perhaps this is what Dr. Qumman wants me to be like."

"And how were you raised, from a young age?"

"It makes me feel, from what Qumman has explained to me, that I am in this world for the sole purpose of giving pleasure to men."

Mugdi wishes Gacalo, Timiro, or Qumman were here to hear what Saafi has just said. They would be so proud of the girl.

After Naciim has showered, Mugdi asks him if he'd like to join Saafi and himself for a bite to eat.

"I promised Mouna I would go to Auntie Himmo's home and give her a game and she would help me with my Norwegian," replies Naciim.

"Give our best to Auntie Himmo."

"Auntie Himmo is at work."

"But Mouna is there?"

"She is expecting me."

"She is lovely, isn't she, Mouna?"

"She is kind, she is gentle, she is sweet, and I learn a great deal from her. I love her so much. She treats me as though I were her younger brother."

"And are you coming back here or going to your mother's, when you are done?" asks Mugdi.

"Maybe I'll go and see Mum after that."

# CHAPTER TWENTY

----------

NACIIM AWAKENS TO LOW VOICES OF WOMEN. HE LIES IN BED, TRYING TO work out what is happening and why the women are speaking in whispers. Then his mother is at his bedroom door shouting, "You promised you'd bring back my daughter, your sister! Tell me, did you see her yesterday and where is she?"

"Who are these women in our home, Mum?"

"Answer me, son. Did you see Saafi?"

"I did. She was at the home of Grandpa and Grandma and she is fine. Unwilling to return here, but fine."

One of the women, who comes out of his mother's room, almost jumps out of her skin when she spots Naciim, and runs back inside.

"Did you see the way that woman ran, Mum? She ran because she saw there was a man in the house. And from now on, if I am to stay, you must treat me as one!"

"To be thought of as a man, you must behave like a man," says Waliya. "You must say all five of your prayers and fast Ramadan without fail. These are the obligations you must meet, and only then will I refer to you as one, never before."

"Who are these women, Mum?"

"Zubair's sisters and cousins."

"What business brings them here?"

"They've come to commiserate with me."

"Commiserate how?"

"Commiserate with me in my moment of sorrow," she says. "So what did you do when you were staying with Mugdi?"

Naciim tells her that he went to a gym with him, but makes a point of not informing her that Saafi was there as well. He knows his mother has never been to a gym and is unlikely to ever go to one.

"Does Mugdi go to a gym at his age?"

"He is healthier than most younger men."

She then wants to know the setup of the gym and he tells her that it is a private club, with one section for men, another for women, and a third larger section where men and women mingle and share the facilities, stretching, squatting, lifting weights, riding exercise bikes and treadmills, even swimming together.

She is appalled. "Is that Mugdi's idea of fun? Men of venerable age mingling with scantily dressed women? What does Gacalo think of this?"

"This is Norway, Mum. Not Saudi Arabia."

"I wish we had never come here."

Naciim is not surprised that he does not recognize any of the women who appear to have taken up residence in the apartment. His closeness to Gacalo, Timiro, and Mugdi, so precious in his life, has set him more and more apart. He has stayed on the periphery of his mother's concerns and she his.

There's a knock on his bedroom door and he opens it to find a very large, sweaty woman with no top teeth, carrying a plate covered with a lid, presumably his breakfast. She says something he does not instantly comprehend on account of her heavy accent, but which he interprets to mean, "Here is your breakfast."

He decides to ask why the women are here, since he is sure there is more that his mother is not telling him. Years ago, when Saafi was raped, his mother moved her to Arla's house, where several women took turns caring for her. Naciim only found out what happened to his sister because another woman, a total stranger, told him. Later, when he was older, he confronted his mother about it, who merely responded, "It's in bad taste for a brother to inquire about his sister's private matters."

He asks the woman, "Why are you all here? Is it really just to commiserate with my mother?"

"Your mother is my younger brother Zubair's wife," the woman says. "Several of us, her new in-laws, have come to celebrate her marriage to Zubair and to get to know her. It all happened in such haste."

Then the woman departs, leaving Naciim agape at her words. He feels suddenly feverish, and the smell of the food reminds him of nothing so much as an out-of-order toilet at a soccer stadium. He is considering what to do when his mother appears. She says, "Why haven't you eaten the breakfast my sister-in-law made for you? That's right, she shared with me what she told you."

"How can this happen without my knowing?"

"When did you last show interest in my affairs? Or bother to share my life or ask how I am doing? You were always off with your Norwegian friends, or with Mugdi, Timiro, and Gacalo, as if you were their son, not mine."

"Even so, how could you not let me know? When did this even take place?"

"We married a day before he was taken," she says. A trace of a smile on her lips, she continues, "Still, we are family, bound by blood and loyalty. And Zubair, who has been unjustly detained, accused of terrorism of which he knows nothing, is your step-dad now."

Naciim pauses, intending to say that he knows he has spent more time with his mates and Grandpa Mugdi and Grandma Gacalo than he has with his mother, but it was because of the kindness they have shown to him. But he keeps silent, knowing it will only upset her if he speaks his thoughts. He is about to speak when the woman who brought him his breakfast says to his mother, "Please come urgently."

He takes the opportunity to slip out of the apartment, ready to share the disheartening news with Saafi, Gacalo, and Mugdi. As he heads for the bus stop, he calls Mugdi, saying, "You'll be surprised to hear what I have to tell you."

Saafi is not shocked, as she claims to have had intimations of her mother and Zubair's affair.

"With both of you out of the house, Saafi with us and you, Naciim, at school from morning until late afternoon, the two no doubt had all the time in the world to meet, mate, and make their secret plans," says Mugdi.

"What's is wrong with her? What are we to do?" asks Naciim.

"There is nothing to give you worry," says Mugdi. "We would love for you both to think of this home as your home for as long as you need."

Saafi and Naciim exchange happy looks before she goes over to the old man and prepares to hug him. Just as she embraces Mugdi, Gacalo walks in. She catches Naciim's eye and the two smile. It is the first time that Saafi has come into welcome physical contact with any man since her rape, evidence that she has changed.

Then Gacalo shares with them the new intelligence she has gathered from reading the Somali websites. "According to one of the outlets, the Norwegian antiterror unit is accusing Zubair of serving as a liaison for Bin Laden's associate Mohamed Atef, aka Abu Hafs, that Egyptian tasked with the job of training men how to down helicopters in 1993. Zubair apparently served as his liaison and interpreter. And the terror unit has the documents to prove this."

# CHAPTER TWENTY-ONE

----------

SIX MONTHS LATER, ANDERS BEHRING BREIVIK, A NATIVE NORWEGIAN, after a lengthy planning process, first detonated a bomb close to the Norwegian premier's office in the center of Oslo, in which eight people lost their lives, before heading to the wooded island of Utøya, where the young acolytes of the country's governing Labor Party were attending youth camp, and proceeded to mow down sixty-nine more, most of them teenagers.

One of the dead was Mouna: charming, exuberant, barely eighteen, soccer-playing Mouna, Himmo's daughter, loved deeply by all who knew her, especially Naciim. He mourns her intensely, his sense of grief knowing no bounds—his survivor's guilt more traumatic than the sorrow he felt when his stepfather died. He wonders if he has done something to lose two people whom he loved profoundly. Mouna's younger sister and brother are equally devastated, the girl weepy, the boy, having withdrawn into absolute silence, sitting swaddled in indescribable sorrow. For company they have Mouna's close friends, who have come to comfort them.

Mouna is buried in Høybråten, in a Muslim funeral ceremony

attended by, among others, the prime minister of Norway and his wife. Commiserating with Himmo, the premier stresses that as a parent, he feels her pain and knows her loss. Naciim and Saafi huddle together, distraught. Saafi's cheeks are wet with tears, her lips astir with Koranic verses, as Naciim stares blankly at Mouna's coffin, draped with the flags of Somalia and Norway. Afterward, at Himmo's apartment, Mugdi thinks of the ill-timed scene he has just translated from *Giants in the Earth*, in which a mother, Kari, goes insane with grief over the death of her son, Paul, whom she and her husband were forced to bury in a makeshift coffin on the prairie, without so much as a proper service to bless his departed soul. In her desperate desire to give her son a proper burial, the mother urges everyone to hunt for and exhume Paul's corpse to place it in a better coffin. A search party is dispatched, only to return saying the coffin is empty.

At the first opportunity presented to her, before Gacalo greets another flood of mourners, Saafi asks if Gacalo has managed to arrange another session with Qumman, the therapist. Gacalo looks at Saafi and straightaway can tell that Mouna's death has affected the girl keenly.

"You like Qumman, don't you?" says Gacalo.

"She listens in the way wise people do."

"And you talk, is that right?"

"I talk in the way fools talk."

Himmo and Mugdi stand in a corner of the living room, Himmo's face streaked with tears and her voice gruff. "Evil sleeps until a wicked monster wakes it up, but once awakened, it stirs into deadly action and there is no safe place to hide; everyone is vulnerable and at risk," she says. She pauses, and then adds, "We are caught between a small group of Nazi-inspired vigilantes and a small group of radical jihadis claiming to belong to a purer strain of Islam. And my precious daughter was forced to pay the price. I say, 'A plague on both their houses.'"

As Himmo gazes fixedly past him, Mugdi thinks that, because of the ongoing ideology-driven violent confrontations between the anti-immigrant hard right and the radical jihadists, everybody becomes a collateral casualty and there is no safe refuge anywhere and we are all doomed.

Every few minutes more mourners arrive, Somali and Norwegian alike, some of them Himmo's friends from work, others classmates of Mouna's, and yet more acquaintances and neighbors.

Mugdi stands aside as they stream past to say a prayer or speak words of commiseration to Himmo, bowing to hug and kiss her, some more inconsolable than others. He observes that Himmo's large eyes, which are charcoal-dark and set wide apart, subject their surroundings to a thorough search, as if she is keen to know who among her friends has shown up and who has not. Mugdi's memory takes him back to when he and Gacalo first met up with Himmo, in Europe. She was pregnant with Mouna and her marriage to the father was already shaky. Mugdi and Gacalo offered their support and advice, though Himmo, a woman of dignity, made it clear she would not rush into any hasty decision, but would consider separation or divorce only if there was no possibility of the two of them reconciling their differences. "I don't like the idea, if I can help it, of raising a child in Europe as a single mother," she said. In the end, she and her husband eventually went their different ways.

One large Norwegian woman, whom Himmo knows only vaguely, kneels down before her and says, "I can't believe this is happening in my country; that such a monster has taken the life of your lovely, lovely daughter. How can that be?"

Himmo is calm as she says, "I wish I knew why, madam. And he didn't kill only my daughter, he murdered many other beloved teenagers as well."

"We've never properly met," the woman confesses, "but I live across the way. Over the years, I've exchanged a few words with your daughter. My son, who is her age, had a crush on her but being shy, he couldn't bring himself to tell her. Now he is distraught and so are we all, every member of our family."

Then Himmo and the woman weep in unison, with the line of mourners lengthening, until Gacalo appears and takes the neighbor by the arm, leading her to the kitchen.

Mugdi is now face-to-face with Birgitta, who asks, "How does Himmo manage to look so dignified, given the circumstances? I couldn't do it."

"There is honesty to her dignity," he says. "That is what sets her apart from many others."

He has always believed that the key to understanding Himmo, as a woman and a human being, is in understanding her marked commitment to her children's well-being, her absolute devotion to her career, and her insistence that her future depends on her own hard work and her efforts as a Somali-Norwegian. "She told me once that, out of gratitude to the kindness shown to her here, she can no longer think of herself as Somali without also thinking that she is Norwegian. And she raised her daughter that way, to embrace her hyphenated identity."

"I remember how I loved Mouna's warmhearted smile on the occasion I met her at your home," Birgitta says.

There are heavy bags under her eyes; she appears to have barely slept. Johan, who has wandered over to join them, thinks it is indeed a miracle that his wife can talk at all without bursting into tears. "Look at what this monster of a murderer has turned us into!" she exclaims. "He has made us lose touch with our Norwegianness! Nor can we any longer lay claim to our sense of innocence."

"Us innocent? Where have you been, my darling?" Johan says. "This hate has always been here. Even the so-called Progressive Party has expressed visceral hate of liberals, immigrants, and Muslims. We've always seen ourselves as uniquely generous to the immigrants we have hosted, to whom we've been kind and welcoming. The fact is, there is no truth to the claims we make."

Mugdi remembers how panicked he felt when word went out that a radical Islamist was on the rampage, only for everyone to be proven wrong—that it was instead one of their own.

Birgitta, fired up, says, "No doubt it was a most terrible day. But here is another element of my grief. Why is this tragedy being compared to those that have taken place elsewhere in the world, when those countries are in no way similar to Norway in terms of population size or history?"

"What on earth are you talking about?" Johan asks.

"This tragedy is not our September eleventh, as some Norwegian journalists have said," she replies. "After all, the differences between the US and Norway are clear to everyone. For one thing, the perpetrators of September eleventh were foreign to the US, whereas the monster that perpetrated these crimes is one of us. Why, he even claimed to be beholden to Odin, the pre-Christian Viking deity!"

Gacalo, who has been managing the kitchen, preparing meals and hot drinks with several other women, turns up carrying a tray with tea, coffee, and glasses of water. She hands it over to Naciim, who has stayed close by the elders, listening to their conversation as if he were attending a lecture at a college. Johan, Mugdi, and Birgitta help themselves to drinks, then Mugdi says to Johan, "Earlier, you wanted to talk to us about Norwegians losing their innocence in one fell swoop?"

"I didn't say that exactly," says Johan.

"Well, what did you mean by Norway never being innocent?"

"We in Scandinavia are under the impression that we lost our innocence when we began hosting hordes of immigrants. Personally, I trace our loss of innocence back to our response to the presence of the first foreigners among us, the Jews, whom we did not welcome as we should have. Instead we deported them, handing them over to the Nazis and certain death. And how many deaths of dark-skinned immigrants at the hands of neo-Nazi skinheads never even merited a thorough investigation or punishment? We as a nation have no problem focusing on what we view as an Islamist threat, when in my view, the much more serious menace is the presence of right-wing, neo-Nazi groups. That's what poses a real risk to our continued existence and peace. In case today wasn't enough of an indication."

"Surely we would be naive if we didn't pay attention to both these radical groups?" says Birgitta.

"In Sweden, a man known as 'the laserman,' as he favored a gun with a laser sight, shot eleven immigrants between 1991 and 1992, though he killed only one, because he was a terrible marksman. His first victim was an Eritrean. He believed that by shooting them, he would chase many thousands more out of Sweden. And do you know what the laserman, who is now rotting in jail with a life sentence, and Breivik have in common?"

Mugdi says, "No, what?"

"We are too slow to square up to the threat of right-wing xenophobes who enjoy the backing of nativists who look to the past, not the multicultural, globalist present. The world has moved on but they haven't, and they will do anything for us to remain backward."

After a while, Birgitta observes that Himmo is sitting by herself and she suggests that the three of them join her. As they do so, Himmo says, "You've all been kind. Thanks."

"We'll miss Mouna, all of us," Mugdi says.

Birgitta and Johan nod their heads in agreement and Birgitta pats Himmo on the shoulder.

Himmo says, "Like many others, I was fooled into assuming that once we'd settled in Norway, a land famous for its peaceful-ness, our young would not precede us into their graves in the way so many of the young do in Somalia's ongoing civil war." Angrily gesticulating as she speaks, she strikes the glass of water closest to her, upsetting it over herself. As if nothing has happened, she con-tinues, "Alas, we've become victims of the very evil we strove so hard to avoid by leaving our homeland and taking refuge here. We thought that by fleeing Somalia when we did, our lives would be spared and our triumph complete."

Mugdi is aware that he will be viewed as an insensitive fool if he asks her whether she knows that she has lost a daughter but gained her new nation's empathy; that her name and that of her daughter have now entered the country's history. Instead, he says, "We have no words to express our sorrow when the unexpected happens."

"Even though it feels good to receive so much empathy from almost all quarters, the undeniable fact is that no amount of empa-thy can bring my daughter back."

"But of course."

"As a mother, I'm resigned to hearing the stuttering rattle of the madman's assault rifle firing his shots into his innocent victims for as long as I live. And this is happening everywhere. As we try to recover from what happened on the island, you hear of a school in Sweden being attacked by a Nazi helmet–wearing, sword-brandishing lunatic." Himmo suppresses a yawn as Mugdi and the others shift in their seats. Himmo is much too polite to tell them to go home, though plainly she is exhausted. Finally Mugdi says, "Folks, time to disperse."

Before leaving for home, Gacalo and Mugdi ask Naciim and Saafi if they want to stay behind or go home with them. Saafi says, "I'll be more useful to Auntie Himmo if I don't go."

Naciim is still so disconsolate he can't speak.

As it's now rush hour, the sidewalks are clogged with commuters and so they walk in single file to the Metro. On the train, Gacalo sits, the wells of her eyes filling with tears, which she dabs with her wet handkerchief. Mugdi remains standing, looking in his wife's direction every now and then. There are so many things they might say to each other, but neither speaks. It is tradition in Somalia when a woman gives birth or there is a death in a family for those near and dear to provide companionship and helping hands. This is why Gacalo will shower, change, and then return to Himmo's, she explains to Naciim. "Death, especially the death of one so young, empties a house of energy, deprives every member living in it of his or her strength."

Mugdi says, "How Himmo will miss Mouna. Do you know what she once said to me? Out of all her children, Mouna was the one who gave her life shape."

"It is very difficult, if not impossible, for a mother to make peace with the death of her eighteen-year-old daughter," says Gacalo.

When they reach their house, Gacalo gives a furtive look at her watch. "I'll just pack a bag and then call a taxi."

"But we just arrived. Aren't you going to have a shower at least?" Mugdi says.

"I don't want to leave her for long," Gacalo says.

As she heads up the stairs, Mugdi wonders if Waliya has offered her condolences to Himmo, who had been so kind to her. At least Saafi and Naciim were there. They have all the heart she never will.

# CHAPTER TWENTY-TWO

------------

TIMIRO, CARRYING RIYO IN A SLING, KALUUN, AND EUGENIA ARE ALL BACK in Oslo with the aim of paying their respects to Himmo the day after the funeral. They set out in a rental car driven by Mugdi, with Naciim in front, Kaluun, Eugenia, and Timiro crowded in the back, and Riyo in her car seat. Gacalo and Saafi have spent the night at Himmo's, keeping Himmo and her children company.

On occasions such as this the sexes are segregated, with the women gathered in the inner chambers of the house, the men in the front, and the young folks in a separate location. Beneath the hush that dominates the scene is a continuous hum, resembling the buzzing of unsettled insects. The Somalis, many of whom arrived here as refugees, never expected something like this to happen in Europe, least of all in Norway. Now nothing matters more than togetherness, as if mere proximity might stave off the sadness that has befallen the family.

Himmo feels deeply moved at the sight of Kaluun, whom she has not set eyes on for a very long time, and the woman he introduces as his partner, Eugenia, whom she has met only once before, many years ago in London. A fine-looking woman dressed exquisitely in black that matches her beautiful dark skin. Eugenia removes her Armani sunglasses as they touch cheeks, and Himmo's forehead collides with the edge of her large hat, which reminds Himmo of one of the fashion items in the form of headwear African American women put on for church. Now Eugenia brings out a Kleenex with which she wipes away her tears and says, "I loved Mouna too and will miss her. I'm so sorry that the bad man killed her."

Touched, Himmo finds it hard to contain her emotions and, overwhelmed, does not know where to turn or what to do when her eyes, brimmed with tears, lock on Riyo, Timiro's little girl, who has just woken up in her car seat. Himmo stretches her hand out to touch Riyo's, but the girl is wary and she avoids all contact. Timiro unstraps the harness tying Riyo down to the car seat and makes an attempt to deliver her into Himmo's waiting embrace. Riyo, however, resists being handed over to a stranger and makes a fuss.

Just then, as if on cue, Saafi appears on the horizon and with a bottle in her hand, stands in the doorway, waiting for Timiro to tell her what to do. Riyo follows her mother's eyes and, spotting Saafi, welcomes "the bringer of the bottle" with a radiant smile; she wants to go to Saafi and Saafi is ready to receive her, take her away, and feed her in another room.

Then, in the protracted silence following Saafi's and Riyo's departure, Himmo's daughter, Isniino, walks in, rubbing the sleep out of her eyes that have gone red from crying. She acknowledges the guests' presence, going around hugging, kissing, and shaking hands with the timidity youngsters feel when they are meeting their parents' friends. At one point, she exchanges murmured words with Himmo, who appears enclosed in the tattered fabric of sorrow.

Then half a dozen Urdu-speaking women, all shawled and

dressed in the proper Islamic way, arrive together, fanning out and filling the living room.

One says to Himmo, "Everything happens for a reason. We have come to pay our respects and to tell you to trust in Allah and He will give you strength."

Soon a group of Himmo's colleagues arrive, and the women rise in unison and take their leave.

Himmo seems rather shaky; at one point she excuses herself to her visitors and shuts herself inside Mouna's room. Perhaps she is remembering the last time she saw her daughter, when the girl was exuberantly happy and full of life.

Mugdi thinks once more of Kari, from *Giants in the Earth*, her baby buried in his mother's best skirt, as they could afford no coffin. He wishes he could think of something less distressing when Himmo returns, sits down next to him, and sobs. He is silent for a long time, waiting for her body to stop trembling before uttering the standard Islamic phrase spoken by those offering their condolences. She murmurs a few words that he cannot make out, words similar but less intense than those she used yesterday.

With the front door of the apartment open, people come and go, taking turns to speak to Himmo and sit by her side. Then she excuses herself once more, and her departure elicits an immediate reconfiguring of the conversation. Kaluun turns to his older brother and says, "Is it true what the newscasters are saying—that at no time in the recent past have Norwegians felt more united than after this tragedy?"

Mugdi replies, "You hear that kind of thing a lot, but we need time to know if this oversubscribed idea will hold. In any case, you'd be naive to expect this to last forever."

"Still, no politician worth the name will openly admit to

supporting Breivik," says Timiro. "Every one of them will put visible distance between Breivik's action and the Progressive Party, to which he belonged for a long time."

Mugdi asks Eugenia, "What was your reaction when you first heard the news?"

Eugenia says, "I was shocked."

"With little or no information to go on," says Kaluun, "we all assumed that the perpetrator was a radical Islamist and we wondered what effect that would have on your lives."

Eugenia adds, "A different kind of shock hit me when we learned that the perpetrator was a native Norwegian diagnosed as psychotic."

"Isn't it curious," says Kaluun, "that when a native European is responsible for such a rampage, every attempt is made to prove that he was suffering from some form of mental disorder or is emotionally impaired. If Breivik is described as mad, then why not describe the radical Muslim groups as mad too? Rather than 'haters of the West' or some such."

It is Timiro's turn to speak. "Remember what Jens Stoltenberg, the Norwegian premier, said at Mouna's burial ceremony: that Breivik turned the paradise island of Utøya into an inferno. That is precisely what both lots do: they turn our world into hell."

With Himmo not yet back and Riyo now awake and fussing, Mugdi gathers his granddaughter into his embrace, speaking to her in calming tones.

Shortly after, Mugdi sends word to Himmo via Naciim that they are ready to leave. And she returns in no time to thank every single one of them and bid them farewell.

Back at Mugdi and Gacalo's, Timiro is off upstairs after telling her mother that she needs to take a long, hot shower to ease the exhaustion in her bones after her early flight from Geneva, nursing a colicky Riyo, and then waiting for Kaluun and Eugenia's plane to arrive.

"Go. We'll hold the fort," says Eugenia.

When Timiro is gone, Gacalo says, "I wonder if there is more to what is bothering Timiro than mere tension in her neck. Do you and Kaluun know more than Mugdi and I?"

"I've always had the feeling that she is unable to compartmentalize her life," Eugenia says. "As a single mother with a busy office to run, I think at times she barely knows where she is."

"I'm not talking about that," says Gacalo.

"Then it is imperative you talk to your daughter," Eugenia demurs. "No doubt she will tell you if there are things that are bothering her. Or talk to Kaluun, who will definitely know more than I do."

A knock at the door announces the arrival of Johan and Birgitta, whom Mugdi ushers into the living room, where Kaluun has already taken a seat. Mugdi offers them all drinks, then he mixes his own.

Kaluun has a sip of his red wine and then turns to Johan and asks, "Do you think the fact that every police officer assumed the perpetrator was a Muslim terrorist, and did not bother to stop Breivik, who was in police uniform, gave him more time to get on with the business of killing, unhindered?"

"The fact that no one would suspect a man in an officer's uniform most certainly played a part in his ability to evade capture," replies Johan.

Birgitta adds, "And if it weren't for those blunders, Breivik might not have killed many of the teenagers on the island."

There is a long silence until Kaluun finds the courage to say,

"When you are Muslim and black, in the way Somalis are, you belong at one and the same time to the two minority groups most hated nearly everywhere. This is the reason why the onus is on Somalis to improve their chance of success wherever they happen to be. Ideally, we should do well enough in every sphere. Unfortunately, we are at the lowest rung of every ladder."

"We Norwegians tolerate one another," says Birgitta. "We don't necessarily feel close to one another. I think it is probably difficult for foreigners to come to terms with this. The darkness of the long winter plays a role as well, let's face it."

Then Johan launches into the story of when he proposed to Birgitta. He says to Kaluun, "Birgitta is from the west coast of Norway and I am from Stavanger. When we decided to marry, it was very difficult to bring our respective families onboard. As communities living apart for centuries, we have mutual suspicions of one another. We perceive ourselves to be different. But we tolerate one another to the extent that we've accepted that we are one people."

"I too am unable to convince Somalis that the distances between us as members of different clan families are smaller than those separating someone from Kent and another from Yorkshire," says Kaluun.

"As colonials, we started thinking of ourselves as Norwegians only after we adopted a flag and a constitution and agreed to live together in mutual tolerance. We were once a colony of Sweden, and of Denmark too, and our loyalties to Norway were often questionable. But since becoming a free country with a constitution, we've worked hard at staying united. Basically, we want the immigrants who have joined and become Norwegian to work just as hard at it as we have," Birgitta says. "The way I see it, when the media questions the loyalty of Somalis or other immigrants, they are accusing them of working less hard at integrating. However, much of what the popular media writes about immigrants is mostly a lie dressed up as truth."

Mugdi offers to top up her drink, but she shakes her head and says, "No. Maybe another glass of white wine at dinner."

Johan says, "However, almost all Norwegians respect Himmo's strength of character, and they mourn with her because she has lost a daughter in the same way many Norwegian parents lost theirs."

Many memories revisit Mugdi: Himmo as a young girl asking him to lend her books to read; Himmo as a basketball player in Mogadiscio, leading her team from the front and scoring points; Himmo visiting them in Bonn on a few months' refresher course, staying up late practicing her German to ensure that she mastered the language in the shortest time possible; Himmo announcing the collapse of her first marriage, and then her second, both times working hard to pull herself together and succeeding. No matter the challenge, she has always survived, and she produced three wonderful children. The tragedy is that one of them is now dead at the hands of Breivik.

Gacalo calls them to the table. Timiro appears looking refreshed. When dinner is served and everyone at the table is eating, Johan asks Naciim, "Can I ask a few of the questions that I've meant to put to you?"

"By all means. Please ask," says Naciim.

"You don't answer them, if you don't want. But if you are able, tell us a bit about Shabaab. I'm curious—did you hate them, love them, hope to join them?"

"I could've joined them, but didn't."

"Why didn't you?"

"Because they seldom told you the truth."

"Did anyone ever try to recruit you, knowing your stepdad was already active in the movement?" Birgitta asks.

"On the contrary, my stepdad advised me against joining."

"Why did he do that?" Kaluun wonders.

"Though he did their bidding and died serving Shabaab's cause, my stepdad wanted peace at home and so he mostly kept me out of it. As a general rule, men at the top of the chain of command never recruit their immediate family members into the militia," says Naciim.

Timiro asks, "Where are the children of the men at the top of Shabaab's chain of command?"

Kaluum says, "As you are all aware, there is a cottage industry of populist politicians in much of Western Europe and in the US who aim their propaganda at the least educated among their citizenry. It is strange but true, that like these populist politicians, Shabaab recruiters also go for the least educated among Somalis: semi-literate adults, school dropouts, boys or girls with no parents. What is more, both groups do not hesitate to spread lies about their ideological foes."

"How right you are!" Johan says, reaching for the tumbler of water, only to knock his half-full wineglass onto Naciim's front, the boy's shirt becoming beetroot-red. Johan is up in no time, apologizing, dipping his cloth napkin in water and dabbing at the stain.

Mugdi, too, is up and waiting for Johan to be done so he may sprinkle the entire area with salt. "There's nothing like salt to remove red wine stains."

Gacalo says, "Wasn't Naciim going to spend tonight with his mother? What will she say? She'll think we gave him wine."

"Wash it, Mum, and then put it in the dryer and voilà, his shirt will be ready to be worn inside an hour," Timiro says.

Naciim cuts a calm figure as he says, "Not to worry. I will tell my mother the truth of what has happened."

"What if she throws a fit?" asks Gacalo.

"It won't be the first time nor will it be the last. But, as you can see, I am still here. In any case, I hate lying, because eventually the lie will catch up with me and then I will speak more lies. And that is no good at all."

# CHAPTER TWENTY-THREE

----------

IT IS EIGHT THIRTY IN THE EVENING WHEN NACIIM LETS HIMSELF INTO
his mother's apartment and hears a man reciting a Koranic verse
and his mother repeating it. He has barely removed the key from
the door and taken a step forward when he discerns an abrupt ces-
sation of the reading, a drop so sudden that it puts him in mind of
a silk dress falling from its hanger. As he walks into the silence,
readying to hurry to his room and change his shirt—for all his bra-
vado at dinner, he would rather not discuss the wine stain with his
mother—he hears footsteps coming from the living room and
comes face-to-face with Imam Fanax, the man with the lecherous
gaze to whom Waliya has promised Saafi's hand in marriage.

"There you are," Fanax says.

"Fancy seeing you this time of the night in our apartment. What
are you doing here? Don't you have a wife and children to care
for?" Naciim retorts.

In response, Fanax only smiles smugly. Naciim wonders if he
can smell the alcohol on him.

"Where have *you* been?" asks Fanax.

"I've been at a funeral."

"Ah, but the funeral was yesterday."

"What's this? An interrogation?"

"Your mother said you'd be home and you weren't." Then Fanax raises his voice a notch and asks, "Have you been drinking? Is that what you've been doing when, God bless her, your mother and a small community of the faithful have been reading the Koran and praying?"

Fanax's loud questions prompt the appearance of Axado, Waliya's niqaab-wearing nursery assistant. She stands to the side, listening, with a grimace on her face. She asks, "What have you done, Naciim?"

Naciim is silent as his mother and Cumar, a tall, bearded man in his mid-forties, who has replaced Zubair as Fanax's deputy, appear. Fanax then ups the ante, smirking at the boy as he asks, "Do you mind if Axado comes closer to you, smells your shirt and tells us what she discovers?"

"There's no need," says Naciim.

Fanax closes in for the kill, like a hunter after fresh prey. "Answer yes or no. Is the stain that we all see and the smell we can all pick up on that of liquor? Yes or no."

"It is," says Naciim. "But let me explain."

At hearing this, Waliya's heart strains, her mind in utter confusion. She leans this way and that before dropping to the floor in a dead faint. Those gathered spread out to make space for Waliya and then congregate around her, their voices dropping into murmurs in the shape of curses as well as invocations of the divine.

After a few moments, Waliya comes to, and with Axado's as-

sistance, gradually tries to rise. With everyone's eyes on her, she finally speaks. "Why have you abandoned the tenets of your noble
faith?"

"The man is a liar," says Naciim.

"Who is a liar?" she asks.

"The imam has had it in for me."

Waliya shakes her head in surprise, disturbed at the thought
that Naciim is blaming a man she holds in such great esteem.

"What has the imam to do with your liquor-taking? Has he
given it to you on the sly? Or known where you've consumed it?"

"He has driven a wedge between us."

"Why would he do that?"

"Because I won't allow him to marry Saafi."

Waliya stares at her son, speechless, until at last she says, "What
must I do with you now?"

"Mother, I've done nothing to deserve your reprimand. You will
have to believe me."

"Dare you address her as 'Mother' after all you've done?" says
Cumar.

"I'm not his mother," Waliya curses.

"You are my mother and you must listen to me."

"How can I listen to you when all you've done since coming to
this country is to dishonor me and the faith for which you have no
respect?"

Fanax says, "Knowing him, he probably washes his whole body
in liquor and then convenes with Satan!"

"Mother, I've done nothing to dishonor you or the faith, nothing. You can ask Mugdi and Gacalo. They will tell you what actually happened," Naciim replies.

"How can we, as God-fearing Muslims, rely on the word of those two, knowing they are apostates and proud of it?" Fanax says.

"How dare you!" says Naciim.

Cumar shakes his head in disavowal. "I've never heard a young boy show such disrespect to a man of the imam's stature."

"What does this gathering suggest we do about him? I promise I'll follow your suggestions to the letter," Waliya says.

"I can set him on the right path," the imam says. "Come with me to the living room, young man. In fact, I suggest all of you join me there."

Naciim says, "Who are you to tell me what to do?"

Waliya advises him to do as the imam says.

It is uncharacteristic of him to agree to what his mother has suggested, but he does not wish to continue quarreling with her. In any case, he is aware that the odds are stacked against him and there is nothing he can do at this moment to turn matters in his favor. So he joins the others.

Once they are all in the living room, the imam organizes the seating, telling the five women and Cumar to sit in the row facing him, as though members of a jury. He sits apart from them, in the largest seat, as though he were the judge.

He says to Naciim, "You stand to the side."

"Is this theater and are we playacting?" Naciim says.

"This is serious, not theater."

"But you've put together a mock court, haven't you?"

"You'll be judged by your Muslim peers."

"Well, I know I won't receive a fair hearing, but tell me—how is it that you've dispensed altogether with the curtain customarily separating the men from the women?"

The imam is noticeably discomfited by Naciim's challenge and he can see that the others are ill at ease too. "As a judge, I dismiss the young man's question as having no bearing on the decision of the court."

Waliya says, "Let's get on with it."

Fanax runs the rules by the jury: how and when they can offer input or ask questions. When they confirm that they comprehend the rules, he says, "We are gathered here as a group of good Muslims representing the faith to ask the erring young man named Naciim, who has lost his way, to explain why he has imbibed drinks that are forbidden to the faithful. Boy, do you have anything to say in exoneration?"

"My lips have not touched a drop of liquor."

"Any witnesses to that?" Cumar asks.

"Ask Mugdi, Gacalo, Johan, and Birgitta," he says.

"Do you have any other witnesses besides those mentioned, since the imam has ruled that Mugdi and Gacalo are apostates and Johan and Birgitta are Christians and therefore not credible as witnesses?"

"He's wasting our time," says Axado.

Waliya says, "I'd like him punished severely."

"I second the proposal," says Axado.

The seriousness of what is unfolding dawns on Naciim with startling suddenness. It is clear this is no mere entertainment at his expense.

Cumar says, "I propose that he receive fifty lashes, half for his unpardonable sin of drinking, and the other half for liaising with apostates."

"You can't be serious," Naciim says.

"We are," says his mother.

The imam feels even more emboldened when he hears Waliya's supportive remarks, and he passes his judgment, saying, "This gathering adjudges you to have committed grave sins and you've been found guilty. You are to receive fifty lashes."

"And who dares to administer them? You?"

"Yes, I'll deal it out to you," says the imam.

"And where is your whip?"

"Here." The imam points at his belt, which he now unfastens. "In the absence of a bullwhip, this will do."

Naciim then brings out his phone—he will call his grandparents he decides, or even the police—but Cumar makes a quick dash and before the boy knows it, he has taken possession of the mobile and thrown it as far as he can. Then, with equal speed, he wrestles Naciim to the floor, pins his hands behind his back, picks him up, and frog marches him to the next room, shutting the door. Then he rejoins the group, telling the imam, "He is all yours."

Fanax struts toward the room, pleased that he will be allowed to punish the boy. He will strike him with as much force as possible, he thinks. He wants everyone to know that the belt has made its mark, and the longer it takes for Naciim to issue a groaning sound of pain the harder he will hit.

After half an hour, the imam reemerges, breathing unevenly and wiping the sweat from his brow. Naciim stays inside for a long time, without making a sound. When he finally emerges, he cuts a relaxed figure despite the traces of blood on the back of his shirt. Waliya makes as if she wants to comfort him and she moves in his direction, but he waves her away, unwilling to accept her sympathy or pity. He moves about with single-minded focus, searching for his mobile phone, then finding the parts and reassembling it. Then he goes to his room and bolts it from the inside.

As the men and women resume reciting the Koran, Naciim telephones his friend Edvart and tells him what has happened. Edvart immediately suggests that Naciim stay with him, but Naciim thanks him for his concern and says, "I am on my way back to my grandparents'. But please tell Ms. Koht, the school adviser, what I've just told you in case I do not come to class tomorrow." Then he slips out of the apartment.

It is a quarter to eleven by the time he arrives at Mugdi and Gacalo's. They are both so incensed that they advise immediately reporting what has happened to the police. Mugdi goes with him to the station to file a criminal charge.

Naciim makes a lengthy statement in the presence of a police officer, with Mugdi serving as witness. Then the officer refers them to the hospital emergency unit. The nurse on duty takes photographs of Naciim's contusions and bruises, noting the discoloration on his back and the cuts that will require care for a month at least. She says, "Someone needs to tear a strip or two off the person who hit you with a belt and caused so much damage."

Mugdi asks, "How long do you think it will take for the emergency unit to prepare a report and send it to the police station?"

"I'll do it before I end my shift," the nurse says. "And since I have your contact details, someone will telephone you if your presence is required."

At home, Mugdi is in such a rage that he can't get his words out. Gacalo has started running a fever, no doubt due to all the stress, and keeps repeating Waliya's name, saying, "What are we to do with you?"

As for Naciim, unable to sleep, he stays up reading and snacking on salted nuts, a rare treat. His insomnia has done him good, affording him the necessary time to sort out a number of things in his head. He will put up as much resistance as need be to make sure that Fanax and his mother do not have their way when it comes to Saafi.

The following morning, as he showers, his body burns with pain from the lashes he received, and his mind wanders to when he was younger and Dhaqaneh was still alive. How little he could have imagined that the man whom he had loved and called "Dad" was a terrorist. He remembers Mugdi saying that it is only later that a parent can truly comprehend what their child is up to, whether it be leaving their spouse or conspiring to blow up a bridge. And what of his mother? What did she know of his stepfather's character, and when? And what did she know about his grandparents? She seemed to have no problem accepting the funds Gacalo sent her son for food and clothing. Did she consider them "apostates" then as well?

After his shower, Naciim sends a text to Edvart, asking for an update on Ms. Koht's reaction to his news. Edvart replies that their teacher has contacted the Child Protection Unit and reported the case. "Ms. Koht wants you to come in tomorrow and talk to the officers in her presence." Then Naciim emerges from his room, wrapped in a large gown Mugdi has given him, and goes to talk to Saafi, who is back from Himmo's, to bring her up to speed about what he and Mugdi have set in motion.

"Will the imam go to jail for whipping you?" Saafi asks.

"You can bet he will be prosecuted. The nurse said we could be looking at several years, minimum."

"And our mother? What will happen to her?"

"She may face jail time too."

"But she didn't strike you, did she?"

"No, but she could've put a stop to it. Instead she did nothing."

Saafi weeps feebly, in a manner he has always found distressing.

"I wish I had been there," she says.

"What would you've done?"

"I would've put a stop to the whipping."

As Naciim knows there is nothing he can do to reassure his sister, he says, "I am going down to have breakfast with Grandpa. Are you coming down?"

"I'll wait until later, after the men have eaten."

At four in the afternoon on the following day, Naciim as arranged goes to meet with Ms. Koht. She introduces him to the two women from the Child Protection Unit there to interview him. One is short, large, and with a scatter of freckles on her face; the other is slim, darker and handsomer. The darker one, her voice reedy, asks Naciim to repeat, in detail, what happened. The larger one takes notes, often consulting the police report she has in front of her.

When they've finished questioning him, Ms. Koht says to Naciim, "If you don't mind, please take off your shirt and show us the injuries?"

Naciim removes his shirt to show them. Ms. Koht sucks in her breath, then says she feels bound to remind him that it is part of her job to make sure children his age are safe both at home and at school.

He asks the two women from the Protection Unit what they expect to happen. The larger one says, "Leave it to us and we'll make certain that the culprits are punished for what they did to you."

Naciim goes home and tells Gacalo and Mugdi what the women said. He finds that Gacalo is doing a little better, but Mugdi looks just as worried as he did the day before.

Just before dinner, Ms. Koht telephones Naciim to say that Imam Fanax is currently at the police station answering questions.

"What about your mother?" Mugdi asks Naciim, when he's off the phone.

"I told them this afternoon that I don't want her punished," says Naciim.

"Why not?"

"What is the point? Life has already punished my mother in so many ways. I do not wish to impose a further penalty."

"What are your plans then? Moving back with her or staying here until your situation is sorted? The choice is yours."

"We'll talk after the courts have decided," says Naciim.

# CHAPTER TWENTY-FOUR

----------

A FORTNIGHT LATER, GACALO TAKES TO HER BED ONCE AGAIN PLEADING AN upset stomach, after coming home early from the court hearing in which the Child Protection Unit's case against Fanax resulted in the imam's being convicted and sentenced to several years in prison.

The judge, on advice from Child Welfare Services, interviews Naciim to decide whether Waliya deserves severe punishment for the role she played that night. The court makes an interim arrangement: Naciim is to spend the majority of his time at Mugdi and Gacalo's, though he may have as much access to his mother as he wishes. She will avoid jail time.

Saafi is enraged at Fanax, though not at her mother. She says, "Whatever else she may be, our mother is not evil."

Mugdi is moved to say, "No one has said she is."

"She loves us and means well," Saafi insists. "Even her trying to marry me to that terrible man. Every one of her actions is inspired by her total devotion to us."

Naciim says to Saafi, "Our mother is weak."

Despite her brother's protests, Saafi returns to the apartment in the company of Timiro, with Gacalo unable to stomach looking at Waliya and Mugdi unwilling to get involved.

As Timiro glowers at Waliya in the background, Saafi dictates all her conditions: that she'll divide her time between Himmo's, her mother's, and her grandparents', the latter being where she feels most comfortable. That she wants to attend school, but won't tolerate her mother's interference; and that her mother must promise never to try to marry her off a second time.

Waliya is in no position to raise objections, and so she does not, merely admitting her sense of relief that she and Saafi are back together. She then surprises Timiro by thanking her for accompanying her daughter. Timiro leaves Saafi in the apartment to talk matters over, safe in the knowledge that Waliya is powerless to stop Saafi's progression toward independence. She says to Saafi, "I am off to see to my mum. Call me, okay?," then hugs the girl and sees herself out.

Later that day, Timiro, for whom relocating to Oslo has remained only a pipe dream, departs for Geneva, and to everybody's delight, Saafi presents herself at Mugdi and Gacalo's, affirming that she would like to be of service to Grandma. She also refuses to speak of what exactly transpired between herself and her mother, contenting herself with a vague statement: that she and her mother are now on steadier ground.

Gacalo's "stomach upset" persists.

As Saafi sits by her bed, reading one of her textbooks, Gacalo is silent for long periods, sleeping or trying to sleep, a mask covering her eyes. Most worryingly, she refuses to see a doctor. Saafi leaves the room whenever Mugdi enters it, to give the elderly couple privacy.

"Why can't we consult a physician?" he asks.

She answers huffily, "I don't like surprises."

Mugdi now remembers how, many years ago, when he was

Somalia's ambassador to Moscow, he pestered his wife over her failing to make an appointment for an annual physical, something she had previously never neglected to do. He had figured that if she was reluctant to do so in Moscow, it was because she had no faith in what she called "Russian quackery." Finally she had gone to a clinic, and came home appearing sicker than someone with rabies.

But the clinic refused to release her results until she saw the specialist they had referred her to. After a round of tests, the specialist told her that she had an irregular heartbeat, but that for the moment, there was no problem with her.

When she asked what that meant, he said that while some arrhythmic hearts may cause sudden death, he did not think hers was in that category of seriousness and therefore there was no need to worry. She was also asked if her parents or grandparents had suffered from a weak heart.

Gacalo had no idea, never having known the medical history of either of her parents, who, to the best of her memory, were never ill for a single day all their lives. In fact, both her parents, like all four grandparents, died at the ripe old age of ninety-something. "The family myth on which I've been brought up is that we are born with strong genes," she'd said. When Gacalo and Mugdi were transferred to Oslo several years later, Gacalo had the medical checkup required of every new state employee. The examination showed nothing that worried the clinicians, and so Gacalo put what the doctor in Moscow had said out of her mind.

Mugdi, his voice touched by anxiety, now asks again how she is. The expression on her face makes clear that she doesn't wish to answer.

"Any idea what kind of pain you have?" he asks.

"As if pains have kinds or categories," she says.

"Is it physical pain or is it mental pain?"

"It is difficult to say," says Gacalo, and proceeds to speak instead of a dream she had the night before, in which she was alone in the house as a swarm of beetles chased her from room to room, their appearance like nothing she'd ever seen, metamorphosing into something arachnid-like and eventually into locusts.

Mugdi, wishing to reassure Gacalo, reminds her that he's just been working on a similar scene from *Giants in the Earth*, in which a swarm of locusts invade and cause devastating damage to the crops of the Norwegian farmers in South Dakota. "No doubt hearing me speak of it caused the nightmare."

He can't help but compare Gacalo's unfounded panic to Beret's illogical anxiety in *Giants* to Gacalo's unreasonableness, the one refusing to listen to reason, the other hiding in the family emigrant chest, as though it were her burial chamber.

Mugdi hedges at Birgitta's pleas for updates on Gacalo's health, and so Birgitta telephones Timiro instead. Timiro tells her that her mother hasn't left her bed since the conclusion of the court case against Fanax. "She hasn't gone to work, and from what Dad has said, she refuses to consult a doctor, despite his insistence."

"What can we do?" asks Birgitta.

"Maybe Mum would listen to you if you went round to talk her out of her obduracy. I am in no position to leave Geneva at the moment, with Riyo and the pressure of work."

Birgitta says, "We're not in Oslo right now. We're vacationing in our summer house across the border in Sweden, several hours' drive away. Let me talk to Johan. I'll suggest we head back."

Johan, irritated with Mugdi for dodging his wife's inquiries, quotes Dame Ivy Compton-Burnett, who once said, "The true index of a man's character is the health of his wife."

Birgitta, exasperated, says, "You can't expect the poor man to act in a normal way at a time when his dear wife is in such ill health."

And before the day ends, they are knocking on their friends' door. Saafi lets them in and then retreats into her bedroom, awaiting further instructions.

Mugdi is surprised to find Birgitta and Johan stomping in. It is uncharacteristic of them to show up unannounced. He offers to make them tea or coffee and Johan, his voice gathering a sense of urgency, says, "We've come to see Gacalo. Where is she?"

"Upstairs," he replies.

"Asleep or awake?" Birgitta asks.

"I believe awake."

Birgitta and Johan proceed up the stairs, Birgitta saying, "I want answers. I won't go away until I have them."

Mugdi, following them, says, "I too want answers."

They pause a third of the way up the stairs, Johan huffing and puffing from his exertions. He needs to exercise more, thinks Mugdi. After a moment's respite, they enter the bedroom and find Gacalo sitting up, her head propped against two large pillows. Birgitta and Johan take turns to kiss her on the cheeks.

"How are you?" Birgitta asks.

"There's no need for any of you to get into such a sweat over my health. I'll be up before long and will be coming to work," Gacalo says.

Mugdi looks from Gacalo to Birgitta and back. He frets, wondering how much of his thoughts he should share. In the end, he does not speak, but points Birgitta to the chair at Gacalo's bedside. He makes as though to bring in a chair from his study, but Johan discourages him from doing so with a wave of his hand.

Birgitta asks, "What would you say is ailing you?"

"What if I told you I feel as if an adult female, the size of Waliya, is sitting in a fetal posture inside my stomach?" Gacalo replies.

Mugdi takes her reply as evidence of what he has believed all along: that Gacalo's problems are mental and not physical, though he will not say this to her face or share it with their friends, who seem stunned by his wife's response.

Not wishing to offend, Johan speaks with great care. "I am wondering if Gacalo's statement can be understood only by someone familiar with the Somali culture. Birgitta and I feel we lack the background to comprehend."

Mugdi considers. Should he answer Johan's question with the sincerity it deserves? One interpretation of Gacalo's words—a more "Somali" interpretation—could be that demons, representing the spirit cult commonly known as "Zar" in the Horn of Africa— have taken full possession of his wife and are "residing in her" in the form of Waliya.

Gacalo stares at Mugdi, as if she is daring him to speak what is on his mind. If Mugdi hesitates to bring this into the conversation now, it is because he knows that without elaborate explanations, neither of their Norwegian friends will understand the place of the spirit in the lives of women, who are often its principal hosts. Moreover, if she is truly possessed, ousting the spirit demands the attendance of a shaman-like priestess who can exorcise the demon through ecstatic dancing rituals.

Birgitta pulls Mugdi aside. "Is this the first time she has said this?"

"Yes," he says.

"Is she talking in tongues?" asks Birgitta.

Plodding on gamely, Johan says, "Maybe Gacalo means that she is suffering from a discomfiting disease to be known from now on as 'Waliyatitis.' But the question is, does this new form of sickness have a cure?"

"What answer would you give to that?" Birgitta asks Gacalo.

"I'm neither a doctor nor a shaman," says Gacalo.

Johan repeats the term "Waliyatitis" a couple of times, looking both pleased with himself for coining it and slightly disturbed. Then he turns to Gacalo, as if to ask her another question, before thinking better of it, and asking Mugdi instead, "Does the host, namely Gacalo, have to cooperate for the cure to be effective? As you well know, you need a fair dose of faith in the cure to drive out an evil spirit."

"If the subject doesn't cooperate with the shaman attempting to exorcise the spirit, then it is likely that the bouts of Waliyatitis will continue to discomfort the subject," says Mugdi.

"So finding a cure may not be easy?"

"I'm a bit tired and would very much like to take a nap," says Gacalo loudly, repositioning her pillows and closing her eyes.

"But of course," says Birgitta.

Birgitta, Johan, and Mugdi retreat to the kitchen, where Mugdi boils water to make coffee for everyone. Birgitta, the first to speak, says, "Your thoughts?"

Mugdi says, "My patience is at an end and I am finding it hard to believe her when she gives me assurances that she will be back at work in a day or two. She has been saying this for days now. And her ailments keep changing—one day it is a terrible headache, the next it is indigestion, the third day something altogether different."

"Like Waliyatitis," says Birgitta.

"Yes, indeed. Like Waliyatitis."

Johan says, "Surely a modern, educated, secular Norwegian, which is what Gacalo is, will find it hard to believe in spirit cults and the like. Surely she cannot think herself truly possessed."

Mugdi says he will go up to his study and fetch one of the definitive texts about the Zar spirit. He dashes up the stairs and returns shortly after with a large book in his hand.

"*Wombs and Alien Spirits*," Johan reads. "No mention of Waliyatitis here?"

"You have the book. You find out," says Mugdi.

When Birgitta and Johan depart, Mugdi goes to check on Gacalo. "They've left," he says. "Can I bring you anything?"

"Like what?"

"Anything that takes your fancy?"

"No, thank you." She then proceeds to climb out of bed with some difficulty, ignoring Mugdi's offer of assistance. Once her feet are on the floor, she stays still for a moment, as if the world turns round in her head and she fears that she will fall flat on her forehead if she moves forward. Then she takes a few shaky steps. Mugdi tries to give her support and she pushes him away gently, a smile forming around her very dry lips. She says, "I am okay. Thanks, darling."

She walks down the stairs into the living room.

"What are you looking for?" asks Mugdi.

Riffling through their music collection she says, "I've found it. Here!"

"What is it? What have you found?"

She hands him a CD called *Sleepwalking* and asks him to play it. Mugdi's mild surprise—he can't imagine when they would have acquired music from a heavy metal band—turns to shock when he puts on the CD and she sings along with it. He is of two minds whether to celebrate, as Gacalo sounds happier than he has seen her in days, or to feel sad, as he knew nothing of his wife's apparent liking of heavy metal music despite being married to her for over forty years. He finds it much harder to admit that there are so many things that he does not know about Gacalo.

"This is great. Thanks for bringing the song to my attention," says Mugdi tentatively.

He's reminded of when the mother of a childhood neighbor of his developed some sort of sleep disorder which had never before been seen in his village. She would wake in the small hours, at times to go to the latrine or get herself a glass of water, sometimes leaving the village altogether. If she ran into someone, she would hold a lengthy conversation, but when morning came, she remembered nothing. She eventually sleepwalked herself to death, falling into a neighbor's latrine.

Gacalo plays the CD again, dancing to it and singing along. Mugdi stares as her entire body sways to the rhythm of the music, not so much moved as astounded.

Over the coming weeks, other visitors arrive—Himmo with her daughter Isniino; Kaluun and Eugenia; Saafi and Naciim; Timiro quietly carrying Riyo in a sling. Yet rather than the guests soothing Gacalo, they only increase her discomfort, until she goes so far as to accuse Mugdi of conspiring with friends and family to unsettle her.

Mugdi is disturbed by Gacalo's attack. When Timiro urges her mother to stop remonstrating with Mugdi, knowing that he is innocent, mother and daughter engage in a feisty set-to, and Gacalo locks herself in the bedroom, refusing to see anyone.

A debate ensues about what to do next. Timiro suggests that either they break the door down themselves or else call a locksmith, while Kaluun says that they should give her time to come to her senses. Eugenia wonders if they should recruit Saafi to plead with her.

"Surely you have an opinion on this?" Kaluun says to his brother.

"Who am I to invent a cure for a new disease called 'Waliyatitis,' especially because I may have contracted it myself?" Mugdi says.

Ill at ease and with no one speaking, Timiro trains her eyes on the stairs, as if hoping against all hope that her mother will appear and come down. Her father, worn to a frazzle, rises to his feet with the suddenness of somebody stung by the urgency of finding a solution to a family crisis. As everyone looks at him with fearful apprehension, they hear a door squeak and then open. A moment laden with the excitement of waiting lapses before they see Gacalo descending and they stay silent and watch her as she walks past the gathering and stops just short of the kitchen door. Timiro, the first to break the silence, says, "How wonderful to welcome you back from wherever you have been, Mum. Truly comforting."

Gacalo, paying her daughter no heed, goes into the kitchen and, without bothering to explain herself, puts on her favorite apron, ready to chop onions before emptying the freezer of its frozen contents, defrosting the chicken, the steaks, and fish and then marinating them.

Timiro gets up and, with care, gets to her feet and puts down Riyo, who is now falling asleep on the closest couch. Then she joins her mother in the kitchen, to whom she says, "That's a lot of food, Mum. How many people you expecting?"

"We have guests to feed," Gacalo replies.

Mugdi obliges in providing her with all the help she asks, including going to the supermarket with a long list of items to purchase. He humors her the way you humor people sick in the head. He also advises everyone else to give her a wide berth.

When Mugdi has returned and she is done with the cooking, she lays the table for as many people as there are plates and other family dishes, after which she washes the floors and vacuums the rooms where there are carpets, paying special attention to the living room and every public space in the house.

Then she showers, changes into a comfortable outfit, suggests that everybody help himself or herself, and hugs them all, before telling each person how much she loves them and how important they have been in her life. At the day's end, as Gacalo has not yet retreated to her room, those gathered begin to relax, convinced that the Gacalo they have always known and loved is back in their midst. Still, Saafi asks, "How do you feel now, Grandma?"

Gacalo replies, "I feel like a purchaser of contraband goods from an illegal outlet bought at bargain prices, with no warranty period to return them, if they turn out to be unsuitable."

"I don't understand you, Grandma."

"One day you will. One day everyone will."

Then Gacalo goes to her bedroom, draws the curtains and pretends to go to sleep. However, she leaves the door open so she can hear everything everyone in the kitchen is saying about her. An hour later, Saafi, who checks on her several times, says, "Grandma is not answering my questions. Maybe she truly is asleep."

# CHAPTER TWENTY-FIVE

----------

MUGDI STRUGGLES TO CONTAIN HIS EMOTIONS; WHEN GOING DOWN-stairs, he comes upon a scene of startling impact: Gacalo's glass-framed photo that has crashed to the floor, the glass splintered into shards and the photo out on its own, facedown. He sits morosely on one of the steps, and not knowing what to do, weeps one moment and recovers control of his emotions the next. He then thinks deeply not only about the significance of what has occurred but also about death, Gacalo's and his. But when he tries to contemplate what shape a future without Gacalo might take, he gets nowhere with his thoughts. He gets up and, with his gait unsteady, looks for and finds a broom and sweeps the glass fragments into a dustpan, which he dumps into the waste bin. But he saves the photo and takes it to his study, and stands it against the wall in full view of where he normally sits when he works or reads, determined not to speak of any of this to anyone.

He returns to Gacalo's room to check Gacalo's pulse, and then his forefinger goes to her throat to detect if her heart is beating, even faintly or irregularly. He is convinced he can feel a pulse one moment, only for it to vanish the next. He cannot seem to follow why, of all the variables possible, this catastrophe had to happen. Eugenia and Kaluun are the first to arrive, followed by a frantic Timiro.

"Not for a moment did it occur to me that she had a bottle of painkillers with her," says Mugdi, distraught. "When we awoke in the middle of the night, she said she was going downstairs to get some water. I recall her gone for a long time and then she was back, but we didn't talk."

"Is there anything else of importance that you remember?" asks Eugenia.

"Even though asleep, I felt her weight beside me a few minutes before I opened my eyes and checked on her."

Mugdi hears the drumming of his heart in his ears as Timiro hugs him. He fears it is beating at such a pace that he may collapse. He holds Timiro for support before sliding into the chair by the bedside.

Timiro's gaze, meanwhile, is fixed upon nothing, her expression that of someone desperate to release her emotions but unable to do so. "She was alive when you came back to bed then?" she says.

At his daughter's question Mugdi breaks down and then motions to everybody to leave him alone with Gacalo's body, after which he takes hold of Gacalo's hand in his and imagines what the others will do if he refuses to let go of his dead wife. Would they think he had gone insane and commit him to a madhouse?

After a couple of hours pass, Timiro and Kaluun reenter the bedroom to find Mugdi weeping the tears of a much older man.

Eugenia soon follows, wrapping her cardigan tighter around herself, as if she has suddenly found the room too cold. Suddenly Timiro begins to wail and Eugenia pats her on the back, commiserating. It is as if Gacalo's death has just dawned on her, and her wailing grows a notch louder than before.

Now Saafi walks in, looks around, and makes a feeble whimper conveying a mix of helplessness and fear for her own and Naciim's future.

Eventually Saafi's wailing awakens Riyo, who is on her rocker. The little girl looks this way and that and then, with a worrying suddenness, lets out a screech, as if she is in pain. Then Riyo's high-pitched weeping results in the adults stopping their wailing. Timiro picks up her daughter and thinks that maybe Riyo has an instinctive understanding that something terrible has happened and she whispers a few comforting words in her daughter's ear, holds the girl close to her chest, and rocks her back and forth until the little girl falls silent. Saafi brings a glass of orange juice for Riyo to drink and this quiets her down.

Kaluun says, "What do we do now?"

"We wait for the ambulance that's on its way here, with the paramedics," says Mugdi. "What else is there to do?"

All of a sudden, a long line of questions forms in Mugdi's head, questions as to whether to bury Gacalo in loyalty to the Islamic faith or to the secular beliefs prevailing in Norway, with each thought touching on a sensitive aspect of religion or cultural tradition, and each answer bringing further uncertainties as to how to proceed.

Kaluun asks, "I take it you have no objections to a postmortem."

"Of course not," says Mugdi.

Kaluun is happy with the clarity of Mugdi's answer. After all, some Muslims are loath to sanction postmortem examinations of their loved ones, even though there are no express injunctions on the matter either in the Koran or in the Prophet's traditions. But Mugdi's consent has a sobering effect on Kaluun.

Not long after that, a police van and an ambulance arrive almost at the same time. They enter together and the police officers ask the preliminary questions, check Mugdi and Gacalo's names against the owner-occupant of the property, and take down the names of all the others who are in the house and their relationship to the woman on the bed. One of the police officers says that, following the paramedics' initial findings, he has called a coroner, whose job it is, essentially, to pronounce whether Gacalo is alive or dead. The officer adds, "You understand, this is the procedure."

In his grief, Mugdi does not register what the officer has just said to him, and so the police officer assumes that Mugdi has no Norwegian and has not understood anything. As the officer looks for someone to translate, Mugdi feels a great wave of loss crash over him, a gulf opening between what he might say if he were able to speak and what the coroner may declare has taken place. And because he thinks that any explanation he proffers will elicit only raised eyebrows, he decides he will continue to say nothing.

When the police officers and the paramedics finally depart, Mugdi's thoughts drift to a novel he read as a child, about a fourteen-year-old boy and his siblings whose mother dies. The children decide to encase their mother's corpse in cement in a cellar, understandably worried that if the body is discovered, they will be made wards of the Social Welfare Division and farmed out to other families. If no one knows of their mother's death they can continue living together in the comfort of their own home. If only he could do the same.

Mugdi decides that his first big task as a widower will be to help set up Saafi's and Naciim's future in a way that gets the monkey that is Waliya off everyone's back. That way, Waliya can decide what to do with her life—to truly make a home for herself in Oslo, wait until Zubair is released from detention, or return to Somalia on an International Office of Migration grant that helps people like her relocate to their homes.

As they wait for the coroner to arrive, every time Mugdi's eyes fall on Gacalo, he thinks of the stretch of time when she was in the kitchen. What did she do there? Did she take the fatal overdose of pills with her glass of water and then come up to lie down beside him?

Kaluun says, "I, for one, thought that if ever there was a storm-proof marriage, yours and Gacalo's was it. And now look! You'd think she knew."

"Knew what?"

"That she was on her way out."

"What makes you say that?" Mugdi asks.

"First she prepared large amounts of food. She did a huge amount of laundry, although there was no need for that, and then she spring-cleaned the house as best she could."

"Do you, like me, suspect that the pills overdose was intentional?" asks Mugdi.

"I know nothing you don't," says Kaluun.

Mugdi had looked forward to the day of Gacalo's retirement, in two or three years' time. They had often spoken about making similar trips as Birgitta and Johan, and simply enjoying life together in old age. Now there is no such possibility of that. The thought of her no longer with him is incomprehensible; even more so if her absence was deliberate.

It takes him a moment to realize that his brother is still speaking to him.

"Are you coming with us? Wouldn't you rather not be here when the coroner arrives?"

"Where to?"

"For a walk in the park."

"Who else is coming?"

"Timiro with Riyo, you, me."

For a moment, Mugdi seems not to remember who these people are, or how they have come to be in his home. What is more, even after he decides to get to his feet and join them, he is unable to move; he feels as if his feet are stuck in quicksand and he can't stop sinking.

"Life is a sham," says Mugdi.

"So you're not coming?"

"I would like to be alone with Gacalo and to think things through, before she's taken from me."

Alone with Gacalo's body, Mugdi is initially at a loss for words. However, rather than grieve in silence, he makes every attempt to talk to her, as if she were alive. He tells her how much he will continue to love her and that he regrets every mishap he has caused, and apologizes for every ill-conceived plan he came up with to stop her having her way. At a certain moment, he is sure her eyes are open, her breathing is back, even if feeble, like an ailing person's. He pauses between his words and focuses on her face, convinced that she is responding to his monologue and maybe nodding her head in agreement.

His outstretched hand touches her wrist and for a moment he feels as though there is a faint pulse, but he loses it in the second instance. As he considers whether it is worthwhile insisting that perhaps she is still alive, he hears footsteps approaching and then sees men carrying a stretcher walking in.

One of the men introduces himself as the coroner. And when two of the other men indicate that they want Mugdi out of the room, he does so with the obsequiousness of someone with nothing to say.

They take away the body and he feels very lonely, wishing that he had someone to talk to, now that Gacalo is no longer there.

Mugdi welcomes back Kaluun and Timiro after their walk. Himmo, who has just heard the sad news from Saafi and Naciim, joins them. Still grieving the loss of Mouna, Himmo seems completely undone by Gacalo's death. Her weeping sets off Timiro again, and their crying becomes more jarring when Riyo adds hers to theirs. Mugdi cringes at the dissonance of the sounds, sadly aware that there will not be many mourners at Gacalo's funeral unless he hires paid moirologists to swell the numbers. Unlike the dozens and dozens who mourned with Himmo, they do not have many friends among the Somali community, nor have they cultivated a sufficient number of friends among the Norwegians.

Mugdi says, "Please," and both Timiro and Himmo take a pause in their crying, with no guarantee that they will not resume. Soon the landline starts ringing. First it is Birgitta in an uncontrollable state. Johan takes the phone and announces briefly that they are coming. More phone calls follow, many of them Gacalo's co-workers ringing to condole the family, men and women who praise her character and her work ethic and say they will miss her friendship and sense of humor.

Johan and Birgitta arrive at a moment when Mugdi is busy taking these calls, many from people whom he may have met casually at this or that reception but whose names mean nothing to him; he has never known them personally. As his friends stand close by, waiting to offer support, they listen to his formal conversation and are struck by the interregnum into which they have walked, with Gacalo's body now in the morgue. They will have to wait three or four days for the pathologist to perform the autopsy and release the findings.

Now that he is done with the phone calls, Mugdi is on his feet, his arms open wide, ready to receive his friends. Johan pays his respects and the two hug, neither speaking. Then Birgitta takes Mugdi in a long, hard embrace, determined to cry her heart out as if that would bring Gacalo back. Her husband pays her no heed.

Johan says, "It is the intervening period between her dying and her eventual burial that will no doubt prove most difficult."

"I dread the thought," says Mugdi.

"You know the origin of the English word 'wake'?" asks Johan, and then without waiting for an answer, he goes on, "*Vaka* is the term from the Old Norse."

"The dourness of our funerals!" says Mugdi.

Johan silently interprets this Mugdi-speak as, "How I wish we could organize a boisterous wake!" Alas, he knows he will not.

In Norway, sudden deaths require certification from the authorities before the corpse can be buried. Johan recalls that with people of the Muslim faith, burials are simple and occur within hours of death, hordes of visitors and well-wishers arriving at the home of the bereaved family. Meanwhile the corpse is bathed and then wrapped in lengths of white cotton or linen, after which the community offers its collective prayer—the Janaaza prayer ritual. Mourning lasts only for a few days, and takes the form of more frequent devotions. Grieving is done with dignity.

Johan also knows of wakes among the Irish and the Yoruba, where the vigil is celebrated with wild dancing, a junketing fit to wake the dead. Timiro and Himmo have resumed their sobbing, until Kaluun censures their behavior, saying, "You sound like paid mourners in Rajasthan, you are so loud."

Himmo is upset, but says nothing.

Mugdi goes on, "Imagine if we continued crying like that for three or four days while waiting for the body to be released."

The silence, prompted by Mugdi's plea, becomes protracted. Himmo, her eyes red, whispers, "Why do they die, the people I love most? First Mouna and now Gacalo, alive one minute, dead the next."

Mugdi wishes he could impose total silence on everyone present.

Johan says with concern, "From your current expression, it seems as if there is something bothering you terribly—besides the obvious. Can Birgitta and I be of any assistance?"

It takes Mugdi a long time to air his thoughts. "Gacalo and I were so self-contained as a couple," he says, "that we allowed only family members, Himmo and her children and yourselves into our small, private circle."

"What are you saying?" asks Johan.

"I am wondering if this is because we've been in exile for a long time and so had no problem severing all ties with Somalis, including those who are here, or whether this is because Norway, which we've chosen as a home, is a country in which it is difficult to make friends."

"All of the above."

# CHAPTER TWENTY-SIX

----------

A TRADITIONAL MUSLIM FUNERAL IS HELD AT A MOSQUE FOUR DAYS AFTER Gacalo's death and the day after the pathologist's verdict that Gacalo died of possible overdose. Himmo made the arrangements once the hospital confirmed that the body was ready for collection, first with a Pakistani-owned funeral parlor specializing in preparing Muslim bodies for burial and then with the imam of the mosque where she attends Friday prayers.

"Very sweet of Himmo to set all this up. Thanks to her," says Eugenia.

"Y'know what has surprised me most?" says Kaluun. "That Waliya has provided the incense that's burning. Incense burning is traditional in our culture and it lends an odiferous liveliness to the burial process."

Gacalo's casket now rests on a stand in the anteroom of the mosque, having arrived in a funeral van in time for the midday prayer. Himmo, Kaluun, Timiro, with Riyo in a toddler carrier backpack—Waliya absent for reasons not given—catch their first sight of Gacalo in the mosque's antechamber. Eugenia, Johan, and

Birgitta stay behind, because they are not Muslim and have no idea how to comply with the ritual demands of a mosque; and because somebody has had to volunteer to look after Riyo. Being local, Birgitta smooth-talked two girls Riyo's age, the granddaughters of a friend, to come and play with her. So while the girls play, Eugenia and Birgitta prepare finger food for the guests, who may come after the burial.

It surprises both women that Johan, on his authority and against her objections, has removed the liquor and wine from the drinks cabinet in the living room, hiding them in Mugdi's upstairs study in case Somalis or other Muslims express disapproval—though not before serving himself two tots of whiskey on the rocks and a generous glass of wine each for Birgitta and Eugenia.

Birgitta says to Johan, "Are you sure Mugdi will like what you've done in removing his drinks?" Eugenia listens to the conversation in silence.

"I can't think why he won't," Johan says.

"It's presumptuous of you."

"Think, darling. Where is he now, as we speak?"

"He is at the mosque, of course."

He says, "Let's ask Eugenia for her view on this."

Turning to Eugenia, Johan says, "Would you agree that Mugdi is culturally a Muslim in the way that you and we are culturally of the Christian faith?"

"I would," says Eugenia.

"We were baptized as infants, confirmed during our teens, attend weddings, funerals, and the odd Christmas mass. However, we are Evangelical Lutherans only by name. And just as we are secular religiously, so are they. Any guests they may have with them are another story." Birgitta, to switch topics, says to Eugenia, "It's strange that Waliya has not called or otherwise bothered to condole with the family."

Saafi, standing close by, gently corrects Birgitta. "Mum has not stopped praying for Gacalo's soul, from the moment she received the sad news, and we are sure she will be here."

When Saafi is out of sight, Birgitta murmurs, "Waliyatitis indeed," seeming to like the sound of the undiagnosed ailment. She continues, "How does one explain that woman's perverse resolve to cut off all ties to Gacalo and the rest of the family?"

"Perhaps one reason is that Waliya became aware that no amends are possible when your closest associates—in her case, Zubair and Imam Fanax—label your in-laws 'apostates' and you defend their name," Eugenia says.

"Why would it matter to Gacalo and Mugdi that Zubair and Fanax called them apostates? Surely there are worse things."

"Kaluun has explained to me that by calling them apostates, Zubair and Fanax turned them into vulnerable clay pigeons, fair targets that jihadi terrorists could take potshots at."

Johan says, "I had no idea."

Birgitta, who is deeply upset, says, "What can Mugdi do to counter it?"

Eugenia says, "This is why Mugdi has agreed to let Himmo organize the funeral service at the mosque and have a highly respected imam speak at the burial."

At the sound of voices at the door, they all fall silent. Kaluun is the first to enter, looking as weak as a plant deprived of sunlight. No one says anything until he has poured himself a glass of water and drunk it. Eugenia then wraps her arms around him and asks, "How did it all go?"

"Death is the new great reality," says Kaluun.

Eugenia exchanges looks with Birgitta and Johan, then waits for Kaluun to hug them with equal warmth.

"What was the attendance like?" asks Johan.

"There were far more mourners than we had hoped for," he says. "At the mosque, the attendance was mostly Somali, with a trickle of Arabs and Pakistanis. And at the cemetery, there was a mix of Somalis and Norwegians. A number of Gacalo's fellow Norwegian workers said they would come to the open house."

Birgitta says, "I'm glad to hear that some of them will come, as Gacalo was much loved, she really was."

Kaluun nods his head in agreement and says, "Some of the women asked why you weren't at the cemetery, and I told them you were helping out at the house."

"Where are Mugdi, Timiro, and Naciim?"

Kaluun says, "They'll be here shortly."

Birgitta takes him aside and informs him that Johan has commandeered the drinks to a room upstairs. "Do you think this will please Mugdi?"

Kaluun says, "I've been meaning to do just that."

"How do we go about serving guests who might actually want a drink?" she then asks.

"You serve the wine in coffee mugs, not glasses."

"The way they serve liquor in Saudi Arabia?"

"So no one knows the contents of a mug."

"What hypocrisy!"

"In any event, you'll see that, on arrival, the mourners will separate into groups, Somalis forming a clutch of their own, and the Norwegians likewise feeling more comfortable among themselves."

Now Mugdi arrives, appearing unsettled, perhaps from his near accident at the cemetery. As Gacalo's corpse was being lowered into the grave, he spotted Waliya among the women. The unexpected sight of her made Mugdi unbalanced, and he would have fallen right into the tomb had Kaluun not moved fast to take hold of his arm and help him regain his equilibrium.

Kaluun asks Mugdi, "Where is Naciim?"

"He is with his friend Edvart, who was also at the cemetery," replies Mugdi. "The two are coming together by bus, as there was no space for them in the cars, with all the mourners."

Mugdi turns to face the ten or so mourners who have come with him. He cuts the figure of a confused elder. Kaluun says, "Why don't you go upstairs and let me take over? You deserve a bit of rest after all you've been through."

Kaluun feels a deep anxiety about his brother. He thinks of how during the funeral, as Gacalo's face was turned toward Mecca and the men recited one religious solemnity after another, all the while repeating, "We commit you to earth, in the name of Allah and in the religion of the Prophet," Mugdi, as if out of a momentary madness, leaned forward and almost fell right into the open grave. Perhaps he could not imagine his beloved wife buried without him.

"Welcome, my friend," Kaluun now greets Suudi, a Somali man he has known for a long time. The woman by his side is Ingrid, his Norwegian wife. Suudi is very dark, large and plump, a jovial character given to rolling with laughter at his own jokes. He is buckle-kneed from the immense weight of his paunch and waddles as he walks. For some reason, Suudi puts Kaluun in mind of the bottom of a huge cauldron used for cooking food in a smoky lean-to kitchen. Ingrid, by contrast, is a very slim, flat-chested blonde, taller than her husband and much quieter, rarely speaking in front of company. The couple lives in Bergen, with a much-loved dog that shares their bed at night and eats its food off their plates. Kaluun believes this to be a tall tale that Suudi is fond of repeating to his fellow Somalis to demonstrate that he is no longer a member of their community. There is nothing wrong in stressing how he has struck out on his own, but what good has Suudi done for other Somalis, culturally, politically, or in any other way? None.

Kaluun points Suudi and Ingrid in the direction where he knows like-minded mourners are congregated, and where nearly everyone is drinking wine or liquor from mugs.

"You and Ingrid belong in this room," he says.

"As long as the drinks flow," Suudi replies.

"Less cracking of jokes, please," says Kaluun.

"Who do you think I am?"

"The occasion demands that you behave."

"Fear not. I will behave," vows Suudi.

As Kaluun circulates among the guests, he comes upon a Somali woman who asks for wine and refuses to drink it out of a mug, insisting that wine consumed from a mug will taste different.

"Besides, it'll be dosed with a sizable shot of hypocrisy and I don't like it one bit," she says.

"Fair enough," Kaluun says, pouring her wine into a glass and moving on.

Kaluun ambles through the living room, where a number of Somalis are slouched on couches, eating and creating a mess. Grains of rice and other droppings are scattered on side tables and on the floor, possibly as a consequence of their eating with their fingers from plates on their laps.

Meanwhile, the Norwegians are having a ball, drinking rowdily as though at an Irish wake. Suudi stands in the center of those gathered, Ingrid by his side, arms locked with hers, maybe worried she will walk away and he will never set eyes on her again. Kaluun greets many of the Norwegians, but he does not linger in conversation. Then he goes upstairs to Mugdi's room, finds the door ajar, knocks and waits for an answer, which does not come. Craning his head inside to get a better view, he sees his brother is lying on his back, his face covered with a pillow, his breathing faint.

Mugdi, meanwhile, is deep in thought, comparing the death of his wife to that of Beret's husband Per Hansa, who meets his death in a fatal trek; his corpse never recovered, it perishes unburied. At least, Mugdi tells himself under his pillow, they have given Gacalo a decent burial.

Kaluun is worried by Mugdi's ominous stillness and calls his name. The old man replies in a muffled voice without removing the pillow from his face.

Mugdi says, "Are there any more recent disasters that you have come to report? If so, please be quick."

"I'm sorry."

"What about?" Mugdi asks.

"I must apologize for disturbing you," Kaluun says, advancing into the room.

Mugdi sits up and pushes the pillow to one side. "Have you noticed how the sick, the ailing, the very young, and the very old have no right to privacy? So please do not apologize on my account. It is not necessary."

Kaluun has a flash of an image of Mugdi as a lonely old man, refusing to commune with friends or family or to answer his phone or emails; an agoraphobic recluse.

Mugdi says, "I am recently bereaved and I'm more than aware that I'll require time to get used to the great loss I've suffered."

"We're here to serve as your safety net."

"Be that as it may, it stirs my ire to realize that someone has taken decisions that will forever impact my life in irreversible ways, without seeking my input. Which proves my point that the ailing, the very young, and the very old have no right to privacy."

"What are you talking about?"

"I know that everything is being done for my own good," he says. "Himmo organizes a funeral service at a mosque and I go along. Another invites half a dozen sheikhs to the cemetery. Johan removes the drinks from the cabinet, which now stands bereft of its usual contents. All for my own good; everything."

"We've meant well," says Kaluun.

"Whenever I've thought of complaining about any of this, I hear Gacalo's ghost of a voice advising me not to return people's kindness with ingratitude."

The two are silent for a few moments, then Kaluun asks, "Coming down to greet the visitors?"

"Give me a few minutes and I will," says Mugdi.

Timiro is happy that Riyo has fallen asleep, giving her time to change her dress, which is wet in the back with sweat, and to welcome more guests arriving together from the cemetery. Himmo guides a group of men from the mosque, including the imam who led the funeral service. It touches her to see Naciim and Edvart walk in together and then to watch as Saafi rushes toward them to say hello. Edvart described Gacalo and Mugdi as "cool" to Timiro, and they exchanged a few kind words at the cemetery, as clods of earth were being thrown onto the grave.

Timiro, circulating—her back now wet from having carried Riyo in the backpack—introduces herself to those whom she does not know and thanks them for coming. At one point she finds herself face-to-face with Kaluun, who takes her by the arm and tells her about his conversation with Mugdi. She says, "Give him time and space and he will start to heal."

Just then Himmo joins them and Kaluun repeats his dialogue with Mugdi.

Himmo says, "He feels hard done by at having to go along with our advice. Maybe he thinks we've continued from where Gacalo left off."

Timiro says, "What would Mum have done if she were alive? She would have told him to behave." She then strides up the stairs to talk to Mugdi. Entering the room, she cannot tell if he is asleep. But when she sits down on the edge of the bed, he turns and says, "What's up?"

"People are wondering why you aren't coming down."

He says, his voice tight, "I'm much too emotional to talk to people, especially when I'm unsure what to say."

"Maybe you shouldn't be alone," says Timiro.

He disregards her comment and goes on, "She slept on this side of the bed, closer to the door and the telephone, which she always answered. I slept on the side nearer the clock and the bathroom. We knew our roles. With her gone forever, I wonder how I'll cope."

Timiro's eyes well and, as she dabs them with a napkin, she realizes she has been wrongheaded in her assumptions and needs to rethink.

"I need a measure of something strong," he says.

"How would you like it served? In a mug or a glass?"

"In a mug, please."

As they go downstairs hand in hand, Mugdi says, "To die does not mean one has ended one's relationship with those whom one has loved. You see, your mother will always love us back, even if she is dead; and I'll love her as I've always loved her, even if I am alone."

Mugdi's sudden appearance stirs the mourners into silence. He moves about, shaking hands, nodding in acknowledgment, and thanking them for their kind words. The imam, who is sitting close to Himmo, rises to his feet and recites a few verses of the Koran. Then he says, "Order, Order," and when everyone grows quiet once more, he says, "Please, a Faatixa prayer," and reads the first chapter of the Koran. Mugdi thanks them all and soon the mourners begin trickling out.

When Edvart and Naciim announce to Timiro that they are ready to leave, she asks if they have eaten enough or would like a doggy bag. Edvart shakes his head, but Naciim, who says they have an exam in a couple of days for which they must cram, agrees to take some leftover chicken. And Saafi offers to look after Riyo, now that the little one has woken up.

By eight o'clock, all the Somalis with the exception of Suudi have gone and Kaluun assigns himself the job of walking the stragglers out to the gate and chatting with them until they depart.

Then he and Mugdi join the Norwegians. The party—Johan calls it a *vaka*—lasts until close to midnight, by which time nearly everyone is soused. It is as though they are all determined to drown their sorrows and Mugdi has no regrets either way.

Eventually when everyone is ready to go home, Johan tells Mugdi to remember to call any time, day or night. "Don't hesitate, especially after Kaluun, Timiro, and her daughter depart and you are by yourself. Come for meals often, join us when we are going to a show at the museum."

Birgitta says, "We'll make sure a life full of new adventures is waiting for you in the wings and we'll help you explore it."

After hugs and kisses, they leave. Kaluun prepares to do the dishes and Timiro checks on Riyo and Saafi. Mugdi, meanwhile, locks himself in his study, his family unsure whether he intends to resume work on his translations or simply derive comfort from his self-isolation.

# CHAPTER TWENTY-SEVEN

----------

NACIIM TOWELS HIMSELF OFF AFTER SHOWERING AND HUMS NANCY SINA-tra's "These Boots Are Made for Walking," his favorite song. He likes the lyrics so much that he has committed them to memory and adapts them to suit various purposes. He imagines singing the song to his mother, who's been "a'messin'" in his life where she shouldn't have been, devoting her love and her best to others, and telling lies, since arriving in Oslo, when she "oughta be truthin'." He prays that someone will tell her "what's right is right."

He stops humming briefly and listens for sounds from his moth-er's room, surprised not only that she is not yet moving about the apartment, but also that her Koranic recitation tapes are not play-ing as they usually are, a persistent background soundtrack. Daily, nightly, for many an hour, his mother plays the tapes of her favorite sheikh reading the Koran. He recalls the tapes weren't playing last night either, when he returned home from the funeral. Instead, he arrived to find the apartment strangely still, his mother's door shut, and from it emanating two low female voices. He wondered whom the other woman's voice belonged to. He waited some hours for them to emerge, before giving up and going to bed.

Naciim and his mother have seldom met the past few weeks. He leaves for school very early and returns very late, and when he is not at school or with Edvart, he is with Mugdi, whom he and Saafi have spent more time with since Gacalo's death, switching off visiting him to make sure he is not in want of company. On the rare occasions Naciim is in his room, he moves about with stealth, and at times pretends not to be in when she knocks. Too often when he and his mother would meet in the kitchen or the corridor, she would just harangue him about one alleged wrongdoing or another, though he has tried to be increasingly polite with her, recalling Mugdi's wise counsel to never abandon yourself to youthful anger, if you wish to survive. Mugdi had said, "Woe to anyone who surrenders to the violence of uncontrollable rage. You must always remember she is your mother even when she is wrong."

"But what can I do to fight her off?"

"You do nothing. And if you are of a mind to say something, be polite. Always."

So he has held back, kept his anger in check, and avoided all-out confrontations. And knowing that neither of them relies on the other anymore, mother and son have arrived at a compromise common among married couples, each spouse content with the concession he or she makes to the other for the sake of sustainable peace. Mugdi believes one can trace the problem between mother and son to within a few days of their arrival. The initial mistake was Waliya's, when she singled Naciim out for his maleness in a household of females and assigned him the role of Mahram, with the authority to protect the honor of the family and determine who may or may not enter the sanctified space. For a while, he behaved the way tin-pot despots behave, believing in his absolute authority over his mother and sister. Mugdi would say, "You were no different from children in plastic helmets who thought of themselves as real soldiers."

"But I didn't ask to be made a Mahram," he said.

"You were too young to carry the burden your mother placed on your head," said Mugdi. "You had no idea what it meant to be a Mahram, nor did you receive the required guidance from anyone."

Naciim would agree that he felt caught up in his mother's web of restrictive rules when he knew little about the nexus between his life and the faith he was expected to adhere to. His mother discouraged him from listening to the Beatles or even Somali music, and her religious cohorts forbade him to watch soccer on TV for fear that he would see half-naked women among the spectators, or ads selling liquor, or infomercials for condoms that openly discussed sex among the young. And so Naciim chose not to share his life's secrets with his mother.

Naciim looks at his watch, now that he is fully dressed, and checks that his textbooks and notebooks are all in his satchel. He stands one more time in front of the full-length mirror, and, nodding to his reflection, decides it is time to go and meet Janine, the classmate with whom he first went out a week ago, when they saw a movie together and held hands in the darkened cinema. She is the one who lent him Nancy Sinatra's song, after he confided in her that he and his mother were not always on the best of terms. He hopes that he will get to know her much better.

He is about to head out when he hears a knock on his bedroom door. Opening it, he finds himself face-to-face with a woman he hasn't seen since he was a child.

"How you've grown!" Arla says.

He holds her gaze, smiling, before allowing his eyes the unfettered freedom to roam. He remembers that he last saw Arla, the woman now in front of him, clad in an almost see-through pair of loose pajamas, nearly a decade ago. She was his mother's best friend and lived across a dirt road in a zinc shack directly opposite theirs. As a young boy, he was in awe at the way she carried herself, a large woman partial to beautiful dresses, and proud of her assets, which she showed off at every opportunity. Now and then, she would babysit him and his sister when his mother went out after dark. Even though she no longer inspires awe in him, her presence in his mother's life makes him worry. For all of her kindness, there was always fire to her and he must be wary, lest he be burned.

"Do you remember me?" she asks.

"How can I forget you?"

He looks at his watch again and realizes that he will be late for his appointment with Janine, whom he has arranged to meet at a corner café for a quick breakfast on their way to school.

He says to Arla, "Just a moment, please."

"Late for class?"

He sends Janine a text message: "I'll be late."

"Who have you texted just now?"

"Does it matter?"

She asks, "Do you have a girlfriend?"

Naciim glares at Arla, who buttons up her pajama top and crosses her arms over her front.

"You were tiny when I last saw you."

"You were slimmer and very fetching."

"Age plays havoc on one's body."

"I won't ask how old you are."

"You are a gentleman and I thank you."

She's heavy everywhere now, her girth wide, her breasts larger and no longer shaped like plantains, her thighs huge. "When did you arrive?" Naciim asks.

"I got here yesterday afternoon."

"Married?"

"Sort of."

"What did you tell Mum?" he asks.

"We haven't come to that part of the story yet."

"How I'd like to be a fly on the wall when you and Mum talk," he says. "Tell me anyhow. Are you someone's mistress? Or better still, a common-law wife?"

"Not too fast, young man."

He looks at his watch again.

"I mustn't hold you hostage any longer. Though I wish you were coming with us, Saafi and me."

"Where are you taking Saafi?"

"Clothes shopping and then job hunting."

"What sort of job?"

"I know someone who runs a Danish-owned company in Oslo, a friend of the man whom I am sort of married to. He has suggested that I escort her to the interview."

"And what has Mum said to that?"

"We'll find out, won't we?"

"Well, as much as I'd like to see Mum's reaction to your arrival, I must be off." As he slips past Arla, he calls Janine and says, "I'm sorry, I've been held up at home. I suggest we meet in class."

After school, Naciim goes to Mugdi's. As he enters the house, he calls out, "It's Naciim, Grandpa. Are you okay, and where are you?"

Naciim hears Mugdi's faint reply, "I'm here."

"Here where?"

Mugdi says, "Bedroom."

Naciim goes upstairs and turns right into the bedroom, where the door is wide open and the curtains still drawn. Mugdi, who is fully dressed, is lying on his back on a bed that appears unmade since he got out of it this morning.

"How are you doing, Grandpa?"

"I've just enjoyed a siesta."

Mugdi's eyes follow Naciim's movements but he remains supine, hardly showing interest in sitting up or changing position. Naciim opens the curtains to let in the late afternoon light.

"What time is it?" asks Mugdi.

"Time I made tea for two. Interested?"

"Thanks, dear. I could do with a cup."

Naciim heads downstairs to make tea.

In the kitchen, Naciim tells Mugdi about Arla's arrival. Mugdi listens, takes a sip of tea, and makes a face as if involuntarily. Then with his cup still in the clutch of his right hand he asks, "Are you saying that we are in uncharted territory?"

Naciim says, "I believe we are."

"You say the Koranic tape has been off since her arrival?"

"It wasn't on when I got back last night and wasn't on when I left for school this morning."

"And you didn't see your mum this morning?"

"No, we didn't meet. On the bright side, it is possible that Arla's presence for a few days will help moderate Mum's extremist views," says Naciim. "And that is not a bad thing."

"Moderate your Mum's extremist views—how?"

"Arla is taking Saafi clothes shopping, and she says she knows someone who may be able to offer her a couple of hours' worth of a part-time job that would give her pocket money."

Mugdi says, "Are you headed home now?"

"I was going to head out shortly. I thought perhaps as a good-will gesture, I would make them dinner."

"I have a better idea." Mugdi opens the fridge and brings out a parcel of takeaways, sealed and ready to eat, from his favorite Indian restaurant. He hands them over to Naciim and says, "Here. All you have to do is to put these in the microwave and serve them."

"What are they?"

"Fish rogan josh, spicy lentil, roti and a brinjal curry dish and okra in tomato sauce," says Mugdi, who puts the parcels on the table and then finds a hefty carrier bag.

"Thanks, Grandpa. I am sure they will enjoy it."

"Unless your mother objects to eating the food, because it doesn't bear the stamp of halal," says Mugdi.

"Is the restaurant Pakistani and Muslim?"

"It's Punjabi."

"They are not Hindu, are they?"

"There is a Punjab Province in Pakistan," says Mugdi, "and there is the State of Punjab, in India. The people who own the restaurant are Indian Punjabi and Sikh, not Muslim. To ease her mind, you can tell her the restaurant owner is a Pakistani."

"Fish is always halal, isn't it?"

"I understand it is."

"Lentil and eggplant are vegetarian and halal."

"Yes," says Mugdi.

Naciim, relaxed, leaves for home.

As he walks into the apartment, he feels a greater sense of light-heartedness than ever before. Again, he notices that the Koranic tape is not on. Even though it is eerily quiet, he adjusts to the new normal by the time he goes into his room and puts his school satchel away, reemerging with the food parcels in his hand. He heads for the kitchen, aiming to empty the food into bowls.

Saafi follows him in and says, "I've got a part-time job at a toy shop as a customer service clerk."

"Where?"

"It's a showroom for Lego, a bus ride away. We're all women, five of us, and our boss is a woman too," says Saafi. "She is lovely. I like her a lot. She speaks some Arabic—she has worked in Lebanon and knows how to recite the Faatixa."

"Has Mum agreed to this?" he asks.

"She has."

"So what's the catch?"

"How do you know there is one?"

"Mum won't allow you to work outside the home, among total strangers, unless there is a catch. So what is it?"

"You have to collect me every evening from work without fail," she says. "Will you be willing to do that?"

"When are you supposed to start?"

"A week from Monday," she replies.

"Okay. I'll be happy to do so," he promises.

Saafi goes to tell her mum the good news.

Naciim hears Arla's clipped tones, as if she is telling his mother off, when the bedroom door opens and Arla emerges. She stops dead in her tracks and says, "Oh, there you are!"

She is in a see-through *dirac*, a dress with a floral pattern fashionable in the Somali Peninsula from the late eighties onward. He notes that both the color of her bra and the shape of her breasts are visible to him. He cannot help thinking that she's coming on to him. She steps closer, takes his left hand, and looks him in the eyes, as his heart misses a beat. Then she hugs him and says, "Welcome back. It's good to see you. How was school?"

"Very good."

"You are an A-student, I hear. I've always known you would do well, given the chance."

That she has bothered to find out how well he is doing at school is heartening to him, given that his mother has never shown the least interest in his studies. "So, did you accompany Saafi to her interview dressed like this?"

"No. I had the full Muslim outdoor gear."

"Niqaab, hijab, and all?"

"When I am outside the house, I comply, but when I am indoors I dress the Somali way," she says. "Here I am in *dirac*, maybe tomorrow I'll be in traditional Somali *guntiino*. I am a woman for all seasons."

"And where's Mum?"

"I've just told her off and she is changing."

"Why did you tell her off?"

"She had on a niqaab and hijab inside the house."

"What did you suggest she wear, then?"

"I've suggested she put on indoor summer wear."

He cannot wait to see his mother come out.

"How do you manage to make her do what you say?"

"I know your mum far better than anyone else does. She and I have been soul mates for a very long time. I know her weaknesses and her strengths," says Arla. "We've been through a lot together, she and I. We've seen happy days together and cried over each other's shoulder on sad nights."

"That's probably true, but it doesn't answer my question," he says.

"I am coming to it. Don't rush me."

"I won't. I promise. But go on, please."

And he starts to set the table for four.

Arla asks, "Are we having a sit-down dinner?"

"Yes, we are. To honor your presence."

Arla gives him her hand and says, "I did not mince my words with your mum. I've told her that it is all well and good to engage in self-reinvention in the way she has done, but that it doesn't make sense if there is no gain in it for her. I was there when she met Dhaqaneh, and I encouraged her to make herself into the woman your stepdad would be happy with, a devout woman, dressed accordingly. I expected that when she got here and saw the situation, met Mugdi and Gacalo and got to know their attitude, she would give up all her pretenses and get on with life."

"Why did she not do what you suggested?"

"She became a victim of self-deception. She fell for that awful man and his offer of marriage."

The table set, he puts the food in the microwave.

Barely has Naciim asked Arla to let his mother know dinner is ready when Waliya appears in the kitchen doorway. With shock he notes how completely she has transformed: she's wearing a floral summer dress, perhaps bought earlier today when they all went shopping; her long hair is gathered into a bun with a Somali headscarf; on her feet are flat-heeled shoes with the buckle loose; and most strikingly, on her face is the lightest trace of lipstick and kohl eye makeup.

"Did you cook dinner for us, son?" she asks.

Naciim suddenly feels so furious he cannot bear to speak. For most of his young life, it is now clear, his mother has lived a life of pretense, which has spawned terrible miseries not only for her but for them all.

Naciim suggests that they serve themselves and pushes one dish toward Arla and another toward his mother. Waliya asks, "What do we have here, dear?"

He does not recall her addressing him as "dear" in all the time they have been in Oslo. Again this disturbs him, but not to the point of expressing his fury.

He says, "This food is from a Punjabi restaurant."

"Punjab is in India, am I right?"

"There are two Punjabs, one is a state in India and another is a province in Pakistan."

"Is this food halal or not?" asks his mother.

"Stop the fuss and eat," says Arla, addressing her words to Waliya as though to a misbehaving child. "One dish is fish and, as you know, fish is always halal. The other two are vegetarian. So say 'Bismillah, thank you, son,' and eat up."

As instructed, she says the Bismillah, and with a sheepish grin, helps herself to the fish and takes a couple of spoonfuls of rice.

"Good?" asks Arla.

"It tastes nice, considering," says Waliya.

Naciim refuses to allow his mother's words to get to him. He helps himself to a small portion and eats without engaging anyone in a conversation, worried he might make snarky backtalk.

# CHAPTER TWENTY-EIGHT

----------

NEARLY EVERYTHING IS IN A STATE OF FLUX, WITH NACIIM REPORTING daily to Timiro and Kaluun after he has called on Mugdi. Timiro and Kaluun confer frequently in the hopes of finding a way to slow down the old man's descent into despair. When they have studied the situation from various angles and Kaluun suggests there is little else to be done short of moving to Oslo to look after him, Timiro bristles, knowing what this means: that in likelihood everyone expects her to relocate to Norway, being Mugdi's daughter and a female at that. But although the idea of moving back to Oslo has appealed to her, it has remained only a fanciful scheme. In Geneva, where she resides and where a number of UN agencies are headquartered, Timiro often lands well-paying consultation. In Oslo, there are no similar work opportunities.

She says, "Let me talk to Birgitta."

"What's the point?" Kaluun asks.

"I've an idea. Let me discuss it with her."

"Birgitta and Johan are globetrotters," says Kaluun. "One week they are in the Caribbean, the next week they are in the Alps. They don't have the willingness to help more than they do already. Like it or not, it falls to us. One of us has to move there."

Birgitta wants to introduce Mugdi to a former schoolmate of hers, a couple of years her junior, who is in charge of the Norwegian literature section at the National Library. She tells Timiro, "She is sixty-two years old, a widow, no children, very well read, a very fine person, empathic about immigrants and multiculturalism, and she speaks French."

"Widow, no children. I like that," says Timiro. "How often do you see her?"

"Our second homes in Sweden are two kilometers apart," says Birgitta. "We meet when we are there and at times go together for long walks. She brings along her dog, and either we go to her or she comes to us. I've no idea why I didn't think of this sooner."

Timiro asks, "What is her name?"

"Her name is Nadia Stein."

Timiro says, "I like that, too. Nadia."

"I'd be happy to introduce them."

By way of introduction, Birgitta writes one email to Nadia and another to Mugdi. Then, as though it were an afterthought and she is a matchmaker, she sends them both a second long email, detailing the pertinent particulars each needs to know about the other. This second missive gives her a chance to express her heartfelt desire for the two of them to get together.

Mugdi may deny it, but his anal retentiveness displays itself in the time it takes him to mull matters over instead of initiating communication, and he allows days to pass after receiving Nadia's email, even though he is as keen as she sounds to meet up.

Finally, Nadia takes the initiative to make a phone call and, listening to Mugdi, she feels that, despite his reticence, he is a man whom it will be a pleasure to get to know. She suggests they rendezvous for brunch the next day at a café close to the National Library.

Nadia and Mugdi meet at noon, on what has turned into the most beautiful day in July thus far, with the sun on splendid display and crowds milling in the streets. Mugdi is a few inches taller and nearly a decade older; Nadia is half a dozen kilos heavier. They discover to their pleasant surprise that they have actually known each other by sight; she admits to having seen him more than once at the library from her cubicle.

As they wait in silence for their orders, Nadia remembers what Birgitta has told her about Mugdi's late wife and son, and the widow and children who survived him. Birgitta said that Mugdi felt honor-bound to avoid confrontation with the widow because of the promise he made to his late wife in the weeks before she died. Birgitta also explained the pride of place occupied by the boy Naciim in the old man's heart and mind.

Mugdi, for his part, recalls how Birgitta wrote that Nadia was truly enamored of Africa, having worked in Tanzania, Ghana, Namibia, South Africa, and Burkina Faso, training librarians while on assignment from the Norwegian government. She found her African colleagues more amiable than her colleagues at home, and made several friends, mostly women. She did become close to a Tanzanian man as her marriage neared collapse, but nothing came of it after she discovered that he was married to two other women, one in church and one by tradition.

Mugdi distantly reminds her of the Tanzanian man in more ways than one: he too was soft of speech and delicate in his manner. And like the Tanzanian, Mugdi possesses a chest so narrow he seems birdlike.

The waitress delivers their order and the two of them eat in silence.

Then Nadia says, "Have you been to India?"

"No, I haven't. Why do you ask?"

"I was there recently for research and had to get a visa," she says. "I've become interested in the questions they insist you answer on visa forms. The Indian application form asks about which of the three 'sex' categories you belong to: female, male, or transgender. But when it comes to marital status, there are only two categories: married or single. Here, you are not required to give an answer to the third category, divorced. Religion, as a defining category, is important to both India and Iran, where I've also traveled, but not to Norway."

"Is divorcing in India anathema?"

"The forms have to cater to a variety of applicants, some of whom are divorced. Or, as in the case of Iran, there are transgender people—but this is not considered a category worth belonging to. Now, can you imagine Africans giving space to transgender folks in the visa forms?"

"I haven't seen an American nonimmigrant visa application since becoming Norwegian, but when I last filled one in, I remember a question asking if you were ever a Communist," he says.

"What about the obligatory question now asking if you have a mental or physical disorder that poses a danger to others?"

Mugdi says, "In colonial times in Somalia, you had to state the name of the clan to which you belonged. This was part of the divide-and-rule policy of that era. The question was removed from forms several years before independence, but to apply for your ID or passport, you still have to state the color of your eyes, hair, or skin—a reminder, if one is needed, that the form has not undergone all the changes necessary."

"You are a dual national, aren't you?"

"In name only."

"How so?"

"Because I haven't applied for a new biometric Somali passport. As you may know, for over two decades during the Somali civil war, Somali passports were not accepted anywhere as valid travel documents, because there was no central government, and you could purchase counterfeit passports at supermarkets along with your food."

She asks, "How easy has it been to travel on a Norwegian passport? Are you accepted as Norwegian or do Norway's immigration officers question your Norwegianness in the same way that Breivik and right-wing ideologues might?"

He replies, "I believe that it has required a great deal of soul-searching on the part of many a Norwegian to accept that someone who is black and has a Muslim name can be as Norwegian as a white native. I am often labeled a refugee, even though I am now a national."

As Nadia is about to speak, two young men walk past their table on their way out of the café. Both handsome and in tight jeans, they are holding hands. The shorter one is talking about the "preponderance of foreigners" in Oslo and how the city has lost its character and charm.

"Did you hear that?" asks Mugdi.

Nadia says, "Sadly I did. Maybe if these two as schoolboys had read the history of Norwegian migration, which I am certain you are more familiar with than they are, neither of them would hold such a view."

Mugdi motions to the waitress to bring him the bill. Nadia, meanwhile, stares into the void, lost in thought. After he has paid and before they leave, she asks him questions about the translations he has been working on. He sounds unhappy about the slowness of his production.

She says, "Maybe you need to go out a bit."

"I am sure I do," he says.

"In that case, would you join me for dinner one of these days?" she asks.

"I would love to."

"What about a week from now at my place? Eight o'clock?"

He replies, "Yes, I look forward to it."

They hug as they part, and she kisses him with warmth on both cheeks and says, "Next week at eight."

He leaves the café, takes a tram, and sits with a book in his hand, facing a group of rowdy teenagers, the boys beltless and wearing their trousers low on their hips, one of them proudly showing off the top of his underwear. The girls are in flimsy summer outfits, a few showing tongues pierced with silver buttons, or their lower lips weighted with custom-designed discs to create an effect similar to that of the Mursi women in Ethiopia. Mugdi amusedly watches the antics of these youngsters, kissing and cracking jokes in Norwegian and English, oblivious to the world around them; they feel comfortable with who they are.

In the farthest corner of the same tramcar, to Mugdi's right, are several Somali women, variously covered in different types of veil, from the moderate scarf to the all-engulfing body tent, albeit with the face uncovered. The niqaab-wearing woman is fair-skinned and bespectacled, and Mugdi thinks she has probably singed some hair off her cheeks, judging by their roughness. Another wearing a hijab has covered her face and neck with a piece of polyester: itchy, and not at all comfortable, he thinks.

Of all the veiled women, the one who seems keenest on ogling the young Norwegian women in their robust self-expressions, and who follows every move they make, is the one in the body tent. She watches everything from behind the veil, smiling whenever she hears something funny, which she translates for her neighbor, covered in a more severe double-layered veil—with scarves, face veils, gloves: the works. She appears to have brought along the full extent of her religious wardrobe. Then the two women laugh, modestly covering their mouths with their hands.

The young Norwegian women are self-centered in the way of the young anywhere in the world. They take no notice of the old men or of the Somali women, who perhaps appear to them, as a Norwegian friend of his once put it, "like crows gathered in an open air piazza on a bright summer's day, mourning the death of one of their mates, killed by a stone thrower."

Mugdi moves to a seat nearer the Somali women and pretends to read, even though his aim is to eavesdrop on their conversation. From the few words he is able to pick up, he infers that they think the young Norwegians behave as though they belong to a home with no adults to show them what matters in life. To Mugdi, this sounds far more damning than anything he can say about the young women of either group. When his stop comes, he gets off the tram, disturbed.

Naciim visits Mugdi after school and is very happy to observe that the old man is in a brighter mood than he has been in a long while. They chat briefly, updating each other on their latest doings. Then Mugdi asks, "How are things at home?"

"The tape of the Koran is back on," says Naciim.

"Since when?"

"Since yesterday evening."

"And whatever has become of Arla?"

"The tape is back on and Arla is gone."

"But her coming has been positive, hasn't it?" says Mugdi. "She has managed to get Saafi a job and, more important, convinced your mother not to make any fuss about her daughter working outside the home."

Naciim says, "Arla's disappearance is as much a mystery as was her arrival."

So much for the empathy Arla has shown, thinks Mugdi. So much for the words of comfort she has spoken to Naciim or the changes her presence has brought. Arla is a holdover from the past that she and Waliya shared, and Mugdi has been wary of the possible dangers that she might pose if he ever met her. The woman is wild and no one can tell what she may do, given the chance.

"Have you asked your mum where she's gone?"

"Mum won't say. But I can find out."

"How?"

"Well, she left behind a bunch of stuff, bank documents and the like. My guess is that she'll return at some point to collect them. So I've hidden them in my bedroom to make sure I at least get to speak with her when she does. I want to get to the bottom of the mystery that is Arla."

# CHAPTER TWENTY-NINE

----------

NEARLY NINE MONTHS AFTER ARLA'S DISAPPEARANCE, WITH HIS MOTHER unwilling to answer his questions as to her whereabouts, Naciim and Saafi return home late one afternoon to discover they cannot let themselves in. They take turns trying the key, knocking the door, all to no avail. But because they hear the tape of the Koran running, they assume that their mother is at home. And so they pound on the door some more and call their mother by name. Naciim wonders to himself—he doesn't share his inner worries with Saafi, who panics easily—if the antiterror unit has taken her away or—here he is mischievous and he knows it—if Zubair has been released and he and his mother are having it off or something.

He turns to Saafi, asks, "Do you know where Mum might be?"

"Last time was talked, she was heading for town to meet up with Arla."

"Would you ring her and ask why we can't get in?"

Waliya's phone rings on and on, no answer.

"Do you by any chance have Arla's Danish mobile number?"

Naciim imagines Arla moving around the city and putting up

with an array of friends after her partner-beating Dane has given her the beating of her life; he also imagines the Dane to be on the run, changing hotels, like the criminal he is, to avoid apprehension.

"Mum thinks you have an unhealthy interest in Arla."

"Forget about calling Arla," he says curtly. "Let's go."

"Admit it. You have a crush on the woman."

"You are out of your mind."

"Mum doesn't like the way you undress her with your eyes."

"Old women don't interest me, especially when I have plenty of girls my age to chase."

"That's an idle boast," she says.

"I have a girlfriend I can introduce you to, if you like."

Then it flashes through his mind that talking this way to his sister about having a girlfriend when at her age she has never had the chance to date anyone is cruel and unfair. He says, "Let us go."

"Where?"

"To Grandpa," he says.

Then he telephones Mugdi, telling him that he and Saafi can't get into the apartment and his mother is not there. He says to the old man, "Can Saafi, and I come to your place, cook, have dinner, and wait until they know why we can't gain access into it and what has become of our mum, who seems not to be here, nor answering the phone?"

"Of course, please come."

So with his satchel on his back, tired, angry and hungry, Naciim and Saafi take the tram to Mugdi's. Immediately they are there, Naciim, with little prompting from the old man, prepares an improvised meal for all three in no time at all. They sit to eat and Mugdi asks Saafi, "How's work?"

"I'm enjoying it more than I imagined possible," Saafi says. "My manager wants me to think of myself as the face of the Lego show-room."

"And what do you do?"

"I answer people's questions, I show the parents and the children who come together how the interlocking bricks work. I answer the telephone at the reception desk. We're busy and I like it, because the effort I put into mastering Norwegian has at long last come in handy."

"Is your mother happy you're working?"

"You know Mum no longer runs the nursery?"

If Mugdi does not mention Zubair and Fanax's names, the two men who in one way or another were linked to her mother's running the nursery, it is because he feels this will embarrass Saafi and there is no need to do that.

"Mum is happy I bring in income," she says.

"The decision not to object to Saafi working, if anything, proves that Mum is guided more by practical matters than by religious idealism," Naciim says.

"Is anything wrong with that?" Saafi asks.

Mugdi takes a sip of water and watches Naciim, who makes small movements with his hands, expressive of pronounced restlessness, as if he wishes to change the subject of their conversation. Mugdi says, "Is something bothering you?"

"Saafi and I had a conversation on the way here—she asked why it takes a country that has collapsed into total anarchy like Somalia such a long time to recover from the strife and mayhem."

Mugdi replies, "Imagine a single house collapsing and causing a handful of deaths. Then think of the damage that would be caused if an entire country collapsed in on itself, the way Somalia did in

1991. Keep in mind that the implosion has not been limited to the country and those who live in it. The collapse has had repercussions for every Somali around the world, no matter if they are still in the country or if they abandoned the country to its tragic fate and sought refuge in other lands. These seismic consequences haunt even those Somalis who have never known the country, whether because they left when very young, or were born elsewhere to parents who had fled the fighting."

"What are you saying, Grandpa?" says Saafi.

"I am saying that the disintegration of Somalia remains a live issue, very much still unfolding. Nothing quite like it has happened before, in Africa or anywhere else—an entire country collapsing in on itself like a tower of cards."

"And we're victims of it?" Saafi asks.

"More like products of the collapse."

"Why do you think some countries come to the aid of other communities that are in full-fledged disaster, when others don't?"

"Because not everyone helps a needy old blind man cross a busy intersection," replies Mugdi. "Some do and some don't."

Naciim remembers riding a tram with Janine when they happened to sit across the aisle from an elderly Norwegian man, most likely blind, who had half-dried phlegm sticking to his white shirt and two buttons in the wrong holes. The two of them debated whether to bring these blemishes to the old man's attention, Janine arguing against bothering him, saying it could not matter to him in the least if the buttons were misaligned or his shirt stained, as he would never see it; Naciim suggesting that that they at least remove the thick mucus or bring it to his attention.

He asks, "Why would some help, others not?"

"It is an emotional thing, helping or not helping," says Mugdi.

"A country is bigger than one's emotions."

"What happened in Somalia is of a different order from the horror that occurred in Rwanda," says Mugdi. "But it is just as frightening to the victims caught in the snares of its cruelty. And it is terrible that so far no reconciliation efforts have been possible. And the world is oblivious."

"Is that right?" asks Naciim.

Mugdi says, "The world could not decipher the signposts. A people with the same singular culture, the same religion, and the same language tearing into one another for reasons that make no sense to those outside the peninsula: that is why. As the saying goes, a stream cannot rise above its own source."

Saafi is about to say something when Naciim's phone rings. The caller ID identifies the number as Danish and he answers it, his voice playful. "There you are, at long last," he says. Then, because of Mugdi and Saafi's quizzical look, he becomes self-conscious and he opts to put on the speaker, so everyone can hear everything.

"Where are you?" Arla asks.

Instead of answering her question, he asks, "Do you or does Mum know why we couldn't get into the apartment, Saafi and I?"

"We couldn't open the door ourselves and we went away."

He shares his supposition with everyone listening. He says, "Here's what I think happened: someone, perhaps unwittingly, engaged the night latch snib on the Yale lock on the apartment door. The key won't unlock from the outside if the night latch button is in the wrong position."

Arla says, "I've no idea what you are talking about."

Then he says, "Let me talk to Mum, please."

A few minutes pass before Waliya comes on the line. And as soon as she does, she wants to know if he has remembered to pick up his sister from work. He says, "Yes, Mum. We are both here, at Grandpa's," and then he repeats his theory about the lock aloud.

She says, "How are we going to get back in?"

"I'll call out a locksmith."

"Where do you want us to meet and when?"

"Right in front of the apartment, maybe in two hours max."

He hangs up, calls a locksmith from Mugdi's landline, and arranges to meet the man at the apartment. When Saafi and Naciim are ready to leave, Mugdi gives him enough cash to cover both the cost of the call-out charge as well as the cab fare home.

Just before the taxi arrives, Saafi takes herself into the toilet. While she is gone, the old man asks the boy how he knows about night latch knobs on the Yale lock and how they work. Naciim explains that he has once toyed with the idea of keeping an unwanted intruder from entering the apartment and experimented with the Yale lock on the apartment door.

"And who might this undesirable visitor be?" asks Mugdi.

"I didn't like Imam Fanax's frequent visits to our home."

Saafi reenters the kitchen and she concludes from Mugdi and Naciim's small, albeit subtle, nervous movements that she may have been the subject of Grandpa and Naciim's conversation while she was in the lavatory.

But no one says and they depart to take the waiting taxi home.

Naciim and Saafi arrive by taxi a few minutes before the locksmith. The man has barely begun working when Waliya and Arla emerge from the lift, seemingly exhausted.

Naciim says nothing until the door to the apartment is open. His mother rushes in, mouthing the word "bathroom." As Saafi pays the locksmith, Arla calls the lift.

"Aren't you coming in?" he asks her.

Arla says, "I'll see you soon."

Naciim and Saafi exchange surprised looks when Arla shares the lift going down with the locksmith, waving them goodbye.

When he and Saafi finally enter, his mother's door is shut and the tape of the Koran is back on.

# CHAPTER THIRTY

----------

MUGDI IS AT THE GYM RELAXING AFTER A LONG WORKOUT, BUOYED BY THE thought that he will go home, shave, and shower, before joining Nadia in the evening for dinner. He knows she has taken the day off to do the shopping and the cooking, proof that she is taking the occasion seriously.

Of course, he wishes Gacalo were alive and that she was joining him at Nadia's. Furthermore, he reminds himself that on the few occasions when he and Nadia have met—once at the café, following Birgitta's emails introducing them, and three more times at the library for a chat—Mugdi has impressed on Nadia how much he misses Gacalo, almost a year and a half after her passing.

On the tram home, Mugdi winces and shifts uneasily when he spots his face faintly mirrored in the window. As he turns away, avoiding his own reflection, he remembers his dream from the previous night. In the dream, Mugdi is traveling to Geneva to visit Timiro and her daughter. At the Oslo airport, he stands at the check-in counter, and asked to show his passport, rummages in his shoulder bag, but discovers it is missing. He checks many pockets, first of the bag, then of his trousers, his jacket, and his shirt. He finds the printout of his ticket, his Norwegian ID, but he knows that is no good because "You are traveling international, sir," says the young woman at the counter, "so you must show me your passport." Realizing there is no way he will be allowed to board his flight, he decides to return to the house to search for it, telephone his daughter to tell her what has happened, and catch a later flight.

He searches in the drawers of his desk, and near the printer, and behind the computer. He remembers the Somali proverb that when desperately searching for a lost camel, one may be tempted to look for it in the small milk container. He is going through the pockets of his shoulder bag again when his phone rings and his daughter asks him for an update. "I can't find it," he says.

"So what are you going to do?"

"I'll apply for an emergency passport."

After a long silence, Timiro says, "You wouldn't misplace your passport if Mum were around."

Seated in the tram, Mugdi thinks it would be easy to dismiss his daughter's assertion in his dream as utter nonsense. Still, he is aware that he acquired Norwegian nationality thanks to his wife, who was an employee of the state, and he one of her dependents, his name and destiny linked to hers, just as the widow and her children later became tied to her. No doubt if Gacalo were alive, he would get his emergency passport faster and with fewer questions asked. He remembers the bureaucratic obstacles when, as a widower, he wanted to change their joint bank account to his name only, the bank insisting that he complete half a dozen forms. His hyphenated nationality is unclear to many Norwegians who cannot help assuming that he must have obtained his status as a refugee.

That evening, he takes a taxi to Nadia's place, arrives early, and dawdles around the block before he knocks on her door at precisely eight o'clock. Nadia appears and they hug. She leads him into the living room and points him to a seat, waiting until he is comfortable to ask what he would like to drink.

"A glass of water please," he says.

"Mineral or tap?"

"I am happy with either."

She returns carrying a tray with a glass of water, a piece of lemon floating in it, and bowls of nuts, raisins, and savory snacks; the half-drunk glass of white wine is apparently for her. She sits down on the couch facing him.

She says, "Tell me, did you not come to the reference desk at the library a few years ago and ask me for a religious text in Geez?"

"I did indeed. But why do you ask now?"

"Because it struck me earlier today that I had met you a long time ago," she says. "The memory that I had filed away unconsciously popped back and there it was."

"I remember asking about the religious texts because I came across an article by Professor Pankhurst that awakened in me an interest in ancient Ethiopic religious writings."

"But you never came back to collect it?"

"It was a passing interest, so I didn't."

"And what about the writings interested you?"

"Maybe deep down sacred texts have always held a certain fascination for me, as do secular classics of other nations. I've always wanted to hold each of the sacred texts and the world's classics in my hands, in deference to the history and the culture that produced them." He pauses, then speaking with tremendous care, says, "Born and raised in the oral tradition, I have a soft spot for anything written, perhaps because I assume societies without written traditions will forever remain beholden to those who belong to nations with scripts and to the technology that is integral to their history and culture."

"I've never thought about it that way."

Nadia is, after all, head of the special reference collections at the National Library, responsible for antique, rare, and irreplaceable books. Mugdi is in no position to read the Ethiopic text any more than he can decipher ancient Greek. But his passing interest was in evaluating the literary contributions Professor Pankhurst had elucidated, and Mugdi, as a layperson, wished to know as much as he could. But when it took Nadia a long time to return with the text, he left, telling Nadia's colleague that he would be back tomorrow. The next day, he received the devastating news of his son's suicide.

As he sits in Nadia's house and looks back on that day, Mugdi cannot determine if it is the anger he felt on receiving the terrible news that is resurfacing now, or if it is the pain that has grown worse over the years and keeps revisiting him in his nightmares. When Nadia asks him if he is okay, he sits up straight, startled, his eyes open wide and his breathing uneven. Eventually he says, "I am okay."

Nadia takes a deep breath and excuses herself. As she heads toward the kitchen, she says, "I am hungry and presume you are too."

She offers him a glass of red wine with dinner.

Mugdi fusses with the table napkin, which he ties round his throat, in the way he remembers from his days in Italy, to protect the front of his white shirt. As he eats, he takes care not to spill even a drop.

He says, "Wonderful, the tomato soup."

"I love simple eating," she says.

"Definitely, it is healthier."

He enjoys the first course, a little surprised that tomato soup might taste as good as this. Neither says anything for a while. Then Nadia breaks the silence with evident reluctance, her voice low and hesitant. She asks, "How is the young man?"

Nadia has never met Naciim or Saafi. But from what Birgitta has told her, Mugdi is very fond of his young charges. Birgitta has also told her that an unhealthy tension pervades the relationship between their mother, whom she also hasn't met, and Mugdi. Anyhow, the rapport between the boy and Mugdi reminds her of an African boy she had the good luck to get to know and help, when she worked as a librarian in Tanzania.

Now she asks, "How are they, the boy and the girl?"

"They're both fine."

"Birgitta describes the boy as ambitious, hardworking, and full of charm, and she tells me that the girl has lately recovered her sense of self-worth, given what she has been through."

"There is much to admire in both my young charges," he says.

Nadia says, "In Tanzania, I once met a boy of a similar age as Naciim, bright and self-reliant, who would come to the library often and sometimes go to sleep in the middle of the afternoon, his head painfully falling forward. His name was Isaac. After I made friends with him, I discovered that he came from a poor family, which couldn't afford more than one meal a day. He was the oldest of six children, four boys and two girls."

Mugdi senses a fresh surge of emotion as he relives the instant when he first met Naciim at the airport: he knew right away that they would get along. He asks Nadia, "Did you go out of your way to get acquainted with Isaac?"

"Yes, I did. But I had a problem with Isaac's parents the moment they found out that, although I am nominally Christian, I never attended church. They made it clear they didn't want the boy to have anything to do with me. But the boy acted in a clever way, telling them one thing and doing something else. We would meet secretly at the home of a pastor, a friend of mine. In the end, I not only helped him to graduate from high school, but I also arranged a scholarship for him to Sweden, with help from a group of proselytizers busy converting the Tanzanian poor to the faith."

"Where is he now?"

"Back home, in Dar es Salaam, working as a GP at a hospital, where I hear he is much liked. His parents are now happy with his achievements."

Mugdi cannot help venting a broadside about shortsighted parents. He says, "I dislike adults standing in the way of their children getting a good education, only to make their claim on them later when they succeed, despite their obstruction."

"What's the children's mother like?" she asks.

Mugdi explains, "Waliya is very austere and so for a long time the boy and the girl felt tied down, constrained by their mother's monastic tendencies. Her religious convictions do not even allow the boy to listen to music, or the girl to live the life of a girl to the fullest. She discourages them from watching TV because they may glimpse men or women in flimsy summer wear. She wants them to devote their entire lives to the service of the faith, and, whereas the girl is more religious, the boy doesn't appear comfortable with that."

"Did he get along with your late wife?"

"He loved Gacalo. Everybody loved Gacalo."

Tears come into his eyes, blinding him. And he shifts uneasily, embarrassed.

"He must be a joy to have around."

"Yes, he is. To me, he is family."

They fall silent, and Nadia gets up to gather the dishes, taking them to the sink and returning with a tray on which there are small plates, a pint of ice cream, and a bowl of fruit. Mugdi points at the fruit, chooses an easy-peel orange and, without waiting for a knife, uses his fingers.

She asks, "Dessert wine?"

"No, thanks."

They move to the living room and sit in more comfortable chairs. "I know that you're busy translating Rolvaag's *Giants*. But tell me, how close are you to completing the work?"

He says, "Nowhere near, because of the interruptions, some due to the arrival of the widow and her children, and more recently, because of my wife's passing."

"Does anyone apart from Birgitta, Johan, and myself know that you're trying to bring the two communities closer together, the Somali and the Norwegian?" she asks.

"I've not spoken to anyone myself."

She asks, "Would you mind if I mentioned it to a friend of mine who works in the Ministry of Culture? I think she'll be interested in setting aside a special grant to help you complete the work."

The coffee is bubbling loudly, evidence that it is ready. When Nadia returns with their cups, he says, "Thanks. I'm not interested in grants."

"But can I mention it to him anyway?"

"You may mention it to anyone you like."

His mind wanders off in the silence that follows. And before he knows it, he is thinking of the reason why he opposes the idea of getting a grant to translate Rolvaag. Doing the work has been a joy and he is not keen on obtaining a grant for it. He hopes that Somali readers will be happy when they come across it and read it for their own edification.

"In your research into the period when the first Norwegians migrated to the Dakota territories, is there something you've learned that has shocked you?" Nadia asks.

He says, "It did shock me, I have no idea why, when one of the newly arrived Norwegians said he wanted to purchase a slave to liberate him from his farm labor."

"Anything else?"

"When one of them writes a letter home describing Sitting Bull, the Native American revered by people as a holy man, to be a rogue."

"How did the resistance fighter die, again?"

"He died at the hand of a police officer at Standing Rock," says Mugdi. "Perhaps we can agree that one group's resistance fighter is another group's rogue. The Norwegian fishermen-turned-landowners weren't seen as any different from the other white Americans, who massacred the natives to lay their hands on more land. Rolvaag, however, exudes goodwill toward the Indians. And that pleases me a lot."

"You are saying that art is a humanizer?"

"That is one way of putting it."

When Nadia yawns, Mugdi takes it as a sign that it is time to call for a taxi. As he leaves, he promises that he will have her over for dinner one of these days.

# CHAPTER THIRTY-ONE

----------

NACIIM IS DOLLED UP IN HIS FAVORITE NEWLY ACQUIRED WINTER WEAR: A
Canadian down jacket, well-insulated secondhand heavy-duty
boots, and a full fur hat. His heart beating with frenzied joy, he
thinks, "What a pretty sight," at the fresh snow falling, the earth
before him serene, and the scene, with which he is surrounded, quiet.
Not only is he now at long last used to the weather in Oslo, but he
is also starting to love the long-drawn winter darkness, maybe because he had only known the dreariness, the heat, the dust, and the
aridness of a refugee camp—and he is now in a place with contrast-
able seasons.

It is rush hour and everyone is equally wrapped up against the
falling snow, the scarves heavy and the hats furred. Naciim recalls
his mother complaining during their first Norwegian winter that
she felt as if the marrow in her bones had been replaced with newly
melted ice. He now feels the chill in the wind and the unrelenting
arrows benumbing his senses.

He is on his way to a computer repair shop, taking the tram
after leaving school. He is planning to pick up his computer and

then meet with Janine at a café to take her to Mugdi's house, in hopes that the two of them can enjoy an hour's privacy in his room before Mugdi gets back from the library.

The tram arrives and he collides with a clutch of boys and girls gathered at its door, pushing his way into a pocket of untaken space where he can stand and read if he so wishes. He is about to bring out a book when his wandering gaze falls on a woman in a niqaab, only her eyes visible. He has a view of the woman from the side, with the advantage that he can see her but she cannot see him. The woman, in silhouette, is facing forward and communicating, he suspects, with the European man sitting next to her. Naciim observes the pattern of their conversation: the man, also facing forward, speaks, the woman listens, her head a little inclined, then she speaks, but he doesn't reply, either nodding his head yes or shaking his head no. At no time do they look each other directly in the face. It is when the woman smiles and he sees her teeth, stained brown from drinking the well water in the region of Somalia where she comes from, that Naciim, shocked, realizes it's Arla. He assumes that the man she is with is her partner to whom she is "sort of married."

Then she rises, pushing her way past other passengers to the tram's door, apparently ready to alight. Naciim waits until both she and the man have gotten out, then darts out after them. He runs to catch up and then thinks better of it, slowing down to ensure that Arla is unaware he is following her.

The pair take their first left, then right, before coming to a stop in front of a tall, eight-story building. The man takes something out of his pocket, which Naciim presumes to be a bunch of keys. Arla waits as the man opens the heavy metal door and motions to her to go in ahead of him.

Naciim stops less than fifty meters away and, just in case one of them looks in his direction, turns his back and waits, his heart pounding. He half turns and watches as the door opens, Arla entering first and then the man. Naciim gives them no more than a minute. Then he does as he has seen film actors in thrillers do: he moves with great speed and gets to the heavy door before the pneumatic device locks it shut. By the time he arrives in the lobby, Arla and the man have already taken one of the lifts. Again, as he has seen actors shadowing prey do, he watches the lift monitor until it stops at the seventh floor.

Naciim enters the second lift, and presses the button not for the seventh floor but for the sixth, intending to walk up the stairs to the seventh. There he waits at the corner and sees Arla's companion come out of Apartment 11 and pull the door shut. The man is whistling a happy tune with which Naciim is not familiar, and takes the lift down.

Naciim realizes that he does not have enough time to collect his computer if he is to meet Janine. Worried about being late, he hurries toward the Metro stop. Fortunately, he has just gone through the turnstile when a train pulls in and he hops on, thinking how lucky he has been in his pursuit.

He moves like greased lightning and is at the café huffing and puffing.

"You okay?" asks Janine, as they kiss.

Mugdi has barely saved the day's translation work when he hears someone entering the house. As he heads downstairs he practically collides with Naciim.

They are delighted to see each other—the boy has been spending most of his afternoons with Janine—and he and the old man hug. Naciim has made a point of telephoning him often, but hasn't come round for nearly two weeks. Now he puts down his school satchel and replaces Mugdi's house key in one of its small compartments, undecided what to do.

Naciim starts to speak but trails off and cranes his neck, looking out. Mugdi asks, "Is there a problem, young man?"

"I am not alone," replies Naciim.

Mugdi discerns a faint shadow in the near distance approaching the door with caution—a tall, slim, flat-chested girl Naciim's age, wearing tight jeans and tennis shoes that were once white but are currently scrawled with messages similar to the missives scribbled on the cast of a broken leg, wishing its wearer a speedy recovery. The girl's lips are thick, her blond hair wafer thin on her scalp. Mugdi says, "Well, ask her in!" As Janine steps inside, he says "Welcome" to her.

Naciim closes the door with extra care. Then, looking embarrassed, he says, "My friend's name is Janine."

They shake hands. "Grandpa Mugdi," he says.

"I'm pleased to meet you, sir."

Naciim says, in Somali, "I'm sorry. I didn't think you would be here and I hope we are not disturbing you."

Mugdi remembers going through this many years ago, when Timiro and Dhaqaneh were teenagers and at the cinema or somewhere else with someone they were involved with and happened to bump into him, their father. It embarrassed them to the extent that they might pretend not to see him, or that they were not serious about the boy or girl they were with.

Naciim says, "We've brought a film by an Iranian director called *A Separation*. Have you seen it, Grandpa?"

"Yes," says Mugdi.

"Did you like it?"

"Grandma and I both loved it."

Mugdi checks his sports bag and discovers that he has forgotten his water bottle as well as his mobile phone upstairs and so he retrieves them.

Upstairs, Mugdi thinks that despite Naciim's being the well-behaved teenager he knows him to be, there is no denying that the boy has lived a life haunted by sex, from what Dhaqaneh told Gacalo and what she, in turn, shared with him. Dhaqaneh met Waliya when she could be described as a loose woman, so promiscuous that she had several male friends whom she went to nightclubs with, often leaving Saafi and Naciim with the neighbors—or that enigma, Arla—and not coming home until the small hours. Or sometimes, when there was no one to watch the children, she would simply take them along, especially when they were babies, and make love to a man in the same house, or even room, while they slept. Dhaqaneh made it his life's mission to make her a good woman and provide for her children.

Mugdi comes downstairs, happy that the boy thinks well enough of him to bring his girlfriend to the house. In any event, there is nowhere else the two can meet and delight in a moment's privacy; his mother would be up in arms with the idea. Maybe the girl's parents wouldn't be happy either, if she took home a dark-skinned Muslim refugee who had been given papers only recently.

He shouts to Naciim, "I am off now," from the kitchen, a safe distance from the TV room where the young man and Janine are supposedly watching a film.

Mugdi slams the door shut.

Naciim and Janine pretend they are watching the movie on the big screen in a cinema. To this end, he makes popcorn and gets two Cokes, and they sit side by side on the couch.

However, it does not take long before Janine moves closer to Naciim and her hand touches his, and his other hand is all over her, her face, her breasts, and her lips. There is a wildness to their actions, motivated by the wish to satisfy each other, as would any boy and girl, both seventeen, never mind that they come from different backgrounds or will return home to parents who would not want them to be together.

By the time they are ready for the serious business that has brought them here, Naciim suggests they leave the movie running and go to his room, where they take off their clothes and make love in privacy, certain Mugdi will not disturb them if he returns before or after they are done. This being his first time, he is nervous initially. But Janine is very sweet and gentle about it and does not tease him about his ineptness—and he is very grateful to her, although he does not say it.

# CHAPTER THIRTY-TWO

----------

IT IS FOUR IN THE MORNING WHEN, AWAKENED BY POUNDING ON THE DOOR of his mother's apartment, Naciim sits up and rubs the sleep from his eyes, wondering who could be at the door at this hour, and why they were pounding so heavily on it. When the heavy knocking resumes and he hears no movement coming from his mother's or sister's rooms, he puts on a robe, his mobile phone in the pocket of his dressing gown, and heads to the entryway. When he looks through the peephole, he makes out at least four or five uniformed officers, two of whom are bearing short-armed guns. They seem to be speaking urgently in Norwegian, though he cannot work out exactly what they are saying. He immediately realizes the seriousness of the situation but instead of panicking, he tells himself it is time he stood up to these men and played the role of the Mahram assigned to him by tradition. His voice firm and unafraid, he says, "Who is it?"

A male voice says, "Open the door."

"Spesialkommando. Open up. Or we will break the door."

Naciim opens the door, taking photos of the men as they enter in single file, as evidence of the raid which he could share with the press or the courts. The men are clearly unhappy about this and debate among themselves whether to confiscate his phone.

He can see Saafi peering around the corner and he shakes his head at her, wanting her to stay put. Her becoming hysterical would only make things worse. To the men he says, "Why a dawn raid with guns?"

"Where is your mother?" Mustachioed asks. The man takes a piece of official-looking paper out of his pocket, consults it and says, "Where is Waliya Adan Ahmed?"

Naciim considers being cocky and correcting the man's pronunciation of his mother's name, but tells himself that challenging an officer in uniform on how to say a Somali name will in no way help his cause; it will only make the officers angrier. Nor will it assist him or his mother if he tells the officers he has borne witness to the damage guns cause and how they destroyed the fabric of Somali society; or how naive he once was to believe he would be safe from guns the moment he arrived in Norway.

"With all due respect, Officers, why the guns?"

Mustachioed says, "You are wasting our time."

"I don't suppose you have a warrant, do you?"

"Let's be quick about it," says Mustachioed.

The men move with speed, their guns raised.

"Wait," says Naciim, and when they turn to face him, ready to listen, he aims his camera in the general direction of the officers and snaps away at them in a photographically organized manner. Then before any of them speak, he says, "Are you taking liberties you wouldn't take with native Norwegians, because we are black and Muslim?"

A door opening startles the men into adopting crouched positions, their guns at full cock and their fingers on the triggers. Waliya emerges, dressed in all-enveloping body tent, and looks around and asks Naciim in Somali, "Have these men come for me?"

Mustachioed tells his men to stand down.

"Yes, they're here for you, Mum," he says.

"Then I had better go with them, hadn't I?" she says.

Mustachioed asks Naciim, "What is she saying?"

"She's expecting you and is willing to come along with you," says Naciim.

Naciim is disturbed, because he can't work out how she knew they were coming or what they have said, when she does not understand Norwegian. Did someone ring to alert her to the raid and advise her to go with them without any fuss?

"*Waa ika ee nawada,*" she says to Mustachioed.

Mustachioed is dumbfounded at being addressed in a language he is unfamiliar with. The man asks Naciim, "What did she say?"

"She is ready to go with you."

Two of the armed men flank Waliya, ready to shepherd her out of the apartment, with the others forming a secure ring around her. Naciim takes several more snapshots for his records.

She tells him to alert Arla as to what has happened.

"Do you know where they are taking you?"

"She'll know someone who may."

The men surrounding her are impatient and one of them uses the butt of his gun to push her from behind, loudly instructing her to move with speed.

Waliya angrily tells the man in Somali not to touch her with the butt of his gun, "Or else!"

"What did she say?" Mustachioed asks Naciim again.

Naciim translates what his mother has said into Norwegian.

After a brief pause, Mustachioed tells his men to go easy on her and let her finish talking to her son.

"You have Arla's phone number, don't you? Call her and let her know what's happened."

"I will. Keep well, Mum."

"Promise to pray for me."

Unafraid, she turns around and opens her arms to embrace Naciim. Again, Mustachioed gestures to his men to let her be.

As soon as the uniformed men are gone, Naciim tells Saafi that there is no more danger and she can come out. But she is quivering involuntarily and so he wraps himself around her in an effort to comfort her. "Trust me. Everything will be all right."

Then he tells her to go and shower, because he will make them both breakfast. When she joins him in the kitchen, her omelet ready, she asks, "Do you think it is safe for me to go to work?"

"Why do you ask?"

"Have you forgotten that it is thanks to Arla that I've landed the job at Lego?" she says. "You see, if Arla is in trouble with the authorities, then it is possible that anyone linked to her in any way will be affected."

"Let me worry about that," he says.

"So I should act as if everything is normal?"

"Did you ever hear the proverb that says that one must prepare for the worst, even if one hopes for the best? Please do and you'll see that everything will turn out well."

He goes to take his shower and she goes to work. They are agreed that they will meet at Mugdi's. He assures her once more that things will work out in the end. She adds, "With Allah's help."

Naciim, adrenalized with rage, goes to school earlier than usual, eager to share the photos with Edvart and Janine and to talk to Ms.

Koht, his school adviser, about the dawn raid and how the men terrorized and took away his mother without the authority of a judge's warrant. He knows Ms. Koht's partner is a reporter on *Aftenbladet*; perhaps he will want to write about the raid.

When Ms. Koht finds him standing with Edvart and Janine in the corridor, the three students talking in low voices, Naciim indicates that he wishes to see her. Ms. Koht motions to him to follow her into her empty classroom. She goes ahead of him and closes the door.

"What's the problem?" she asks.

Naciim pulls out his phone and shows her the pictures he has taken. She flips through them one at a time, the better to study them.

"Please send these to me," she says, giving him both her mobile phone number and email address. He forwards them to her before the school bell rings.

"A parent is a parent, never mind how shitty they are," says Edvart, as he, Naciim, and Janine sit on the school steps after classes. "I know there are times when I wish I could kill my dad, he is so insensitive. I remember the terrible things your mother did to you and how she upsets you."

When it is Janine's turn to speak, she says, "My uncle is a criminal lawyer." She pauses, reflects for a moment and then goes on, "I am not suggesting that he can act as your mother's lawyer. But I am sure he would give me the name of a colleague of his who may be of assistance, even do it on a pro-bono basis. Would you like me to call and ask what he thinks and if he can help?"

Naciim is touched and he thanks them both. He says, "Let us wait for a day or two. Maybe then we'll know more, know if she'll be charged with something."

Edvart says, "Still, tell us how we can help."

"I'll call if I need your assistance," he says.

When Janine and Edvart have gone their separate ways, Naciim takes a tram to Mugdi's to bring him up to speed on the latest developments. No doubt, he will spell out the details for her with the tact this requires when he picks her up from work.

Mugdi broods over the meaning of this raid, aware that there is no way of knowing where the antiterrorist unit is holding Waliya. He also believes that nothing can be done to help her until she is brought before the courts and charged, or released. They will have to wait, and Mugdi is worried about Naciim's state of mind in the meantime.

Finally he says, "You have no idea why your mother thought that Arla would know where the unit would take her?"

"None at all."

"You haven't been in touch with Arla, have you?"

"I am on my way there now."

"So you know where to find her?"

"I do. Remember, I told you how I followed her and a man a few weeks ago to the apartment where I believe they are staying."

Mugdi brings out his wallet and hands Naciim a wad of cash. "This is a stopgap, for your taxis and other incidentals. If you need more, please don't hesitate to let me know."

"Thanks, Grandpa," says Naciim.

"I suggest you and Saafi stay here until your mother's situation becomes clearer one way or the other."

------

Naciim rings Arla's apartment doorbell and she lets him in, but she does not seem happy to see him.

"How did you know I live here?" she asks.

Arla has on a see-through robe, her hair fashionably coiffured, her neck adorned with silver pendants. She is also wearing very bright pink lipstick. He is struck by her smooth skin and comely appearance. He would be ecstatic if he could lay his head between her breasts and if she would be his guide. He imagines there is nothing like having sex with a woman of Arla's age and experience.

"Did you not hear me? How do you know where I live?" she snaps.

Snapping out of his reverie, he says, "I have a message from my mother."

She darts an angry look down the hall and says, "You can come in, but just for a moment. I am going to change, and when I am back, I want you to tell me how you found me."

"Maybe my mother told me?"

"I don't believe you," she says and walks off.

This gives him the opportunity to look around the apartment. He wanders into the room that serves as a study, where he observes a number of papers carrying the name "Christian Christiansen." He also notes the expensive furniture.

Arla returns, dressed a bit more modestly in an expensive, patterned frock.

"The truth is, my mother didn't tell me."

"I knew she wouldn't know."

"I tailed you and a huge white man from the tram stop, and you led me here."

"I wonder: do I know a huge white man?"

"His name is Christian Christiansen."

Her eyes twinkle a little mischievously.

"When you're ready, I'll give you the message."

She says, "That is old news."

"Have you news that is more recent?"

"Have you been home?"

"Not yet. I've just come from school."

"As you speak, your mother is home."

"Did she explain the reason for the raid?"

"She didn't volunteer and I asked. Apparently the antiterror unit recently took a woman named Axado into detention and when they questioned her, they found a number of things that linked her to your mother. The woman is from Stavanger and she worked at the nursery as your mother's assistant. Do you remember her?"

"Vaguely. What is Axado accused of?"

"She is a sister of a Somali-born Norwegian citizen suspected of being a member of the Shabaab unit that is responsible for the Westgate shopping mall massacre in Nairobi, in which many people were killed," says Arla.

"And what has my mother got to do with this?"

"Your mother's name is linked to Axado and thence to a Somali-Norwegian terrorist who once lived in the same block as your mother. Some money was wired to this man using your mother's bank details. Or so she told me herself."

"Does Mum acknowledge knowing the man?"

"She swears she doesn't."

"You say she has been released, right?"

"She's been let go, pending more investigation."

"Why did she say you would know where she was?"

"Because Axado, who has a way of reaching me, has alerted me to what is afoot," says Arla. "That is how I know."

Then Arla's phone rings. "Hi," she says, her whole demeanor visibly changing. Naciim understands from the way her body melts into something soft and gentle and sweet that sex is on her mind now, perhaps because her secret lover is on his way here. He hears the voice of a man saying in English, "I am close by."

When she hangs up, she sighs. Naciim is about to comment on how happy she looks when she forcibly pushes him out of the apartment and closes the door.

He goes home and finds his mother weeping. But she will not answer his questions about where the men took her or what happened to make her cry this way.

# CHAPTER THIRTY-THREE

----------

EARLY ONE EVENING A COUPLE OF WEEKS LATER, ARLA TURNS UP AT WALI-
ya's apartment in a taxi, laden with two huge suitcases.

Naciim observes that his mother turns off her Koran tape,
though he is not enthused over her request that he help with Arla's
luggage. He drags his feet and although he has heard her request,
he wants her to repeat it. "What is it you want me to do?"

"Please go down and help Auntie Arla."

"Help her how, Mum?"

"Go down and meet her. She's in a taxi."

"What's the problem?"

"She has two huge suitcases to bring up."

"Is Arla moving in with us, Mum?"

"Why must you jump to hasty conclusions?"

"I bet she's had a nasty fight with her man."

She looks stunned. "What man?"

"It beats me why you pretend not to know."

"I've no idea what you're talking about."

"Mum, I know stuff. I'm not a child."

"Just help bring her suitcases up."

"I don't know if I want her to move in with us."

"It is not your place to decide who moves in and who doesn't," she says. "And in any case, who says that Arla is moving in?"

"Would you like a bet?" says Naciim.

"On what?"

"That her man has beaten her to near death."

As Naciim goes down to meet her, he notices there is less of Arla's usual bluster and more of a sense of defeat about her. As testament to her mood, she has donned a large body tent, supplemented by a niqaab that covers her entire face. Nor does she bother to return his greeting or respond when he says, "Are you okay?"

His gut feeling is that Arla is going to be staying with them for a long time.

"Can you help with the suitcases, please?" she asks.

Her lips and eyes are swollen, as if her face has been struck several times with vengeful force. The visible parts of her body are bruised all over. When her full-length abaya slips down as she rummages in her handbag for the taxi fare, Naciim is able to see more of her face. He steps aside to study her every move, and waits, as she wraps herself afresh with the niqaab and a face veil.

"Who's done this to you?" he asks.

He catches sight of the discolored skin on her wrist, elbow, and neck. There is dried blood here and there and he thinks the swollen section of her finger joints must be hurting her, for they look stiff as wood. Eventually, she brings out a wad of cash and manages to say, "Here," as she passes the money to him and gestures in the direction of the driver. Naciim takes the initiative to ask the taxi driver how much the lady owes him. When he mentions a sum, Naciim counts the money and pays.

The taxi driver gives back the change that is due. As before, Arla says something to Naciim, who of his own accord gives the loose coins to the driver, suspecting that he may need his help to take the huge suitcases up to the apartment. Arla appears to disapprove of the huge tip but says nothing. She points a finger and says, "Suitcases?"

Naciim tells himself that this can only mean that she and Christian Christiansen, her common-law husband, are done with each other, unless—like many victims of wife-beating—Arla decides to return.

The driver releases the trunk. Naciim tries to bring out the suitcases, but they are too heavy for him to lift. The taxi driver, maybe offering to give him a hand, asks, "What floor?"

"Sixth."

The driver asks, "Is there a lift and does it work?"

Naciim nods in the affirmative.

The man says, "Then I'll help you."

When Arla heads for the lift, Naciim and the taxi driver watch in silence, as though certain that the suitcases will be brought up somehow. Meanwhile, the automatic door opens and she disappears into the lift. The taxi driver says to Naciim, "Do you know what happened to her?"

"No idea," says Naciim.

Naciim and the taxi driver wait for the lift to return to the ground floor, neither speaking.

When they hear the loud thud of the lift arriving, Naciim places his hands below one of the suitcases and says, "Ready? Shall we?"

The driver says, "I'll carry one and help you with the other."

Naciim insists he can carry one. He says, "I am strong enough to meet my responsibility," as if they are dealing with more than suitcases. He adds, "A man my age should not shirk his duty."

The driver says, "We need to take up one suitcase at a time. There is either gold or stones in them, they are so tightly packed."

They take the lift up to the sixth floor. When the taxi driver has helped him get the suitcases to the door, Naciim gives him an extra tip, thanks him and says, "I can manage from now on."

The driver shakes Naciim's hand with renewed warmth, and he says, "If I were you, I would tell the lady to report the brute to the police and to have him reined in. This is not Somalia. This is Norway, where they take wife-beating seriously."

"You may be right," says Naciim.

The driver speaks his parting shot. "I'd rather you didn't shirk your responsibility and that you reported the incident to the authorities."

"Thanks for your suggestion."

For the first day or so, Arla keeps to herself, eating in her room and seldom coming out.

In the days following, she avoids Naciim, venturing to the bathroom only when she is sure he is out of the apartment. On the odd occasions when he has reason to knock on her door, she does not answer.

However, she spends a lot of time with Waliya and Saafi, the three often talking in conspiratorial tones, so low that Naciim cannot make out what they are saying. Yet today, almost a week after Arla has moved in, and with Saafi out at work, he manages to finally decipher part of Arla and his mother's conversation. He is able to pick out Mugdi's name, which occurs more than once. Naciim feels troubled when he figures out why they have spoken the old man's name: Arla, from what he hears, suggests that she and Waliya work on an elaborate pretext that will make it possible for them to move in with Mugdi, who now lives alone in a very big house.

"We move in and then we take over," says Arla.

Waliya asks, "Take over how?"

"I'll think of a way."

"I don't like the idea," Waliya says.

There is a pause and he hears footsteps heading his way. Deftly maneuvering from where he has been eavesdropping, in no time he is in the kitchen, where he opens the fridge, retrieves an onion, and takes hold of the chopping board.

His mother asks him, "What are you preparing?"

"Depends on what you would like to eat."

Waliya fixes her gaze on the wall before her. She says, "We both liked the chicken you made yesterday with rice."

He boasts that he has a couple of fish dishes in his repertoire. "Would you like me to make fish and would Auntie Arla like it too?"

"I'm sure she would."

"A bit of salad as well?"

"But not with the dressing you make."

"What is wrong with the dressing I make, Mum?"

"Your dressing has that French thing, what do you call it?"

"It's called 'mustard,'" he says.

"It has alcohol as an essential ingredient, yes?"

"I can make a dressing with no alcohol in it."

"Forget about salad. Make us chicken and rice."

"Will Auntie Arla join us at the table then?"

"I'll ask her."

Naciim avoids his mother's stare, certain that it is time he engages Arla in a serious conversation about how she came by the bruises and the bandaged, maybe broken, nose. He remembers his own mother's bruises not long after they arrived in Oslo, when she said she had slipped in the bathroom. (He thought "Mea culpa," at the time, because it was he who had left the wet soap in the shower.) The two bruises, his mother's and Arla's, look remarkably similar. He wonders to himself if his mother lied about her contusions in the first place and whether it is now Arla's turn to do just that.

Arla shows no eagerness to join Naciim in the kitchen. However, she does so at Waliya's insistence when the young man's mother announces that she will shower and then say her afternoon prayer. Now that Naciim is alone with Arla, he asks, "Will you not tell me what happened?"

She says, "I was alone when I fell and I will leave it at that."

Naciim sighs and goes to fetch Saafi from work.

Dinner ready, Saafi, Waliya, and Arla join Naciim at the table. Naciim serves the meal, offering a plate each to Arla, Saafi, and his mother and then serving himself a small portion. He watches Arla pushing the food around, like a child who has had enough to eat and is ready to play.

Arla's question blindsides him. "Any idea how many unoccupied rooms there are in Mugdi's house?"

He gives himself a moment's pause and says, "Mugdi won't rent a room to you or anyone else, if that's what you have in mind."

"Who's talking about renting?"

His bone-deep suspicion comes to the surface and he looks at his mother. Saafi says, "All the rooms are accounted for. One is the old man's, one is Timiro's, the third is Naciim's, and I use Riyo's room when I stay over now and then."

"But they're not always there at the same time, surely," she says.

Naciim says, "Nothing would make him share his home with you or anyone else. He values his privacy."

"Not even in case of an emergency?" she asks.

"What kind of an emergency?"

Arla says, "What would he do in such a case?"

"I would advise you to rein your fantasy in."

Naciim knows that if Arla puts her mind to moving into Mugdi's, she will find a way to do so. But he thinks it would be difficult for her to take over.

When Naciim's protracted silence makes both women nervous, Arla resorts to whispering audibly to Waliya in her frenzied attempt to assure the boy that she had no intention to harm Mugdi in any way. He thinks he knows what her ultimate goal is and he is confident that he will subvert it.

"The house is much too a big for one man," she says. "Why not share it? Is there anything wrong in finding out if he'll mind us moving in?" She turns to Waliya. "We don't mean to do anyone harm, least of all an old man, who has shown kindness to Naciim, Saafi, and you."

Naciim says to his mother, "Having been mostly unfriendly, you cannot expect any kindness from the old man, who will never forget the outrageous comments Zubair made and which you didn't challenge."

Waliya falls silent.

"Doesn't he need young female company now that his wife is dead?" Arla asks.

"He is content being alone," says Naciim.

Arla goes on, "Most Somali men of his age remarry. I've known many old men who secretly pine for the company of younger women."

Naciim says to Arla, "Mind if I ask you a question?"

His mother says, "Not if you'll be rude."

Arla says, "Let him ask whatever he wants."

"Are you offering your services to him?"

"Of course not."

"It sounded as if you were."

Waliya says, "How dare you talk to Auntie Arla in that rude way! She is not a prostitute."

"I never said she was."

Waliya then storms out of the kitchen, followed by Saafi.

Alone with Naciim, Arla says, "This is good-natured banter and neither I nor your mother mean to do ill to Mugdi, who is a likable old man, from what I hear. In fact, we're proud that you are protective of him."

And she leaves him in the kitchen.

# CHAPTER THIRTY-FOUR

----------

IT HAS TAKEN ARLA ABOUT FIVE MORE MONTHS FROM THE MOMENT SHE thinks about the idea and whispers it to Waliya to the instant she believes that it is mature enough of a plot to act on. Then the disaster her scheming has set in motion strikes. Waliya is in the living room, praying, Saafi at work, and Naciim at school when Arla, as per claim, happens to see a fire igniting with such suddenness and ferocity that within a few seconds the white smoke turns black and the walls burst into flames.

Waliya, entering the kitchen, halts in mid-stride, shocked. She prepares for danger while Arla's eyes open wider, transfixed as she stares at the fire and then at Waliya, as though daring her to do something. Waliya does not need reminding that Arla has long had a fascination with fires.

A formidable tension divides the two women as much as it unites them. When Arla extends her hand toward Waliya, preparing to say, "Come," Waliya sees the severe burn that left an indelible mark on Arla's skin many years ago when they were both young in Somalia.

"The fire is still hungry," says Arla.

Waliya says, "I should phone the fire brigade. We can't just wait and watch as the fire destroys where we live."

As Waliya moves to the phone, Arla takes her by the hand and stops her, saying, "It must continue to burn."

Waliya, turning, sees that Arla has packed suitcases by the door and her handbag is slung over her shoulder, ready to call a taxi and leave. Waliya regrets agreeing to Arla's plot, remembering Arla telling her years ago that she was born holding a box of matches in the clutch of her fingers. This gave her mother such a fright that she considered abandoning the baby. Arla says, "I can say I've done what we've agreed on."

"You and I remember things differently."

Arla looks at Waliya but remains silent. The fire burns steadily, the flames continuing to feed on everything around.

Waliya, panicked, brings pails of water from the bathroom and pours them on the flames, in the hope that the fire will not spread through the wall and ceiling into the other apartments above and below.

Just then Naciim arrives on the landing and sees smoke pouring out of the apartment. He pounds loudly on the door and enters, his heartbeat quickening and his state of confusion playing havoc with his reasoning. When he stumbles in, the combined heat and smoke from the burning fire increases his uncertainty. He raises his hand to protect his face and closes his eyes against the smoke. Though he can now hear his mother speaking, Naciim is unable to spot her until he rubs his eyes and moves with caution in the direction of the sound the two women are making.

"Let's go," he says to his mother.

In the kitchen, the fire has almost slowed to a stop, but it has gathered momentum elsewhere. Arla, he eventually observes, is nearer the door, her handbag firmly in her grasp and her packed suitcases by her side. Naciim has the sense to run to his room to retrieve his identity papers, which he stuffs hurriedly into his school satchel. He also fills another shoulder bag with a handful of valuables and his favorite books.

He says to his mother, "Any idea where your essential papers are?"

"Why would I bother about papers?" she says.

"In that case, let's get going then, quickly."

"Given the choice, I wouldn't go anywhere."

He scans the fire with rising panic and asks, "What's the problem?"

"We came here as refugees after living for years in zinc-sheet shacks in the refugee camp in Kenya," she says. "Now we're homeless. So what is the point of going anywhere else and starting over? There's no point."

"What do you suggest we do? Burn in this mindless fire?"

"I am a cursed woman," she says.

He grabs her by the hand to pull her out. But she is too unwilling to help. She says, "With one husband dead in a suicide blast, another in jail, the apartment burning, my children lost to me, why would I want to continue living this life?"

A Norwegian woman comes to assist and the two of them drag his mother out. Once safe, the thought of rushing back in and giving a hand to Arla with her suitcases fleetingly crosses his mind, but he thinks better of it and stays with his mother. A man shouts at the top of his voice to warn people not to take the lifts. As he prepares to support his mother down the flight of stairs, Naciim spots Arla charming a young Norwegian into giving her a hand to carry her stuff down to the hall.

When they are in the vestibule and are waiting for something to happen, with the residents milling about and talking anxiously, Naciim asks his mother if she remembers where she was when the fire started.

"As if any of this or anything else matters anymore," she says.

Arla joins them and says, "Finding us somewhere to stay is the one thing that matters most now."

He says, "We'll book ourselves into a cheap hotel."

Arla asks, "A hotel? For how long?"

"Until the city sorts out something for us."

Waliya says, "Allah has willed the fire to start and only He knows where we'll find a temporary home."

Eventually, they hear the fire brigade sirens coming closer. Naciim thinks it is the most opportune time to ask Arla if she knows who Prometheus is.

"How should I know?"

Waliya asks, "What are you two talking about?"

Arla declares, "Your son is a show-off."

"Will you let my son be, after all the trouble you've caused, from which we'll find it difficult to recover?" She turns to Naciim and says, "As for you, son—really, do you need to parade your knowledge?"

Naciim helps Arla with her suitcases after his mother begs him to. When they are outside the building, it dawns on all three of them that they have no idea where to go or where they will stay. Naciim knows he and Saafi are guaranteed a place in Mugdi's house, but is not enthusiastic about Arla and his mother sharing the home with them, fearful of the menace Arla poses. Still, he feels weighed down with the burden of arranging a place for his mother until something else is sorted for her. As he rubs the residual smoke out of his eyes, Naciim now relives his memories of the refugee camp in Kenya, and then recalls his arrival in Oslo with his mother and sister.

With crowds milling at the entrance to the building, Naciim decides to call a taxi, which takes a long time to come. He gives the driver the name of a cheap hotel in Groenland, which he knows about thanks to Janine, with whom he has rented a room a couple of times for privacy's sake.

At the hotel, Naciim reserves a room for his mother. He has no objections to Arla staying with her, if that is what she wants. He then phones Saafi to let her know what has happened. He gives her the address of the hotel and asks if she can get herself there in a taxi. He then telephones Mugdi to inform him where he is and the disaster that has struck.

Mugdi says to Naciim, "Come and let's talk."

Naciim knocks on the door and waits, worried that he may disturb Mugdi, who has lately been hosting Nadia often. He wonders if moving in may upset the elderly couple's tête-à-tête.

Mugdi lets him in and says, "Welcome, my dear."

"Thanks, Grandpa," says Naciim, soon realizing, as he prepares to deposit his school satchel and shoulder bag in his room, that Mugdi is not alone; Nadia is in the living room, where she and Mugdi had been watching a BBC cultural program on TV. Naciim says, "I am sorry." But Nadia greets him with enthusiasm.

Mugdi speaks in Norwegian, wanting to include Nadia in the conversation. He says, "There is no reason to be sorry. Anyhow, give us your latest news."

Telling them what has happened, Naciim says that he has made temporary arrangements for his mother in the hotel in Groenland, and he tells Mugdi that even though the idea of allowing Arla to share it with his mother does not sit well with him, yet he has raised no objections when his mother insists on hosting the woman. Then, in an effort to reinforce his total trust in Mugdi, Naciim says he did not have sufficient funds for a cash deposit—Mugdi knows that the boy doesn't have a debit or credit card.

"Why did you take them to a hotel?" Mugdi asks.

"Where else could I take them?"

Mugdi remembers that when they first arrived, he and Gacalo gave a formal undertaking that they were responsible for Waliya and her two children. Since then, much water has flowed under the bridge, but he owes it to Gacalo's memory and feels, too, that he is under a moral obligation to help the three of them. But he is unsure if he wants to host Arla, unless Naciim suggests that he, Mugdi, extend this goodwill gesture to the woman, because she is an inseparable friend of his mother's.

He says to Naciim, "We'll call the city authorities about the possibility of finding you, your sister, and your mother accommodation, somewhere close to your school and Saafi's place of work. I take it that is what you want?"

"Yes, Grandpa. That's what I want."

"But you know you are always welcome here."

Naciim, his voice betraying a little tremor, says, "Thanks, Grandpa."

"We don't yet know how the fire started?"

"Arla blames it on a short circuit."

"She would, wouldn't she?" says Mugdi. "The self is never to blame."

After a pause, Mugdi asks, "Did you say you didn't have sufficient funds to deposit at the hotel?"

"That's right," says Naciim.

"Would you like me to lend you my credit card?"

"The manager has agreed to wait until Monday, when the banks
open, when I'll pay the remainder," says Naciim.

"How many days have you reserved the room for?"

"A couple of nights."

"But do you need to keep them at the hotel?"

"What other options are there?"

"Why not move them here?"

Naciim closes his eyes and clenches his hands. Then he opens his
eyes and looks this way and that, as though he is in a burning house
and is in search of a fire exit. He knows what he overheard from his
mother and Arla, yet he cannot bring himself to share what he
knows with Mugdi.

"I don't think it is a good idea."

Nadia asks, "Why not?"

Naciim wears a guilty expression and looks monumentally sad.
He loves the old man and does not want Arla to have the opportunity to hurt him.

"Think about it," suggests Mugdi.

Naciim says, "Let us take our time on it."

Mugdi excuses himself and goes to the upstairs bedroom. Meanwhile, Nadia says to Naciim, "You don't know how the fire started?"

"No idea," says Naciim.

"Oslo's fire department, one of the best in the world, will con-
duct tests and they will tell us all we need to know."

When he has rejoined Naciim, Mugdi brings out some money,

which he spreads on the low table in the manner of a poker player fanning out his cards.

"This is all I have now in the way of cash. You take it. Unless you want us to go together right away to get some more from an ATM to tide you over."

Naciim thanks him for the funds, even as he regrets his inability to confide fully in Mugdi.

# CHAPTER THIRTY-FIVE

----------

SAAFI, AT NACIIM'S GENTLE PRODDING, AGREES TO PAY THE MONTHLY RENT of a two-bedroom apartment he has found a block away from their old flat and which guarantees them immediate occupancy while they wait for the city to find them more permanent shelter. Naciim cuts school for a day to help his mother and Saafi pack the little they have in the way of possessions into suitcases and plastic carrier bags. But there is a problem: Arla wants to relocate with them. Naciim is firmly against this; however, he says that he will pay for one or two more nights for her at the hotel until she finds alternative accommodation.

His mother asks, "Where did you get the money for her two-night stay at the hotel?"

"From Grandpa Mugdi," replies Naciim.

Arla is chain-smoking before the sign that says in several languages that the room is nonsmoking. Naciim stares at her, incredulous, but she merely smirks. And he grows even angrier when she says, "Either you get more money from him and pay for more nights here, or else I'm coming with you."

Naciim makes as if to leave the room but Arla blocks his escape. Her hand on his chest, pushing him with all her might, she says, "Where do you think you are going? We haven't yet settled on a solution."

He says to his mother, "Please ask your friend to move out of my way."

Arla removes her hand, but continues to stand in his way.

He continues, "Please tell her to prepare to pay the fine for smoking in a nonsmoking room. I've got less than a quarter of an hour until checkout time, when I also expect a taxi to take you and your stuff to the new place."

"I hope you are coming with me," his mother says.

"When have I not come with you?"

Naciim takes the heaviest of the suitcases down in the lift, inwardly seething with rage. How he wishes his mother would stand up to Arla and tell her to eff off.

After he has settled the bill for two more nights, he calls the room from reception so as to spare himself another unpleasant encounter with Arla. When his mother comes down, she subjects him to a harangue, saying, "Why do you always go out of your way to embarrass me in front of my friends? I find it insulting that you determine if Arla, who has nowhere else to go, can or cannot stay with us."

He is silent as she grows more agitated. She says, "There's enough space. The three of us women can stay in one room, and you, the big man and Mahram, can have your own." Then she quotes a Somali proverb with the gist that "those who love one another can crowd into a small space without the slightest annoyance."

He says, "You're being unreasonable, Mum."

She is tearful as she says, "You have Mugdi to help you out, your white friends, your classmates, and a life full of daily excitement. Saafi has a job that keeps her busy all day. I have no friend, except Arla. I'll be alone with my weeping, with my thoughts."

He searches through one of the suitcases for her tape player and Koranic tapes and puts on her favorite surah. The chanting of the holy text always calms her. He allows the tape to run for quite a while, waiting for his mother to fall under the influence of the recitation.

Then he says, "One reason why Arla has been no good for you, insofar as I am concerned, is that she has no tolerance for the Koranic tapes to run when she is around you. Besides, if she stays in the hotel, she is only a couple minutes' walk from here and you can visit each other often."

Waliya reaches for the nearest object she can lay her hand on. She finds a slipper, which she throws at Naciim in anger, and he ducks his head low to avoid the missile. She bursts into tears and storms outside.

In the taxi, he gets a call from Saafi, who asks him to fetch her from work. He says, "Is there a problem? It's not yet midday."

She says, "I've just been fired."

"Why? What did you do?"

"The manager called me into her office half an hour ago and she sacked me, no reason given. So please come and maybe we can do a bit of shopping for food and other stuff."

Saafi and Naciim do the necessary shopping with the money Grandpa Mugdi has given him. He suggests that they do not tell their mother that she has been fired. She fusses a little, arguing that there is no point postponing the inevitable, since their mother will find out as soon as tomorrow that she no longer has a job.

"That'll buy us time," he says.

"I want Mum to know I've been fired," she says.

"Trust me. I know what I'm doing," he says.

They arrive at the new apartment with their mother in a pliant mood, ready to help by making the beds, cleaning and cooking. The tape is blessedly running and Saafi keeps quiet, as per Naciim's suggestion.

When they are settled, Naciim heads out to see Mugdi.

Naciim senses that Grandpa seems eager to revisit the position he took last night about whom he wants to host and whom not. Maybe Nadia has talked him out of accommodating Arla after he briefed her about the kind of person she is, from what Naciim has told him.

"What's your stand on Arla? Would you host her along with the three of you, if you were in my position? I have to make a decision on this one way or another if there is need before we have the result of the investigation into what caused the fire."

"Mum, Saafi, and I are well sorted for at least two months. Saafi has paid two months' rent of the apartment we are now in. I've paid two nights at the hotel on behalf of Arla, after which she is on her own, and where she stays is her business and is not of our concern. In short, I would rather Arla did not set foot in your house," says Naciim.

Mugdi's eyes meet Naciim's, and each waits for the other to say what is on his mind. Mugdi, the first to speak, says, "I can feel there is another problem that is bothering you and of which you haven't spoken. So out with it."

Naciim says, "Saafi has been fired."

"What a great pity!"

"But we haven't told Mum."

"How do you explain your action?"

"Ladders are climbed step by step," says Naciim. "We'll tackle one problem at a time. But we won't rush into doing anything foolish."

Naciim and Mugdi are in their separate rooms, the young man studying for an exam, and the old man working in his study, when someone from the city calls Naciim's mobile to inform him that they have found an apartment the same size as the previous one and that it will be available in a few days.

Naciim surprises Mugdi with his quick thinking. He says, "I am thinking of not letting anyone else apart from you know about the availability of the city apartment."

"And why would you do that?"

"I want Arla to sort out her problems before she hears that the city has provided us with another apartment," says Naciim.

Mugdi, after Naciim's departure, returns upstairs and, restless, decides to do a bit of vacuuming, something he hasn't done in a long while.

He sneezes a few times, the vacuum having stirred up quite a cloud of dust, and goes to the bathroom to wash his hands and face.

As he looks in the mirror, he seems shaken, remembering the superstitious belief among Somalis that one is on the verge of death every time one sneezes. In Islam, one thanks Allah after sneezing. Among Russians, one is told to avoid sneezing a third time, a sign perhaps that one's death is gaining on one. Mugdi is disinclined to take superstitions seriously, yet the sight of a black cat crossing his path from his right to his left would make him think about bad omens. Doubtless he is ready for his death, having lived a fruitful life, and he is now prepared to clear up the mess he has caused, given the chance. Maybe it is time he has made it clear to Waliya how her wrongheadedness has created mayhem. And because of this he will be glad to show her the door. There is no other way around it.

As afternoon turns to evening, someone knocks on the back entrance. When he goes to answer the door, Mugdi finds himself face-to-face with a woman he does not like the look of. The woman is in an all-enclosing veil and she takes a long time to gather the courage to make as if to speak. He waits, focusing on her eyes through the slits in the veil covering her face.

"I'm looking for Naciim," she says in Somali.

"He's not in," says Mugdi.

"Did he tell you when he'll be back?"

"And who are you and what do you want with him?"

She says, "Isn't it inhospitable of you to keep Naciim's visitor waiting outside, rather than letting her in, giving her a glass of water, offering her a seat, and then asking whatever other questions you would like answered?"

"Please forgive my manners. Come in," he says.

Mugdi gives her a glass of water, which she holds in her gloved hands. She lifts the piece of cloth covering her mouth to take a sip and gulps the water heartily.

"Tell me who you are. I'm sure Naciim will want to know that you've called round when he isn't here."

"May I use one of your bathrooms?" she asks.

His wariness again raises its head.

"How do you know I have more than one bathroom?"

"A big house like this usually does."

"Tell me who you are first and what you want with Naciim," he says. "For all I know, you could be a woman with evil intentions toward the boy."

"My name is Arla," she says.

Mugdi does not bother to ask how she discovered where he lives. There is no doubt in his mind that she has cased the joint in the same way as Naciim tailed her and her man to their apartment.

"Let me use the upstairs bathroom and I'll leave."

"There is one downstairs," he says.

"I'd prefer the one upstairs, if you don't mind."

"Please explain why."

"It's more private than the one down here."

"The one down here is cleaner, as no one has used it for a good two days."

"Upstairs is more intimate," the woman says, "and I like it."

The woman comes down, thanks him, and then departs without bothering to explain the real purport of her visit. When he is alone, he goes upstairs in his effort to work out why she called on him. He discovers nothing missing and no trace of any item or items that she might have left behind.

His wariness of any hidden dangers that might result from the woman's visit prompts him to talk about the woman's visit to Timiro and Nadia, believing that it is wiser to be preemptively cautious than to wait until it is too late.

# CHAPTER THIRTY-SIX

----------

IN ALL RESPECTS EXCEPT FOR HER VOICE, THE WOMAN AT HIS DOOR IS UN-
familiar to him. It is close to midnight and Nadia has been with
him from before six in the evening. The voice reminds him of Arla,
but this woman seems to have had some sort of an encounter with
a pugilist: her face bleeding, eyes swollen shut, the blood around
her nostrils congealing, and her cheeks puffing up by the second
like a balloon. The front of her low-cut dress is torn haphazardly,
and her right breast seems to be spilling out of her bra. Mugdi has
no idea what to do. When she was here earlier, she asked for a glass
of water. Now she needs to get herself to an emergency unit for
those injuries to be attended to.

She also seems to have had too much to drink, her gesticulations
those of someone who is propped up in a bar. He wonders how she
got here, then remembers hearing a car arriving, a door opening
then closing, then the engine revving up and driving off. But who
was in the car and why did this person or persons drop her here?

"You can't be looking for Naciim," he says.

"How clever of you. Is he here?"

"He is at his mum's and, I presume, in bed."

"Did you tell him about my visit?"

"I'm afraid I didn't."

"Why didn't you? You naughty old man."

"I feared what his mum might think."

"His mum knows he is infatuated with me. Won't you allow me to come in?"

"I'd rather not," he says.

"What could happen if you invited me in?"

"Please leave. I have a guest."

"Shouldn't you be asking what happened to me?"

He keeps her at the doorsill, ready to pull the door shut. She begs him in the name of Islam, in the name of the Somaliness that they share, to let her in. When none of her pleas move him, she threatens to scream so loud the neighbors will turn their house lights on inside and watch from behind their windows.

She says, "You'll see what happens to you."

He hears footsteps behind him, but he doesn't need to look, because he knows they are Nadia's. But Arla takes an interest in the person behind him. "Is the white woman your lover?"

"I don't know you well enough to talk about my private life," he says.

Again he hears Nadia's footsteps as she goes back up the stairs, the door still open, Arla presently sprawled in an ungainly way on the steps. The scene before her reminds Nadia of Tanzania, whose bars crawled with drunk men and women. She senses that Mugdi is currently in total control of the situation and, in any event, he will tell her all about it when he comes back upstairs.

Arla says, "Give me a hand, so I can get up."

Mugdi does as instructed.

She says, swaying this way and that, getting so close he can see the color of her corneas, "I bet I can give a better fuck than your white woman. And I can show you, if you'll allow it."

When he relaxes himself into believing that she is all talk and wind, Arla hurls herself at him with shocking suddenness and gets a good grip on his pajama top and pulls him toward her. They lose their balance, and in the process she yanks his shirt open and he falls on top of her. He scrambles to his feet before she does and Arla says before she leaves, "Remember what I said earlier. You'll regret you haven't let me in."

He closes the door right away, and when he is up in the bedroom with Nadia, Mugdi tells her everything the best he can.

Four days after his embarrassing late-night encounter with Arla, Mugdi telephones Naciim just as the young fellow and his mother are discussing a topic close to Waliya's heart: praying. Waliya, her lips astir with the susurrations of a surah she has just recited, is telling Naciim off for not praying with her and Saafi.

"It's a lot easier to follow one's sinful thoughts here in Europe in ways you couldn't if we were still in Somalia. But I am wondering why, since you must sin, you can't even the score by also praying, or fasting Ramadan. Why can't you be a good Muslim? Families praying together are blessed."

"We were all good once, Mum, every one of us."

"What do you mean?"

"We were good before our country collapsed," he says. "When you were young, our people were good people, friendly toward one another, kind to one another, and tolerant of one another's failures. No more. Somalis are no longer as good as the Somalis of those long-gone days. How can you expect me to be good when a great number of our people kill, when the weak are massacred with impunity? We

Somalis pay lip service to the faith while we live a life of lies. This is why the dissonance in our hearts continues to flourish, why there is no letup in the usual struggles within our minds, why the strife in our land rages on unabated."

Waliya prepares to retort to her son when his phone rings. The caller ID tells him it is Mugdi. He says, "Mum, I must take this. It's important."

"More important than our discussion about prayer?"

"Don't let us push it, Mum. Please."

"I can tell it is Mugdi," she says. "To you, he's more important than any discussions we may have about anything."

He says in Norwegian, to Mugdi, "Yes please?"

Saafi stands, folds up her prayer mat, putting it in its usual corner, and watches as her brother takes a few steps away to talk on the phone. Her mother switches on the Koranic tape and turns up the volume so she cannot hear Naciim's conversation.

Mugdi is saying, "Something urgent has come up. If it is not an imposition, I wonder if you have the time to help me out today?"

Naciim senses that Mugdi's voice is weak, as if suffering from an early onset of laryngitis. Anyhow, he says, "Grandpa, I have all the time in the world for you. Please tell me what do you want done, when and where."

"Could you meet Timiro and Riyo's flight?"

Naciim says, "I had no idea they were coming."

"Nor had I," says Mugdi. "But they are."

"Is everything okay with them?"

"I've just received a call from Timiro telling me they're coming and nothing else. She may need assistance with Riyo and it would be good if you were with her when she takes a taxi home."

"I'll be glad to meet their flight," says Naciim.

Mugdi gives Naciim the flight details, then asks Naciim to repeat everything.

Mugdi says, "Do you have the debit card I gave you a week ago? I suggest you go to an ATM first and collect sufficient cash to pay for your express train and other expenses."

"Consider it done, Grandpa," says Naciim.

"Send me a text message if there is a problem."

"I understand, Grandpa."

"Off you go then," says Mugdi.

Naciim, who is supposed to be meeting Janine, tells her of the change of plans. Naciim asks Janine either to postpone their meeting until another day or go with him to the airport.

Janine says, "Nothing would give me more joy than to come with you and to make their acquaintance."

"Central Station in half an hour?"

"Done," says Janine.

As he changes into his favorite clothes, Naciim wonders what might be stopping the old man from meeting Timiro and Riyo's flight. When Gacalo was alive, the couple would rent a car in which to drive Timiro and Riyo around. Then he remembers seeing an envelope with the Oslo Police insignia on Mugdi's kitchen table. Naciim is innocent of the contents of the envelope, but is it at all possible that Mugdi is answering a summons from the police?

Naciim and Janine meet at the Central Station as arranged and they hop on the first available express train to Gardermoen, happy to sit beside each other and hold hands until they reach their destination.

Timiro is the last to emerge into the arrivals hall, carrying a heavy backpack, a computer bag slung over her right shoulder, and also pushing a carriage in which Riyo is playing host to a temper tantrum. She stops moving when Naciim comes into view and hugs him. Then she and Janine shake hands clumsily. She bends down and, with Riyo still irascible, she says, "Look who's here?"

Naciim adopts a crouching position, his eyes level with Riyo's, and takes Riyo's hand, squeezing and kissing it playfully, he says, "Look, I am here." Riyo falls silent and, recognizing Naciim, smiles.

Janine, meanwhile, relieves Timiro of the heavy backpack and as they walk through the throng in the direction of the lift, Timiro asks, "What about the tickets for the express?"

"We have them," assures Naciim.

In the train, Riyo falls asleep, her head resting on Naciim's lap. Timiro says to Naciim, "What's the plan?"

"The express and then a taxi home."

They fall silent and stare at the countryside through the window of the fast-moving train. When the train conductor arrives to stamp their tickets, Naciim cannot find them and becomes frantic, emptying his pockets one after the other.

Janine then says, "I have the tickets here, dear."

Timiro interprets this as a touching moment, as if she and Naciim were an old couple that have been married for a long time. Nor does it take long before she remembers that her father now has a girlfriend a few years his junior. Deep in thought, she is happy to devote more time to her work and to her daughter, now that she is divorced from Xirsi and her father seems to have found a loving, caring partner in Nadia. She looks at Riyo, whose eyes are closed and asleep.

Then she asks Naciim how Saafi is doing. Naciim updates Timiro on the latest events, including the fire.

From the Central Station, they take a taxi home.

Again, Janine and Naciim help with the luggage and Timiro

carries Riyo in her arms. Naciim opens the door with his key, deposits the suitcase in Timiro's bedroom upstairs, and leaves Timiro to sort her daughter and herself out.

As they're heading out, Timiro says, "What a lovely thought, sending you and Janine to the airport, when the old man couldn't come. A bonus. That's what I call it."

"It's been a pleasure to meet you," says Janine.

"Likewise here," says Timiro, and the two hug.

"Wonderful to welcome you home," Naciim says.

"Thanks, my love," says Timiro, and kisses him on the cheeks.

Naciim's phone pings with a text message: Mugdi asking how things are at the airport. Naciim lets the old man know that all is well and that Timiro and Riyo are home and happy.

"Was that my dad?" she asks.

"He says he'll be here shortly," says Naciim.

# CHAPTER THIRTY-SEVEN

------------

MUGDI IS AT SEA AS HE ENTERS THE CENTRAL OSLO POLICE STATION, CON-
fused as to why he could be of interest to the police, who sent him
a letter, which he received the previous day, requesting that he present himself at three o'clock this afternoon. Apart from the one time
he went to the police station with Naciim, he has never been in a
police station to answer questions of any sort, never filed a statement as an accused man or appeared as a witness in a trial. Somalis
say, "Do not tell me who you are, tell me who your associates are
and I'll decide if you are virtuous or wicked." In other words, by
associating with Waliya and, by extension, Zubair, Imam Fanax,
and Arla, Mugdi has crossed a line that now makes him of interest
to the police. That the officer even suggested that he could bring
along a lawyer points to the seriousness of why the inspector wishes
to interview him. When he consulted Nadia, her feeling was the
invitation had less to do with Waliya and more with Arla, whose
wiliness sets her apart so far from his former daughter-in-law.

Entering the station, Mugdi reconnoiters the room for faces
known to him and, finding none, takes his number and a seat, his

heartbeat drumming in his ears. He waits alongside men with tattoos bearing messages that mean nothing to him and women with cleavage, wearing lipstick so bright he thinks of a semaphore. It irks him that he is sharing a bench with the city's lowlifes.

A woman sporting a ring in her tongue, another in her nose, and several more of various sizes in her ears, asks him, "Why are you here, old man?"

"No idea," he replies.

She says, "I know of a man your age and appearance who lives in my neighborhood and who is given to buggering street boys. Has one of the boys you buggered reported you?"

This puts him clean out of countenance. "I've done no such thing," says Mugdi.

He gets to his feet, urgently desirous of placing some distance between himself and these riffraff, lest another engage him in untoward talk. Mugdi waits for his name or number to be called. Such is Mugdi's frustration that the longer he waits, the more convinced he becomes that Nadia is right and Arla is his accuser. He remembers her threats as he closed the door in her face and fled up the stairs to tell Nadia about it.

He wonders if she has filed a complaint again him. Even if she has, if Mugdi is sure of one thing, it is that he is innocent and therefore free from both fear and guilt. And if it ever comes to a trial, he has a witness: Nadia, who was with him that night and who would verify that Arla never set foot inside his home.

Mugdi startles when a female officer calls out his name. After he has identified himself, she leads him down a corridor to the farthest room. She knocks on the door and a male voice inside says to enter. The female officer tells Mugdi to go in, then she pulls the door shut and departs.

A man in uniform rises like a huge mountain behind an immense desk. The man has on a shirt that is half tucked in and a loose necktie. He is bald, tall, and broad in the shoulders, as though he devotes a large amount of time to working out at a gym. His knotted muscles, comparable to Arnold Schwarzenegger's, resemble the nodulated roots of an ancient tree. Mugdi thinks that each of the man's arms is as big as his own thighs.

"My name is Inspector Lonn. Thanks for coming."

Mugdi nods. The inspector turns the tape recorder on and requests that Mugdi give his full name, his date and place of birth, and his current address. Mugdi does as asked. Then his phone gives a *bing* sound, indicating he has just received a message. Begging the inspector's pardon, he asks, "May I take a look at the message, please?"

Inspector Lonn nods his head.

The message is from Naciim, giving an update about Timiro's arrival. Mugdi closes his phone and then encourages the inspector to begin his questioning.

"Do you know a woman called Arla Mahmoud?"

Mugdi replies, "Yes, I do."

"How long have you known her?"

"I knew of her as a friend of my daughter-in-law's, though I had not met her until she turned up at my house five days ago, clad in an all-enclosed body tent." Then he tells the inspector about their conversation, relays what transpired between him and the woman, what he said, what she said, and how she left when he was still none the wiser why she visited him in the first place.

"Would you say you don't know her well?"

"I would say I don't know her well, yes," he says. "And she and I were never alone at any time, except on the two brief occasions when she showed up at my home, the first of which I've explained. On the second occasion, she turned up late at night and knocked on my door. When I answered it, she seemed hurt, with blood streaming down her cheeks, the front of her party dress torn. She begged me to let her in, but because I had female company and sensed Arla would be worth more trouble than I was ready for, I wouldn't allow her into my house the second time."

The inspector asks, "Did your female guest come down from upstairs when you and Ms. Mahmoud were conversing?"

"Nadia Stein came down to get a drink of water from the kitchen and she could hear me and Ms. Mahmoud speaking, even though she couldn't understand what was being said, as we were speaking in Somali, and Nadia is Norwegian."

"And Ms. Stein and Ms. Mahmoud did not meet before that night and have never met since? In other words, to the best of your knowledge, the two women don't know each other?"

"That's right. They never met."

"You never laid a finger on Ms. Mahmoud?"

"I've never laid a finger on her."

"Not even after she tore your nightgown?"

"Not before then and not after either."

"You did not have sex with Ms. Mahmoud?"

"We never had sex, Ms. Mahmoud and I."

"Do you remember when you last set eyes on her?"

"I would say a quarter past midnight."

Inspector Lonn takes a bit of time taking notes. Then he asks Mugdi, "Did you tell your female guest what the noise downstairs was all about?"

"I did soon after going upstairs," replies Mugdi.

The phone on Inspector Lonn's desk rings. He allows it to keep ringing as he jots down some points. Finally he answers it, listens for a long time, and then covering the phone and speaking through only one side of his mouth, the inspector says he will give "him" a referral letter to take to the forensics folks at the hospital tomorrow so they can have their shot at "him." Mugdi suspects that the inspector is talking about him and that he will have to give samples of blood and semen to determine his innocence. And that is fine with him.

Inspector Lonn says, "In her statement, Ms. Mahmoud speaks of you forcing yourself on her and that she fought you off."

"But that is not true."

"Ms. Mahmoud claims that you were alone, inside."

"That is another blatant fabrication."

"Would you please give me the name, phone number, and address of the woman you claim was with you in your house when Ms. Mahmoud visited you?"

Mugdi reads Nadia Stein's details into the record.

"Now I would like you to give me the name, phone number, and address of your daughter-in-law, whom you describe as Ms. Mahmoud's friend," says Inspector Lonn.

Mugdi provides the details the officer wants.

Inspector Lonn says, "We're almost done."

At the end of a long wait, he asks Mugdi to sign the printout of his statement, having notified him of the dire consequences including possible imprisonment if he is found to be giving false information. Then a young female officer arrives with a referral that Mugdi is supposed to take to a nearby hospital, where he is to offer blood and urine samples.

Mugdi telephones Nadia to tell her to expect a phone call from

Inspector Lonn. Nadia says, "I have no idea why but I felt that woman was trouble."

------

He arrives at home, exhausted, and after greeting his daughter, who tells him that Riyo is upstairs, asleep, Mugdi apologizes for not being at the airport to welcome them. "But I did what I could, sent you Naciim, and I understand he didn't come alone, but brought a charming girl."

"I liked her a lot," says Timiro.

"I am glad to hear they helped."

"But why didn't you come to meet us, like you always do?" she asks.

"Arla, Waliya's friend, has accused me of rape."

"Is the woman mad? Waliya must have egged her on."

"I'm not sure about that."

"Did you meet your accuser, and where?"

"She came to this home uninvited twice, once disguised as a devout Muslim, and in her next visit, she turned up with her face bleeding and with cuts and bruises all over her body."

To spare her the need to question him, he gives his daughter a detailed summary of what he told Inspector Lonn.

"How much trouble are you in, Dad?"

"Not a lot, I think."

"You're not afraid of being arrested?"

"Not at all, darling."

"What makes you so sure?"

"My blood and semen samples, which I am to provide tomorrow

morning, will prove her wrong," he says. "Besides, I didn't have sex with that woman."

She remembers hearing a famous politician say something similar after having oral sex with his intern. But she is certain of her father's innocence. She says, "You're not violent by nature, and in any event, you've been seeing Nadia. From what Birgitta has told me, things are serious between the two of you. I feel deep in my heart that you are innocent of the crime which this woman accuses you of."

"It's heartening to hear you think I am innocent."

"What do the police think?"

"The police don't share your view of me."

"Well, I pity Arla if she wished rape on herself. Sexual trauma resides in the mind as well as in the body of the victim."

"I feel as terrible as a victim does," he says.

"I am relieved Mum isn't around to hear this."

"So am I," he says.

"If Mum were alive, Waliya wouldn't encourage Arla to accuse you of rape," says Timiro. "You can be sure of that."

"Your mother was tough. I am not."

"What will happen to Arla if she is found guilty of perjury?"

"She'll end up in jail for a long time."

# EPILOGUE

----------

WALIYA SAYS TO NACIIM, WITH SAAFI SITTING CLOSE BY IN TOTAL SI-
lence, "I feel the past has caught up with me and it is time I dealt
with it. And the best way to deal with it is for me to go home."

Naciim knows what his mother means about the past catching
up with her. Lately, especially after Gacalo's death and the humili-
ating raid, he thinks that Dhaqaneh must be uppermost in her
thoughts.

Indeed, Mum says, "How I miss your stepdad, a man unlike any
I've known. Gentle. Kind. Sweet. Generous. Had your stepdad
been alive, we wouldn't have come to Norway, and our lives would
have been much happier."

He says, "I'm not so sure about that. Our lives would have been
different, but not safer, nor as happy as Saafi and I are at present
here in Norway."

His mother circles back to Dhaqaneh, speaking of their years
together with nostalgia and enthusiasm. She is sufficiently heart-
ened to bracket her late husband's name with Zubair's, his comrade
in arms, whom she visited in prison earlier that day.

She says, "Zubair is a good Muslim, whom I would describe as a victim of injustice. He did nothing to deserve a long-term detention. What he did was this: he took up arms against infidels, whom he killed, and there's nothing wrong with that. Zubair too, like Dhaqaneh his comrade in arms, picked up a gun only after the Ethiopians invaded Mogadiscio. Nor do I think there is anything wrong with that either."

"But Mum," Naciim says. "Many Muslims in this country are not subjected to antiterror unit interrogations. They live and move about freely, without any trouble. So there must be a reason why the antiterror unit has targeted Zubair and Axado."

"I also visited Imam Fanax," Waliya volunteers.

"The cruel imam who whipped me. How can you?"

"I've found him a changed man," she says.

Saafi is interested. She asks, "How so, Mum?"

"He looks and sounds like a broken man."

"Serves him right," says Naciim.

"Imam Fanax doesn't even attend the prayers at the prison mosque, he is so bereft. Some of his fellow prisoners have said he lives in total self-isolation."

"Would you say you've changed too, Mum?"

"I must have changed. I've had nothing but one misery after another since coming," she says. "I've lost weight. I am no longer as active as I used to be. My children are lost to me."

"Didn't you bring so much of the misery upon yourself, Mum?" he asks.

Saafi says, "Will you stop torturing her?"

"I am not torturing her. I'm asking questions."

Naciim knows it cannot have been easy for his mother to be in Oslo when Mugdi associated her with both his son's and his wife's deaths. Mugdi gave the impression that he could not care less whether she left or stayed.

He asks, "What sort of life do you think awaits you in Somalia? A better and a happier life?"

"I've plenty of choices there," his mother said.

"Plenty of choices in a country that's at war with itself? How can that be, Mum?"

"I envisage a life of possibilities."

"Tell us more about the life that awaits you, Mum."

"Allah is my guide and protector," she says.

Naciim thinks his mother does not have a prayer in heaven to succeed in Somalia, where many others much stronger and better educated have known nothing but failure.

He says, "It saddens me to see you leaving just when Saafi is setting up her seamstress business after obtaining her qualifications and when I am about to write my exam to enter university."

"I don't wish to stay here a day longer."

"Why, Mum?"

She replies, "You won't understand."

"Please help me understand."

"You pursue your dreams, and I'll pursue mine."

"What dream is taking you back home?" he asked.

"I've a job waiting there."

"A job? What job, Mum?"

"As a concierge in a hotel in Mogadiscio."

Waliya and Naciim hear Saafi's weeping, distraught that their mother is leaving for Somalia, when they are staying behind. "Who'll look after you when you are old and decrepit?" she says.

Waliya leaves for Somalia a month later, thanks to repatriation assistance from the International Organization for Migration and the Norwegian Directorate of Immigration.

On the day she collects the first Somali passport she has ever owned, thanks to the IOM which has arranged it through the offices of the only Somali embassy in Scandinavia, Waliya speaks of it as one of life's delicious ironies.

She says to Naciim, "No one can question my Somaliness anymore after many years of being a stateless refugee in a camp in Kenya."

Naciim remembers the story of a man, reportedly a friend of Mugdi's, who was once committed to a mental hospital and then released. He had the habit of carrying in his pocket the affidavit given to him by the institution when he was discharged and sent home. He would boast to all and sundry that he was sane and could prove it. "But are you sane or insane?" he would say to the friends he met. "Could you prove it either way?"

Naciim is about to leave the room when his mother calls him back and hands him a thick envelope. When he opens it, he finds an air ticket and reams of documents. She asks him to translate for her the letter in Norwegian that is in the pile she has just received.

He tells her that the letter confirms in detail the packages the IOM is offering her. "They're offering you support in the form of cash as part of the reintegration package, so that you can start a small business venture when you get back."

"What other packages are they offering me?"

"They'll provide you with a one-way air ticket home and someone will meet your flight when you arrive in Mogadiscio. They will help you find a place in which to stay for the first three months after your return."

"I don't need their help once I am in Somalia."

"If I were you, I'd take all the help I can get."

"What else is the letter telling me?"

He tells her about her departure date, plus all the telephone contacts of people who may assist her in case of difficulties in transit. She says, "Can you write down a summary of what these reams of papers say, and give me the names and the numbers on a separate sheet, in Somali? Thanks."

At the approach of Waliya's departure date, Saafi is weepier than a broken faucet. She cannot bear the thought of waving goodbye to her mother. Mugdi telephones Waliya briefly to wish her good luck and to promise he will take care of Naciim and Saafi as best as he can. The next day, Saafi and Naciim accompany their mother to the airport.

Saafi shares a two-seater chair with her mother, with buckets of tears running down both their faces and choked up with excessive emotion. Naciim is up on his feet, across from where they are sitting, his hands in the back pockets of his jeans. He says to his mother, "You think you'll be okay, Mum?"

She nods her head yes.

"What will you do when you get there?"

She makes an effort to say something, but no words come. She bursts into tears and Saafi joins her effortlessly and mother and daughter go into a huddle, and their bodies shake from sobbing, from their ceaseless sniveling. They fall quiet for a moment before they become hysterical in their weeping.

Naciim looks on, as if embarrassed by what the two women are doing, carrying on and crying their hearts out in unison. And he takes a physical distance from these weepy women in all-black body tents sharing a two-seater chair in the airport in Oslo.

When his mother's flight is called and she disengages herself from Saafi's grip, Naciim watches as she moves toward security.

Saafi, however, walks with her to where the sign says PASSENGERS ONLY, and waits until her mother has gone past the uniformed men and women, and turned to wave goodbye to her.

When Waliya lands at Aden Abdulle International Airport in Mogadiscio, three Somali men, unfamiliar to her, meet her flight and take her to the staff quarters of the hotel where she has the job arranged.

Waliya telephones Saafi and Naciim from Mogadiscio three weeks later, a couple of days after the Somali news outlets reported that one Arla Mahmoud had been charged with perjury and sentenced to seven years in prison in Norway. Waliya sounds sanguine about her future prospects when she speaks to Naciim and she talks in a relaxed fashion, perhaps to prove that she is happy to be home.

"I am well, very well," she says.

"What's your job at the hotel, Mum?"

"I do this and that. I go to the vegetable, meat, and fish market with a group of young women and men and we buy provisions for the hotel. Mostly, that keeps me busy."

He asks, "And where do you stay?"

"I share a house with a lovely female coworker."

"On the grounds of the hotel or away in the city?"

Waliya mentions the area of the city where she lives. "Not that you know the city, having never been here yourself. But we're a few hundred meters away from the former Tamarind Market."

"Is the mobile number you are using the best one I can reach you on, Mum?" he asks. When she says yes, he asks for the hotel switchboard number as well, in the event she does not answer her mobile phone.

Naciim presses the redial button a moment after she rings off, with the purpose of checking if his mother's number works. It doesn't. A week later, his mother telephones again, using a new number. When he asks her about these numbers, his mother is cagey, unprepared to tell him where she is, or why her numbers keep changing. Rather than give him a satisfactory answer, she changes the conversation altogether and then hangs up.

Worried, his mother's behavior reminding him of similar incidents in their past, Naciim shares his troubling discovery with Grandpa Mugdi.

The old man asks, "But why are you in such a state about it?"

"Because my stepdad used to change his numbers often too."

# ACKNOWLEDGMENTS

----------

THIS IS A WORK OF FICTION, SET AGAINST THE BACKGROUND OF ACTUAL events, whose retelling I have layered with a membrane of my own manufacture. Many of the characters populating its pages, with the exception of a few—these include Anders Behring Breivik, a hard right progressive politician, and a couple of radical Islamists—have their beginnings in my own imagination.

In writing it, I've benefited from speaking to a great many people in Norway, Nairobi, and Mogadiscio and from reading hundreds of documents, periodicals, and books. On, occasion, I've relied on interviews I conducted in Oslo, Nairobi, and Mogadiscio from the beginning of 2015 and the end of 2017.

The epigram is from *Concerto al-Quds* by the Syrian poet Adonis (translated into English by Khaled Mattawa and published by Yale Press [2017]).

Among the texts I've read, consulted, or borrowed from are: O. E. Rølvaag's *Giants in the Earth* (1924); Asne Seirstad's *One of Us: The Story of Anders Breivik and the Massacre in Norway*; Aage Borchgrovink's *A Norwegian Tragedy* (2013); Sindre Bangstad's

*Anders Breivik and the Rise of Islamophobia* (2014); Unni Turrattini's *The Mystery of the Lone Wolf Killer: Anders Breivik* (2015); Solveig Temple's *In Their Own Voices: Letters from Norwegian Immigrants* (1991); Ingrid Semmingsen's *Norway to America: A History of the Migration*, translated into English by Einar Haugen (1980); Ian Buruma's *Murder in Amsterdam: The Death of Theo van Gogh and the Limits of Tolerance* (2006); Ben Doherty's "Hate-filled Narratives Target Minorities Globally, Says Amnesty International" (*The Guardian*, February 22, 2018); Raekha Prasad and Khalil Dawoud's "Cairo Writer Threatened with Divorce" (*The Guardian*, June 17, 2001). The other texts that I've read and borrowed from are too numerous to list here. However, I am grateful to every single one of them.

Foremost among the people to whom I owe a debt is Hodan Gedi Mohamoud, mother to Mona Abdinur, one of two young Somali-Norwegian victims killed by Breivik; she was eighteen when Breivik brutally cut her life short. (In this novel, I've changed Mona's name to Mouna, short for Maimouna, and have also changed her mother Hodan's name to Himmo, the better to suit my storyline.) Hodan was very kind and generous to me: she answered my stupid questions with exemplary patience and clarity, as she spoke about her life and Mona's—may the Heavens bless her! Hodan, in any event, had no idea what I would make of the stories she told me, and to be honest nor had I. I did not know what shape I would give those moving stories, whether I would fashion them into a single article for a newspaper or work them into one of my fictions. As it happens, it has taken me a long time to work Hodan's stories into the new novel and I can only hope that she and her family will approve of the "clean-limbed" reworkings I've given them.

I am also thankful to my friend Lul Hassan Kulmiye, who facilitated my encounters with Hodan whenever I visited Oslo.

Mette Cecille Newth, a very dear friend whom I've known since the mid-1970s, has served as a most reliable springboard on all matters Norwegian from the get-go. Generous with her time, she has answered my questions and introduced me to a lawyer, who answered what the law says about rape in Norway and has even read an early, messy draft. My thanks and love to Mette.

The novel has also benefited from Maya Jaggi's suggestions after she read a very early draft. Her perceptive comments on the manuscript have made the task of rewriting the two subsequent drafts a lot easier and more manageable, and I heartily thank her for her insightful input.

The last person in order of mention, but by no means least in importance, is Umar Abdi Mohmed Affey, a Somali-Norwegian who has gone out of his way and volunteered to do research for me and who, on occasion, has had to translate Norwegian texts for me so I could gain a full understanding of the intricacies governing asylum seeking and refugee statuses in Norway.

Need I add that I alone am responsible for the opinions expressed in this novel and for any errors or misinterpretations?

Nuruddin Farah
Cape Town
February 2018